"Who is the *Arab*?"

"I don't know."

Bannerman stretched his arms. He sat back.

"What are you going to do with me?"

"Peel your face off."

"Peel . . ."

Bannerman closed his eyes.

"What are you talking about?" the Jamaican asked.

"It will be done on an operating table." Bannerman stifled a yawn. "Then you will be taken back to New York and released on the street where you live. You will have no face, no eyes, no tongue. Your friends will find you stumbling about, trying to scream. I need them to see you that way."

Hector tried to spit. His mouth was dry.

Neither man moved or spoke for several minutes. Bannerman appeared to doze. He waited, giving Hector Manley's imagination time to see himself groping from one parked car to another, hearing the screams of women, children running from him, older boys tearing at his pockets, taking his jewelry.

"I don't believe you," he said finally.

"I know you don't. Get some rest."

"This, I take it, is to frighten me? To make me talk?"

"Talking won't save you. But you will talk. Trust me."

Other books by John Maxim

Novels
Platforms
Abel Baker Charlie
Time Out of Mind
The Bannerman Solution

Non-Fiction
Dark Star

The Bannerman Effect

— John R. Maxim —

BANTAM BOOKS
NEW YORK · TORONTO · LONDON · SYDNEY · AUCKLAND

THE BANNERMAN EFFECT
A Bantam Book / November 1990

All rights reserved.
Copyright © 1990 by John R. Maxim.
Cover art copyright © 1990 by Tom Galasinski.
No part of this book may be reproduced or transmitted
in any form or by any means, electronic or mechanical,
including photocopying, recording, or by any information
storage and retrieval system, without permission in writing from
the publisher.
For information address: Bantam Books.

ISBN 0-553-28559-9

Published simultaneously in the United States and Canada

PRINTED IN THE UNITED STATES OF AMERICA

OPM   0 9 8 7 6 5 4 3 2 1

For John Waldo

The Bannerman Effect

—1—

December. Alexandria, Virginia.

The secretary of state, Barton Fuller, had never been entirely comfortable with computers. Least of all where intelligence operations were concerned.

While fully appreciating their capabilities, he considered that they tended to encourage the gathering of information rather than the decisive use of it. An endless flood of data from a million different sources, all needing to be processed and stored. Too much processing, not enough thinking. Need an opinion? A forecast? An assessment of the tottering Soviet economy or of Syria's capacity to produce nuclear weapons? Ask the computer. Never mind that it's almost always wrong. Not enough data, they'll say. Let's pump in some more and ask it again.

It was the computer, in his opinion, more than the Congress, that had pulled the teeth of the CIA. Reduced them all to clerks and analysts. And filled his desk daily with a mound of intelligence reports that he'd long since given up trying to read.

Then, too, he couldn't help feeling that there was something terribly unconfidential about a network of computers. He could never seem to call up a classified file or read the printout of an eyes-only telex without wondering whether some pale and pimply faced hacker in Silicon Valley or some damned place had found a way to read over his shoulder.

His own hackers, of course, had done their best to reassure him. Such a thing was not possible, they said. The system used by the State Department, right down to the machine he kept in the study of his home, was absolutely impenetrable. They were certain of it because their security system was itself designed by computer. There was, he felt sure, a flaw in that logic.

For these reasons alone, therefore, Barton Fuller would have been less than pleased when, on this bright Sunday morning, Roger Clew appeared at his home and produced a laptop Toshiba from a bag that was supposed to contain the wherewithal for their regular Sunday game of platform tennis.

Clew was also two hours early. Barton Fuller was still in his robe, his first cup of coffee in hand, the *Washington Post* crossword puzzle open but untouched beside his favorite chair. The solitude of an early Sunday was one of his few indulgences. Now young Roger had shattered it, no explanation, just a series of incomplete sentences and mysterious bear-with-me gestures as he busied himself, unbidden, setting up the Toshiba next to Fuller's IBM station, fiddling with cables, connecting the two.

"Unless we're at war and I haven't been told"—Fuller made a show of searching the front page of the *Washington Post*—"can't whatever that is wait until Monday?"

He made it a rule: Sunday mornings at Briarwood were for platform tennis in winter and clay-court tennis in summer. Or some half-court basketball, depending on the athleticism of the day's guests. But, barring a legitimate emergency, no shoptalk. Not until noon when a few department heads and the odd senator arrived for an informal working lunch. One's oases were where one finds them. Sunday mornings at Briarwood were his. They restored the body and flushed the mind.

Clew straightened. "Um . . . actually, it can't, sir. The fact is, after you see this, you might tell me not to bother coming in on Monday."

Fuller released a sigh. He had been afraid of this. High

drama. It was usually on Monday mornings that the world seemed about to come to end. Or on an evening for which he had theater tickets. It rarely happened on Sunday mornings, Pearl Harbor notwithstanding.

"This is not personal, is it?" he asked. "You're not in some sort of trouble."

"No, sir. Well—um, no."

Certainly clears that up, he thought. "Do I gather then, that this is something Harry and Irwin may not be privy to?" Harry Hagler was special adviser to the Intelligence Committee of the National Security Council; Irwin Kaplan was director of operations for the Drug Enforcement Administration. Except on Sunday mornings. On Sunday mornings they played platform tennis. In fact, Fuller seemed to recall, it was Roger who had suggested that particular foursome in the first place.

"Sir"—Clew turned to face him—"my position is that they know nothing about it. That position may change depending on how this meeting goes."

Another sigh, deeper than the last. "Roger," he said, grimacing, "one of the most attractive things about you is that you've never seen the inside of a law school. Have you been keeping bad company?"

"Ah—Irwin is a lawyer, sir."

"I'd hoped he'd gotten over it. Please consider that all appropriate asses are covered. What say we get on with this?"

"Yes, sir." He continued fiddling. His tennis tote yielded a box of floppy disks. Clew inserted one into the slot of the IBM, another into his laptop. Fuller studied him. In the nearly twenty years he'd known Roger Clew, first in Europe where Roger had spent most of his career, and, for the last three years, in Washington where Roger had been appointed his undersecretary of state for political affairs, Barton Fuller was not sure he'd ever seen him sweat. Not even at tennis. He might glow a bit from time to time, but actually trickle? Never. It would ruin his image. It would be like having his hair mussed. A bit of spinach between his teeth. Being caught ordering a pizza.

But he was sweating now. All these "yes sirs" and "no

sirs" were another matter. On Sunday mornings, the formalities were to be left in the locker room.

Roger Clew reached for the Toshiba's "power" switch and flipped it. A soft blue light filled the screen. He followed this procedure with the IBM. A title appeared. JTR EFFECT, Fuller thought it said. The younger man quickly advanced past it to what seemed to be a short list of instructions. From his tote, he produced a single sheet, covered in plastic. This he placed beside the keyboard.

"These are some special commands." He pointed. "Otherwise, the system is interactive. It's basically self-explanatory."

"Am I going to hate this, Roger?"

"My hope is you'll. . . ." He pulled out Fuller's chair. "Sir, if you'll just—sit."

An hour later, Barton Fuller had still not moved from the IBM machine. Nor had his eyes left the screen except to consult the list of commands or to glance up, blinking, at Roger Clew.

The younger man watched him in silence, his hands wrapped around a mug of coffee that had long grown cold. He'd watched the secretary's expression change from one of confusion to one of disbelief to one of horrified fascination. But he did not see rejection. He began to hope that, come Monday, he would still have a career after all.

Fuller, a large man, a full head over six feet, leaned back in his chair and stretched. With one huge hand he kneaded the muscles near his neck. His head turned toward the little Toshiba that Clew had set up within arm's length of his machine. Curiously, to no purpose, he reached out to touch it. He found himself reflecting on its size. One of his hands, spread wide, could easily cover the entire keyboard. Such a little thing. Somehow he'd always thought of laptops as more toy than tool. Not any more. This was no toy. This, in theory at least, was a machine that killed.

In the past thirty minutes alone, Barton Fuller had snuffed out the lives of eight men and two women. He had kidnapped three others. He caused four more to vanish without a trace. He made a shambles of two known terrorist organizations, one Libyan, the other Irish. He had paralyzed them, caused defections from their ranks, and caused member to turn on member.

Fuller muttered something. Clew leaned forward. "Sir?" he asked.

"I said it's a game." Fuller's eyes remained fixed to the screen. "It's still only a game."

"No, sir." Clew answered. "I don't think so."

Fuller waggled the fingers of one hand in a signal to be still as his other hand searched the keyboard and his eye returned to the list of commands. At the top of the sheet was that legend again: JTR EFFECT. He'd asked what it meant at the outset. Clew, he thought, had avoided answering. He'd apparently forgotten it was there. "When you're finished, sir," he said. "Please."

An index of organizations appeared on the screen. He scrolled past those of known terrorist groups. There were more than 200 in the Middle East alone. A similar number throughout Europe. More in Africa. More everywhere. A few, even, in the Soviet Union.

Next came the drug traffickers, another long list. Then Mafia families. Then came corporations. Barton Fuller frowned. Corporations?

Then he understood. He recognized the names of a German firm that had helped Libya build a chemical weapons factory, a Danish company that had illegally sold submarine detection devices to the Soviets and an American defense contractor whose greed and shoddy standards had resulted in the deaths of several flight crews.

Fuller returned to the drug traffickers. He was more comfortable there. He selected one at random, a drug distribution network based in Mexico. He touched a key and an organization chart appeared. He touched another and the names became faces. Fuller chose one face at random. A brutish looking man, hooded eyes, thick lips. Fuller ordered his execution, using the keyboard to type in the means. He chose a car bomb. Next he asked the computer to predict the effects of that assassination. A list of consequences appeared on the screen, in order of probability. The primary effect was a relatively peaceful reorganization and a redistribution of the dead man's property among his associates. Fuller then killed his replacement. Another car bomb. Now the effect was panic. He killed two more. The effect was chaos. Incredibly to Fuller, the computer predicted six additional deaths, all men and women who were likely to be suspected of the original killings. The drug distribution network was effectively destroyed. In theory.

Fuller leaned away once more. He took a long breath and exhaled slowly. Roger Clew tried to read his expression. He thought he saw a certain wistfulness, and a measure of satisfaction. Again, his hopes began to rise.

Fuller folded his long arms. He nodded in the direction of the laptop. "Who knows about this? Who programmed it?"

"Basically it's the TENET program adapted to the new Cray-3 computer system. I asked some of the Cray programmers to experiment with a few refinements. No one person has seen all of it."

Fuller nodded.

TENET, an acronym for Terrorist Network, was a data bank that collected and continuously updated all available information on known terrorist organizations. It included estimates of capability, political orientation, and even psychological profiles from the world's leading experts on terrorism. The Cray was simply the world's fastest and most-sophisticated computer. TENET and the Cray-1 had been used to predict terrorist behavior and targets since 1984. Results had been mixed. But the capabilities of the new Cray-3 were said to be nothing short of miraculous. And, even then, Roger Clew had refined them. God knows how long he'd been working on this.

In retrospect, Fuller supposed, he should not have been surprised. He and Clew had had many conversations about this during the past two or three years. Roger had complained, sometimes bitterly, that the intelligence services had a system that could identify an enemy, tell us what he's done in the past and what he's likely to do in the future, and yet we do practically nothing with it. It's not a failure of capability, he'd argue. It's a failure of will.

"Roger," the secretary asked quietly, "by any chance, are we talking about government death squads here? Argentine style?"

"Absolutely not."

Fuller gestured toward the screen. "But I see a great

many unpleasant people dying in many exotic ways. How else does this come about?"

"The actions I have in mind do not necessarily involve killing. And I do not propose to use government personnel."

Fine distinctions, thought Fuller. Perhaps young Roger is a closet lawyer after all. "What, then, do you have in mind?"

"Sir, at this time I'm still really just exploring potential. But these actions would not be unlike many of the covert operations, past and present, of our intelligence services."

"Those operations fall, for better or worse, under a legally constituted charter. Does this?"

"No, sir. It can't work if it does."

"Do I gather, then, that I have just been lured into a criminal conspiracy with you, Mr. Hagler, and Mr. Kaplan?"

"Not at all. We're just . . . talking."

"Funny, you don't look hypothetical," Fuller said, dead pan. "But as long as we're just talking, what does our expert on counterterrorism think about all this?"

"You know what Hagler wants. He wants his hands untied."

"Who among us does not? But I'm asking about this." He turned his thumb to the laptop.

"In Harry's words, he would like the freedom to hit those fuckers so hard and so often that they'd be afraid to come up for air. Any way he could. Legally or not."

"That's Harry, all right. Where would he draw the line?"

"I asked him that. He said he'd let me know when he reached it."

"Surely he'd stop at murder."

"Naturally. If that's what it was."

"What else could it be and still have the same effect?"

"Punitive action. Preemptive strikes. Pest control. Whatever works for him."

"And Irwin?"

"He was—uneasy in the beginning. He's coming around. It was Kaplan who insisted that I expose this to you before we go any further."

"In search of a godfather, I take it."

"On the contrary, Kaplan doesn't think you'll have the stomach for it. Frankly, I think that's what he's hoping for."

"He might be right. What are you hoping for?"

"That we can all, the four of us, put our minds together. That we can come up with a way to use this technology that is both morally defensible and effective. Above all, sir, I'm with Hagler. I want the enemies of our country to be afraid. TENET can show us how to hit them with random but strategic—*countermeasures.*" He'd almost said *brutality.* "But they will have no idea who is hitting them or why."

"No idea?" Fuller raised an eyebrow. "Does TENET say these people are all stupid? You don't think they'll make some gesture in our direction such as blowing a few more of our airliners out of the sky?"

"Not if our strikes appear to be the work of rival factions. We can have terrorists killing each other off at two or three times their current rate. We can start wars between drug lords, drive them undercover, paralyze their traffic."

"And gang wars between mobsters?"

"Eventually, yes."

"And corporate executives, Roger. Do we start killing them off as well?"

Clew bit his lip. "That was purely . . . an exercise. There are corporations with policies every bit as inimical to the interests of the United States as those of the drug cartels. However, I would—"

"Draw the line?"

"Yes."

Fuller stared at him.

"In any case," Clew continued, "after these—surgical strikes—our own legally constituted agencies would be employed to move in and pick up the pieces. The computer would have told them exactly—"

"I get the picture."

"The beauty of it is," Clew pointed out, "that no one else has to be in on this. Just Kaplan and Hagler. They'll go on directing operations just as they're doing now. No one's going to ask them how they got so smart all of a sudden."

"No CIA?" Fuller asked.

"Not while Palmer Reid is there."

Fuller's eyes narrowed. "Which, I gather, means that your chief surgeon is to be your old friend Mama's Boy."

"There is no more Mama's Boy. He's just Paul Bannerman now. But yes, he'd be my first choice."

"Does he know about this?"

"No one knows. Just the four of us."

"What makes you think he'd be interested?"

"He won't be. Not at first. I'd have to work on him."

Fuller brought his hands to his eyes, rubbing them. He should, he supposed, ask how. Better, probably, not to know. Except he owed that much to Cassie.

"Cassie Bannerman."

He spoke her name in his mind. And he saw her face. The one they called "Mama." He never called her that; to him, she was simply Cassie.

Abruptly, Fuller rose from his chair. He stepped to the sideboard where he filled his mug, slowly, from a thermos pitcher. He kept his back to the younger man. Turning, he wandered toward a painting, a pastoral scene, that hung on the far wall. It was not of any great value. He simply liked it. Or rather she did. Knew the artist. Knew his work. That was why he'd bought it.

"Yes, Cassie. I still have it. I look at it every day."

Sixteen . . . almost seventeen years.

He could still feel the emptiness, although the anger had faded over time. It was more than anger. The closest he'd ever come to taking up the gun himself, to wanting to look into a man's face as he killed him, was on the day he was told that Cassie had been murdered.

The odd thing was, they hadn't even been all that close, at least by modern standards. Met her at an embassy party in Vienna. Had dinner a few times. Took long walks. The nearest they'd come to a tryst was a weekend in Paris. Prowled museums. Went dancing. Separate hotels rooms, not even on the same floor. At the end of it, a hug, a peck on the cheek, a long look into her eyes, nothing more. He was, after all, married to Katherine, rest her soul. And happily so. But that fact did little, it seemed, to keep Cassie Bannerman out of his dreams. Every man, he supposed, has had a fantasy woman. Cassie was his. And, no doubt, that of a few dozen other men as well. More than good looks, there was a tremendous . . . electricity to her. Beautiful, yet totally un-self-conscious about it. Tremendously kind. Quick-witted.

She said she was an art buyer for several museums. Which was true enough. But she was also, as it turned out, an American intelligence operative, code name "Mama," who was the control of a small army of contract agents until she was set up and sold out by her own people.

Her son, Paul—she'd spoken of him. Barely out of college at the time, living back in California. He'd spend his school breaks driving all over Europe with her. Nice young man. Nothing in his history to suggest what he would become. Except that he was Cassie Bannerman's son.

An astonishing story, really: He returned to Europe at the age of twenty-four to find out who and what his mother really was, and why and how she'd been killed. He might well have suffered the same fate had he not been adopted, so to speak, by certain of the contract agents she'd been running.

It was a bit like being raised by wolves. These were men, and women, who did not content themselves with the mere urge to kill. Within a few months, three CIA agents, including one section chief, were dead. So were two, possibly three, corrupt Austrian policemen and a pair of German thugs who were the actual triggermen in Cassie's death.

The CIA, sensible for once, sued for peace. Offered reparations, an apology, and disciplinary action against those involved in his mother's death, that's if any of them still lived. Mostly, they wanted this unexpectedly dangerous young man to go away so that the free-lance agents who had embraced his cause would stop the foolishness and go back to work. They chose as their spokesman a young trade mission diplomat—Roger Clew—in the belief that someone Paul Bannerman's age, borrowed from the State Department, clearly uninvolved, would not be shot on sight.

They were too late. Cassie Bannerman's son had grown larger than life. Paul Bannerman, by that time, had become Mama's Boy. The stuff of legends. A name spoken in a lowered voice. That astonished no one more than Paul Bannerman himself. His newfound friends informed him that, just as they relied on Cassie Bannerman to represent them, negotiate for them, protect their interests, they would now rely on him. He is, after all, his mother's son. He bears her genes as well as her name. He is intelligent, articulate, multilingual, and cool under fire. If he were to abandon them now, any settlement negotiated with the CIA would soon be forgotten. They would be picked off one by one.

And so, at the tender age of twenty-four, Cassie Bannerman's son began running what would soon grow into the most tightly knit, and deadliest, network of contract agents in all of Western Europe. He would work, within limits, for most of the Western intelligence services, including certain of the American services, but he would never again trust the CIA. And Roger Clew, the young innocent who was borrowed via that long-ago phone call to Barton Fuller, built a career on being the only man in the entire United States government with whom Mama's Boy would negotiate.

Pity, thought Fuller, that he hadn't left well enough alone. Bannerman, and Roger, would still be there. But twelve years of that were enough. Roger had earned his reward. Barton Fuller had called in his loan. Still, he should have realized that Palmer Reid would rush into the vacuum left by Roger and try to to reclaim what he considered his feifdom.

"Mr. Fuller?" Roger's voice, behind him.

"Um-hum?"

"Are you okay, sir?"

"Yes." He nodded, still looking at the painting. "Just woolgathering, Roger."

He could not recall ever discussing Cassie with Roger. Certainly not his special feelings for the woman. But they'd certainly discussed the son. Perhaps, on one of those occasions, Roger had seen something in his eyes. And had gone back to his damned computer. God knows what was in those things. Good man, Roger. Could do with being a bit less manipulative, however. Well, Fuller thought, let's see. Roger is not the only one who knows how to access a computer file.

"From what I hear"—he turned from the painting, and from Cassie Bannerman—"Mama's Boy has been knocking off more of us than them lately."

"Palmer Reid's people are not *us*," Clew answered evenly. "If the CIA had its way, he wouldn't be *them*, either. As for

Bannerman, Reid tried to hit him at least twice, and he got bloodied each time. Bannerman warned him what would happen. So did I."

"It won't surprise you that Reid has a different view. He insists that Bannerman and his killers are a pack of mad dogs, that they have invaded this country, and that Bannerman himself is insubordinate, a thief, and a traitor."

"With all respect, sir, I think you know better."

Fuller shrugged. "I know that he and a dozen or so of his killers returned to this country three years ago, waltzed into a CIA training facility up in Connecticut and handed Reid and his people their walking papers."

"It's not a training facility. That town was one big safe house for Reid's private army and it's illegal as hell."

"The fact remains—"

"And Bannerman didn't waltz in. Reid lured him there. Reid meant to kill him."

"He denies that as well."

Clew made a face.

Fuller tried not to smile. "The fact remains," he pressed, "that Bannerman and his people have taken over an entire American town. Wouldn't you say that borders on bending the law?"

"Bannerman took and held a number of properties that Reid acquired with unaudited funds. There's a clinic, a restaurant, some houses, and a few retail businesses to give his people something to do. Bannerman himself runs a travel agency. He has not taken over the town. He simply lives there."

"Westport, Connecticut." Fuller returned to his seat at the machine. "A nice place. I'm told the crime rate is remarkably low."

"Bannerman takes care of his own. He always has."

"The local residents—they know nothing?"

"There's no reason why they should. Bannerman doesn't bother them. If anything, he protects them."

"Still, you'd think someone would notice that—"

Clew shook his head. "Westport is a commuter town. New people come and go all the time. Bannerman's people don't have horns. Most were born in this country. They look like everyone else."

"Back to Reid. You say he's tried to dislodge them?"

"Not dislodge them, kill them."

"Then what's kept Mama's Boy from killing Reid?"

"My opinion? He uses the threat of Reid to keep his people on their toes. You can lose your edge in a place like Westport. Anyway, he knows Reid won't try to retake the place in force because that would leave bodies all over the street. The media would notice."

"I dare say."

"And Reid would have to explain why he's conducting operations within the borders of this country. He's the one who's breaking the law, not Bannerman."

"I take it you've been to Westport."

"I stay in touch."

"And you're satisfied that Bannerman and his people have no other agenda? That they're simply trying to live normal lives?"

"No question." Clew gestured toward the Toshiba. "That's what's going to make this a hard sell. You have to realize that contract agents are people. They get tired. They get lonely. In Westport they've made friends, new neighbors, who treat them like ordinary human beings. In Europe, everyone was afraid of them. In Westport, nobody is."

"Except, presumably, burglars, car thieves, and the odd drug pusher."

"I'm told that such people have . . . moved along."

"All except Palmer Reid."

"Except Reid. Yes."

"May I have a few more minutes with that machine?" He gestured toward the IBM.

Clew looked at his watch. "You have almost an hour before Hagler and Kaplan get here."

"I'd like twenty minutes. Alone, if you don't mind."

Roger Clew spent that time wandering the grounds of Briarwood, calming himself, wanting to shout out loud. The subject had been raised. It had not been rejected out of hand. It was a beginning. He balled his hands into fists and shook them, a silent cheer. He turned back toward the house.

A German shepherd, one of two, trotted by, paused to

pick up his scent and then, satisfied that his odd behavior posed no threat, resumed patrolling. There were no other guards. Not on Sunday, not even Fuller's chauffeur. Only the gatekeeper. There were two household staff, an elderly couple, but they had gone to church. They would be back soon to begin preparing lunch. Clew reached the French doors off the broad flagstone terrace and stepped through, allowing one of them to slam behind him.

Barton Fuller was still at the machine. Not using it. Just staring at it. Clew cleared his throat. Fuller raised a finger, using it to beckon the younger man to his side. He brought the finger down on the plastic-covered list of commands and tapped a finger against its heading.

"Are you ready to tell me what JTR EFFECT means?" Fuller asked.

"It's not important." Clew seemed faintly embarrassed. "Just a name I gave it."

"Well? Tell me. That way we'll both know."

Clew took a breath. "I had to call it something. I call it the 'Ripper Effect.' "

"As in Jack the Ripper?"

"Yes."

"Melodramatic." Fuller raised an eyebrow. "But apt. Random terror. Tied up an entire police force. Kept people at home nights."

"And," Clew added pointedly, "the Ripper was never identified."

Fuller sipped thoughtfully from his mug. "No one else, beyond you and me, Kaplan and Hagler, would have to know?"

"And Bannerman, if he'll do it."

"No records would be kept?"

"None."

"No accountability?"

"You might wish to tell the president. That's up to you."

Fuller threw him a look. He did not bother to comment. "When Hagler and Kaplan arrive, we will play platform tennis. That's all."

"Can I tell them you'll . . ."

"You can tell them I'll think about this. If you wish, I'll

say something cryptic to that effect. But the four of us will never sit down and discuss it."

"I understand." A sigh of satisfaction. Relief.

"It's a fascinating premise, Roger. Not just counterterrorism. Terrorists, America's own, striking back, taking the initiative for a change. But it's hardly the answer to all the world's problems. And your friend Bannerman is just one man. I assume you do not expect him to eradicate both the terrorist threat and the drug problem single-handedly."

"Of course not. But he can start giving us the experience we need. Let me work with him. A test. Find out if what works in theory will work in the field."

"And if he refuses?"

"I won't let him. He owes me."

Fuller didn't doubt it. Palmer Reid had, however uncharacteristically, tried to harass Bannerman by legal means. Getting his passport lifted; trying to interest the IRS in his financial affairs; and demanding the arrest of Anton Zivic, a former colonel in Soviet Military Intelligence, in the country illegally and now, apparently, Bannerman's second in command. Roger Clew had blocked him at every turn. A thought struck him. "That computer of yours . . ." He pointed with his mug. "Is Bannerman's organization in it?"

"Yes."

"And is Reid's?"

Clew hesitated.

"I thought so."

Clew remained silent.

"No further action, Roger. No experiments. No computer games. Do nothing at all. I've said I'll think about it, and I will."

"Yes, sir."

"Why aren't you arguing?"

"The truth? This is already more than I'd hoped for. I was afraid you'd ask me to resign."

"I still might. You're a very good man, Roger, but you may have spent too many years with Mama's Boy. I hope it hasn't damaged you."

"He says the same thing about my years in Washington."

Fuller frowned. "You took an oath. He didn't."

". . . Yes, sir."

"May I hold on to that laptop for a few days? I'd like to become more familiar with some of these groups."

"Sir, if someone should get into this room—"

"Take the list of commands. I've memorized them."

"Yes, sir."

"Yes, Bart," Fuller corrected him. "The meeting is over."

The Ripper Effect, indeed, mused Barton Fuller, returning to his painting. The Ripper was small potatoes compared to some of Bannerman's crowd. As Roger knows perfectly well. Why not call it The Bannerman Effect and be done with it?

The Bannerman Effect.

"Oh, Cassie," he whispered. "What have we created, you and I?"

—2—

Harry Hagler arrived. Irwin Kaplan appeared moments later. The platform tennis was subdued, played almost in silence until Fuller, true to his word, held up his serve long enough to indicate that he had seen the proposal and had not at once summoned the FBI or a State Department psychiatrist. It was enough.

Clew did not stay for lunch. He would not have been able to bear it. He doubted that Barton Fuller would be an especially attentive host that day either. His briefing of Hagler and Kaplan, held in the parking lot of a nearby Dunkin' Donuts, was punctuated by the smacking of Hagler's fist into an open palm. Irwin Kaplan merely sighed. Kaplan was always sighing.

Hagler—red haired, thick-set, pugnacious, the face and temperament of a saloon brawler. Irwin Kaplan—paunchy, balding, thoughtful, cautious yet relentless. The pit bull and the bloodhound, Clew called them. Different men, different styles. But both excellent. Personal reputations: superb. Prior achievements: stunning. Record of accomplishment in their current jobs: dismal.

Especially Hagler. In two years, not one of his offensive

strategies aimed at terrorist organizations or at freeing hostages had been implemented. Only his defensive measures. And only those deemed politically safe. He had hoped for a positive change with the coming of a new administration. But it, if anything, was worse. No more of that ludicrous "make-my-day" posturing but no air strikes either. Just lots of earnestness, niceness, wringing of hands. It was humiliating.

Kaplan had at least put people in prison and had seized billions in drugs, cash, boats, planes, and Florida real estate. But he was, as even he realized, just a finger in the dike. No more. He despaired for the country in which his two young daughters must grow up. His vision of it frightened him. Made him sigh. Made him angry. It had taken Roger Clew many lunches with Kaplan, many walks along the Potomac, and an entire summer of tennis matches, making little progress with him, before he realized that the way to reach Kaplan was through his children. Within days of that revelation, shortly after their return to junior high school, their principal, acting on an anonymous tip, found vials of crack in both their lockers. They denied any knowledge of them, of course. And Kaplan believed his children. He knew that the drugs had been planted, perhaps by a schoolmate, perhaps by someone who wanted to cause him pain. It made him angry. Another step forward.

The three shook hands in the Dunkin' Donuts lot. Patience, Clew told them. Just a little further, a push here, a push there, and nobody will be able to stop it.

At his townhouse on N Street in Georgetown, Roger Clew tapped out the digital code that disconnected the alarm system and another that permitted him to open his safe.

From the safe, he drew out a Toshiba that was a duplicate of the one he'd left with Fuller and a file of hard 3½-inch disks. He selected a disk marked "auto-repair records" and booted it into the machine. He scanned past the repair records, some genuine, some fictitious, until he came to the most recent entry. Now he typed in an access code. The repair records blinked off and a file titled "Westport" appeared on the screen.

He hit the "scroll" button, then sat back as the machine scanned a series of files on Bannerman and his people, occasionally stopping the scroll as a photo appeared. There were nine, counting Bannerman, who were positively identified as being in Westport. He had photographs of the nine, mostly passport photos, plus a few others taken over the years, always with a telescopic lens.

Clew had no purpose in calling up his Westport file. Except to see them. To count them. To be with them. He scrolled upward again, stopping to linger over each of the photographs. Anton Zivic. He smiled. The only extant photograph, as far as he knew, and he had it. Dapper little man. Cultivated. Looks more like an Italian sports-car maker than a Russian. Very smart. Once Bannerman's enemy, now his right hand.

Billy McHugh—huge, Bannerman's monster, the most frightening of the bunch, had been with Bannerman the longest. Carla Benedict—who likes to play with them, get laid by them, before she kills them. Janet Herzog—never says much, just kills them. John Waldo—once a Navy seal, still likes to work at night. Glenn Cook—ex-FBI, Bannerman's long-distance shooter. These last five, between them, Clew reflected, have probably killed more people than smallpox.

Clew went on, stopping at Gary Russo. Dr. Russo. Their resident surgeon. Also their interrogator. Could make a stump talk, they say. Reputed to be Carla's boyfriend, more or less. Hard to imagine, Clew thought, unless he could also make a stump come. Otherwise, it has to be like fucking a black widow, saying so far so good.

Molly Farrell. The nice one. The youngest. Been with Bannerman since Iran, probably his closest friend after Billy. Also the hardest to figure. Comes from money. Radcliffe grad, nationally ranked college tennis player. Went abroad for her junior year. Something happened. Clew never knew what. But five years later she's making bombs and tapping phones for Bannerman. Now a Westport saloonkeeper. Runs a restaurant called Mario's, more or less their headquarters.

There were at least four more, Clew was reasonably sure. Bannerman wouldn't say. Not even to him. It was another reason why Reid had not dared to raid Westport in force.

Reid could never be sure of getting all of them. Any he missed would vanish. And then they would begin hunting him. There were few things that frightened a man more than the knowledge that he was being stalked by someone who lived only to kill him.

Clew stopped at Bannerman's most recent photograph. It was taken, like the others, with a telephoto lens. He had just left a restaurant on Manhattan's Upper West Side, smiling at some remark made by a female companion whose face, except for a bit of her hair, had been cropped. Clew sat back and studied him.

Clew shook his head. It's amazing, he thought. On the surface, as nice a guy as you could want to meet. Soft spoken. Never swears. A good face. His mother's looks, but rugged. A scar high on one cheek that probably drives women crazy. Not that he'd notice. Or know what to do about it if he did. Almost forty years old and he's still basically a klutz with women, straight ones, anyway. Sticks mostly with his own kind. Says it's just as well, says he's never won an argument with a woman. Molly, Clew suspected, probably takes care of his needs from time to time. What are friends for?

Anyway, he's more of a man's man, really. Good guy, good neighbor. The kind who would not only lend you his tools but would probably drop whatever he's doing and come over to help you. You want company watching a Yankees game on TV or you want to play some one-on-one in your driveway? Call Bannerman. You got troubles? Someone screwing you over and you want a sympathetic ear? Call Bannerman. Good listener, never lectures. The best part is, just talking to Bannerman has a way of making your troubles disappear. The guy who's harassing you suddenly seems to lose interest. Maybe he woke up in the night to see Billy McHugh leaning over his face. Next thing you know, he's a recluse, hardly leaving his house anymore which, by the way, is suddenly up for sale.

Bannerman takes care of his own.

Clew moved on. He scrolled through the dossiers on Bannerman's known agents, past a list of fifty or more possibles —agents who'd been known to work for him at least twice— and reached a set of supplementary files listing various other people known to have had a business or personal relationship with him. He tapped a key to stop it and backed up to the photograph of the young woman whose face had been cropped out of the other shot. Her name was Susan Lesko. Bannerman's current lady friend. A straight one. He called up her file. The more he read, the more he frowned.

The relationship had been going on for several months now and showed no sign of ending. That was not like Bannerman. He tended to stay in his own world. He'd had occasional affairs with outsiders before but he tended to end them at the first sign that they might intensify. Before they could become a distraction. This one seemed not only distracting but foolhardy. The girl, aside from being too young for him, worked for a newspaper. A reporter. She'd been sniffing around Westport, but not on an assignment. On her own. Apparently she'd been helping a friend move into a new house in Westport and had come across a Welcome Wagon brochure that bragged about the unusually low crime rate. She wondered why, dug some more, and then came on another set of figures showing that Westport's suicide and accidental death rates were remarkably high for a town that size. Her curiosity was aroused. Thought there might be a story in it. Stress among the affluent, maybe. Or another rash of teen suicides.

Clew couldn't imagine Bannerman getting nervous about this. But for some reason he'd contrived to meet her, get close to her, see what sort of questions she was asking. Possibly to see whether she just might have stumbled on something that might lead to him or his people. To do some distracting of his own. He might even have done it to save her life.

Whatever. She did lose interest in the story. There was no reason for Bannerman to keep seeing her. Now she was nothing but trouble.

For one thing, he thought, Palmer Reid almost certainly knows about her by now and is bound to be wondering what Bannerman is doing with a reporter. He probably also knows that Bannerman and this girl are about to take off together on a ski trip to Europe. That in itself would be enough to make him crazy—that Bannerman is allowed to come and go as he pleases and yet he has the gall to tell Reid never to set foot inside Westport. But this reporter business would be the real kicker. Reid will toss and turn over it. He'll see a conspiracy in it because he sees conspiracies everywhere. Ask Reid for the time of day and he'll wonder if you're trying to establish an alibi. Fuck him. Let him stew.

Another concern was the girl's father. Roger Clew hit the "scroll" button again. He stopped at a photograph taken from newspaper files. A huge man. The build of a wrestler. Mean face. Daughter must have been adopted. In the photograph, a television reporter was asking him a question he must not have liked. Lesko looked like he was about to eat him.

Raymond Lesko. Former New York City police detective. Highly decorated. Retired two years ago under a cloud. Suspected of a triple murder. Story is that Lesko's partner went bad. Was ripping off drug dealers. Did it once too often. They blew his head off in the driveway of his home. A few days later, Lesko slaughtered two Bolivian nationals and one Colombian in the back room of a Brooklyn barbershop. Or so they say. Lesko was never charged. But Irwin Kaplan, who knows Lesko from way back, says it's true. Says Lesko splattered them all over the walls, reloaded his shotgun, then emptied it into a million dollars worth of cocaine until the whole room turned red and white.

Lots of stories about Lesko. One says there was a woman in that barbershop. And that she was the one who ordered the hit on Lesko's partner. Lesko blew all the others to hell but not her. He left her standing there. Some say he just couldn't kill a woman. Others say he didn't know who she was until later. A few say that he did know her and was on the take from her and wanted to teach her a lesson. Irwin Kaplan says that's horseshit; he says the partner turned out to be a thief but Lesko was straight as they come, and the partner was lucky to get killed before Lesko could get his hands on him.

Which brings up one of the weirder Lesko stories. Kaplan says that Lesko doesn't seem to want to let the partner, whose name was David Katz, stay dead. Says he still talks to him sometimes. Maybe it's not so weird. You work with the same partner for ten years, day in and day out, counting on each other, you find yourself finishing each other's sentences after a while. You develop a kind of ESP. Same way, maybe, that a widower would go on talking to his dead wife as if she were still out in the kitchen. Or that people visit graves and have long talks with the person buried there. Not so weird. Maybe it's just lonely.

Anyway, Kaplan says this woman, known only as Elena, never photographed, dropped out of sight. Retired. Some say to La Paz, some say to Zürich. If you want to know more, Kaplan suggested, ask Reid. Reid had some kind of connection with her. *"Ask me,"* Kaplan said, *"Reid was probably protecting her in return for a cut of her action."* Clew wasn't surprised. He knew that there were some in the CIA who saw all that drug money as a way to fund other activities that would not survive congressional scrutiny. If they couldn't stop the drug traffic, they felt, they might as well get some use out of it.

Whatever. Clew wasn't interested in Elena, especially not in Reid, and he didn't really care about Raymond Lesko. Except that, retired or not, Lesko was a cop, a very formidable cop, and except that he was a father who presumably took an interest in his daughter's choice of lovers. Especially one who was pushing forty. Especially one who was about to take her on a ski trip to Switzerland. Bannerman had to realize that. Clew could only hope that Bannerman knew what he was doing. And that he was not in love. *That,* Clew thought, *is all we need.*

Switzerland.

Clew made a face.

Zürich.

Kaplan said the woman, Elena, might be in Zürich. Reid had to know that as well.

Damn.

He tried to imagine what Palmer Reid would make of this. Paul Bannerman had almost certainly never heard of Elena. He'd never even met Lesko. Has probably been ducking him. Yet here we have a neat little circle that seems to run from Bannerman, to the girl, to the father, to Elena, to Reid, and back again to Bannerman. Reid hates and fears Bannerman. But he doesn't dare move against him. And Bannerman has promised to live and let live as long as Reid keeps his distance. But now here's Bannerman, all of a sudden, apparently developing a connection with a woman who could, conceivably, blow the whistle on Reid. Yes, definitely; Reid would see a plot unfolding here. The topper would be Bannerman's upcoming trip. Where is he going? Switzerland. Who else lives in Switzerland? Elena. What could be clearer?

"But," he muttered softly, "what will you do about it, Palmer?"

Roger Clew stared at the telephone on his desk. He should, he knew, call Bannerman. Tell him about Lesko, about Elena, and what Palmer Reid was likely to be thinking. But what might Palmer Reid actually do?

Wouldn't it be great, Clew wondered, if he could ask the computer. What if the Cray-3 system were programmed to predict Palmer Reid's behavior? It would take a while but it ought to be possible. Even for a mind like Reid's. Reid might be borderline crazy but probably no more so than any terrorist. If he fed the computer everything they had on file about Reid, his personal and professional history, his psychological profile, the mind of a probable paranoid schizophrenic who does nothing except circuitously, he would be able to tell Bannerman what actions Reid is most likely to consider in ranking order of probability.

And how Bannerman should respond. For maximum effectiveness and maximum damage. Bannerman would be grateful. He'd owe him big.

But what if the computer turned out to be wrong? Clew leaned forward on his elbows, his hands cupped over his mouth, his expression distant. How would he know whether he fed the right information? Or enough information? Garbage in, garbage out. Do this wrong and Bannerman might never trust it again.

And the Ripper Effect would be just one more idea that died in committee. Better, maybe, to say nothing. But do a trial run. Program the computer, ask it what Reid will do. Even ask it how Bannerman might respond. If it turns out to be right, Bannerman's got to be impressed.

If it doesn't, who's to know?

—3—

Mid-January. Southeastern Switzerland

Elena had noticed the van. It had followed her silver Mercedes since Davos. It stayed fifty meters behind, not passing when invited to do so, keeping its distance even when the Mercedes paused at stop signs.

Her cousin Josef Brugg, driving up front, had noticed it as well. It seemed strange to him that the van made no attempt to pass. The road ahead was clear. And he was driving slowly, in part not to risk being stopped by the Swiss police, and in part not to jar the bleeding American who was rapidly sinking into shock.

Still he was not greatly alarmed. The van, colored maroon and brown, with German plates, had a ski rack on its roof. There were many like it on this road every day. And the driver, as best he could make out, seemed no more than a boy, traveling alone. At one point, driving through the town of Küblis, Josef had seen the boy honk and wave at a knot of skiers who were trudging along the road in their heavy boots, their skis on their shoulders. Two or three of the skiers had raised their arms in response. That their response was tentative, even questioning, Josef Brugg did not notice. He relaxed. Josef tugged the hem of his trench coat so that it covered the automatic pistol that rested on his lap and concentrated on the road ahead. Soon, in any case, his brother, Willem, would be catching up to them in the other Mercedes. Willem would not be far behind, perhaps five kilometers, depending on how long it took him to help the other Americans clean up the mess they had left in Davos.

He adjusted his rearview mirror so that he could see the back seat. The van snapped out of sight. Slouched directly behind him was the wounded American doctor, Russo. He was barely conscious now. His head lolled in rhythm with the springs of the Mercedes. Elena was holding him, her arm around his shoulder. With her free hand, she kept pressure against the most serious of his injuries, low on his chest, where the assassin's knife had entered. The others, those under his right armpit, were flesh wounds made by bullets. Elena had torn her cotton blouse to make a packing for them.

Elena was talking to the American, encouraging him. Only a little farther, she said. The clinic is not far. They know we are coming.

Russo grunted. He lifted his head and nodded feebly.

He felt no fear. Only humiliation. There was not much pain where the knife had entered. But there was a sense of fullness, a coldness, which he knew to be a sign of internal bleeding. It was the bullet wounds, although far less serious, that hurt the most. The bullets had only grazed him but the muzzle blast from Bannerman's pistol had also seared his flesh and set his clothing afire. And yet he knew that Bannerman, in shooting through him, had probably saved his life.

The man, Carmody, had taken him from behind. So stupid. So careless. Carmody was in the act of killing him, driving the knife into his heart, and would surely have finished him had the knife not squarely hit a rib. It gave Russo time to struggle. It gave the others time to reach him. But by then the knife had penetrated a full three inches and had twisted. Carmody had held him like that, pinioned, his body a shield now that Carmody saw that he was trapped and tried to bargain his own life for what remained of Russo's. Bannerman had not hesitated. He stepped forward, lifted Russo's right arm and thrust his pistol into Russo's armpit, then clamped the arm back down to muffle the sound of the shots. He fired three times, through Russo, into Carmody's heart.

The next ten minutes had been a blur. The others had broken into a shop where he could be kept warm until cars could be brought up. Davos Hospital was near but there could be no question of bringing him there. That would mean police. His carelessness had done enough damage already. Then he heard the woman's voice. Elena—Bannerman must have sent for her. She was nodding. Yes, she said. There was a clinic this side of Zürich that her family had funded. Treatment would be swift and discreet. She and her cousins would take him there. And she tried. No one expected the van.

The killers were patient. They had waited for the silver Mercedes at the edge of Davos, knowing that it must eventually return the way it came. There was only one road back to Zürich.

True, there had been many places along the winding mountain road where the Mercedes could have been overtaken. But if, as was likely, it ran off the road at the first burst of fire, even if it then plunged down through the trees, its occupants might well have survived. Worse, escape would be difficult. If the attack were witnessed, and an alarm given, this single road was too easily sealed.

And so, keeping their distance, they followed. Another thirty kilometers and the Mercedes would reach the junction town of Landquart on the valley floor. There, the mountain road connected to an autobahn. Plenty of room to pass, not much traffic at this hour, farmland on either side. Best of all, there were many exits, several main roads branching off it, a wide choice of escape routes.

On the autobahn, the van had dropped farther back, the driver biding time. Now, gradually, it closed the distance, ready to ease off if the Mercedes, which could easily outrun the van, accelerated. If it did, they would wait. It did not.

They were near the town of Sargans, where the autobahn would soon branch off toward Austria, and where the morning fog had begun to thicken, when the killers made their move. The Mercedes had remained in the right-hand lane, the van in the center. Now it moved up, slowly, until it had drawn abreast.

Elena Brugg saw the shape. She raised her eyes. The van's driver, a young man, no, a woman, thin, bad skin, was looking back at her. Shouting something. Not watching the road. What is it, she wondered. A low tire?

But then she knew. Even before the side door of the van swung open, she knew. She called a warning to Josef. But the door sprang back. Two men. One was tall, fair skinned. The other was short, dark, with a cigar between bared teeth. That was all she had time to see. Except for the weapons now appearing from behind their backs. The dark one fired first, at Josef.

One short burst, then a longer one. She saw his body shudder under the impact but still he tried to fight. She could see him groping for his weapon as he steered the big Mercedes into the open side of the van in an effort to block its line of fire. But the van swung wide and accelerated. She could see the two gunmen again.

They seemed to hesitate. They had clear shots at Russo and yet they were looking beyond him. They shifted their sights. It was then that Elena knew that she, not Dr. Russo, was their target. As Josef slumped forward, and as the slowing Mercedes drifted onto the soft shoulder of the road, they emptied their clips at her.

Flying glass ripped her scalp. One bullet shattered the forearm that held Russo. Another found her right shoulder, slamming her backward onto the seat. Russo, his last breath a scream of rage, his body jerking wildly under the impact of two dozen slugs, seemed to turn, deliberately, and hurl himself across her body.

She could see nothing. But she felt the bouncing of the Mercedes as it crossed the shoulder and tore through a signpost. It was in a field now, a plowed field, pitching over furrows, turning, tilting, then rolling, so slowly, onto its side. The Mercedes' engine coughed and quit. Now she could hear the screech of brakes, and then running feet as the two from the van rushed to finish their work.

But suddenly, new gunfire. This from a distance. She felt a thrill of hope as, in her mind, she saw her cousin Willem racing up the road from Landquart, his own machine pistol spewing bursts of fire out the window of his car. The running feet stopped, then turned away. Doors slammed. Tires squealed.

Soon there was only Willem. His manner anguished but efficient, feeling the throats of first Russo, then Josef, nodding to her as if to say they were alive although the pain in his eyes told her that his brother, at least, was dead. Then there were sirens. Policemen. Paramedics dressed in orange jumpsuits. Men tugging at her, their voices distant. Then only dreams.

—4—

The nuns had told her, when she was a girl, that one's life passed in review at the moment of death. This was God's mercy, they said. He permitted his children that brief instant in which to remember all their sins, the better to make a good act of contrition.

That had not happened. It was probably for the best. Her thoughts at that time might not have been pleasing to God. The first was of revenge.

Even as the bullets screamed through glass and flesh, she knew who had sent these men. It seemed to her that she had prayed. That she had asked God to spare her long enough to send them to hell.

There were other thoughts, astonishing in their variety and clarity for so short a time. Two seconds. Three at the most. Perhaps the nuns were correct after all.

There were regrets. But more a sense of resignation. She could hardly complain. For much of her life she had played a dangerous game. She knew the risks. She, too, had sent out killers in her time. Still, it seemed less than fair. That life was behind her now. She had been to confession. She had given away millions. She had walked away from millions more.

Nor might God have been pleased that, at the moment of imminent death, she committed the sin of vanity. It was true. She would never tell her priest about it because, even as he gave her absolution he would bring a hand to his face so that she could not see him laugh. For at one point, for one of those seconds, what had seemed foremost in her mind was a concern for the appearance of her corpse. She saw a vision of herself as the police would find her: face bloodied, eyes staring at nothing, mouth gaping, hair dripping and matted, her body in an indecorous sprawl, legs apart, across the backseat of the Mercedes. They would take photographs. And so, even as Russo threw her backward and the car began to roll, she had curled up like a fetus and was struggling to hold her long leather skirt against her calves.

But most of all, she'd thought of Lesko. And whether he would come to see her body. And if he did, would he be sorry that he had hurt her.

And that, Elena knew full well, was the greatest absurdity of all. It was ludicrous. About to meet her maker and yet mooning like a schoolgirl over this great beast of a man who, two years earlier, would happily have seen her in prison and had himself come within a whisper of killing her.

It had happened in New York. Brooklyn. The back room of an abandoned barbershop on a street of gutted tenements. He was still a policeman then. He'd come with a shotgun in one hand, a pistol in the other and vengeance in his heart. He left death all around her. Yet, in the end, he could not pull his trigger that one last time. He'd left her standing there.

Josef had once remarked that she was born again that day. But she knew it was nothing of the sort. A time simply comes when enough is enough. She'd stood there, trembling, long after Lesko had turned away from her and had gone. Then, composing herself, she'd stepped over the bodies of the men he slaughtered, walked out onto the dead street of a dying city, and never again looked back. She would not return to Bolivia. There was no reason. The last of her relatives, on her mother's side, were dead. Her house had been bombed in the drug wars, the servants frightened away. Her only home was a hotel suite in La Paz.

Nor could she have remained in the United States. There were two warrants for her arrest, one from the federal government, the other from the state of New York as a material witness to that so-called barbershop massacre that had filled the front pages of the city's newspapers.

But there was still Switzerland. Where her money was. Where her second family was—that of the Swiss father she had never been permitted to meet until, at age twenty, she telephoned him herself, then met him in Zürich soon after. He, too, was dead now. He had died in the same climbing accident that had crippled Uncle Urs. But Uncle Urs, no less formidable for being confined to a wheelchair, no less the head of the family, had now become her protector. And there were aunts, nephews, and many cousins. All of them welcomed her. Loved her. She felt alive again. Her past, her mistakes, were behind her. All of it. Except for Lesko.

In the two years since the barbershop he was never far from her thoughts. Not for a day. The priest had tried to explain it. This man, the priest said, this policeman, was the instrument of your salvation. Granted, this was not his intention. But your life did turn on your encounter with him. It is perfectly natural to feel certain emotions toward those who have importantly touched our lives.

"Certain emotions?" she asked softly. "The man despises me."

"And you wish he did not?"

"Yes."

"This too seems natural. If he was the instrument of your salvation, perhaps you would like him to know it. Perhaps you wish his forgiveness."

"Father," she closed her eyes, "I ordered the death of his partner."

"The corrupt detective? The one who was stealing from you?"

"Yes."

"And yet, in avenging the partner, Lesko spared you. He must have seen something in you, Elena."

"He saw a small frightened woman who traffics in cocaine. If I were a man I would have been dead."

"And what did you see?"

"In Lesko?"

"Yes."

"An honorable man."

"To whom you told the truth. Even if you would die for it."

"Yes."

"Then perhaps he saw honor in you as well."

"Perhaps," she said quietly. "Father?"

"Yes?"

"If I ask this, you will not laugh?"

"I will not laugh, Elena."

"Is it possible to love such a man?"

"It is clearly possible to become obsessed with such a man. Elena." The priest took her hand in his. "By your own account you saw this Lesko once in your life for no more than five minutes. And afterward, you sent out word among your former associates that, on the lives of their own women and children, neither Lesko nor any member of his family was to be harmed. For that reason alone you might feel a certain bonding with him. But love? I do not think so."

"I suppose not," she said. Her cheeks were burning.

"May I now ask you a question?"

"Of course."

"If he, or a member of his family had been harmed, would you have made good your threat?"

"Immediately."

"But not now. You have renounced all violence just as you have renounced your past."

"It has been two years, Father. The question no longer arises."

"But if it did," he pressed.

"I have not attained sainthood, Father. I owe the man a debt. I will pay it if I can."

Then, perhaps, he could forgive. Even if God and her priest would not. At least, then, she could be free of him.

The two years in Zürich were a cleansing time in a place of peace and beauty. It was one of the few cities in the world that had no slums, no stink of poverty. She made new friends, first those of her cousins and then her own. She began to entertain, as often as before, but now it was for the pleasure of good company. No more strutting Bolivian generals and fawning politicians. No more swinish Colombians with gold crosses on their chests and knives in their pockets who came for the coca leaf with trunks full of American dollars. No more Americans in their suits and ties with the struggle against Marxism on their lips and the rape of her country in their hearts.

In all the ways that she could think of, she remade herself. She allowed herself to gain two kilos of weight. Her cousins said that it became her. She had long been too thin. But she kept her body firm through long solitary hikes in summer and ski lessons in winter. She lightened her hair, to look all the more European, and she cut it short. She wondered if Lesko would like it. She knew that was foolish, the conceit that he would care enough to comment, that he would even remember her face. But she wondered nonetheless.

She remembered him. She'd even painted him. Or tried. It was near the end of the first year. The horror of that day in Brooklyn had begun to fade. Even the lines of Lesko's face, which she saw now and again in dreams, began to soften. It was a massive face, more square than oval. Hair combed straight back, thinning just a bit on top, the color of steel at the sides. It was also a hard face. The eyes were menacing, the mouth was cruel. And yet, she felt, it was not life that made them so, because Lesko's face could be frightening even in repose. His teeth were white, even, and cosmetically perfect and yet, when she tried painting a smile, the result was as intimidating as a Lesko scowl. Unfortunate. An accident of physiognomy. And the eyes, quick, intelligent, cunning, must certainly have been capable of expressing tenderness at some time in Lesko's life—he had, after all, been married once, and had held a child—but her brushes could not find it.

She put the painting away. But she felt good that it was near. She felt safe. Her new life went forward, a season at a time.

And then, one day in January, the phone rang, and the flesh-and-blood Lesko was back in her life. A part of her had never expected otherwise.

It was Josef who called.

"Elena," he asked, "do you know a man named Raymond Lesko?"

Her throat became full.

"This man, Lesko," Josef told her, "has been calling from America. He calls every Brugg in the Zürich directory. He is quite insistent. He says he knows that you are here and you must call him back. He says it concerns not himself but his daughter."

His daughter. Elena bit her lip. Could they have harmed her after all? Fearfully, she placed the call to the number Lesko had left.

She had prepared herself for . . . she did not know what. The worst of news. Threats. Contempt. The hard voice of a hard man who loathed everything she had been. But his voice, when he answered the phone and she said her name, became quiet, gentle, sometimes halting and shy in the manner of a bashful boy. He must have realized how he sounded because he abruptly cleared his throat.

His daughter was well, he told her. What's more, he knew that Elena had protected her. Lesko stammered as he acknowledged this. He could not, Elena knew, quite bring himself to express gratitude. It was in his tone and manner nonetheless.

"Listen," he said. "Susan, my daughter, is on her way over there. She's going skiing with this guy. His name is Paul Bannerman. The story is he owns a travel agency in Westport, Connecticut. Do you know him, by any chance?"

"No," she answered. "The name means nothing to me."

"What about Palmer Reid?"

She frowned. "How are you involved with him?"

"Not me," he said. "The Bannerman guy. I had a friend make some calls. He asked a few people what they had on Bannerman and all of a sudden this CIA guy, Reid, gets very interested in why he's asking. Next thing I know, my friend disappears, but not before he tells me you used to know Reid."

"I knew him. Yes." One of those Americans in suits and ties. The worst of them. A loathsome man. She told Lesko what she thought of Reid. Very powerful. He seemed to answer to no one. Thought to be unstable. He and his people had extorted millions from the *trafficantes* in return for protection from raids and from competitors.

"One more name. Did you know a Robert Loftus?"

She did. "He worked for Reid. Not . . . comfortably, I think. That was my impression."

"That's what I hear, too. I've been leaning on him pretty good."

"This man, Bannerman," she asked. "You think he works for Reid as well?"

"Loftus says no. He says there's bad blood but that's all he'll tell me for now. I'm trying to piece it together but in the meantime I don't want Susan caught in the middle of anything. I'm just finding things out, otherwise I would have broken the guy's legs before I let him take off with her."

"But you believe that Bannerman is involved in drugs. This is why you called?"

"I called because . . . you're in Switzerland, Susan's on her way . . . it just seemed worth a shot."

"I see."

Lesko hesitated. He'd begun to stammer again. "Anyway." He cleared his throat once more. "People tell me he isn't. They say he's straight. But they say it in a funny way, you know what I mean? Like there's more to Bannerman than they want to let on they know."

"I can make inquiries. Do you wish me to do so?"

"Yeah. Yeah, I do."

"Where will your daughter be staying?"

The line fell silent.

"As you wish." She tried not to sound hurt.

"Look . . . Elena."

"Never mind, Mr. Lesko."

"Will you listen?" She heard the sucking in of breath, the choosing of words. "It's not like I think you'd—it's just—sometimes I get a little nervous where my daughter is concerned." Another pause. Another breath. "They got an apartment in a town called Klosters." He gave her the address.

"Thank you, Mr. Lesko."

"Like I said, I know you protected her. If I knew a way, I'd make it up to you."

"It is forgotten." Another long silence. "And what of you, Mr. Lesko? You are well?"

"Not too bad. I'm not a cop anymore."

"I know. I have inquired. You are a man not easily forgotten, Mr. Lesko."

"I don't meet too many like you either."

"Well . . . good-bye."

"Wait a second. If I need to call you again, how do I get you?"

"As you did this time, I think. Call my cousin Josef."

"Direct dialing would be quicker."

"Perhaps . . . perhaps it is best we keep some distance between us, Mr. Lesko." To be in communication with him, this easily, even after two years, she was not prepared for it.

"I guess." He was trying to envision her. A small woman who looked bigger because she stood with her back straight and her chin high. Guts of a bandit. Very classy. Eyes that looked right at you and were a little sad. Pretty. Shiny black hair that kind of flowed down one side of her face and across her throat. A real good, honest face considering the kind of shit she was into. "Listen . . . Elena . . ."

"Yes?" Her voice was soft, expectant. But he had no idea what he wanted to say to her. Or why he wanted to keep her on the phone.

"You take care of yourself, okay?"

He heard a sound. Like words begun, then bitten off.

"Mr. Lesko," she said finally, "we have friends in Klosters. They are reliable people."

"Yeah?"

"If you wish it, I can have them look after your daughter while she is here."

Lesko hesitated, but only for a beat. "She can't know about it, okay? She'd have me for breakfast if she knew."

"She will not be told."

"Then, yeah," he said. "Yeah, I'd appreciate that."

"Good-bye, Mr. Lesko."

"Okay . . . well, good-bye Elena."

It was a small favor, easily done. She broke the connection and dialed the number of Uncle Urs. He would place a call or two. The Klosters police would agree to keep an eye on Lesko's daughter. Perhaps he would send Josef as well.

Then he would ask one of his friends with Interpol to see what, if anything, they could learn about a man named Paul Bannerman. Simple enough.

And yet her hand was shaking.

She did not know what caused it more. The sound of Lesko's voice. Or the name of Palmer Reid.

Two days later, Urs Brugg had learned everything and not enough about Paul Bannerman.

His contact at Interpol, a man he had known since their days at the university, was curiously reticent. He would say only that whatever file that might have existed was not criminal in nature and that the man's activities, therefore, were of no "official" interest to Interpol.

His choice of words, Urs Brugg realized, was deliberately tantalizing. They were those of a man who was already saying more than he should.

"Who, then," he asked, "would have a file, whatever its nature?"

"You have friends with the intelligence services? Ask them."

"Which intelligence services? The Swiss?"

"Any of them. But to save time, do not ask about Paul Bannerman. Ask about Mama's Boy."

Urs Brugg had heard the name. And the whispers. "Paul Bannerman works for this Mama's Boy?"

"Paul Bannerman *is* this Mama's Boy."

By the end of the second day, Urs Brugg had filled the better part of his scratch pad with facts, rumors, legends, and probable lies about the man. The composite that emerged was awash with contradictions. So gray, so unknowable was the overall picture that, Urs Brugg concluded, it was probably clouded by design.

The most balanced view, curiously, came from the KGB station chief in Bern, a man with whom he occasionally played chess. He told Urs Brugg what he could of Bannerman's history. A dangerous man, certainly, but one who kept his word when given. A contract agent, loyal to no particular flag although some bias in favor of the United States must be assumed. Hardly a friend of Soviet interests but even less so to those of the Central Intelligence Agency.

He was said to have retired. Withdrawn from the field. Returned to America. Many of his agents simultaneously vanished from sight. They were said to be with him. Wanting only to be left in peace. No one believed this, the KGB least of all. Two things argued against it. One was that a Soviet defector, a colonel in the GRU, once Mama's Boy's opposite number, had gone with him to America and Bannerman had effectively resisted all efforts to interrogate him. The other was that Bannerman had apparently chosen a known CIA training facility as his new home and had brazenly appropriated it. In the KGB's view, it was inconceivable that either of these would be tolerated by the United States government unless there was a very substantial quid pro quo in the offing. If Urs Brugg could shed some light on its nature, his chess companion told him, the KGB would consider itself in his debt.

Urs Brugg considered all this. But he was soon distracted. Because the same two days later, two boys, hiking with their dog up a snowy mountain path near Klosters, chanced upon the beaten and comatose body of Susan Lesko.

—5—

Elena's telephone chirped. She bolted for it before her maid could dry her hands. Behind her, her evening meal lay untouched.

"Uncle Urs," she closed her eyes. "What have you learned?"

"The girl is alive, but barely," he told her. "Elena. It was done with cocaine."

"Cocai—" Elena gasped. "But the police said she was beaten."

"She was, into unconsciousness," he told her. "Then the powder was forced into her mouth. There are finger marks of a gloved hand across her cheek. It forced her to swallow or to suffocate."

Elena sank into a chair. "But will she survive?"

"The doctor in charge is hopeful but not optimistic. Much depends on the amount she ingested. The cold may also have helped by slowing her metabolism. Still, she is in a deep coma. The next twenty-four hours will tell."

"Uncle Urs," she swallowed hard and lowered her voice. "Please tell her doctor that the girl must be examined for the presence of a suppository. It will be made of cocaine. It is intended as insurance."

A brief silence on the line. His distaste, that his niece would know such things, was palpable. "I will see to it," was all he said.

"This Paul Bannerman," she asked, "He is at the hospital?" The question was asked with bitterness. But for him, the girl would still be in New York. Working. Meeting decent boys. She would be with her father. And Elena would not have failed him.

"He is there now, yes. He seems to have brought at least two bodyguards of his own with him. A man named Russo and a woman named Benedict. The police have picked them up for questioning. It was the woman, Benedict, who assaulted Josef."

Josef had been in Klosters when Bannerman and the girl arrived. On the second day, when heavy snow had closed the ski lifts, the girl had taken the train to visit the shops of nearby Davos. She had gone alone. Josef followed. A woman, an American, had intercepted him in Davos. It seemed that she too had been sent to protect the girl. Each saw the other as a possible assassin. A tragedy of errors. In interfering with Josef, the Benedict woman caused both of them to lose sight of Lesko's daughter. She was left unprotected. The killers, clearly, had been waiting nearby for their opportunity. It came as a gift.

"Elena," he asked, "Do you know who did this thing?"

She took a breath and let it out. "No. Not yet."

"But, Elena, it was done with cocaine," he said gently. "To kill in that manner is to send a message. Whatever else this Bannerman might have been, I am assured that he had no involvement whatsoever with drug traffickers. Not even as their enemy. Could the girl have been involved in drugs?"

"Impossible," she answered flatly. Not Raymond Lesko's daughter.

"Then it must be said. You were involved, as their associate. The father was involved, as their enemy. If the girl herself is innocent, and if this attack was a message, that message must have been meant for either you or the father. Is this not so?"

"Perhaps," she said slowly. "I do not think so."

"Tell me why."

"Because a message is pointless unless its meaning is clear. If this was done because of me, or because of Lesko, they would have called me within the hour to boast of it, to hear my anguish. It is their way."

"Do we then conclude," Urs Brugg asked, "that it must have been done because of Bannerman?"

"If that is so, why this method? Why cocaine? You said he had no connection with it."

"There is one common thread," he reminded her. "It is your former associate, Palmer Reid."

Elena fell silent as she considered the suggestion. Palmer Reid. Even the name, when mouthed, formed the beginnings of a sneer. Lesko had spoken of a connection between Reid and Bannerman. Uncle Urs had confirmed it. But their relationship was far from what Lesko may have imagined. By all accounts, they despised each other.

"Uncle Urs?"

"I am still here."

"It was Palmer Reid."

A long silence. "You say he is responsible? For the attack on the girl?"

"You will ask me why," she said quietly. "You will ask me his motives. I do not have those answers. But Reid is behind this. I feel it."

Urs Brugg started to speak, to argue other possibilities, to point out that no action could be taken on mere intuition. He chose not to state the obvious. "What would Lesko do if you shared that conviction with him?"

"He would go after Reid. And Reid would crush him."

"In that case, Elena, I suggest that we leave the matter in the hands of Mr. Bannerman. He seems more than equal to the task. Has Mr. Lesko been told about his daughter?"

"I have left a message. I will wait here for his call."

"Elena." A thoughtful pause. "I am posting armed guards at your house. If you leave it, I want Josef and Willem with you at all times."

"It is not necessary," she argued. "If Palmer Reid wanted to harm me he would have done it two years ago."

"Not Reid," he said. "Bannerman. Perhaps even Lesko."

The line went silent for a moment. "Lesko would not harm me," she said, her voice small.

"Elena, listen to me." His tone became stern. "I have intuitions of my own in this matter. Neither Bannerman nor Lesko are likely to be behaving dispassionately, especially if the girl dies. The use of cocaine points to you, if not as the killer than as the indirect cause. If you are right about Reid, this may well have been his intention. To set you, Bannerman, and Lesko one against the other."

"Lesko will not harm me," she said stubbornly.

In the intensive care unit of Davos Hospital, a nurse approached the bed where Susan lay. She checked the flow of glucose into Susan's arm, then checked her pulse and jotted the result. Next she lifted the patient's head with one hand and tugged at a bloodstained pad with the other. She replaced it briskly, a bit roughly. The man sitting by the bed looked up at her. The nurse met his gaze, hesitated for a moment, then withdrew. For the remainder of her shift, she would shudder at the look she saw in that man's eyes.

Bannerman stood up. Carefully, tenderly, as if in apology, he smoothed the edges of her pillow. The right side of her face was now in view. He had deliberately placed his chair where he could only see the left side, the less damaged part. Her right eye was swollen shut. The brow was held together by sutures. The cheekbone was fractured. The impression of a gloved hand was still visible across her mouth. An oxygen tube was taped to her nostrils. Her left eye remained partly open, seeing nothing.

"I am so sorry, Susan," he whispered.

In his mind, he saw her as she had been. Lovely. Young. Full of life. A childlike enthusiasm at the prospect of her first trip abroad. Delighting in everything she saw.

They'd gone to London first. She'd never been there. She adored it, she said. Thrilling to all the sights that he barely noticed anymore. She made them fresh again. From London, they boarded a boat train, reaching Paris by early evening, Zürich by the next morning, then on to Landquart at the foot of the Engadine Alps. She was in heaven, every moment of it.

As he sat by her bed, whatever the direction of his

thought, Bannerman's mind would drift back to that train
ride. She was so happy then. So excited. She'd met new
friends. They were charmed by her. They exchanged addresses. One couple, Americans, promised to visit them in
Klosters. He hoped they would not come. Not to see her like
this. Her father would be enough to deal with. He was coming. Anton had arranged it. Bannerman wanted him there
even less but he could not decently have prevented it.

"Our choice," Anton Zivic had told him, "was to fly him
there under escort or to leave him to his own devices. The
man is barely rational. This way we will be better able to
control him."

"Who else are you sending?"

There was an edge to the question. Zivic, on his own
authority, had dispatched the team of Carla Benedict and
Dr. Russo to be in place before he and Susan reached Klosters. Bannerman, he had decided, could pretend all he
wished that he was just another American on holiday, but
someone had to be a realist.

"Molly Farrell and Billy McHugh," he answered. "Until
your mind is clear, I suggest you leave all operational decisions to Miss Farrell. If there is a confrontation between
yourself and Mr. Lesko, I have instructed Billy to deal with
him."

"Anton, I don't want him harmed." Enough is enough.

"That may not be your choice, Paul. Lesko knows who
you are."

"From whom? You told him?"

"He has his own sources. The man has been busy. So have
we. Miss Farrell will brief you when she arrives. In the
meantime," Zivic warned, "Lesko is certain to conclude that
his daughter's present condition is a result of her involvement with you."

"We don't know that," he answered, stung. "The father
made enemies of his own. This is more their style."

"The father," Zivic pointed out, "will be no more willing
to see himself as the cause of this than you are. This is
human. It is foreseeable. You should assume, therefore, that
it is foreseen by someone else as well. Until we know who
that is, let us try not to oblige him."

Zivic was right. Bannerman knew it. And he knew that he

was not thinking clearly. Trying to put this on Lesko's head may have been human but it was also stupid, not to say petty. Still . . .

"Mr. Bannerman?" A nurse, a different one, touched his shoulder. He turned. "There is a call for you," she said. "It is a Mr. Lesko."

Bannerman took it in a private waiting room. He picked up the phone and said his name.

"This is Lesko." The voice was pitched low, little more than a hoarse whisper. Bannerman could hear a rage, and a hatred, held barely under control. In the background he heard a flight announcement in English. The father was calling from Kennedy Airport. "How is she?" he asked.

Bannerman told him all that the doctor had said. Coma. Waiting for tests. Twenty-four hours would tell. He chose not to mention the battering of her face.

"Who did it?" Lesko hissed.

"I don't know."

"Then fucking guess. Who did it?"

"Mr. Lesko"—Bannerman sighed—"it depends on whether this was done to you or to me. Nobody had anything against Susan. I don't know whether she had worse luck being my friend or your daughter."

Lesko took a breath. He had the sound of a man biting his tongue. "What about who did the hit? You got anything there?"

"No."

"No? What's no?"

The question caught him off guard. He had, he realized, answered it almost dismissively because the habit of his years in Europe was rarely to concern himself with trigger men but rather those who sent them. Chasing after hired hands was a waste of time and energy. But a policeman, he realized, would not think that way. In this case, when he thought of it, neither did he.

"So far, no one seems to have seen anything," he said wearily. "All we know is that she took the train to Davos to do some shopping. Then she stopped for lunch at a mountainside restaurant. It was walking down from it that she . . ." Bannerman stopped. In his mind he was staring at an American Express receipt that the Swiss police had shown him earlier. It was from the Schatzalp Restaurant where she paid for her lunch by credit card. The amount. What she paid for the lunch. He'd seen it but it hadn't registered. Almost eighty Swiss Francs. Enough for two lunches. More likely three. When Bannerman spoke again, his voice was soft and distant. "She had lunch with them," he said. "She paid for it."

"Lunch with who? Whoever did it?"

"Unless she ran into . . . I don't know . . . someone she knew from the states."

"Come on, Bannerman. Wake up." Lesko's voice was rising. "Her friends from the states don't hang around Davos and they don't try to kill her. Who did she know in all fucking Europe well enough she'd buy them lunch?"

Bannerman felt the blood drain from his face. Suddenly, he knew. He more than suspected. He knew.

"You there, Bannerman?"

"I'm here."

"Our flight's in a few minutes. We'll get there in about ten hours. Do you think maybe you can give this a little thought in the meantime? Maybe keep an eye on her for a change?"

"I'll see you in ten hours." He replaced the phone.

—6—

Bannerman's eyes were burning. He returned to Susan's bedside where he dampened a towel in a pitcher of ice water and pressed it to his face. It helped him to separate the sting of Lesko's words from their content.

Lesko, of course, was right. Even with his daughter lying close to death, his cop's mind had continued to work while Bannerman's had become paralyzed by the pain of what he'd brought on Susan. The killers had to have been people she knew. People she was so pleased to see again that her own plans for the day could wait. And as clearly as he knew that, he knew that sooner or later the phone would ring and he would hear the voice of the man or woman, the American couple, that they'd met on the train.

They would announce that they were in Klosters, passing through, had hoped to find them free for dinner, and had somehow heard the terrible news of what had happened to Susan. Maybe they stopped at the apartment. Heard it from the housekeeper. In a village the size of Klosters, an attempted murder would be on everyone's lips. They would be shocked. Horrified. Eager to help in any way they could. And, as long as they heard no suspicion in his voice, and as long as they were sure that she was still in a coma, they would insist on coming to the hospital. Good old Ray and Caroline. Middle-aged southerners. Salt of the earth. First trip to Europe. They would volunteer to forego it. To come sit with her. Take up the vigil. Share his burden. Let him get some sleep. And then, because they were paid for results, they would finish her.

Bannerman even knew how.

The Swiss doctor had told him, not an hour before, when he came into the room to describe Susan's condition. Almost lost in his litany of tests they had run and treatments they had given was the mention that no suppository had been found.

"Wait a minute," he'd said. "No what?"

"No suppository. No more cocaine."

"Doctor," Bannerman tried to shake off the fog, "what are you talking about?"

The doctor, his expression now confused, explained about the suppository and its purpose. A guarantee. A time bomb. In the event that the original dose failed to kill her. Bannerman, for a long moment, could only stare. During his years in Europe, he thought that he had seen every possible way one human being could kill another.

"Yes, but," he managed finally, "how would you know to look for such a thing?"

"There was a phone call," the doctor told him. "A man. He suggested that we check for a suppository. Until this moment, I assumed it was you."

"Then you didn't speak to him."

"No. Another doctor. In the emergency room."

"I would like to see him."

The doctor who had taken the call was a younger man, a resident, who had gone with the paramedics to the scene of the attack and had stayed with her until her condition stabilized. The call, he told Bannerman, had been brief. Only a sentence or two but quite insistent. It was taken seriously for two reasons. First, he saw that the girl's ski pants had been torn at the waist as if someone had tried to rip them open but had apparently not succeeded. Perhaps the assailants heard the boys and their dog coming. Second, if there had been a suppository, and it had released its contents, even though the machinery that monitored her vital signs would have reacted violently to it, it probably would have killed her before they could find the cause.

"This man who called," Bannerman asked, "can you tell me anything about him?"

"A deep voice," the doctor shrugged. "A mature voice. Educated. A Zürich accent."

"He was Swiss? You're sure?"

"Definitely Swiss."

Bannerman was more troubled than before. He was not at all in control. Events were controlling him. Too many question marks. Why would a Swiss national be involved? Why would he want to help? How would he know about killing with cocaine?

But after Lesko's call, the most urgent question, at least, had come into focus. Ray and Caroline. If they now appeared, they would be the ones.

They would come to the hospital and they would try again. They would wait until he left them alone with Susan. To make a phone call or go to the washroom. They would need only seconds. He would let them try. Susan would be helpless, he'd be putting her at risk. But if they used cocaine, as he was sure they would, the risk would not be great as long as he was near.

And he would have them. Russo would question them. Inside an hour they would beg to tell who sent them.

Wait.

He closed his eyes.

Hold on a minute.

It's one thing, he reminded himself, to trust his instincts, and another to become obsessive about a possibly harmless American couple he and Susan had met on a train.

Zivic had said it. He was not thinking clearly. Chasing at shadows. On the other hand, the call from the mysterious Swiss reminded him of something he should have thought about earlier. Ray and Caroline, if they were the ones, would have called already, maybe claiming to be relatives, maybe using other names.

Leaving the emergency room, he took the stairs two at a time back up to the main floor corridor where he found a sign marking the cubicle of the hospital's telephone receptionist. There was a woman there, seated at a switchboard. She was young, no more than twenty, bespectacled, no makeup. Probably a farm girl earning extra money between growing seasons. A plastic strip pinned to her blouse said her name was Helge. She looked up at him, questioningly. Her eyes dropped to the two 100-franc notes he was holding in his hand.

"My name is Bannerman," he told her. "I am here with a patient who is in intensive care. Her name is Susan Lesko."

"I know," she nodded sympathetically, "The girl who was beaten. Have they found the one who did this?"

"Not yet," Bannerman shook his head. "There is a chance, a small one, that the person who did it might call to ask about her condition."

"There have been several such calls."

"Several?" They must have come while the police were questioning him. "From whom please?"

"With names? One American, two Swiss. The American said he was her father. The Swiss were from the police here in Davos."

"The father," Bannerman asked, "what did he sound like? I mean, what sort of voice?"

"Like a gangster, I think."

Bannerman nodded. That was Lesko. "There were more calls? People who did not leave names?"

"Three Americans. One Swiss."

"Swiss? Can you describe him?"

"It was a lady. Her accent was . . . I don't know . . . from Zürich but also perhaps Italian or Spanish. She was very sad."

Bannerman frowned inwardly. Another mystery Swiss. "And the Americans? What did they sound like?"

"One man, old. Another man, soft voice like you, most upset. The third man, not young, not so old, a cowboy."

"A cowboy?"

"Like this." She mimicked an accent that was vaguely Texan.

"When did this man call?"

"Just now. Two minutes."

He placed the 100-franc notes on her desk. "If the cowboy calls again, will you let me know right away?"

"This is a matter for the police, no?"

"This is personal. However, you may tell the police anything you think they should know as long as you tell me first."

"I will do it, yes." She picked up the money and held it out to him. "The gratuity is unnecessary. Your friend should not have been beaten."

"You're a decent young woman. Thank you. Can you describe the older American?"

"You know the actor who plays General Patton?"

"Um . . . George C. Scott?"

"Yes," she brightened. "Similar voice. But not so strong. Said he will pray for her."

Bannerman frowned. A raspy voice, authoritative, pious, like General Patton. The description fit Palmer Reid. He was annoyed but not alarmed. Reid might or might not have had him watched. But with satellites, instant global communications, every intelligence network, friendly or otherwise, would probably be reading the Davos police reports by morning.

The other American, young, upset, sounded like Roger Clew. Odd that he left no name. Bannerman needed to call him in any case. Have him get Carla and Russo released by the Davos police in time to be useful for a change. So far, the most useful person he'd talked to all day was a telephone operator named . . .

"Helge," he forced a smile. "May I call you Helge?"

She shrugged. "It is my name."

The money was still in his hand. He raised it "Are you sure you won't . . ."

"Go to your lady, Mr. Bannerman."

Less than an hour passed. A nurse brought him a note from Helge. There had been another call from a cowboy. This time a woman. Still no name given.

Now Bannerman knew he was right. The first cowboy would have been Ray, the second, Caroline. To Helge, an apparent fan of American films and television, their Mississippi accents would be cowboy voices. They were the ones. And they knew that Susan was still alive.

Bannerman checked his watch. It was after nine. By now,

he guessed, they would be somewhere outside. In a car. Slowly circling the hospital building. Looking for signs of a trap. Once satisfied, they would drive away, back to Klosters, where they would go through the motions of a surprise visit. They would find a credible means of learning the terrible news. Soon they would call. This time they would give their names.

From the first-class lounge of JFK's Swissair terminal, Lesko dialed into the answering machine at his apartment and listened to his messages. The first two were from Loftus, almost a day old. One nervous, the next scared. Reid was on to him. He was heading for Westport. Meet him there.

He never made it. Not in one piece. By the time Lesko got to him his face looked like it was meat axed. But he was alive, just barely. The two men who did that to him, according to Bannerman's Westport pals, were not.

Elena's voice came on. His jaw tightened. Although she said little, he could hear the anguish. She left a number, this time her own. He pulled a credit card from his pocket and, turning his back on the two escorts who hovered within earshot, tapped out a series of digits. Elena picked up on the second ring.

"I heard," he said, brushing aside an attempt to tell him gently. "I'm coming over."

He listened, impatiently, as she expressed her sorrow and her remorse over her failure to protect his daughter. "All I want to know," he said, "is who did it."

A small hesitation. "Just come, Lesko. Come to Zürich."

"Was this about us? About what happened in Brooklyn?"

"I am not sure." Another pause. "It is not so simple."

"Then who? Who the hell else kills that way?"

"I . . ." she fell silent.

"Elena," he hissed, "don't hold out on me."

"I will not," she promised. "Come to Zürich. We will talk."

"Where will you be?"

"I will meet your flight. I will provide anything you need. Cars. Bodyguards. Money."

Lesko made a face. The last time she provided bodyguards they weren't worth a shit. But he didn't say it. "What I need is some answers. And I need a gun."

"We will talk."

"What about the gun?"

"We will talk, Mr. Lesko."

"Mr. Lesko . . ." The woman, Molly Farrell, waited until he replaced the phone and stepped close to him, almost touching. She was tall, almost his height. He guessed her to be about thirty-two. With the fingernail of one hand, she began scraping a spot on his suit that may or may not have been there. "Have you looked at your passport?" she asked.

He had. His face was on it. But everything else was false. The name was Dumbrowski. "What about it?"

"If you make one more phone call," she said quietly, "or give us trouble in any way, I will give your real name to the nearest customs officer, or to the nearest Swiss policeman."

He glared at her.

"Further, if you do manage to get your hands on a weapon, I will take it from you, even if Billy here," she gestured toward the silent, burly man who waited several feet away, "has to cripple you first."

Lesko showed his teeth. She touched a finger to his lips.

"You're a proud man, Mr. Lesko," she told him, her expression pained, her manner almost apologetic, "a very tough man. I know that you find it hard to take me seriously. But for all our sakes, please try."

He looked at the eyes. They were more than thirty-two.

"There's one more thing." She took his hand in both of her own and held it against her breast, trapping him. "I also know that you're hurting, and angry, and that for want of a better target you're probably going to lash out at Paul. If you even look as if you intend to harm him, if you do anything whatsoever that might endanger him, I will shoot you dead on the spot. No more talk. No other warning."

He could feel the warmth of her body. Her heartbeat. The rise and fall of her chest. His own pulse had quickened but her's had not. He felt himself becoming flustered. But not angry. If the man, Billy, had said those words, Lesko knew that one of them would have been on the floor by now. And he knew that she knew it. From her tone, the words aside, she could have been talking to some drunk in that Westport bar she ran, saying she likes him, she cares about him, and that's why she won't pour him another vodka and she won't let him drive home and maybe hurt himself or somebody else.

Except for the eyes.

Lesko took her seriously.

Nearly four hours elapsed since Helge told Bannerman of the second call and before the third call came. He took it at Helge's desk. It was the one he'd been waiting for. It was Caroline.

"Paul?" Her voice was tight with concern. "We just heard. Is Susan all right?"

"We don't know yet. Caroline, are you in town?"

"We're still in Zürich. But we were heading down your way and tried to call you to make sure you'd be around. Ray suggested I try leaving a message at your local real estate office, said there probably isn't but one place in town that rents out apartments. The woman there told us Susan got hurt real bad."

Zürich, thought Bannerman. That was better. Less transparent than a sudden appearance in Klosters. And it gave them more distance in case they detected any strangeness in his manner.

"It's bad. It's just as well you didn't come. She may not make it."

"God in heaven," she gasped. "Paul, what happened?"

Bannerman, through gestures, asked Helge to confirm that this was same voice she'd heard earlier in the evening. Helge nodded.

"Sorry," he said, his voice weary, "I thought you knew. Someone tried to kill her."

"Oh, my stars. We thought . . . we just assumed a ski accident. Paul, me and Ray can be there in two hours."

"No," he told her. "No use ruining your own vacation. Anyway it's late and the doctor says there won't be any change until at least this time tomorrow. Of course, if you're coming this way in the morning . . ."

"Just say it, Paul. What can we do?"

"Maybe you can stop in, spell me for a while. I'll need some sleep by then."

Bannerman could hear a muffled conference on the other end. He could make out none of the words but he could guess their content. A weighing of risks. The morning might be better. She could be dead by then. If not, he would be exhausted. They might still decide to come at once but he dared not press them to wait.

"Paul?" Caroline came back on the line. "Ray says no way we're not coming. We'll be there at first light if not before."

"Thank you," he said. He broke the connection.

Helge stared up at him.

"It was these people?" she asked.

"Perhaps. I'm not sure."

She shook her head. "She called before this. She knew what happened to your lady. Now she calls and she does not know. I think you are sure."

"Helge"—he spread his hands—"I need time. In the morning I will have help. If they see police they will not come. My friends are better than police."

She looked at her hands. "I was beaten once," she said quietly. "It was a young man I was seeing. He was drunk."

Bannerman blinked but said nothing.

"His father was rich. The police did not arrest him. He left me with these." She touched a bump where her nose had been broken and traced a scar high on her cheek.

"I'm sorry. I truly am."

"Your friends are better, you say?"

"Yes."

"I will wait for them as well."

Bannerman could think of nothing to say. He reached out, he did not know why, and touched her hair. It seemed to please her. He walked from the room and returned to Susan's bedside. He allowed himself to doze.

Elena Brugg's telephone rang. Reluctantly, she reached for it, first making the sign of the cross. It would not be Lesko. He would be on his flight by now. More likely it would be Uncle Urs with news of the girl. She said her name, then held her breath.

"Good evening, Elena." An oily voice. In Spanish. Or- tirez? No, not possible.

"Who is this, please?"

"You forget old friends so soon, dear lady?"

"Ortirez." She spoke the name drippingly. "Where are you?"

"At my house," he said, his manner cheerful, "enjoying a fine lunch on this beautiful day."

She could hear birds in the background. And children. "What do you want, Colonel?"

"Ah, but I am now a general. And I live in a grand house. Indeed, it was once your house, Elena."

"You are scum, Ortirez." This man a general. The uni- form must have cost him millions.

He laughed aloud. "Such brave words. But from such a distance."

"Then come to Zürich and I will say them to your pig face."

"Ah, but I am there in spirit, Elena. This very day I have made you a present of the daughter of Detective Lesko."

Elena put a hand to her mouth. It was as she feared. She had suspected the *trafficantes,* certainly. But Ortirez? He was a fool and a brute, not given to poetic methods of kill- ing. He would have poured gasoline on the girl and watched her dance.

"Did you hear what I said, great lady?"

"I heard it."

"And when your detective has suffered enough pain, I will make you a present of him as well. I will save you for last, Elena. I will . . ."

"Do I hear the laughter of children, Ortirez?" she asked calmly.

The line went silent. He had covered his mouthpiece.

"Ortirez, do you know what a perpetual trust is?"

He said nothing. Even his silence, she thought, sounded stupid.

"It is a fund of money that carries out one's wishes even after death. This fund will contain two million Swiss francs. Do you know how much that is in pesos, Ortirez?"

"Tell me about your fund," he said, attempting scorn, "and I will laugh at you."

"Oh, the bounty will not be on your life, Ortirez. That would be merciful."

He waited.

"First it will be for the eyes of your children and the noses of your women. I will keep them here in a box where I can count them. Next it will be for your disease-ridden cock, Ortirez. I will dry it and frame it so that those who come to my house may make jokes about the great General Ortirez."

At six in the morning, Helge shook Bannerman awake. He bolted to his feet. She calmed him. The cowboy, she said, had called again. Again he asked if Susan Lesko had yet regained consciousness. She told him she had not. Bannerman composed himself. He thanked her.

He stepped inside the curtain that surrounded Susan's bed. No change. He tried not to look at her face, at the bruises and swelling. It would anger him, make him hate. He needed his head clear. At any moment now, their friends from the train would come walking through the front entrance. He took a towel from her nightstand and dipped it into a small pitcher of ice water. This he dabbed against his face. It was better.

But he was still not ready for them. No word from Carla or Russo. Those coming from Westport would not arrive for three hours at best. Until they were in place, he could not leave Susan's side. He hurried to the washroom where he freshened himself, then to a vending machine where he bought two cups of coffee in plastic containers. He settled in to wait.

It was not yet sunrise when the killers came.

Ray and Caroline—he in his cashmere topcoat, hat of Irish tweed, his expression pained, compassionate, she in a silver fox, eyes wide, questioning, caring. In Ray's hands, a thermos of coffee and a box lunch with the logo of Zürich's Dolder Grand Hotel on it. A nice touch, he thought bitterly. He put it aside. Then he hugged them.

He declined their offer, several times repeated, of croissant sandwiches and good Swiss coffee to replace the metallic brew he'd taken from the machine. It was vile but it was coffee. And it contained no chemicals that might, at the very least, have caused him to sleep.

For three hours they sat or paced, making small talk, sharing words of encouragement. Caroline Bass busied herself gently brushing the tangles out of Susan's hair, running a piece of ice over her parched and swollen lips. Bannerman stood by the bed, watching her every move, doing his best not to seem unduly suspicious. They were cool. He had to give them that. And patient. They also seemed thoroughly genuine. In their eyes, their actions, he could see nothing but kindness. No unspoken signals flashed between them. None of those searching looks that often follow a lie. There were moments in which he almost began to doubt that they were anything other than what they seemed. Perhaps it was his own fatigue, his own guilt, that led him to embrace suspicions that might not outlast a good night's sleep. Adding to the doubt was the fact that he had never heard of them. A folksy husband and wife hit team of late middle-age seemed likely to have been the subject of an anecdote or two over the years. On the other hand, the only Americans he knew much about were those who had worked Europe and the Middle East. And, in addition, Ray and Caroline gave no sign of having heard of him either. Perhaps that, more than anything, was at the root of his doubts. He could not imagine a team being sent after someone who touched his life without at least being cautioned that he wasn't quite what he seemed to be. It was a conceit, he realized, but a reasonable one.

But then Helge came into the room and his doubts faded. She nodded politely and handed him two slips of message paper. The first was from Molly Farrell. Their flight had landed. She was awaiting instructions. Bannerman scribbled a reply. The second was from Helge. It said, *I have listened. These are the voices from the telephone.*

By the end of the second hour, Bannerman's bladder began to ache. In his mind he saw the car that should now be en route from the airport at Zürich after first securing weapons from a local source. He willed it to hurry. A nurse entered the room carrying towels and a tray of bathing materials. Caroline stood up. She'd been a hospital volunteer back home, she said. If the men would like to stretch their legs, she would bathe Susan herself. It would help her to feel useful. Bannerman thanked her but said it could wait. The third hour passed.

They were well into the fourth hour of their vigil when Bannerman heard, from the corridor outside, the sound of a woman's footsteps followed by a quiet cough. The footsteps went back the way they came. It was all he could do to show no reaction. He let a full two minutes pass before he rose stiffly to his feet. "Too much coffee," he said, moving toward the door. "While I'm gone I'll see if I can find some newspapers."

"You take your time," Ray smiled and nodded. "We'll be right here with Susan."

The men's toilet was just off the main lobby. On his way to it he saw the woman who coughed. She was seated just inside the main entrance, reading a magazine. Bannerman stopped to relieve himself. He took his time washing his hands. Emerging, he saw that Ray was now in the corridor outside the intensive care unit. Bannerman knew what was being done to Susan. He tried to block it from his mind. He stretched and yawned, then turned his back on Caroline's sentry and strolled toward the entrance where he stopped, pretending to watch the passing traffic, within a few feet of Molly Farrell.

"You got my message?" he asked.

"Uh-huh." She did not look up. "Who's Helge?"

"A new friend. Who's outside?"

"Billy's watching the front. Carla and Russo are covering the back and side."

"How long have they been there?"

"Maybe two hours."

"It's nice someone told me."

"Count your blessings," she said through stilled lips. "Lesko and three others are down by the railroad station."

"Three others? What others?"

"More new friends," Molly Farrell said simply. "They're keeping Lesko away. You have ten minutes tops. Don't push it."

He had less than five. Lesko had agreed to ten minutes while Molly scouted the hospital area. It seemed only prudent but the time passed too slowly and he had come too far. His daughter was in there. Shaking off Elena's hand, he opened the door of her Mercedes and began pounding up the hill in the direction indicated by hospital signs. It was a one-way street. The car could not follow. She ran after him on foot. Her two cousins in a second car sped off to intercept him by a different route.

At the hospital's front desk, Bannerman purchased a copy of the *Herald Tribune* and returned at a measured pace to the intensive care unit. By the time he arrived, Ray and Caroline were slipping into their coats.

"I cleaned up her face a bit," Caroline told Paul. "Gave her a little of my Shalimar behind the ear."

"She'd appreciate that," he said. "Are you leaving?"

"Wouldn't think of it," Ray shook his head. "Me and Caroline just thought we'd get a breath of air before we settle in for the duration."

"Good idea," he forced a smile. "Listen . . . I don't know how to thank you for . . ."

"Oh, hush." Caroline kissed his cheek. He kissed her in return.

Bannerman listened as their footsteps receded down the corridor. He walked to a supply cabinet where he found a box of plastic gloves. Slipping one over his right hand, he stepped quickly to Susan's bed and drew the curtains fully. Bracing himself, he reached under the sheet that covered her and he parted her legs. He began probing.

A soft moan came from deep within her chest. One knee quivered, then rose. Bannerman felt a thrill of hope. She was reacting. Still, he probed. His gloved fingers found something hard. Carefully, he eased it backward in the direction of his palm. He had it. He looked down. There was the suppository. Sculpted out of paraffin. He pressed his thumbnail into it. The coating cracked, showing a core of white powder.

What he should have done, what he'd intended to do, was withdraw his hand and leave the room at once. To follow the killers, to cut off their retreat. But Susan had moaned. She'd reacted. He wanted to touch her again. To watch her eyes this time, to see her chest rise and fall. His fingers probed once more.

"Come on, Susan," he whispered. "Come on."

She gasped. A sucking in of air. The knee came up higher. "Good girl. That's it. Come on. Come on back . . ."

"What the . . ." A voice behind him.

"You creep. You fucking creep." Bannerman went rigid as Lesko's fist slammed into his kidney.

—7—

His face was burning as he staggered from the room, the glove and suppository still gripped tightly in his fist. His hurts ran deeper than Lesko's blows. He was furious with himself.

Stupid. Unprofessional. Humiliating.

He knew how it must have looked to her father. Bannerman didn't blame him. The man wanted to kill him. He might have, had not that woman rushed into the room just behind him. One of the mystery friends. It was she who'd kept her head. She'd tried to stop Lesko. To pull him off. And failing that, she'd calmly stripped off her stout leather boot and swung it against the side of Lesko's head.

In the corridor, Bannerman gathered himself as two nurses and a security guard rushed to the source of the shouted curses and crashing furniture. The pain was easing as he walked toward the hospital exit. But a crushing sadness had come in its place.

The humiliation, he knew, would pass. Soon enough, Lesko would learn about the suppository. He would be forced to accept that what he saw was not a sick act of manual rape but an attempt to save his daughter's life. But, soon after, he would see the other side of that coin. That Bannerman had used her as bait. And he would want to kill him for that, just as Bannerman would in his place.

The two killers, husband and wife, had intended to leave by the front entrance. Taking their time. Strolling away up toward the Davos shopping promenade where they had left their car rather than risk having it trapped in the hospital lot.

But the woman Bannerman knew as Caroline had just reached the automatic doors when she saw Lesko, head down, coat flying, storming up the hill in their direction. Behind him, calling to him, came a fur-wrapped Elena Brugg. She recognized them both. Caroline had seen their photographs, memorized their faces. She tugged at her husband's arm, drawing him back into the lobby. There was another door. A stairwell. She knew that it led to the emergency room. Her husband nodded. He led her through it.

"You get a gold star for your timing, darlin'," he said, reaching the first landing. "Right now, I'd say we got one too many fellers named Ray around here."

"That was him all right." She glanced toward the ceiling as if she could see him going by. "You do know that was Elena with him, don't you, love?"

He nodded. "Shame we have to leave. Won't likely be another time when we got all three of them practically within the swing of a cat."

"Everything in its time and place, darlin'." They hurried along the ground floor corridor. "For now, let's get at least an hour away, down toward Italy. Then we can call like we're still here in town and get the bad news about poor— Goodness, what was that?" A loud crash echoed from above. A woman's voice shouted. Sounds of running footsteps.

Her husband looked up. "That's about where Susan is," he said. "With all that bangin' and smashin', maybe that suppository wasn't as slow releasin' as advertised."

Caroline frowned. "The suppository was just fine. More likely that big ox, Lesko, tripped over a chair on his way in. Still, we hadn't ought to dawdle."

"Let's not get careless, either. When things start to go funny, they tend to go in bunches."

"After you, darlin'," she said.

Carla Benedict's job, as assigned by Molly Farrell, was to cover the emergency entrance and to cut off any escape uphill toward the town while Molly and Billy McHugh covered the route down toward the railroad station. But Carla, eager to be in on the action wherever it happened, had chosen a position half the distance between the emergency entrance and the main entrance. She and Gary Russo were fifty yards from where they should have been.

Still, when a middle-aged couple stepped arm in arm from behind a row of parked EMS vehicles, Carla spotted them at once. Slowly, her eyes widened. A smile tugged at her mouth. "Well, I'll be damned," she whispered.

"You know them?" Russo asked.

She shushed him. "I'll tell you later," she said. She watched them go.

The couple turned uphill but she waited, expecting Bannerman to appear and signal her to close on them. He was nowhere in sight. When she could wait no longer, she had to choose. Either follow them up a street that offered no real cover or try to get ahead of them and contain them until backup could arrive. She and Russo had scouted every street within three blocks of the hospital. The one to her right ran roughly parallel. If she hurried, sprinting all the way, she could intercept them before they reached a street where there was pedestrian traffic. But Russo, she knew, could never keep up with her.

"You follow from here," she told him. "Stay in the middle of the street where Paul can see you if he comes out. Otherwise, keep them in sight. Do not engage. Don't worry about them spotting you."

Before he could object, she took off at a lope toward the nearest corner and disappeared from view.

It was Russo's pride that would kill him. If not in five minutes, then within the hour. True enough, Russo would admit, he was not the equal of the others when it came to a field action. Nor had he had any special training in the art of surveillance, although he tended to regard it as less an art than a matter of common sense. And, true enough, he had no great experience in the techniques of silent killing, an aptitude that, in his view, reflected more a personality disorder than a talent. Still, so be it. They had their specialties and he had his. But for Carla to use him in this manner was an insult. She'd as much as said, just stay out of the way, distract them if you can, but let me handle them. Well, he decided, he might not be a Billy McHugh or a Carla Benedict but he'd show them he was easily the match of that middle-aged couple now puffing up the hill ahead of him. And he was damned if he would stroll like a dummy up the middle of this street waiting for one of them to decide to turn and put a bullet in him.

Carla Benedict's eyes were shining. The couple that she'd been told to watch for, middle-aged, well dressed, passports identifying them as a Ray and Caroline Bass from Mississippi, were no more from Mississippi than she was. It had been years, fifteen at least. But she'd have known them anywhere.

The man was Harold Carmody. The woman was Lurene, his wife. She also knew the way they liked to work. Get close in. Get friendly. Pick your time. Then vanish. They always had good paper. Somewhere, she knew, there would be a real Mr. and Mrs. Bass. Probably off on a world cruise or touring India by yak. Some damned thing. Harold and Lurene would leave a trail a mile wide but all it would lead to in the end would be a pair of bewildered vacationers someplace wondering what the hell the arresting officers were talking about.

Last she'd heard, they'd retired. Bought a house in Lubbock to be near the grandchildren. They must have gotten bored. Maybe, she wondered as she ran, they got into a drug habit and it got expensive. Maybe, somewhere in there, was an explanation of why they'd use cocaine as a weapon. It didn't sound like them. They never touched drugs that she could recall. Hardly even drank. Anyway, Harold liked to work with a knife. Cocaine was dumb. Iffy. Too slow. Carla made a mental note, if they got a chance to chat, to ask them about that.

Harold and Lurene, as Carla intended, had spotted Russo.

"I'd say we got company, darlin'." Harold Carmody nudged his wife as they trudged up a crooked street lined with old converted warehouses and an occasional shuttered shop selling plumbing or electrical supplies.

She nodded that she'd seen him. "Real sloppy company if you ask me."

Russo may have been the only man in Davos wearing a chesterfield coat and a homburg hat. He walked with both hands in his pockets, elbows out, in the manner of Peter Lorre. Worse, he stayed close to the building line, trying to seem casual, pausing now and then to examine the odd window display of toilet mechanisms and drain snakes.

Carla Benedict's intention was to distract them, to make them wonder. Russo made them certain.

"Two or three more blocks," Lurene said, "and he'll see the car we're driving. We don't have time to idle around so he don't. I suggest we either lose him real fast or you gut him."

Just ahead of them, the street they were on doglegged about twenty degrees to the left. Half a block farther it veered back to the right.

"Darlin'," he said, "we round this little corner here and you just zip on ahead. Wait for me 'round the next one but let that feller see a little piece of you turnin' out of sight."

"All right, but don't linger with him," Lurene said sternly. "Never mind asking any questions. You just kill him and be done with it."

"I wasn't of a mind to socialize, darlin'."

A BMW, Billy McHugh driving, swung into the street a full two blocks below Gary Russo. Bannerman, holding a bloodied handkerchief to his mouth with one hand, pointed with the other. Russo was approaching a blind corner from its near side.

Billy shook his head ruefully. "Hugging that wall's a good way to get his throat cut."

Bannerman could see that. "Maybe you'd better tap your horn."

"They'll hear it too," the bigger man frowned. "Wherever Carla is, she's got something going here by now. We could blow it."

Bannerman hesitated. But Billy was probably right. "Let's just get up there," he said.

Russo, approaching the bend, had hesitated as well. But now he could see the next corner. There was the woman. Just disappearing from view. Looking ahead, not back. Gesturing with her hands. The man must be in front of her. Russo cursed. Lose them and he could look forward to about a month's worth of crap from Carla.

Rounding the dogleg, he lengthened his stride. As he passed a recessed doorway, his eyes locked on the corner beyond and his inner brain tried to shout a warning that something was wrong. There was a shape in that doorway. He sensed movement. His head turned to glance over his shoulder but, before his eyes could focus on the shape, a gloved hand clamped over his face. It jerked him backward. An arm coiled round his waist and, with it, the white hot rip of a knife point as it probed for a space between his ribs. Russo was sure he was dead.

"Car–mo–dyyy . . ."

A distant call. Carla's voice. Then, to his right, the squeal of a car's brakes. The man behind him stiffened. Abruptly, the gloved hand came down from his eyes and grasped him across his burning chest. He could see, through tears of pain, but he could barely breathe. He looked down past the arm and he saw, to his horror, that the long thin knife, blood running down its blade, remained in his chest. He could not tell how far it had penetrated except that he saw no tapering of the blade at all. Only parallel edges of steel.

"You get one chance." A voice to his right. Billy's voice. "Ease it back out or you're dead."

He saw Billy, his face dipped low over the barrel of a silenced pistol that was aimed at a point just behind him. And Paul, in the passenger seat, climbing out now. And Carla. Here comes Carla. She's walking with the woman, half-dragging her. The woman's face is smeared with blood.

"Well, I'll be . . ." Russo heard the voice at his ear. There was no fear in it. More a sense of wonder. "Hello there, Carla, honey. Little rough on an old friend, aren't you?" Russo felt himself being dragged deeper into the doorway. The knife twisted. He began to scream but could only gag.

"Paul?" Billy's voice. "I got no shot."

Carla was close now. With the woman. He saw a knife in Carla's hand as well, its blade held high against her cheek.

"Lurene?" The voice again. "Lurene, darlin', are you okay?"

"I'll mend," she said thickly. "Just don't you let go of that hole card."

"Paul, my friend," Carmody pressed his back against the padlocked door, "I'd say we got ourselves a stand-off here."

Bannerman rounded the car, his eyes, with no expression, locked on those of Harold Carmody. He stepped to the driver's side and held out his hand toward Billy McHugh's pistol. "Billy," he said quietly, "give me that, please, and open the trunk."

"Darn it," Carmody clucked his tongue. "I just knew there was somethin' about you. If you're who I think you are, me and Lurene had a real careless briefin'." Ruefully, he glanced toward Carla Benedict. Hadn't seen her in fifteen years but he'd sure heard about her. Even worse, the feller Paul called Billy, that'd be Billy McHugh himself. *Ah me,* he thought sighing. *And if they're with Paul Bannerman, answerin' to him, the Paul must be . . . damn. Careless ain't the word for it.* "Anyhow, Paul, put that thing up. Shoot me and you as good as kill your friend here."

"Harold," Carla Benedict said through her teeth. "You stick him any more and you'll watch me core old Lurene's eye like a fucking apple."

"Paul?" Carmody's voice went higher as Bannerman shifted the silenced Ruger into his left hand and stepped toward him. "Paul, it weren't personal. Fact is, me and Lurene were gettin' real fond of you and Susan."

"Uh-oh," Carla gestured urgently with her chin. "Paul, on your left."

Bannerman glanced down toward the hospital. There was Lesko, his face white with rage, charging the hill in their direction. Bannerman did not break stride. He reached for Russo's right hand, which had been hovering, quivering, over the knife as if afraid to touch it. Calmly, almost gently, Bannerman took the hand and raised it to shoulder level. He fired three times.

—8—

Lesko was the first to return to the hospital. He came alone. The look in his eyes, thought Elena, was strangely distant.

"Did you find them?" she asked.

Lesko nodded vacantly. "I want to see Susan." He brushed past her and opened the curtain surrounding his daughter's bed.

"The news from the doctor is good," she said to his shoulder. "She is responding. Her lips have been moving. Coma is becoming sleep."

"Yeah, look," he said without turning. "Leave us alone, will you?"

Elena backed out. She closed the curtain. Behind her, a tapping on the glass partition. Molly Farrell was there, her expression anxious.

Elena listened to the events of the last twenty minutes. One man was wounded. He insists that his wounds are not immediately life-threatening but he needs attention where no questions will be asked. Does Elena know of such a place? She did. She and her cousins would take him there at once. She returned to Lesko's shoulder.

"I must go," she said. "One of their men needs help."

"Yeah. Go ahead." He still did not turn.

She brushed against him, reaching to touch Susan, to remove a strand of hair from her face.

"Look," he snapped. "I asked you. Leave us alone."

Elena stepped back. She paused, hugging herself, stung by the unexpected brutality of his dismissal. There seemed nothing to say to it.

"Good-bye, Lesko."

She turned and walked away.

Lurene Carmody, gagged and tightly bound, one eye swollen shut, watched the preparations being made for her interrogation.

A plastic automobile cover, proof against blood stains, had been borrowed from the basement garage and spread over the carpet of Bannerman's Klosters apartment. She was lifted onto it. Now Billy McHugh was drawing the room's upholstered furniture close around her. Next, she assumed, would come the bedroom mattress to serve as the roof of a small soundproof chamber. Carla Benedict had Russo's medical bag. She was sorting through its instruments, laying out the set of probes with which Russo normally began. Lurene caught her attention with a muffled grunt, then shook her head slowly. Carla understood. She approached Bannerman, who was in conference with Molly Farrell, listening intently, and spoke to him quietly. Bannerman glanced at Lurene, hesitated, then nodded. Carla stepped to the older woman and loosened her gag, leaving the scarf in place beneath her chin.

Lurene tried to moisten her lips. Her tongue was dry and thickened. She gestured toward several bottles of wine that sat on a side table. Carla found one that had been opened and poured a glass. She held it to Lurene's mouth. She drank all of it, then nodded gratefully. She looked up at Bannerman.

"Paul?" she asked quietly. "You're Mama's Boy, aren't you."

He said nothing. There was no need.

She shook her head ruefully. Poor Harold. Stuffed into that trunk downstairs. She'd tried to tell him they were getting too old for this.

"Paul?" She made a face, "is there a way in the world to convince you that me and Harold never knew who you were until we saw Carla and Billy here?"

"Would it have made a difference?" he asked coldly.

"Sure as heck would." She raised her eyebrows. "For one thing, we would never have let you see us. For another, even if we took this job, which I'm not real sure we would have, we never would have fooled with drugs. Harold and me don't like 'em anyhow."

"Who hired you?"

"I truly want to answer that, Paul. Like Harold said, we got an awful careless briefin' and I'm not feeling real loyal to the son of a bitch who left out all those details. I got a suggestion."

Paul waited.

"Let me go and I'll let his air out myself. My word on it."

"Carla?" Paul asked.

"She'd keep her word, but no."

"Billy?"

"That's games," he shook his head. "Don't play games."

Bannerman nodded agreement. Saying nothing, he reached into his pocket and pulled out the plastic glove containing the suppository. He held it up for Lurene to see, then placed it on the counter next to Carla.

Lurene understood. She'd just been given a choice. Hard or easy. *Ah, me,* she thought, *there were sure worse ways to die.* She'd take easy. Still, it was going to be damnably unhygienic, considering where that thing had been.

"The man I'd have got for you," she said, "is Oscar Ortirez. He's a general down in La Paz. I swear those people got more generals than bathtubs."

Bannerman frowned. The name meant nothing to him. "How is Palmer Reid involved?"

Her eyebrows went up again. "If he is, Paul, we don't know it. Me and Harold got our standards."

"What's the connection between this Ortirez and Susan?"

"My guess?" she shrugged. "None at all except Lesko. And Lesko's friend, Elena. She used to work with Ortirez. Maybe Lesko did too."

Bannerman had long known about the barbershop killings. The cocaine. But he'd known nothing of Elena Brugg, or her involvement, until Molly, just now, had explained it to him.

"Then why?" he asked. "Why do this to Susan?"

She shrugged. "These people have done whole families. They do them first. It's for the hurt of it."

"To punish Lesko." Bannerman closed his eyes. Deep within himself, he felt a stirring of something akin to relief. He wanted to believe it. That Lesko was the reason. That he himself was not. But when he looked again at Lurene Carmody, she was shaking her head.

"He was next, all right," she said. "Then Elena Brugg. Thing is, no one said we had to give either one time to stew."

Bannerman's jaw tightened. "You think it's me."

She smiled. "Not till today, I didn't. But seein' who you are, Paul, it just don't seem too likely that you're an innocent bystander."

There were more questions. They led nowhere. Lurene Carmody knew nothing more. Bannerman could make no sense of it. Three murder contracts, all with the common thread of cocaine and of events that happened two years before in which he was not involved. If ever these three were to be killed, it should have been then. Or soon after. Why wait so long? Why in Switzerland? Simply because Susan was then on Elena Brugg's doorstep? Bannerman could not believe that. Too much trouble, too little point. And could it be mere chance that an attempted punitive murder of Lesko's daughter came at a time when she was involved with a man who could, if he so chose, field a hundred killers of his own? He didn't think so.

He had to accept, however grudgingly, that Lurene Carmody's intuition was correct. He was not an innocent bystander. Someone, perhaps Reid, perhaps not, was trying to punish him, more likely to manipulate him. But into doing what? Starting a war against some obscure Bolivian? Against the drug traffickers? Against Reid himself? He had no idea.

But if someone was indeed trying to use him, he would soon know it. All he had to do was the unexpected. Which

was to do nothing at all. Then wait and see who suggested
what.

The telephone rang. He took the call. It was the receptionist, Helge, at Davos hospital. Susan Lesko, she told him,
was regaining consciousness. She seemed to recognize her
father. She comes and goes. Too early, the doctors say, to
know if there will be lasting damage. But she would live.
Bannerman let out the breath he had been holding.

"There have been more calls," the young Swiss told him.
"And there are flowers."

"Who called?"

"A Mr. Zivic from Westport. He said he is your friend."

"He is. Who else?"

"A Mr. Clew from Washington. Also a friend. He said he
is flying here today."

"This Mr. Clew. Could he be one of the Americans who
called earlier? The young one?"

"It was the same man, I think. The older man called as
well. A Mr. Reid. It was he who sent the flowers."

Bannerman grunted. Christian charity from Palmer Reid.
"Is there a message?"

"The card said . . . I wrote it down, *You are in my
prayers. A speedy recovery.*"

"No, I mean for me."

"To you he says, *Whatever might be going through your
mind, I know nothing. Whatever our differences, any help
you need, it is yours.*"

Bannerman sighed. Reid was nervous. He was right to be.
But Bannerman could not imagine what Reid had to gain by
trying to hurt him through Susan.

"Thank you, Helge," he told the young Swiss. "You've
been most helpful. I want to do something for you. I'll send
you something."

"We have discussed that sufficiently. You are not coming
to the hospital?" There was rebuke in her tone.

"I don't think so. As long as her father is with her,
I . . ."

"You will come," she said firmly. "It is the correct thing."

A long pause. "Yes. Yes, it is." He surrendered. "I'll be
there shortly."

The correct thing, he thought. But to what purpose? At best, another angry scene with the father who despised him. More lies to Susan. But they would be the last.

He left Carla Benedict and Molly Farrell to finish with Lurene. His word would be kept. Lurene would die peacefully of a cocaine overdose although, if he knew Carla, Carla would make her chew it. Later, after dark, she and Harold would be slid through a hole chopped in the ice of a frozen lake. Possibly, knowing Carla, each minus a thumb that would be neatly boxed and couriered to a Bolivian general named Ortirez.

Billy McHugh came with him. Billy insisted. "We get to the hospital," he told Bannerman, "you let me handle her father. He comes at you again, I'll take him. It wasn't dignified, you rolling around the floor like that."

—9—

On a Zürich-bound TWA flight less than two hours out of Washington, Roger Clew, his expression drawn, stared at the screen of the laptop he'd opened up on his tray table.

He'd reserved two seats, the window for himself, the aisle to be kept vacant, and had asked for the last row in business class so that a bulkhead would be at his back. On the tray table next to him his lunch sat untouched. He was too sickened to eat. And not a little afraid.

Only a few hours before, the Ripper Effect had been theory. Not any longer. Now it was real. It had predicted the murder of Susan Lesko.

Granted there were other predictions, ranked in order of probability. And granted that the attack on the girl was far down the list of the possible courses of action that might be taken by Palmer Reid. Still, it was there. He had seen it. He had known it could happen. He had done nothing to prevent it.

But it was not his fault, he shouted within himself. Who in his right mind would have predicted that Reid would react to the appearance—not the fact, the *appearance*—of a linkage between Bannerman and Elena by moving to destroy the chain? Even the computer predicted that surveillance, not action, was far and away the most likely course he would follow. Even allowing for the fact that Reid was *not* in his right mind. That he hated Bannerman. That Reid, given two or more possible courses of action, would almost always choose the most devious.

True, after surveillance, the computer did assign a better than 90 percent probability to some sort of interdiction. Specifically against Elena, and, although less likely, against Lesko. As for the girl, the probability of action against her was so small it hardly made the chart.

Still, with all of that, he should have known because he knew Reid. The man, crazy or not, was a genius at misdirection. His mind worked with a kind of loony logic that no computer could fathom. Except this one. Because Reid, without realizing it, was employing the premise of the Ripper Effect. The disruptive effect of random terror. Clew asked the computer to forecast the consequences of that act. He typed:

EFFECT/INTERDICTION:
ASSASSINATION/SUSAN LESKO:
FUNCTION/PREDICT

He tapped the "return" key, his eyes on the screen. The reply appeared in milliseconds, again in ranking order.

ENMITY: BANNERMAN/PP UNKNOWN	100.0
ENMITY: LESKO/BANNERMAN	94.0
ENMITY: LESKO/BRUGG	21.4
ENMITY: BANNERMAN/BRUGG	16.3
ENMITY: BANNERMAN/LESKO	11.7
ENMITY: BANNERMAN/REID	0.4

There it was. A 100 percent certainty that Bannerman would now turn all his energy toward hunting down the person or persons unknown. A 94 percent probability that the father, Lesko, would hold Bannerman to blame for what happened to his daughter and was very likely to be in a killing rage when he saw all that had been done to his daughter. A much lower probability that Lesko would blame Elena but, Clew realized, that assessment would change drastically if he told the computer that the weapon was cocaine. Similarly, only a small chance of Bannerman blaming Elena. Or the father. Almost no chance at all that he'd blame Reid. Reid, Clew realized, would not even have appeared on the list had he not built in the presumption that, if Bannerman were harmed in any way, Reid's involvement could never be ruled out entirely.

And yet Reid had done this. He knew it. He could almost see the meeting in which the decision was taken. Reid and his bitchy little assistant, Whitlow.

The girl, Reid would remind them, is a reporter. There can be little doubt what she intends to report. Then he would turn away, his back to Whitlow, and he would say something like, "We can do nothing, of course. We are a nation of laws. The girl's actions, however, have put her at risk with others who do not share our concern for due process." Now, Reid, still not looking at him, would paint a scenario of what those "others" might do about her. The method they might use. And, he would say, it would be no more than just. A case of Elena's chickens coming home to roost. And those of her father. "But, of course," he would add, "we will pray that no such tragedy befalls these people. We will pray that we are mistaken." *Reid, you fucking snake.*

Whitlow would take the cue. He'd farm out the job, outside the company, probably to the traffickers, telling them it's time Lesko and Elena paid their bill. He would say nothing about Bannerman; no use dampening their enthusiasm. And Reid would keep his back turned. Not even Whitlow would see the gleam in his eyes as he envisioned Paul Bannerman, crushed and broken by the girl's death, lashing out in impotent rage, making mistakes, scattering his forces. He would see Bannerman, Elena, and the girl's father all at each other's throats, whatever plot they might have been hatching now in tatters. He would see a vulnerable Bannerman. A careless Bannerman. He would begin to see a day, not far off, perhaps even at hand, when a clean sweep could be made of Westport once and for all. His humiliation avenged.

"Jesus Christ," Clew muttered aloud.

It was all so damnably dumb. So pointless. There was no plot. Nothing. Bannerman *happened* to get involved with a girl whose father *happened* to know Elena Brugg who *happened* to have some dirt on Palmer Reid. You couldn't even call it coincidence. Almost everybody knows somebody who has dirt on somebody else except most times they never know it because the chain never connects.

Anyway, who'd give a shit?

Tell Bannerman you can prove that Reid was extorting drug money and you'd get, at the most, a yawn. But try telling a paranoid son of a bitch like Reid that nobody cares, that everyone just wants to be left alone, that Bannerman has probably never even heard of Elena before now, and you'll get that patronizing little smile of his that says why don't you run along and leave these matters to the professionals.

He should have known. If he'd programmed the computer properly, he would have. But how do you program meanness? Vindictiveness? There had to be a way. He'd work on it.

A more immediate question, he reminded himself, was what to tell Bannerman. That he knows it was Reid? That he saw this coming? No way. Bannerman would ask how he knew. "How, Roger, could you know what Reid knows unless you told him? Is that what you did, Roger? Did you put a bug in his ear? Did you, for example, make a careless phone call over an unsecured line, maybe to Irwin Kaplan's home phone, knowing that Reid almost certainly had a wire on it? Did you ask him a few harmless questions about Lesko, and Elena, and Zürich? Did you remark on the odd coincidence that Lesko's daughter and I just happened to be on our way to Switzerland? Is that why this happened, Roger? Did you set me up?"

No. I mean, I never intended . . .

Christ!

Get a grip, Clew told himself. Bannerman won't ask those questions. No way he could know about that phone call. And even if he did, no way he could conclude that the leak was deliberate. That his friend of more than fifteen years was playing computer games with his life. And he would certainly be in no mood to listen to computer theory, especially if the girl comes out of this with her brain fried.

No. First things first. What was needed now was damage control. What he had to do, one way or the other, was head off a war. At least until he was ready. Until it was his war, fought his way.

"Excuse me?"

Roger Clew looked up, startled. A man was standing in the aisle—young, middle thirties, dressed in a sweater and jeans. Clew had not noticed him. He raised one hand to cover the screen.

"Yes?" he asked.

The man held up a cigarette and gestured toward the front of the business-class section. "I couldn't get a seat in smoking. It looks like you've got two. Mind if I grab a quick one?"

"I'm afraid I do mind," he answered. "I paid for both of them so I'd have room to work."

The man's eyes dropped meaningfully to the vacant seat. No papers, no briefcase. Just the uneaten lunch. "I won't stay but five minutes. One cigarette?" he pleaded.

Clew hesitated. Then he nodded. "Sure," he said. "One cigarette."

In five minutes, the man was gone. Clew was grateful that he'd made no attempt at conversation. No "What brings you to Zürich?" No "Nice machine you have there." No questions that would have made Clew wonder about him more than he did already.

It was so damned exhausting.

—10—

"Mister Bannerman? Wait, please!"

The receptionist, Helge, called his name as he and Billy McHugh passed her cubicle en route to the intensive care unit. He heard her chair scrape against the floor. Ahead, through a glass partition, he could see the bulk of Susan's father rising to intercept him. Billy edged forward, placing himself between the two men. Bannerman turned back. The young Swiss approached him, a message slip in her hand and something, concern perhaps, in her eyes. But his mind was on the confrontation that awaited him.

"Thank you," he said, and began to pocket the slip.

"No." She stopped him. "You must call."

He unfolded the piece of paper. A name and a Zürich number. Urs Brugg. A relative, he assumed, of the woman, Elena. Probably news about Gary Russo's condition. Bannerman looked up at Helge and again he noticed her eyes. He saw more than concern. She was staring at the message slip as if afraid of it.

"What has happened?" he asked quietly.

"Please." She gestured toward her cubicle. "You must call."

* * *

At Helge's desk, as the young Swiss waited in the corridor with Billy, Bannerman listened, his face drained of color, as Urs Brugg described the ambush that had left Gary Russo and Josef Brugg dead and his niece, Elena, dangerously wounded.

The voice on the telephone was softly accented, a deep and gentle bass. It sounded somehow familiar.

"My niece," Urs Brugg told him, "would not accept sedation until I promised I would speak to you. She is alive because she was shielded by the body of the injured man, Russo. She asks me to persuade you that such use of him was inadvertent."

"I . . . understand," he answered, stunned. He had watched them leave. Russo in the left rear, held in the woman's arms.

"It is Elena's impression, however, that your man was unimportant to them. Both gunmen, after first shooting Josef, concentrated their fire on her. My nephew Willem drove them off before they could finish her."

Bannerman's brain was whirling. He groped for a chair and pulled it under him. Beyond the shock of Russo's death and learning that a second team, a back-up team of killers had been near, he found himself trying to envision this man, Urs Brugg, who could speak of ambush and murder with such self-possession. But more than that, he wondered why. Why first Susan and now Elena, two women whose only common thread tied them to Raymond Lesko?

Urs Brugg appeared to read his thoughts. "It is Elena's belief that she and Mama's Boy share a formidable enemy. The policeman, Lesko, is in danger as well."

Mama's Boy. Bannerman let it pass. "Did she name this enemy?"

"Yes." Urs Brugg hesitated. Bannerman could hear the drumming of his fingers against the telephone receiver. "She accuses Palmer Reid."

Bannerman felt suddenly out of control. Too many connections. Too many people knowing more than he did.

That voice. "Mr. Brugg," he asked, "do I know you, sir?"

"We have not met."

"Did you call this hospital yesterday? To advise the doctor who was treating Susan Lesko?"

"Yes. Also at the request of my niece."

"How did you know to look for a suppository?"

"Elena has seen this method before."

"When she trafficked in cocaine?"

He heard a cluck of the tongue. An expression of distaste. "There are more generous ways to characterize what she did," Urs Brugg told him. "I emphasize *did*. Nonetheless, you are correct."

"I'm sorry. I have to know this."

"Yes." A long pause. "Elena asked that I hold nothing back. It is difficult."

"Tell me about Palmer Reid, then. How is he involved?"

"I am asked to explain this to you as well. But I must also tell you that she accuses him without evidence. It is intuition, no more."

Evidence. Bannerman closed his eyes. There is never any evidence. Intuition is everything. "Please tell me."

For the next two minutes, Bannerman listened patiently as Urs Brugg provided a capsule history of Elena's life. Swiss father, Bolivian mother, born in Zürich during the war. At war's end, mother and child went to visit her family in La Paz. Kept from returning. Marriage annulled. Elena then raised in Bolivia where the family plantations had grown coca leaf for nearly 300 years. Did not stop selling it simply because the United States government declared Bolivia's best cash crop to be illegal. Demand soared. Profits huge. Competition became murderous. Elena Brugg forced to protect the interests of her family, many of whom died during the cocaine wars of the eighties.

Bannerman had little interest in her personal history and less in the justification of Bolivia's drug crop. But Urs Brugg needed to say aloud how he had come to terms with the life his niece had lived; Bannerman did not press him.

His head stopped nodding when the narrative reached its first mention of the Central Intelligence Agency. When Palmer Reid saw that cocaine traffic could not be stopped at its source, he decided that some of the enormous profits could be used to fund his own activities. He entered into agreements with certain of the traffickers, offering them pro-

tection in return for huge sums of cash. The Bolivian grow-
ers chose Elena, who was educated, multilingual and non-
Latin in appearance, to be their representative in dealing
with Palmer Reid.

Urs Brugg now described the events that had led to her
retirement, beginning with the murder of a New York police
detective and the retribution exacted by his partner, Raymond Lesko, in a Brooklyn barbershop. One of the dead,
unknown to Lesko, was an agent placed there by Palmer
Reid to protect his interests. The transaction that Lesko
interrupted was actually a transfer of cash and pure cocaine
to Reid's people. Elena, left standing there among the dead,
decided enough was enough. She told Reid she was finished.

Reid threatened her. Elena, by then safely in Zürich, told
him to do his worst. Reid also accused her of complicity
with Lesko, reasoning that he would not have let her live
had there not been an arrangement between them. She denied it. Reid said that Lesko, in any case, would have to die.
His loved ones as well. Reid would not prevent it. He could
not afford to appear weak in the eyes of the traffickers. Elena
swore to Reid that whatever harm came to Lesko or his
family would also be visited on the family and the person of
Palmer Reid.

"Why?" Bannerman interrupted, startled. "Why would
she protect Lesko?"

"It is . . . um, perhaps in the nature of a penance. Perhaps a compulsion. Even Elena cannot explain her emotions
toward this man."

"This threat. Reid took it seriously?"

"I added my voice to it."

"I see," he said politely.

Urs Brugg heard the doubt. "I am not without means,
Mr. Bannerman."

It was said quietly. Not boastfully. Bannerman chose not
to challenge the statement. But the weapons of Urs Brugg's
world were likely to be money, influence, connections. Not
guns and bombs. And yet, apparently, Reid took him at his
word.

"What changed?" he asked. "Why would Reid try to kill
Elena now?"

"Because he saw that Elena had somehow recruited

Mama's Boy to her cause. And that Mama's Boy was clearly in league with Lesko, even to the extent of using Lesko's daughter as the means of exposing his drug dealing on the pages of a New York newspaper."

Bannerman was silent for a long moment. "You do realize," he said slowly, "that none of this is true? That I never set eyes on Lesko or your niece, or even heard her name before today?"

"Of course. But Palmer Reid does not."

Another long silence. "I don't believe it."

"Please tell me why."

"To begin with, I couldn't care less that Reid is involved in cocaine traffic. If it wasn't Reid, it would be someone else. I have no interest in Reid as long as he doesn't bother me."

"Would he believe that? The man hates you. Therefore, he fears you."

Bannerman shook his head. "Which is why he would not dare hurt someone close to me."

"But if he had succeeded, if Lesko's daughter had died, whom would you have blamed?"

Bannerman didn't answer.

"Drug dealers? Lesko himself? My niece? Have not each of these crossed your mind?"

Bannerman hesitated. "Yes," he admitted.

"And were it not for this conversation, Mr. Bannerman, would you have gone home to Westport and licked your wounds or would you have begun a vendetta?"

Again he did not answer. There was no need. The first thing he would have done would be to track down the man named . . . "Ortirez," he said aloud. "Do you know that name?"

A thoughtful pause. "I gather you have heard from him as well."

"As well?"

"He telephoned Elena, last evening, from La Paz. It is clear that he thought your Susan was dead. He *claimed* responsibility. Boasted of it. Elena did a foolish thing. She threatened him, insulted his manhood, apparently frightened him. He reacted more quickly than she anticipated."

Bannerman heard the emphasis on the word *claimed*.

"Do you have reason to doubt that he ordered Susan's death?"

"Oh, he probably did. But on his own? Surely not. The man is a creation. A tool."

"Of Reid's?"

Bannerman heard a grunt. The equivalent of a shrug. "Of the money. The power. Reid's hand can be suspected but not presumed. He does not rule that country. He uses them, they use him."

Bannerman frowned. Twice now, Urs Brugg had stopped short of unequivocally condemning a man he clearly despised. "What would you like me to do?"

"I do not presume to tell Mama's Boy his business."

"And yet you've as much as told me that Palmer Reid is behind all this."

"I have told you," Urs Brugg corrected him, "what my niece thought you should know, and what she believes to be the truth. I do not doubt it. Neither do I rush to accept it. When a truth comes so easily, Mr. Bannerman, I have learned to examine it all the more closely."

"One does not," Bannerman replied slowly, "always have that luxury."

For what seemed a long time, although it might have been measured in seconds, Bannerman stood silently at Susan's bedside. She was breathing easily without the need for oxygen. The tube that had been taped to her nostrils had been taken away and someone, perhaps her father, had arranged her hair so that the damage to her face was less apparent. A part of him wished that she would not waken. That he would have an excuse to back quietly out of the room and out of her life.

"Two minutes, Bannerman," Lesko had said to him. "That's enough to say good-bye. After today, I don't want you near her."

There could have been another brawl. Lesko had raised a hand against his chest as he approached. Billy stepped in close, his body crowding Lesko's, his mouth almost at Lesko's ear. "You don't want to do that," he said, his tone more reasoning than threatening. Bannerman knew that tone. Lesko was within a heartbeat of having his fingers crushed or worse. He had never seen anyone last more than a few seconds against Billy. Not that close. On the other hand, looking into Lesko's eyes, he understood that the same could probably be said of him. Bannerman placed a staying hand on Billy's shoulder. "Two minutes is fine," he said. He stepped past Lesko.

"You know you're a jerk?" Billy stayed with Lesko. They stood, side by side, watching through the glass partition. "You ought to learn who your friends are."

Lesko ignored him. He saw one of Susan's hands reach up as if she'd been startled. Bannerman took it. Now he was leaning over her. Kissing her forehead. Touching her cheek. Come on. Get on with it.

"Helping you, we lost the Doc. He's dead now, too."

The Doc? Oh, yeah. The guy who got knifed and shot up. Funny, he didn't look that badly hurt. But Lesko would never forget what he'd seen Bannerman do. Never hesitated. Never even blinked. Just walked up close and blasted, using his own guy's armpit to muffle the shots. Himself, he couldn't have done that. Not that last part.

The thing with Elena bothered him as well. Maybe he shouldn't have talked to her the way he did. She tried to help. She did help. He wasn't mad anymore about her whacking him. It was just that he didn't want any of this shit, none of it, near Susan anymore. Maybe she'll come back down, he'll apologize. Maybe he'll write her a letter.

"Helping you," Billy turned, poking him as Lesko had poked Bannerman, "even your own friends got shot. You don't care about that either?"

Lesko was in no mood. His impulse was to swing except this guy was a tank and he knew that another fight would get them all thrown out of there for good. "Wait a minute. What?"

"The lady who drove you. When she drove back."

Lesko brushed the hand away. "What the hell are you talking about?" He suddenly felt ill. In his mind, he saw the young woman who'd stopped them in the corridor. She had a message. And when Bannerman finished with her, when he came back up, his eyes were cold and hard, looking past him like he wasn't there.

* * *

Susan Lesko knew that he was there. And that he was saying good-bye. Very softly. Telling her how sorry he is.

She tried to blink away the fog. Other faces swam by. Ray and Caroline from the train. But they couldn't have been there. They were dead. She was sure of that. Her father had as much as said so. They can't hurt you anymore, he'd whispered to her. Their deaths were in his eyes.

"Your father," Paul was saying, "will stay with you. You're going to be okay. He'll explain why I have to . . ."

Will he tell me who you are?

No answer. Not to that. He must not have heard. Now he's saying how he never meant to hurt her. That he did love her. But that it was wrong. A mistake. And it was selfish. He was stepping out of her life. He would never expose her to anything like this again.

Schmucky lines like those.

She wanted to tell him to shut up, give her a minute, let her head clear, but the fog was coming back in waves.

She wanted to say, "Look Bannerman, I'm not stupid. I knew from the start that there was something about you. All those funny looks you get, and I get, from so many people in Westport, as if everybody there knows something I don't. Like, for example, that you're two different people. That's right, isn't it? Like my father, all the time he was a cop. One person while he was working, someone else when he was home. You're that way too.

"And the way you got close to me. Patient. Taking your time. No wrong moves. Me wondering what a guy like you, sophisticated, world traveler, would see in a twenty-four-year-old cop's daughter from Queens.

"What is it about you, Bannerman? What is it about Westport?"

She felt his fingers touching hers. His shadow leaned over her. She felt his lips touching her forehead. They were dry. The shadow backed away. It turned.

Paul?

There were things she wanted to say to him. And ask. She couldn't be sure, through the fog, whether she was saying them or not. Or whether he answered. And now he was going.

This isn't over, she called. *Damn it. You're going to talk to me. Bannerman?*

But he was gone.

"Hold it." Lesko fell in step with him as he hurried down the corridor. "What about Elena?"

"She's been shot. She's in surgery now." He kept walking. Billy had gone ahead for their car.

"Will you wait?" He grabbed Bannerman's arm. "Where is she? How bad?"

Angrily, Bannerman slashed at Lesko's hand as he turned, his nose an inch from Lesko's. "There are two dead," he hissed. "They both tried to protect your daughter. One was a friend of mine. The other was Elena's cousin. Lesko, I don't have time for you right now."

"You going to her? I'm going with you."

"You're staying with Susan. The killing isn't finished." He pulled an automatic pistol from his hip and jammed it into Lesko's belt. "I'm sending Molly Farrell down here to help you."

"I don't need any of your goddamned women. And don't you tell me what I'm going to—" He didn't finish. Paul seized his lapels and slammed him backward against the wall. Bannerman stepped away, eyes burning, and waited.

Lesko made no move. His fists formed into clubs and he dropped into a crouch but that much was reflex. Slowly, he straightened. Paul turned away.

"Bannerman," Lesko said huskily. "Wait. Wait a second."

"Now what?" Paul slowed.

"Okay. Sometimes I can be a prick where my daughter is concerned. Not just with you. Anyone."

Paul listened.

"On top of that, I was a shit to Elena. I don't even know why, because she was never anything but straight with me. One minute I'm ready to break your back for putting Susan in danger and the next I'm ready to leave her alone here while I run off to Elena. I don't know. I . . ."

Bannerman's expression softened a shade. Still, he waited.

"It's okay to send Molly. I appreciate the thought. I'd also appreciate it if you call me when you know something."

"You have a place to stay?"

Lesko shook his head.

"Use my place. Molly will bring you the key and she'll get you a car."

Lesko nodded thanks. "Look . . . if you see Elena, if you talk to her, tell her for me . . ."

"Tell her yourself, Lesko." He walked briskly toward the street at the sound of Billy's horn.

—11—

Snow had begun to fall as they drove back to Klosters. The road was becoming slick. But the BMW, its traction improved by the weight of Harold Carmody above its rear wheels, pressed on confidently. Bannerman said little. Billy left him to his thoughts and to his private sorrow. In Klosters, they stopped at a hardware store where Bannerman purchased a hatchet and saw.

Arriving at his apartment, he found the body of Lurene Carmody bound in a dark blanket and readied for removal. Another blanket, this one for Harold, sat on a chair by the door along with some towels and a bottle of household cleanser for later washing the vinyl floor of the BMW's trunk. Bannerman gathered these and Billy hoisted Lurene Carmody under one arm. Carla Benedict went ahead to see that the way was clear. They proceeded to the garage. Bannerman, with Billy, would dispose of the bodies on their way to the Zürich airport.

Molly Farrell had packed his belongings, his and Susan's, holding out her toiletries and a change of clothing to be worn when she was able to travel. She would bring these to the hospital.

It surprised her, somewhat, that he'd asked her to stay with Susan. It was not like him. His normal practice would have been to disperse them all, see them out of Switzerland as quickly as possible and by different routes. If he needed people to stay behind as observers or, as in this case, bodyguards, he would have hired free-lance talent rather than ask one of his own to take on a job that was outside her specialty. A single call, Molly knew, could have had a dozen armed men speeding toward Davos within the hour, probably refusing payment, preferring to be able to say that when Mama's Boy needed reliable people, they were the ones he chose. A more immediate alternative would have been to send Carla or Billy. Both deadly in close quarters. But he'd asked her, an electronics expert, to do the job of a shooter. She questioned him with her eyes and he looked away. Then she understood.

The BMW, Billy driving, continued northward through thickening snow. They reached Landquart and the autobahn as the sun went down. Twenty kilometers farther, the sky nearly dark, they saw slowed traffic and flashing lights at the place where Elena's car had been overtaken. Billy slowed, staying to the right. The Mercedes was still there, on its side, illuminated by spotlights and by the glow of flares that funneled all traffic into a single lane. Several cars marked *Polizei* lined the shoulder of the road, their blue lights strobing. Two uniformed policemen paced the shoulder, heads down, searching for shell casings with the aid of a metal detector. But for that, it seemed the scene of an ordinary wet-road accident. Cars crawling past, children pointing, windows being rolled down to ask hushed questions. A silent policeman, shaking his head, not answering, waved them forward.

"A cowboy job," Billy muttered contemptuously.

"Uh-huh," Bannerman nodded, agreeing. It had been hastily conceived. Messy. Too many ways for it to go wrong. Whoever hired them, apparently this Ortirez, either didn't know how to pick the right men or was desperate to see that Elena never lived to make good her threat. Probably both.

Billy glanced at him. "You okay? You want to talk?"

"I need to think. But thank you, Billy."

The BMW sped on. In another fifteen minutes, darkness

was total. Their headlights picked up signs leading to the Wallensee, a deep freshwater lake that had frozen over during this unusually cold January. Billy flicked his turn signal and climbed the exit ramp.

The shore of the Walensee was less than two kilometers to the east. A single lane road led to a cluster of boarded-up summer cottages. He backed the BMW between two of them, its rear end a few feet from the shore. There they waited for thirty minutes as their eyes adjusted to the night. Billy nodded that he was ready. Taking the hatchet and saw, he walked out onto the ice where he cut two holes fifty yards from shore and as far apart. Returning to the car and satisfied that they were unobserved, Billy hoisted Harold Carmody over his shoulder and made his way to the larger of the two holes. He slid Harold through the ice, then returned for Lurene. Bannerman, meanwhile, made a bundle of the Carmodys' legitimate travel documents, weighted by their weapons and Billy's as well, and dropped these through the smaller hole. Their false papers, identifying them as Ray and Caroline Bass of Mississippi, had been left in their pockets and purse. Bannerman replaced the disk of sawed ice, then returned to the larger hole, dropped in the tools, and did the same there. He could feel, through his feet, the two bodies gently bumping against the underside of the ice. They would sink within the hour. The holes would freeze solid by morning. Fresh snow would probably cover all traces. If not, any visible signs that remained would look like the work of ice fisherman. The bodies would surface sometime in April. They might never be correctly identified by the police. But the people who lived in his world would know who they were and who put them there. He would see to that. Satisfied, Bannerman returned to the car.

His mind now clear of that task, Bannerman tried to focus on the conversation he'd had with Urs Brugg and on the action that he must now take as the result of it. But it was difficult. There was the road to watch, ahead and behind. They were vulnerable here and unarmed. And there was Susan. He saw her in his mind. Sitting up by now. Moved to a private room. Hearing, from her father, all the lies she'd been told. But he'd never lied. He wanted her to know that. Perhaps Molly would help her to understand.

Molly.

He had no business asking her to stay. He knew it and so did she. What's more, he would soon have need of her back home. A job more suited to her skills. Not that Molly couldn't protect Susan. He had bet his own life on her more than once. It was just that she and Susan knew and liked each other. They'd had lunch together several times, played tennis once. Susan would talk to Molly. Listen to her. Trust her. Maybe.

He'd considered sending Carla, to keep her mind off Gary Russo. Maybe he should have. Carla would have jumped at the chance to drive the last nail into that relationship. Good riddance, she'd say. You shouldn't have let yourself get involved with an outsider anyway. Especially a reporter whose father is a cop. Especially that cop. Besides, Carla had told him more than once, she's just a kid. You need your ashes hauled, find a hooker or pick one of us. We're all happy to oblige. You won't have to tell us you love us and we won't ask any questions you can't answer. Try telling the truth to that kid, she'll run screaming from the room, first back to daddy and then to her city editor. Next day we'll have the network news all over Westport.

Bannerman knew she was probably right.

Even so, he could have choked her.

Molly, on the other hand, had encouraged him. Susan was young, she said, but not *that* young. And forty-ish was hardly old. Susan was also bright, thoughtful, energetic, had a good sense of fun and she was kind. Being her father's daughter, she was not likely to be fragile. *"She could be good for you,"* Molly had said. Could it last? Long-term, probably not. But most relationships end. Why treat this one any differently? Everyone has secrets that they can't or shouldn't share. Get what you can out of it, give what you can, tell her what lies you must for her own sake as well as your own.

Susan, he hoped, would open up with Molly. People just naturally did. Molly would tell her what she could, help her understand, take some of the edge off whatever her father was saying to her.

"You're thinking about Susan, right?" Billy asked quietly. They had entered the airport grounds. He was following the signs for rental car returns.

Bannerman sat up. "Among other things."

"I liked her," he said. "And you know what? She liked me too, I think."

"Everyone likes you, Billy." Bannerman turned his head toward Westport's favorite bartender. "You've made more friends than any of us."

"That's what Molly says." A shy smile. The statement pleased him. It still felt funny, a little, but he was getting used to it. All those people, every day, getting off the train and coming into Mario's for a drink. Talking to him. Not afraid of him. Telling him jokes. In his whole life, before, he couldn't remember anyone ever telling him a joke. Or talking sports with him. Mostly, before Westport, they'd just stare for a second and then look down. Sometimes they'd get smart with him to show they weren't scared. He'd look back at them, not saying anything, wondering why they were being jerks. Then their spit would dry up. For certain people, it was good they were afraid. But for others, sometimes that hurt his feelings.

People did like him. He had friends. And it didn't feel funny any more and it didn't cause problems for Paul like in the beginning. Back then, before he got used to it, he figured that if you got a friend, and the friend gets in trouble, you help him out. His friends would come into Mario's and sometimes they weren't smiling. He'd ask what's wrong and mostly they'd tell their Uncle Billy. You'd be surprised, the problems people have. Guys getting sued, or cheated, or fired off their jobs. Burglars working their neighborhood, taking their stuff. Women getting beat up by their husbands but afraid to move out. Women getting raped. And not just by street punks either. One was by her dentist after he gave her gas. Another was by her shrink.

He had helped them out. Some of them. He made it look good. Like accidents and suicides. Before you knew it they were smiling at their Uncle Billy again and talking about nicer things. He never said anything. For a couple of years, nobody even noticed.

Then one day Susan Lesko shows up in Westport to help this friend of hers from college move into her new house and she finds this little book about Connecticut that's full of statistics. It says Westport is a good place because crime, especially the last couple of years, is so low. But it also says people there are more careless than almost anywhere else in the state because they keep drowning in bathtubs or getting electrocuted and that they must worry a lot because a lot of them take the pipe. It wasn't such a lot. It was like eleven. But Susan thinks maybe there's a story for her paper and she starts snooping around. Paul thinks maybe she knows about us so he gets to know her and finds out she doesn't. It's just those statistics. At first he feels better but then he starts wondering about them himself. He asks around. Then he asks straight out. You can't lie to him. It was the only time since he first knew Paul that Paul almost yelled. Anyway, he promised he wouldn't do that any more. Not unless Paul or Molly or Anton Zivic said it was okay and how it should be done. Carla's on the council too but she didn't get a vote on this. She'd always say yes because she's a little mean. Also, she'd suggest complicated stuff like letting a guy wake up with his own cock in his mouth. That's games. He didn't like games. When you go to fix something, you fix it. Speaking of which . . .

"Paul?"

"Yes, Billy."

"All what happened here. It's Palmer Reid, right?"

"He denies it."

"Right. And he sent flowers." Billy curled his lip. "What about this guy, Loftus? He doesn't tie Reid in?"

"Not to this. Not to Susan."

Loftus.

Molly had briefed him. He'd been sent by Reid to watch Lesko. Lesko had spotted him, grabbed him, ended up offering him a way out from under Reid, and probably his life, if he'd cooperate. Loftus told him about Reid and Mama's Boy, also about Reid and Elena. But these, as far as Loftus knew, did not connect. Reid obviously learned that his man was trying to deal. Probably tapped Lesko's phone. Sent two men to silence him. Do it near Westport. Make it look like he, Bannerman, ordered it. But the two men came too close. Anton had Loftus now. Gave him sanctuary. Perhaps they'd get more out of him when he could speak again.

"Tell you what," Billy said. "We'll go home, and me and

Johnny Waldo will disappear for a week or two. Time we get back, you won't have to worry about Reid no more."

"I don't think so, Billy. Not yet."

"The more we wait, the more he's got the edge."

"I know."

"Especially," the bigger man said, "someone's got to pay for Doc Russo. Even if it's the wrong guy. You can't let anyone hit you without you hit back. Otherwise, word gets around."

Bannerman understood that. The Carmodys were a start but they would not be enough. Certainly not for Carla. He shifted uncomfortably in his seat. "Billy?"

"Yeah."

"Is there anything about this that just doesn't feel right to you?"

"Like what?"

"I don't know." They had entered the parking garage. "Roger Clew is on his way over here. Why?"

"To help out, right? Wasn't it him who sprung Carla and the Doc?"

"Probably," Bannerman acknowledged. "But all that took was a call or two. Any other time we've needed Roger's clout, the best thing he could do for us was to stick close to his phone. Why, this one time, would he feel the need to come to Switzerland?"

"The other times weren't personal. They didn't mess up your head."

Bannerman closed one eye. "You're saying he came to save me from myself."

"Don't knock it. So did me and Molly." He found a parking space in the section reserved for Eurocar rentals. "You know what I think is different here?"

Bannerman waited.

"The girl back there. Susan." He jerked a thumb in the general direction of Davos. "She's got you thinking too much. It's the one bad thing about liking women."

"I suppose."

"Take my word."

Bannerman had to smile.

"On Reid too," Billy said firmly. "It's him."

"Or somebody wants us to think so."

"I know." Billy shook his head. "Things aren't always what they seem. But you want to know something else? Most times they are."

"Let's just get home, Billy." Bannerman opened his door.

He had not booked a flight. Better not to announce their intentions. Getting seats on a weekday would not be difficult. Bannerman's more immediate concern was to get through a crowded airline terminal without being shot. Elena's car had been hit on a main highway in broad daylight. Anyone that desperate might not hesitate to shoot up the line at the Swissair check-in counter, especially knowing that the two of them were sure to have discarded their weapons. Bannerman's next concern would be getting through passport control without being detained by the Swiss police. They'd have identified Russo's body by now and connected Russo with him. Urs Brugg had warned him of that. He promised to distract them if he could but he urged Bannerman to waste no time leaving Switzerland. Bannerman would try to call him from the boarding gate. Ask about Elena. See if she's out of surgery. And he'd call Molly. To ask about Susan. And to tell Molly that he'd changed his mind. She should get home as well.

They entered the terminal, each with a ski bag and boot bag. Just two more skiers. Best way to pass unnoticed through a Swiss airport in January.

Dropping the car keys on the Eurocar desk, they proceeded to the Swissair counter. Bannerman paid for their tickets with a credit card, checked their bags, and moved directly to passport control. The official there, in his glass booth, examined their passports then stared at each of them with more than passing interest but he made no move to check their names against the computerized stop list in front of him. Now the official's eyes flicked past Bannerman's shoulder. Bannerman saw a tiny nod. He turned, his stomach tightening. He saw a man, thirty paces away, dressed in a leather topcoat, his arms folded. He glanced around the terminal. Two more men, one on either side, stood facing him. He looked back at the man in the leather coat. The man touched a finger to the brim of his hat, smiled briefly, and turned away.

It was Willem Brugg.

In an eighteenth-century villa overlooking the lights of Zürich, Urs Brugg winced as his chess opponent pounced on a bishop whose bad intentions Brugg hoped he had disguised.

He was man of middle size, made to seem larger by a broad chest and powerful arms and shoulders, which for twenty years had done the work of legs. A thick Hemingway beard added to the impression of mass. The beard and his hair, worn in a near crew cut, were the color of steel wool. His face was unlined, except at the edges of his mouth and around his intelligent blue eyes, where deeply etched creases gave him a look of sustained amusement.

The room in which he spent much of his existence had been a ballroom in another age. The ceiling, blue in the daytime with painted clouds, became a twinkling night sky at sunset, lit by scores of tiny bulbs. The walls were hung with art, all of it light and summery. Outdoor scenes. A mountainscape done by his niece had recently displaced a Monet a thousand times its value although not as prized. The centerpiece of the room, other than Urs Brugg's desk, was an astonishing Turkish carpet, all silk, 2,000 knots to the inch, forty feet in length. It was set on a parquet floor with ample room around it for the passage of his wheelchair. At each end of the room, matching screens of carved Swiss oak concealed the otherwise jarring notes of an electrically adjustable bed and a small gymnasium of weights and pulleys. His desk was in the center. Behind him, French doors opened onto a stone balcony that ran the length of the room. On it, covered now with plastic tents, were many flower boxes whose cultivation was among his hobbies. It was there that he took his midday meal in all but the most inclement weather.

At the left side of his desk, as he sat, was an antique armoire that concealed an elaborate communications center that included two computer consoles, a telefax machine and telex printer, and a voice-activated telephone system that remembered hundreds of unlisted numbers.

The chessboard was to his right. His opponent, a smaller, balding man with the dress and manner of a rumpled academic, pondered his next several moves while absently signaling, with the stem of his pipe, that the light on Urs Brugg's private line was flashing. Urs Brugg spun his chair and picked up the phone.

"Yes, Paul." A short nod to the other man, then he grunted dismissively as Paul Bannerman thanked him for the protection provided by his nephew and for the apparent influence that had been applied on the man at passport control. Urs Brugg gestured toward his opponent and held out a hand for the folder he had brought. The other man pushed it across the desk. Urs Brugg opened it to a photograph of Paul Bannerman, grainy, much enlarged, not recent. His opponent reached to select a second photo, one of several. "McHugh," he mouthed. "The man with him."

Urs Brugg shrugged. His interest in the second man, the brutish one, was limited to his capacity to protect Paul Bannerman. From his appearance, he seemed adequate to the task.

"Yes, Willem called as soon as you were safely past our friend at the booth," he said into the telephone. "You are leaving none too soon. The police think they have the lot of you contained in Davos. They have set up roadblocks."

He listened, hearing no concern in Bannerman's response. He studied the photograph. An interesting face. Curiously gentle. He set it down as Bannerman asked about his niece.

"She is still in surgery. The damage is extensive. And your Susan?"

"I'm about to call," Bannerman told him.

"Please keep me informed."

"I will, sir."

"Today," said Urs Brugg, "I have put a price on the men who shot Elena and killed Josef. If Mama's Boy finds them first, will he give them to me?"

"Mr. Brugg, I would prefer to be called by my name."

"Forgive me. Mr. Bannerman, then."

"Paul is fine. In any case, those men are only shooters. They're a dime a dozen in Europe. I'll try to do better than that."

"It is . . . as we discussed, I take it."

"I'm not sure. I hope to be. Very soon."

"And if you are not?"

Bannerman hesitated.

"You will act nonetheless." Urs Brugg answered for him. "Do others know this about you?"

"Sir?"

"That no assault on you can go unpunished. That an immediate response must be presumed, regardless of any remaining doubt. If others know this about you, Paul, you become predictable. You can be manipulated. You have considered this?"

"The problem with that," he answered, "is that doubt can be manipulated as well."

Urs Brugg understood. Doubt, successfully nourished, can lead to inaction, even misdirected action. He sighed audibly.

"How wearying it must be," he said, "to be Paul Bannerman."

"Sometimes. Yes."

"Safe home, Paul."

"I'll be in touch."

Urs Brugg broke the connection. His opponent reached to retrieve the file he had brought. "An interesting man," he said softly, returning his attention to the chessboard.

"Leo," Urs Brugg said firmly, "I have your word."

The other man nodded. "You have lost a bishop," said the KGB station chief from the Soviet Embassy in Bern. "But perhaps, today, you have gained a knight."

Molly Farrell took his call in Helge's cubicle.

"She goes in and out," Molly told him. "Dozing a lot, having bad dreams. The doctor says that will go on for a while, occasional hallucinations, some memory loss, but he thinks she'll be okay."

"Has she . . ."

"Asked about you? Some."

"How much has her father told her?"

"The basics," she answered. "Not that he knows all that much. He did say that no matter whose side you were on, you're still a killer. Then Susan asked him how that made you different from him. Not a bad question."

"What did he say to that?"

"Same thing you've been saying. She can't live in your world and you can't live in hers. She told him she loved him but he should fuck off."

"Susan said that?"

"And you too."

He let out a breath. "Try to make her understand that . . ."

"Paul," Molly said gently, "don't push."

"Yeah." A long pause. "How is Lesko behaving otherwise?"

"He's calming down. He's . . . did you know he still talks to his partner?"

"What partner?"

"The dead one. When he thinks no one is looking. Susan says it's just force of habit from ten years of working together."

"He's not . . ."

"Wacko? I don't think so. More like lonely. By the way," she glanced back up the corridor, "he's signaling me right now to see if you have any news about Elena."

Bannerman told her what Urs Brugg had said. He gave her the name of the hospital in Zürich. Molly nodded toward Lesko and held up her thumb. Lesko turned away so that she could not see his face.

"Roger Clew," she told Bannerman, "called an hour ago from the airport. He's on his way. You must have passed each other on the road."

"Did you tell him I'm leaving?"

"I just said you weren't here."

"Don't tell him. Don't lie to him either. Let him draw his own conclusions but I'll want to know what sort of questions he asks. Tell him I'd like him to make arrangements to get Susan and her father out of Switzerland as soon as she can travel. Is Lesko's passport legitimate?"

"He didn't have one. The one we gave him is okay but not great. Short notice."

"Then Lesko will need Roger. Bring them both to Westport where we can protect them until this is settled."

"Susan will come. She's not through with you. If she does, so will he. He's not through with you either."

"Fair enough. Until then, get Roger to arrange for more security around that hospital."

"No need," she told him. "There are six men outside with automatic weapons. They're paratroopers, off duty. Their major came in to introduce himself. They're with the Enzian Unit out of Zürich."

Enzian Unit. Swiss commandos. Bannerman was impressed. "Roger works fast."

"Not Roger. Your new friend. Urs Brugg."

He was doubly impressed. He remembered the awe on Helge's face when she first told him that Urs Brugg was on her telephone. There was more to this man than money after all. "Well," he said, "in that case, wait for Roger and then get home. I might have a job for you."

"I thought you might."

Exhausted, Bannerman was asleep before the clouds blurred out the lights of Zürich. The Swissair flight took him only to Geneva where, to confuse possible surveillance, he and Billy boarded a TWA flight to Montreal. There they connected with a Finnair flight that was on its final leg from Helsinki to New York. They arrived at five in the morning. They'd been traveling fourteen hours.

At JFK Airport, they passed through customs without incident. Beyond, a knot of about a dozen people, several of them yawning, waited for arriving passengers. A number of limo drivers were among them. One of these, short, white haired, a sour expression, wearing a chauffeur's cap and a raincoat, held a sign with Bannerman's name on it. He recognized John Waldo. Against the far wall, he spotted the Jewish Afro hairdo and beaded denim jacket favored by Janet Herzog. She was sitting on the marble floor, hugging a knitting bag to her chest, apparently dozing. She could have been a college student traveling on winter break although he knew her to be almost his age. He also knew her to be wide awake. She would not move or be seen to look up until they were safely on their way. The knitting bag would contain an Ingram machine pistol. John Waldo's raincoat probably concealed a shotgun.

Bannerman checked his watch. Nearly noon, Zürich time. He wanted to make one more call. As Billy pushed their

luggage cart toward the stretch limo waiting at curbside,
Bannerman stepped to a bank of phones and, using a credit
card, once more punched out the number of Urs Brugg.

"My niece is out of danger," the familiar bass voice
boomed back at him. Drained of worry, it sounded younger,
fresher. "One bullet shattered her collarbone but it missed
the lung. Her left arm has been reassembled with the aid of
screws and clamps. She may or may not regain full use of it,
yet she is in good spirits. Her primary concern seems to be
the scars and how they will affect her choice of wardrobe."

"That's the best possible news, sir."

"Easy for you to say. You do not wear low cut gowns."

Bannerman smiled at the joke and at the relief that it
implied. "Mr. Brugg, I regret that I did not get the chance
to know her better. She sounds like a very considerable
woman."

"Yes. Yes, she is."

"Susan is also recovering nicely. I hope to get her home in
the next few days."

"That is done," Urs Brugg told him. "They leave tonight
by way of Munich. Your man from the State Department
has arranged transport by military aircraft. She is well
guarded. An army doctor will fly with her. She has agreed
to accept your protection in Westport. The father disdains it
but I think he will follow."

The smile remained, although it twisted a bit. "Mr.
Brugg, I seem to be having trouble keeping up with you."

"I have my turf, as they say. You have yours."

"Which brings me to the other reason for my call. I made
you a promise. Can you stay close to your phone this
week?"

"I am always here. I am in a wheelchair. You have, I
gather, made a decision?"

"Just about."

"Have you slept?"

"On the plane, yes."

"You have had two days with very little rest. Get more
sleep. Then decide."

"I will. Mr. Brugg, I need two favors."

"Ask them."

"Dr. Russo's body. He ought to be buried where his friends are. If you could somehow get it released . . ."

"Give me an address."

"Thank you." Bannerman named a mortician in Westport.

"The second favor?"

"The telephone receptionist at Davos Hospital. Her name is Helge Guler. She's been most helpful and very kind but would not accept a reward. However, she is very much an admirer of Urs Brugg and I thought if you might . . ."

"Perhaps she would join me here for dinner."

"That's more than I would have asked. Thank you."

"Paul . . . this Lesko." Urs Brugg lowered his voice, signaling a topic of an equally personal nature. "He is not, I gather, an especially handsome man."

"I, um, would not say so. No."

"A man of great charm, then."

"Mr. Brugg," Bannerman grimaced, "if you're asking me what your niece sees in him . . ."

"He came to visit her this morning. Elena was greatly touched that he did so. Yes, Paul. I suppose that is what I am asking."

"Mr. Brugg, I don't know the man."

"You know the daughter. How does she speak of him?"

Bannerman glanced apologetically in the direction of the waiting limo. He had more on his mind than whatever emotions existed between Lesko and Elena. Still, with a small sigh, he tried to answer. "Susan speaks of him with great warmth. She has expressed the wish that others could know him as she does. She calls him a pussycat. Do you know the expression?"

"It is similar in German."

"Still, she knows that he can be a brutal man. When he was a policeman, the newspapers called him Raymond 'the Terrible.' He's been in more than his share of shootings but he is known to prefer his fists."

"A humanitarian, then," Urs Brugg said blandly. "And your own observations?"

"He's certainly tough but I don't think he's mean. By all accounts, he is scrupulously honest. For what it's worth, I guess I respect him."

"Would Mama's Boy recruit him?"

"No."

"Beyond the obvious, may I ask why?"

"He is—not like us."

"Yes," Urs Brugg said thoughtfully, "I think I understand."

Bannerman said nothing.

"Elena tells me that she has invited him back to Zürich. For an indefinite visit. Do you think he will come?"

"He might, but he won't stay. All he knows is New York."

"And Elena cannot go there. There are warrants for her arrest. Perhaps it is just as well."

"Perhaps. Yes."

"You have been indulging me, Paul. I appreciate this."

"You care about your niece. You don't want her hurt. I understand that. If you're asking my opinion, this thing with Lesko won't go much further. It's impossible."

"Like yourself and his daughter?"

A long pause. "I think so. Yes."

"You seem to know a great deal about men, Paul. I wonder if you know as much about women."

—12—

Roger Clew, unshaven, his clothing wrinkled, turned his rented car into the Compo Shopping Plaza off Westport's Post Road. It was after six. Most of the shops were dark, the parking lot nearly empty.

Choosing a space, he allowed his headlights to wash over the double storefront of Luxury Travel Limited. He saw no movement inside. The reservations desks were empty, their consoles silent. The only lights came from Bannerman's office in the rear and the small conference room adjoining it. He waited, gathering himself, then stepped from the car. He tried the door. It was unlocked. Bannerman had said it would be.

He heard the clink of ice cubes being dropped into a glass. Then into another. He followed the sound, encouraged by it, to the conference room door. Bannerman turned as he reached it, holding up a Scotch bottle questioningly. Roger Clew nodded. He pulled the nearest chair and sank into it, hoping that his manner seemed weary, harassed, anything but afraid. Bannerman poured three fingers over the ice.

"You realize," Clew asked, taking it, "I've been to Europe and back looking for you? I haven't showered in two days."

"Ships in the night." Bannerman shrugged. He hoisted his own drink, mostly water, by way of welcome. "How's Susan doing?" he asked, although the question was unnecessary. Molly Farrell had called him from Greenfield Hill, the nearby psychiatric clinic where he himself had once been held and from which he had expelled Palmer Reid. The Leskos were being quartered there. Molly was helping them to settle in. *"Yes,"* Molly had told him, *"she knows you're in town. No, she hasn't asked to see you."*

"Shaky but okay," Clew answered. "Her father has a message for you. He's been on the phone calling some New York cops he knows to come up and guard her. His message to you is, 'Nothing personal, he won't tell them much, but don't you try to stop them.' "

Bannerman felt a headache coming on.

"The Swiss have a message for you, too," he said. "Theirs is, 'You even think about going back after whoever hit Russo and the Lesko girl and they'll lock you up for ten years.' "

"I'm not thinking about it."

"What does that mean? You already got them?"

"I'm not interested in shooters, Roger. You know that."

Clew didn't like this. Bannerman should have been full of questions. He should have been asking for help. He looked down at his drink. "I hear you figure it's Reid. Behind all this, I mean."

"There is that chance."

Clew sipped from his glass and sat up in his chair. "That's what I want to talk to you about," he said. "Reid's on his way out. Fuller's got a squeeze going but it has to be done carefully. Story is, Reid has private files on just about everybody, which is how he's lasted this long. We don't want you doing anything until we know what he's got."

"For that you chased me to Europe?"

Bannerman had turned away. But not before Clew saw what he thought was a glint of surprise at being asked to do nothing. "I went over as your friend. And to get you the hell out of there in one piece."

"I did get out. But thank you." Bannerman waited.

Clew stirred his drink with his finger. It gave him something to do with his eyes. "There's more," he said. "You want it straight?"

"That would save time, Roger."

He would have preferred to have eased his way into this subject. Over several weeks if he had them. But events had forced his hand. "Once Reid's out of the way," he said, "and it's done without headlines, we'd like you to come back to work."

"No chance, Roger."

"I'm not talking like before. Not exactly."

"Then how, exactly?"

"You have a hell of a team here, Paul. It's a lot of talent not to be put to good use."

"What do you consider good use?"

Clew gestured with his thumb toward the world in general. "There are some people out there. They do terrible things. We know who they are, even where. Just the other day, the secretary was saying how frustrating it is that we can't touch them."

"And you want us to start killing them off."

Clew raised his brow. "I didn't say that. Barton Fuller certainly didn't say that."

"I'll try to pay closer attention. What did you say?"

"That sometimes . . . occasionally . . . we could use a little outside help. There's a way we can use you, a new way, with almost no risk to you or your people. Besides, after three years in Westport they can probably use the exercise."

"When they need exercise, I'll take them jogging." Bannerman's expression darkened a shade. "Roger, someone probably said that to Palmer Reid once. If those files of his exist, that's how he started building them. In any case, I'm not interested."

Clew brought his glass to his lips and held it there. He knew that he was handling this badly. After months of work, weeks of stewing over the best way to raise this subject with Bannerman, he'd practically blurted it out. But if Bannerman, by any chance, knew anything at all about the Ripper Effect, now was the time to find out. There was a new way, he'd told him. No risk. And Bannerman hadn't even batted an eye. That was how little he cared. That was also how little he knew.

He'd half-expected to walk in here, see those soft gray
eyes staring up at him, watch Bannerman step to the door
and close it, and hear him say, "I'd like the truth this time,
Roger. Tell me how it is that you were heard discussing my
travel plans over an unsecured line. Tell me about this computer that predicted what was done to Susan and what I
might do in response. Tell me why you sat back and let all
this happen. Tell me about the Ripper Effect."

Bannerman could not have known. Clew realized that.
Maybe, just maybe, he could know about the careless phone
call but not the rest of it. But that was the thing about
Bannerman. You just never knew. And if he did know, if he
even suspected that he was being used as an experiment, a
test case, it would be all over. Fifteen years would go right
out the window. Those eyes of Bannerman's would bore
right into him and then they'd turn dead. Clew had seen
that look before. He didn't want to see it again.

But Bannerman didn't know. And yet, there was . . .
something. Clew decided to press it.

"You're not Palmer Reid, Paul," he said quietly. "For
openers, Reid is nuts. Second, the people working for him
are either there to get rich or they're a bunch of fucking
robot flag-wavers all pissed off that we don't kill commies
anymore. Your people are professionals. They get paid, they
do their job, and they go away."

"Roger—"

"Third"—Clew held up his fingers—"people trust you.
No one trusts Reid. Fourth, and because of number three,
you've got resources that Reid could only dream about.
Now I see you're even wired into the Brugg family, which
incidentally has a lot of juice over there, and also the New
York cops by way of Raymond 'the Terrible' Lesko. This is
the basis of a considerable network."

"You're babbling, Roger. Lesko is no friend of mine. I
hardly know the Bruggs at all. In any case, I'm retired."

"I know. To Fortress Westport. Where you're indepen-
dently wealthy, having ripped off a few million of federal
funds and a dozen prime pieces of Westport real estate. But
we're not even going to mention that. No hard feelings."

"Glad to hear it."

"We're just going to stay in touch. Any time you need a

favor, even if you can't do anything in return, being retired and all, boy, I'm going to be right there."

Bannerman waited.

"Speaking of favors, Lesko reminds me that there's a DEA warrant out on Elena Brugg and another one from New York as a material witness to some old shooting. It occurs to me that you might owe her one. So by next Monday, she'll be clean."

"That's very thoughtful of you, Roger."

"What are friends for?"

"Okay." Bannerman softened. "Maybe I owe you one for that."

"I'll try to think of something."

"One, Roger." He held up a finger. "Medium size."

"And you'll leave Reid alone?"

"For the moment."

Clew studied him. "What kind of an answer is that?"

"It will have to do. Until you decide to level with me."

Clew felt his color rising. "You think I haven't?"

"Not entirely. There's something else."

"Like what?"

"I'll know when you tell me."

"I did. It's Reid's private files."

"Stop it."

Clew leaned backward in his chair, folding his arms. Bannerman made a mental note of the body language.

What the hell is it? Clew bit his lip. What's Bannerman got? Was it just that he'd shot over to Europe as soon as he heard? Could that look funny to Bannerman? A little like panic?

Clew suddenly remembered the man on the plane. The one who wanted a smoke. The one who'd stood there, God knows how long, possibly reading the screen of his Toshiba. Could he have been one of Bannerman's people?

No. That's crazy. Still, just in case . . .

"What if I told you," Clew said, grimacing, "that I'm working on something. It involves computers."

He paused. Bannerman's eyes, if anything, glazed slightly.

"I can't tell you any more just yet, but when I do it'll knock your socks off. To go forward, there are some people I need. If you hit Palmer Reid, you will scare them off. This is the truth."

"These people you need. Am I one of them?"

He nodded. "It's that favor we talked about. When I'm ready, I'll ask it. Whether you do it, that's up to you."

"But you'll tell me nothing in the meantime?"

"I can't. Someday, I promise, I'll explain why."

Bannerman stared at him. Those gray eyes. "I'll think about it," he said.

"No hit on Reid?"

"I said I'll think about it. Roger?"

"Yeah?"

"When did you find out what happened to Susan?"

"When I got your message. Why?"

"Just wondered."

Friday afternoon. Westport.

Within an hour of his arrival at the clinic, Lesko was on the phone calling in favors. The first call was to Detective Lieutenant Harry Greenwald, with whom he once worked narcotics, Manhattan South and who had known Susan most of her life. Lesko told him what had happened to her.

What cops, asked Lesko, did they both know and trust, who were currently working undercover and might, therefore, not be missed for a few days? Greenwald named three. He said he would contact them.

The three street cops, Greenwald with them, arrived that evening before nine. They carried duffle bags packed with assault rifles, radios, and assorted weaponry that they had confiscated over the years and kept. Each was assigned a post, two inside with Lesko, two patrolling the grounds. They stood guard through the night. Nothing happened.

Lesko had not encouraged questions. But by late morning Friday, his four cops could not help noticing that nobody else at Greenfield Hill seemed to share Lesko's sense of imminent peril. The clinic's grounds appeared otherwise unguarded. The few people there, apparently staff, went about their routines seeming to find nothing unusual or even noteworthy in seeing four rough-looking men in flak jackets turning guns toward them every time they rounded a corner. They would nod politely, ignoring the weapons, and then go on. The three undercover cops were disappointed. Greenwald had begun to wonder aloud why he had given up several days off. And Lesko was becoming embarrassed. He would like to have revived their interest by telling them that those people passing them in the halls had probably killed more people than the average plane crash, but he had given his word. Unable to confide in the four New York cops and unable to get to Loftus who was stashed, under guard, somewhere else in town, he found himself looking for ways to be alone so that he might talk things over with David Katz.

It had taken a while, the better part of two years, but Lesko had more or less come to terms with his partner's occasional presence. It made people wonder about him, he realized. When they caught him at it. But it wasn't so crazy. Any two cops, working together that long, get into each other's heads. Finish each other's sentences. One of them dies, leaves an empty seat in the car, the other one still talks to it. Or listens to it. It's not the same as talking to yourself. What you're doing, because you know how that person thinks, dead or not, is more like getting a second opinion.

Even Susan said so. Anyway, he'd decided, it's harmless. And it's better than nothing.

The trouble with Katz, though, aside from the fact that he was a fucking thief, for which Lesko still had not forgiven him, was that Katz did not always wait to be spoken to. He would just show up. In the beginning, he would show up mostly in dreams, usually the four-in-the-morning kind, the half-awake kind, walking in with coffee and Danish to pick him up for roll call like he did every morning for ten years because Katz mostly drove. But before long Katz was showing up in other places, too. Wide-awake places. Broad daylight. Lesko would be walking along, he'd see something, wonder about it, to himself, and Katz would answer him. Before long, it got so he couldn't even watch a Knicks game on TV without Katz shooting off his mouth about the Knicks having no bench because of dumb trades and lousy draft choices, which would have been irritating even when Katz was alive because Katz never knew shit about sports.

But it was also good in a way. If Katz never knew basket-ball, but now he does, it couldn't really be him. Right?

The thing was, as much as he hated taking Katz's crap, Lesko missed him. He hadn't been around lately. Wouldn't come, even when he was called. Lesko knew why. What it was, he was sulking. Katz's nose had been all out of joint ever since he hung up from that first call to Elena.

"Hey. Lesko. What the hell was that?"

"Huh? What was what?"

"You and Elena is what, damn it. That broad orders my fucking head blown off and all of a sudden by you she's Doris Day."

"Yeah, well, this is about Susan. Anyway, it's none of your goddamned business."

"Don't give me Susan. I heard you. You were schmoozing with her, Lesko, the lady who killed your partner. But what's to hold a grudge, right? Forgive and forget. Why don't you take her fucking dancing?"

"David—"

"And I'll tell you something else. Forget it. Even if she was straight—"

"She straight now. Shut up about this, David."

"In a pig's ass, she is. But even if she was, she wouldn't touch you with a garbage man's gloves because you're—"

"How would you like me to rip out whatever brains you got left?"

"See that? That's why. It's because you're such a nasty son of a bitch and you got no class, Lesko. Plus which you're ugly and if you think—"

Lesko shook off the memory. Maybe it was just as well that Katz was staying away. He didn't need the grief. It was enough that he was starting to get grief from live cops. And who could blame them? They're hanging around Greenfield Hill, getting no sleep, while the allegedly dangerous Mama's Boy is sitting around his dumb travel agency booking blue-haired old ladies onto cruise ships and his gorilla, McHugh, is home helping his landlady wallpaper her dining room. His cops were getting disgusted. But at least they were keeping their ears open.

That was how, in the halls and washrooms of Greenfield Hill, Lesko picked up two rumors. One was that Palmer

Reid had holed up in his home in Maryland. The second was that two of Bannerman's women plus a long-distance shooter named Glenn Cook had gone to pay him a visit. On hearing this last, he borrowed the car his cops came in and confronted Paul Bannerman at the offices of Luxury Travel Limited.

"This Cook guy, the sniper, he's down there to hit him, right? You promised me a piece of him."

"He's there to observe," Bannerman winced, motioning for Lesko to keep his voice down. It had not occurred to Lesko that Bannerman's reservations clerks might be just what they seemed. "As for Molly and Janet, they're long since back."

"So why'd they go?"

Bannerman hesitated. But better, he thought, to tell at least part of the truth than to let him go on speculating. "They penetrated Reid's house. Molly rigged his phones."

Lesko raised an eyebrow. "With a guy like Reid, it's that easy? He doesn't keep them swept?"

"Molly knows her business." He dismissed the subject with a wave.

"So? What happens now?"

Until Roger Clew's visit, the answer to that had been clear. He could not afford to let Reid, guilty or not, take the initiative. Roger would understand that. And yet Roger had asked him to take no action. If he was being used, therefore, he was clearly not being used to destroy Reid, at least not by Roger. And Roger's friendship was valuable. That of Barton Fuller even more so. Still . . . something about Roger. Roger, unless Helge was mistaken, had lied to him about when he learned of the attack on Susan. Bannerman couldn't think why.

"I haven't decided," he answered.

"What's to decide? You know he's behind what happened to Susan and Elena."

"I don't know it. I think it."

"You talked to Loftus, right? You connected Reid and his greaseball general, right? The guy didn't dig in down there because he's innocent. What more do you want? We sit here waiting for him to drop a bomb on Westport with a signed confession taped to it?"

Bannerman shook his head. "He won't move yet. Not until he knows where all the players are. He probably isn't even sure I'm here." Reid had already tried to contact him twice in Westport and once more at his Klosters apartment. On that occasion, Lesko answered. Apparently, Reid babbled on for some time with offers of sympathy, men and money before he realized he was talking to a stranger. Lesko did not enlighten him.

"Bannerman," Lesko slid into a chair. "I want this guy. I'll work with you or I'll do it alone. But I want him dead."

Paul said nothing. He seemed to sigh.

"Hey, look," Lesko leaned toward him. "The last few days I heard a lot about Mama's Boy. All of a sudden you're not acting much like the guy I heard about. Does Susan, by any chance, have anything to do with the change?"

A small shrug.

"I also hear you're thinking about hanging 'em up, letting this guy, Zivic, run the show here. Is that true?"

"More or less."

"Well, if you think backing off is suddenly going to make you better son-in-law material—"

"I don't."

"Then what do you say you get off your ass?"

Bannerman shook his head. "You're a smooth talker, Lesko." He reached for a pad and scribbled an address. He tore off the sheet and pushed it across his desk. "That's where Reid lives. You want to go after him, be my guest."

"You don't think I will?"

"I think you might. You won't last a day."

Lesko reddened. He stood up, paced the office, struggling to control his temper. "You got a better idea, let's hear it."

Bannerman looked at him coldly. "I don't need you, Lesko. Try to understand that. If my problem was in some New York back alley, you'd be the first one I'd call. You're tough and straight ahead. Reid is devious, cowardly, and probably crazy. But he'll dance rings around you."

Lesko started to speak. He bit his lip. He knew that Bannerman was right. His expression softened. "Look," he said slowly. "They hurt my daughter and I didn't do shit. All I did was almost louse everything up and then watch like a dummy while you take over and blow away the Carmody guy. They hurt Elena, they busted her up bad, and all I can do is go see her with this stupid plant and tell her I'm sorry. I have to do something. I have to at least be in on it."

"Can I ask you a question?"

Lesko made a face. "What's with me and Elena, right?"

Bannerman waited.

"The answer is I don't know. Look at her, look at me, try to figure. Anyway, what's it to you?"

"Just trying to know you a little better."

"We're not going to be pals, Bannerman. All I want from you is one thing, one time. Are you going to do something about Reid or not?"

Bannerman leaned back in his chair. His eyes rested, thoughtfully, on a drawer of his desk. He reached to open it. From it, he pulled out a small address book. He reached for his phone and began punching out a number.

"Who are you calling?"

"It's time to find out what Reid's up to."

"How do you do that?"

He motioned Lesko to the extension at the far end of his office sofa. "I'm going to ask him," he said.

"Paul? . . . Is it you? . . . Where are you?"

Palmer Reid held the phone as if it were a living thing. He snapped his fingers, silently, in the direction of his assistant. Charles Whitlow, lips pursed, one eyebrow raised, carefully lifted an extension from its cradle.

"I'm back in Westport, Palmer. You called. What's on your mind?"

The voice, thought Reid. Not at all cordial. Yet not hostile, especially. Preoccupied. Distant. Weary.

"The girl, Paul. How is she?"

"Look . . . Palmer . . ."

"Paul, we've had our differences." Reid gathered himself. "You know that I would happily see you and all your people behind bars. But you cannot believe that I would have harmed that innocent girl."

"I don't. Necessarily."

Reid let the qualifier pass. "How is she, Paul?"

A brief silence. A sigh. "Somewhat better. She's here. I've been spending most of my time at her bedside." He saw Lesko's eyebrow go up. He touched a finger to his lips.

"Who did this to her? Could she describe them?"

"She has no memory at all of what happened. She's barely lucid. There's apparently brain damage. Thank you for the flowers, by the way."

"The least I could do," Reid mumbled. His attention had turned to Whitlow who was busily scribbling questions on a pad, now holding the pad for him to see. Reid nodded, frowning. "Paul, I called your Klosters apartment two days ago. A man answered, pretending to be you."

"Probably Lesko. He took his daughter's key to collect her things. Do you know where he is, by the way?"

"He's not with you?"

"Hardly. He blames me for what happened to his daughter. He's threatened to kill me for it. For all I know, he's still in Switzerland with that drug dealer of his."

Reid blinked. A smile spread across Whitlow's face. He raised a tiny fist as if in triumph, then scribbled another question on his pad.

"Paul," Reid asked, again nodding toward his assistant, "the Swiss police say the attackers were a man and a woman. Do you know who they are? Any sign of them?"

"They sank out of sight."

"Probably shot your man Russo as well, don't you think?"

"It wouldn't surprise me. But they're only hired hands. I want who sent them. If you didn't do it, tell me who did."

"Paul . . . I have certain . . . evidence . . ." Reid was squinting, trying to make out Whitlow's scrawl.

"Evidence of what, Palmer?"

Whitlow wrote a name in block letters. He underscored it twice. He jabbed at it with his pen.

"Palmer? If you know something, tell me."

"I hesitate because . . . Paul, there are people who would like nothing more than to see the two of us at each other's throats. People who would try to destroy me before I can expose them for the traitors they are."

"Names, Palmer. Who are you talking about?"

"I'll answer with a question. Why would Roger Clew, in a

telephone conversation with Irwin Kaplan of the Drug Enforcement Administration, be so concerned that the purpose of your visit to Switzerland might be to meet with Elena Brugg?"

A long silence. "When did this call take place?"

"The week before you left. Paul, it gets worse. Much worse."

"Tell me."

"Drugs, Paul. And Barton Fuller. That hypocrite has been using his office to facilitate drug traffic for years."

"You can prove that?"

"Not in a court of law, perhaps. My evidence would be ruled inadmissible. But I have tapes that leave no doubt."

"Then why don't you leak them? Let the press destroy him."

"This is a nation of laws, Paul. I want it done correctly, no matter how long it takes."

"If this is true, I'll sentence him myself. How is Roger involved?"

"For your sake, I've tried to believe that he's been an unwitting dupe. But after intercepting that call . . ."

"I'll want to hear the tapes. All of them."

"Only," Reid's voice became firm, "if you'll promise to work closely with me on this. Your people and mine. I can't have you going off half-cocked."

"Show me the proof and you've got a deal."

Reid closed his eyes. "I'm pleased, Paul. Very pleased. We should never have been adversaries."

"Palmer, I'm going to call an immediate council meeting here. Then in, say, two hours, let's have a conference call. Will you be there?"

"Depend on it."

"Palmer?"

"Yes, Paul."

"I owe you one."

Lesko put down his extension. He stared disbelievingly at Bannerman. "What the hell was all that?" he asked.

Bannerman rubbed his eyes. "Apparently, he wants me to kill the secretary of state."

"I heard. You believe any of that shit?"

"No."

"What was that about me blaming you, which I do, and threatening to kill you, which so far I didn't?"

Bannerman stood up, stretching. "Reid likes to hedge his bets. If you go home to Queens he'll probably look you up, show you evidence that I ordered the attacks on Susan and Elena to frame him and try to get you to kill me. You wanted a way to get at Reid, there's your opening. All you have to do is go wait for your doorbell to ring."

"What evidence would he show me?"

Bannerman shrugged. "More tape recordings. We've had any number of phone conversations over the years. He's taped them all. So have I. Give a good editor half a day and Reid could play you conversations proving that I'm a child molester."

"That's what he'll do with Clew and Fuller?"

"Same sort of thing. Yes."

Lesko pondered this. "Let me ask you something."

"Shoot."

"You two do this all the time? In that whole conversation, neither one of you hardly said a word that was true."

"Except I know when I'm lying and when I'm not. I'm not sure Reid knows the difference anymore."

"You don't get tired of that?"

"Yes, I do."

"You made up your mind?"

"Yes. If Anton and the others agree."

"I'm in, right?"

"If you do it my way. And you do as you're told."

"You get first shot. You miss, it's my turn."

"Fair enough." Bannerman checked his watch. Half past three. "Be back here in two hours."

"What happens then?"

"Happy hour."

—13—

Charles Whitlow, a small, windup toy of a man who seemed to flit rather than move, quietly replaced his extension and, raising his chin toward Palmer Reid, applauded him using the fingers of one hand against the back of the other. That done, he cocked his head, smirking, toward the third man in the room. The man answered with a sneer and a hand to his crotch. Whitlow rolled his eyes.

"Enough of that," muttered Palmer Reid distractedly. He sat, one fist against his mouth, staring at the phone on his desk.

Whitlow allowed himself one more smirk in the direction of General Oscar Ortirez. *Pig of a man,* he thought. The Bolivian had arrived in a black business suit that was at least a decade out of style. His embroidered white shirt, already stained, had a collar a full size too small. The necktie was atrocious and four inches wide. Someone, thought Whitlow, probably had to show him how to knot it. Pity they didn't show him how to bathe. Skin shines like a dead fish.

And he had not stopped harping about the failed attempt on Elena since he got here. Machine pistols, he screamed. Two little Jew popguns against a heavy Mercedes on an open highway. One team of gunmen. No cross fire. No chase car. And you wonder that she is still alive? Why should she *not* be alive?

It was hardly Whitlow's fault. He found the best people he could in the time he was given. If Ortirez had not made his appallingly stupid call to Elena, trying to rub her face in the death of the Lesko girl, who, lest we forget, was not dead either, we might have proceeded at a more orderly pace. Even with all that, the attempt should have succeeded. Who would have expected a man like Russo to shield her with his body? And Ortirez is a fine one to talk about the choice of personnel. *"The Carmodys are the very best,"* he said. *"They never miss because they never quit,"* he said. Well, where are they, then?

As for his whining complaint that he should have been told about Bannerman, that Bannerman was something more than a Connecticut travel agent, it was simply none of his business. Everyone he's ever been asked to remove was *something more.* That was the point, don't you see, in removing them.

No matter. It seems that this mess is about to sort itself out after all. With only one thing to be regretted. It might no longer be necessary to sacrifice Ortirez. To show Bannerman his corpse. Pity, after bringing him all this way.

"General Ortirez," Palmer Reid's voice snapped Whitlow out of his reverie. He had brought his knuckle to his mouth. He was biting it. Always a good sign, thought Whitlow. "I would like a few moments alone with Charles."

Whitlow glanced at the man in the dreadful suit. He had stiffened. Flat, stupid face. Pig eyes. "I am here to be consulted," Ortirez raised his chin. "I will stay."

Reid bit harder. Whitlow saw his eyes drift toward the door and then beyond it in the direction of the armed guards who were stationed in his foyer. *Do it,* thought Whitlow. *Call them in. Have them club this oily brute to his knees as a lesson in deportment.* But he did not.

"Events, General Ortirez," Reid said, uncoiling, "have progressed beyond the limits of our relationship. I must now deal with a matter that is vital to the interests of the United States."

Ortirez spat. It was more than a gesture. A spray of

brownish droplets arced onto Palmer Reid's carpet. "This is shit," he said.

Reid stiffened. "What did you say?"

"What you are doing," Ortirez repeated, "it is shit. I stand here listening as you make an allegiance with this Bannerman. You say his great enemy is now his friend, his great friend is now his enemy. Is Bannerman so great a fool that he believes you?"

"He is not a fool," Reid said evenly, although he seethed at the insult. He had just, brilliantly he thought, improvised a strategy that he wished he'd followed from the beginning. "I will show him evidence. Even then he will doubt it. I will show him more. At best, yes, he will make an attempt on the life of the man who seeks to deprive you, not to mention your poor country, of your only source of wealth. Then I will destroy him."

Ortirez heard him. "And at worst?"

"The doubt will remain. The secretary of state will know that and he will fear Bannerman. Whatever protection Bannerman now enjoys will be withdrawn. My hands will then be untied. I will destroy him."

Ortirez pursed his lips as if to spit again, but Whitlow gasped "If you don't mind." And he did not. "This, too, is shit," he said. "You make big plans, big schemes, you and this *maricón.*" He cocked his head toward Whitlow who rolled his eyes in response. "Always you say, when I do this my enemy must do that. And when your enemy does something else, you say it is because he is a fool and you make more big schemes. I tell you how I make a scheme. I say, I will shoot my enemy in the head and when I do that he must die. Do you know what happens? I shoot him and he dies."

Palmer Reid could feel hot liquid rising in his throat. There would be no use, he realized, in explaining the meaning of finesse, the concept of *ruse de guerre,* to this mestizo who would still be walking on all fours had not a few drops of Spanish blood managed to trickle into his veins. No use in pointing out that the true art of diplomacy rests on placing one enemy against another. That as we speak, Bannerman, the Bruggs of Zürich, and Lesko, wherever he is, are beginning to circle each other like so many snarling beasts. And

that now, to that melange, have been added that bumpkin
Barton Fuller and his toady Roger Clew.

*And you, General Oscar Ortirez, will indeed become my
gesture of goodwill toward Mr. Bannerman. Your body, delivered to the town line of Westport, a signed confession pinned
to your nose, will serve as proof of the guilt of some and the
duplicity of others. And if your body is not enough, if there
should be any lingering suspicion that any member of this
intelligence body was in any way involved in profiting from
the sale of drugs, if Elena should live to place such a charge
at my doorstep, then I, to my horror, will discover that I have
had a traitor in my midst. At my right hand. Placed there by
none other than Barton Fuller. His agent. The architect of his
cruel attack on that innocent girl. One Charles Whitlow. He
too will confess. Readily. These pansies never have much tol-
erance for pain. He will be found in his home, his diaries and
financial records in his personal safe, a tape recorder at his
side into which he will have blubbered his guilt before taking
a fatal overdose of the same vile substance with which he
attempted to destroy the moral fiber of this great nation.*

Reid looked at his watch. Twenty past four. What did
Bannerman say? Two hours. He would be calling at six.

"This is shit," he heard Ortirez say again.

Reid wet his lips. His eye drifted toward the place on his
prized Persian carpet, a gift from the Shah, where drops of
Ortirez's spittle still glistened. For that alone he would . . .

Six o'clock.

At six it would be set in motion. This time, his way.

Good man, that Bannerman. Priorities not where they
should be but a good man nonetheless.

It was true, you know.

They should never have been adversaries.

Spilt milk. No help for it now.

The flowers.

They were what did it, he realized suddenly. Showed Bannerman who his friends are. Made him call, one American
to another, ask for help.

The flowers, yes. They were a masterstroke.

"Mr. Brugg? This is Paul Bannerman speaking."

"How are you, Paul?"

"I'm well, sir. How is Elena?"

"Recovering nicely. Her spirits are as high as I have seen them in two years. Your Mr. Lesko seems to have been the best medicine."

Bannerman tried to imagine being cheered by a visit from Lesko. He chose not to comment. "Mr. Brugg, I'm about to place a call to Palmer Reid. Please stay on the line but say nothing at all. Just listen."

"Am I to hear a confession?"

"It will be more in the nature of a repentance, sir."

"I will listen."

The sign on the door of Luxury Travel Limited said Closed. Through drawn blinds, Lesko could see movement inside. As he reached for the door, a latch clicked loudly and it swung open. The Russian, Zivic, smiled and stepped aside. Lesko heard the door shut tight behind him.

Scattered around the agency's front office, Lesko saw what he took to be Bannerman's entire group, minus the shooter who was still down in Maryland. He recognized most of them. The bartender and the two women from Switzerland were there, plus a few he'd seen at Greenfield Hill and a couple more he was sure he'd seen around Westport although he had not connected them with Bannerman before this. There was also Robert Loftus, jaw wired, nose splinted, half his teeth kicked out.

Lesko shook his head. Forgetting Loftus, he could have picked any twelve men and women off the street at random, ages thirty to sixty, and they wouldn't have looked much different. Two jogging suits, a few ski jackets, a Mickey Mouse sweater on the woman with the knitting bag, another in a party dress like she's got a date later, Bannerman in shirtsleeves. The only other guys in suits were Zivic, who runs the local antique store—they say he's definitely not a fag, though—and a guy who someone said was their accountant, and looks it, which probably means he's a world-class money launderer. No wonder nobody in this town noticed.

Billy McHugh was clearing one desk, setting up champagne bottles and plastic glasses. Molly Farrell was at another that had a call director on it. She was wearing headphones and fiddling with a small black box that had assorted gauges on its face, a red plastic switch and an LED readout with blue lights, all zeros. The others, one by one, were picking pairs of headphones and little radios out of an open suitcase. Bannerman was at the rear-most desk, collar open, feet up, looking more relaxed than Lesko had ever seen him. Lesko made his way back.

"What the hell is all this?" he asked Bannerman blankly.

"I told you. Happy hour."

"Happy hour," Lesko repeated.

"Take some earphones. Find a chair."

"Ask a silly question . . ." Lesko muttered.

Reid stared at his watch. The minute hand moved slowly toward six and then past it. Twenty seconds. Thirty seconds. Forty. Stay composed, he told himself. You're in control. Act the part.

He jumped when it rang.

Reid forced a smile. He motioned Charles Whitlow to the extension. Whitlow scurried into the chair nearest it, a notepad on his lap, knees close together.

Four rings.

On a signal from Reid, they picked up together.

At the call director in Bannerman's office, Molly peered at a meter on the instrument she held as Reid answered. The drop in amperage was twice what it should have been. She held up two fingers for Bannerman to see.

"Palmer? It's Paul. Is your phone secure?"

"It is. I had it swept an hour ago."

Molly looked toward the audience, her expression smug. Several of them broke into mimed applause. Lesko scratched his head.

"Are we alone, Palmer?"

Reid considered telling the truth. After all, it was Bannerman who had proposed a conference call. But the lie came by reflex. "We're alone at this end."

"At this end," Paul told him, "we have Molly Farrell monitoring for any cut-ins by listening devices. We also have Anton Zivic, who shares our outrage at all that has happened. You don't object, do you?"

Reid was less than comfortable but he could not object. He did not like being anywhere near an electronic device if the Farrell woman was involved. He knew her file too well. And he was appalled to discover that the Russian defector, Zivic, appeared to have risen to a position of high trust. But soon he would have them as well. Zivic would be taken alive and kept alive, and in pain, until every last bit of intelligence was wrung out of him. "Not at all," he said.

As Reid spoke he saw Whitlow waving vigorously and pointing toward Ortirez. Ortirez had found a third extension and was carefully lifting the receiver. Reid gestured angrily. Ortirez ignored him.

Molly's hand waved. Her meter showed a sudden drop of fifteen milliamperes. The two fingers she'd been holding aloft changed to three. She looked at him questioningly.

He hesitated for a beat. Glenn Cook had reported the arrival of a man, not a bodyguard, possibly important because another of Reid's people had carried his bag. Cook did not know him. No time to explain that now. He shook his head, shrugging. Molly shrugged in return.

"Palmer, our whole group is assembled here." He looked to his left where every available chair and desktop held one or more of his agents. All were seated except Billy, who'd begun pouring champagne. Janet Herzog was engrossed in her knitting. Carla Benedict used the time to balance her checkbook but her eyes were shining. All the rest were eagerly attentive except John Waldo who had worn a sour expression since he arrived and was idly leafing through a Bermuda brochure. "Everyone wanted to be a part of this," Bannerman told Reid.

"I understand . . . of course . . ." Reid's voice trailed off. Paul could almost read his thoughts. Reid was envisioning them, all together, lightly armed at best, all trapped in one place. But his time would come. Bannerman would soon divide his forces and send them out, and they would be caught in the act of murdering the secretary of state. After that, there would be a slaughter. Even if some stayed behind, no one would hide them, protect them. Public outrage would be such that. . . .

"Palmer," Paul interrupted his reverie, "as long as we're being truthful with each other—"

"At long last, Paul."

"—I should tell you that until we talked this afternoon, I

was pretty sure you were behind all this. Mind you, that was before I knew that it's Barton Fuller who's been working with the cocaine traffickers all along. So, a few days ago, Anton sent Molly Farrell down to your house."

Janet Herzog looked up, stared at him.

"Um . . . and Janet Herzog." He tossed his head, apologetically, in her direction. She returned to her knitting.

A long silence. "To what purpose, Paul?"

"You'll see in a minute. I'm afraid I wasn't entirely truthful about Lesko, either. He's here listening in."

"Paul—"

"Palmer, I think it's time we ended this. Don't you?"

"If . . . if you mean the mistrust . . . the suspicion . . ." In the background, Bannerman heard a series of hissing sounds, words, that sounded like *this is shit.* And he heard a growing panic that constricted the throat of Palmer Reid. But he knew that Reid would not hang up. Not while there was another lie to attempt. Bannerman almost felt sorry for him.

"Bear with me, please." Bannerman signaled Robert Loftus. He motioned him toward Molly Farrell's station. "Palmer, I have one more person here who especially wants to say something to you. I believe it's in the nature of a resignation."

Molly, her fingers still aloft to show that all three extensions remained in use, turned an open microphone toward Loftus and guided his hand toward the red plastic switch on her black box. Now Paul raised his arm. The arms of the others rose as well except for those of a confused Raymond Lesko and a sulking John Waldo.

Loftus bent over the microphone.

"Hello, Mr. Reid," he slurred through wired teeth.

A gasp through the line. "Robert?"

"I won't tie up the line. I just wanted to say good-bye."

"Robert! What are you . . ."

"Good-bye, Mr. Reid."

Paul's arm came down. The others fell in unison. Loftus hit the switch. Lesko heard a sharp snapping sound. Then, instantly, a duller *thukk,* like an archer's arrow hitting a target pad. A chorus of birdlike squawks, each at a different pitch. A telephone clattered against a desktop. A glass smashed against a hard surface. Now there were sounds of furniture toppling over and of bodies thumping against a thickly carpeted floor.

Silence now. No sound at all. Lesko, his eyes wide and disbelieving, clung to his earpiece. A loud "Yes" startled him. Carla Benedict, grinning, applauding, rose to her feet. The others joined in. Billy began passing the champagne. Molly listened for a few seconds more, then broke the connection.

Lesko, his headphone still at his ear, his mouth open, said, "What the hell . . . was that what I think it was?"

"I believe," came the voice of Urs Brugg, "that it was a promise being kept. Paul?"

"Yes, Mr. Brugg."

"You will come visit me one day?"

"I'd like that, sir. As soon as the Swiss lose interest in me."

"I will try to hurry them along. Mr. Lesko?"

"Yeah . . . Yes, Mr. Brugg."

"You especially. I think we should talk."

"Well . . . you see, I hardly ever get over to . . ."

"I gather your horizons have expanded considerably in recent days. Come see me, Mr. Lesko."

"I have some things to work out here, but maybe, yeah." Molly broke that connection as well.

John Waldo, who in his mind saw Palmer Reid's lifeless body, eyes wide, blood from both ears, and two more like him—whoever they were—steel darts exploded inside their brains, messing up the rug, would rather have seen a simple hole in Reid's forehead. Not that he'd take anything away from Molly. She was a sweetheart and all. But that was the trouble with the world today. Too much high-tech shit. You lose the personal touch.

—14—

Palmer Reid's obituary, with photograph, ran for three columns in the Sunday *New York Times.* An outstanding career. One of the original "cold warriors." Served under seven presidents. Died suddenly. Cerebral hemorrhage. Alone at home. Working at his desk.

The funeral service was held three days later. The vice president attended, as did the secretary of state and the undersecretary of state for political affairs. Roger Clew witnessed the lowering of his casket, then was immediately flown to Connecticut. An airport taxi brought him to the door of Luxury Travel Limited; Bannerman had been expecting him.

Leading Roger Clew to the soundproof conference room, Bannerman listened patiently to five minutes of well-rehearsed obloquy. The secretary, Clew told him, was furious. The act was insane. It could well have cost Paul every friend he had in Washington. How are they to trust him again? How are they to work with him, if from now on they won't even be able to pick up a telephone without wondering if they've annoyed Paul Bannerman in some way?

"Then the solution"—Bannerman made a time-out sign

with his hands—"is *not* to work with me. They could simply leave us alone."

Clew stared at him. "That's it? That's all you care about?"

"No." Bannerman shook his head. "I care about my friends. Another way to get along with me is not to try to kill them. A third"—he turned to the credenza behind him and picked up a tape recorder and earphones, which he placed in front of Clew—"is not to try to set me up to kill someone else."

Clew felt the color drain from his face. He thought only of his computer. He tried to remember what conversation he'd had, and how damning, that Bannerman might have recorded.

"Go ahead, Roger. Play it."

Hesitantly, he reached for the earphones and slipped them over his head. He pressed the "play" button. Bannerman was watching his eyes.

Palmer Reid's voice. Then Bannerman's. A phone call. Reid saying . . . that it was Fuller. Reid trying to set him up. To get Bannerman to . . . that was it. It wasn't the computer at all. Relief flooded over him. But Bannerman still watched closely. He could only hope that whatever Bannerman saw in his reaction would pass for shock and disbelief. He nodded that he'd heard enough. He pressed the "stop" button.

"There's one more," Bannerman said. He reached into his pocket and withdrew a second cassette. This he snapped into the machine. Again he waited as Roger Clew listened. Clew's eyes, ever widening, told him that he'd reached the instant in which Palmer Reid died. Bannerman shut off the machine.

Clew could not speak for several moments. His mouth was dry. "May I have these?" he asked finally.

"The first one. Not the second."

Clew let out a breath, then nodded. "Did you . . . even begin to believe it? What he said about Bart Fuller?"

"And you."

"The unwitting dupe," Clew nodded.

"No."

"But he claimed he had proof. I know he didn't. But

when Bart Fuller hears this," he held up the first tape, "he's going to ask me what it was."

Bannerman made a dismissive gesture with his hand. "Given time, he would have produced something. Doctored tapes. Ambiguous photographs. He didn't get the time."

"You still should have waited. You could have been sure. And you should have trusted me enough to call me first."

"Roger, it's done."

"Not yet, it isn't. Reid's private files. We can't find them."

"How do you know I don't have them?" The question was asked for the benefit of the concealed microphone that his old friend might just possibly be wearing. Wire or no, the question had its effect. Roger Clew showed a pained expression and gazed longingly in the direction of Bannerman's liquor cabinet. Paul opened it and poured two Scotches.

"Okay," Clew peeled off his coat and threw it over a chair. "It's done. I won't say it's not a relief. The message I'm supposed to bring back, I take it, is that everyone should now leave well enough alone because you're keeping Reid's private files as insurance against anyone bothering you, which, by the way, you and I both know is horseshit."

Bannerman shrugged but said nothing. He handed Clew his glass. "The paper said he died alone."

"If he didn't," Clew curled his lip, "I don't suppose you'll tell me how you managed to get Whitlow and a Bolivian General in the same room with Reid and then get all three to pick up separate booby-trapped telephones. Even for you, that was neatly done."

Bannerman didn't answer. He had presumed one of the eavesdroppers to be Whitlow, but he had not dared hope that the other might be the man who, according to Lurene Carmody, had sent her after Susan. Both bodies, obviously, had been quietly removed along with all physical evidence that they'd ever been there. They would, he imagined, be kept in cold storage until more convenient and unrelated deaths could be arranged for each of them. In any case, Paul was not inclined to correct Clew's assumption that no part of the massacre had been left to chance.

"Roger," Bannerman took a seat, "not that I don't enjoy our visits, but why did you come here?"

"The truth? To find out where your head is. To understand why you did it."

"Assuming I did it," Bannerman corrected him.

"Hey." Clew looked at him curiously. "This is me you're talking to. What's with the hedging?"

"We're discussing a capital crime, Roger."

Clew's expression darkened. "You think I'm wired."

"Are you?"

"You'll take my word? Or would you like me to peel down to my shorts?"

"A simple yes or no would be fine."

"Yeah, well, fuck you, Bannerman. We're supposed to be friends. By now you either know that or you don't."

"The answer, I gather, is no."

"No, the answer is fuck you."

The anger, Bannerman decided, was genuine. As to the truth of it, Bannerman would soon know. Molly Farrell would be outside by now, ready to scan him as he leaves. He was reasonably certain that she would not pick up a wire. He would be saddened if she did. But it would be good to know. He reached for the Scotch bottle and freshened Roger's drink.

"You asked why," he said. "I'll answer your question."

"Assuming that you did it."

"Assuming that, yes."

"I'd rather have an apology."

"Come on, Roger"—Clew was still glowering at him—"We're not playing for marbles here. You have your agenda, I have mine. That's always been true. I trust you within those limits."

Clew sipped from his glass. He put it down. "There's no wire. Not since that first day we met. And even then, I told you about it."

Bannerman remembered. He nodded. "As for Palmer Reid, the problem was not so much what he tried to do to me. The problem was that too many people knew about it. Even if I wanted to, I couldn't let it pass."

"You could have let us handle him. In our own way."

"No, Roger. I couldn't."

"Then you could at least show some appreciation. We covered for you. No one's going to know."

"You're missing the point," Bannerman said quietly, almost gently. "I need it to be known."

Roger Clew lowered his eyes. A tiny nod. He understood. A reputation is a weapon. Use it or lose it. By now, every enemy Bannerman ever made, everyone who'd ever had reason to fear him, but also every friend, had probably heard some version of the story. They would have watched and waited, with great interest, to see what he did about it. All these years, Mama's Boy's only real protection was the knowledge that whatever you tried to do to him, he would do worse to you. Bannerman had no choice. Especially now that everyone knew where he was. And where he'd been during the three years since he dropped out of sight. Clew could see them, in his mind, reaching for maps of the United States, drawing circles around Westport . . .

"Penny for your thoughts?" Bannerman's voice jerked him back.

Clew straightened. He faked a yawn. "Not for a penny. Maybe for a steak. All the trouble you've caused, the least you owe me is dinner."

Bannerman checked his watch. "I'd like to go work out for an hour or so. Then Lesko wants to meet me at seven, my place. Which reminds me, what about those warrants on Elena Brugg?"

"You made it harder for us. But it's done."

"In that case, I'm buying. How's eight o'clock at Mario's?"

"Eight's fine."

"Is this when I find out about that favor you mentioned?"

"Are you kidding?" Clew pushed to his feet. "After last Friday, you're lucky we even talk to you."

"But you're here."

"As a friend."

"I'm glad, Roger." Bannerman leaned forward. "I hope that never changes."

"Fuck you again," Clew scowled. "I'm starting to get very tired of all these little needles lately. If you have something on your mind, say it."

"I would. I'm just not sure what it is. Unless . . ."

"Unless what?"

"It used to be"—Bannerman seemed to be groping—"fifteen years ago, even three years ago, when you said 'us' or 'we,' you usually meant you and me. I guess I miss that. I guess I worry about you."

"As I said, I'm your friend. As you said, we have different agendas. The two don't have to cross."

"I hope not."

"Hey, look." Clew rose to his feet. "If I have to sit through dinner waiting for you to drop the other shoe, I'd just as soon go to a movie."

"Move to Westport, Roger. Get out of Washington."

Clew closed one eye. "Where the hell did that come from?"

"It's all that 'us-ing' and 'we-ing.' Reid used to talk like that. Whatever went wrong with him, you want to try very hard not to catch it."

"Hey, David . . . ?"

Lesko stood in the center of Bannerman's living room, raincoat open, hands in his pockets, waiting as Bannerman showered. It was a condominium unit, very private, guard at the gatehouse, off Greens Farms Road and on the shore of Long Island Sound. "Make yourself at home," Bannerman had said.

"David? What about this guy?" he asked, barely audibly. *"What do you think?"*

There was no answer. He expected none. Force of habit. A hundred times, over the years, they'd walked into someone's house or apartment, sometimes that of a suspect, and they'd try to get a feel for the guy based on the way he lived. Katz was a schmuck in a lot of ways, Lesko thought, but this he was good at. He could look over a guy's apartment and in ten minutes he could tell you more about him than any shrink. He'd add up a hundred little things; how the place was furnished, what kind of mail piled up, the books and music he liked, and he'd *know* the guy.

Even for Katz, though, Bannerman's place would have been tough. Lesko had half-expected it to be your basic bachelor apartment. Chrome furniture, a stacked stereo, a wine rack, maybe a couple of framed posters on the wall so people would know he's sophisticated, one or two ratty plants, a few copies of *The New Yorker* on the coffee table, and a wok in the kitchen so people would also know he's a gourmet cook.

Bannerman's place was nothing like that. The furniture was big, solid, comfortable. Lots of leather and dark wood. Heavy drapes for privacy. A whole wall full of books, most of them old, none looked like they were there for show. Dictionaries in four or five different languages. A lot of history, most of it European. About half the books were fiction but none were current best-sellers. Lesko recognized titles he hadn't seen since required reading in high school. Complete works of Dickens. *Lord Jim. Wuthering Heights.* Short stories of Irwin Shaw. No spy thrillers but a couple of Agatha Christies.

Quite a few record albums. Some of them highbrow but there was also a fair amount of soft rock. The Beatles. ABBA. Carly Simon. Framed paintings on the walls, mostly watercolors, shore scenes, a couple of landscapes in oil. The room had a few touches that seemed feminine, probably gifts from friends, maybe even from Susan, but hardly anything that seemed personal. No mementos from trips, no framed photographs on the mantle, not even of "Mama." He'd avoided peeking into the bedroom. He knew that Susan had probably spent the night there more than once. He did not want Bannerman's bed in his memory.

Lesko tried to imagine what Katz would have guessed about the man who lived here. An author, maybe. Or a college professor. Someone like that. Quiet. Private. Comes here to shut out the world. The kind of guy who walks away from arguments, probably had his last fight in the sixth grade. That definitely did not describe Bannerman. Then again, maybe it did. Come to think of it, he realized, this whole town is a lot like this room.

It was also a room that belonged, if you didn't know him already, to a guy you'd like to know better. Nice guy. Very civilized. Maybe that explained what Susan saw in him. Put the other stuff aside, forget for a minute what a cold-blooded son of a bitch he can be, including making a cocktail party out of a triple murder, and the fact is he's a guy you could almost be friends with.

The shower turned off. Lesko waited. A blow dryer started.

What he did for Elena, for example. He didn't have to, and it probably cost him. Nothing's for nothing. What he also did, letting him listen to Reid getting zapped, giving Loftus the satisfaction of doing it and Elena's uncle the satisfaction of hearing it . . . he didn't have to do any of those either.

A part of Lesko, that afternoon, had wanted to be the one who threw the switch. Another part was relieved that he wasn't asked. He didn't think he could have done it. Not without being dead sure who all was listening on the other end. And especially with half of Westport watching. Which still seemed nuts. This was a killing, not a fucking school play.

The bathroom door opened. Lesko turned. Bannerman entered the room buttoning his shirt.

"You mind telling me something?" Lesko blurted.

Bannerman shrugged, his expression cool, polite. Which was another thing that bothered Lesko. Just once, he would like to see Bannerman lose it. Just once he would like not to have the feeling that Bannerman always knows exactly what he's doing.

"Last Friday," he finished his thought. "The champagne. All those people."

"Why the witnesses?"

"I guess. Yeah."

"I know it seemed a little childish," Bannerman answered. A faint smile. As if mildly embarrassed. "But they had a right to be there. Reid would have killed every one of them if he got the chance."

Lesko twisted his lip. *Childish* was not the word he would have picked. Except maybe for the champagne. Which had been Billy's idea. What the hell? It was happy hour. Why not chips and dip? "So now we're all supposed to spread the word, right? Don't mess with Bannerman? How come you left out Susan? She could have put it in the paper."

"Lesko. . . ." Bannerman's expression darkened.

"Which is what she says she's going to do. An exposé about Westport."

"She won't."

"You're so sure?"

"Not while her father is an accessory to several murders. If for no other reason."

"I'm taking her home tomorrow."

Bannerman nodded, but said nothing.

"Are you going to try to see her?"

"I don't think so."

"What if she tries to see you? You're right about that newspaper thing, by the way. It's a bluff. She wants you to come talk her out of it."

"Just take her home, Lesko."

"I got your word?"

"That I won't contact her? Yes."

"What if she calls you?"

Bannerman hesitated.

"She will. I know her. What I want is for you to just hang up on her."

Bannerman shook his head. "I won't do that."

"Why not?"

He didn't answer.

"You're a pisser, you know that?" Lesko waved his arms. "I've seen you blow away four different people, you never even blinked, but you wouldn't hang up on my daughter because that would be impolite."

"Give me a break, Lesko." Bannerman checked his watch.

"Anyway, that's not why I came."

Bannerman waited.

"What you did for Elena. Maybe I owe you one."

"I didn't do that for you."

"Don't brush it off, Bannerman. Like you said, you might be in a back alley someday."

"I might," he acknowledged. "I appreciate it."

"There's one other thing. This guy, Clew. You trust him?"

Bannerman raised an eyebrow. "What's on your mind?"

"I don't know. A feeling. Forget it. It's none of my business."

"This feeling. Can you put it into words?"

Lesko shrugged. "I shouldn't judge. I never saw the guy before last week. You've known him, what, fifteen years?"

"Just about." Bannerman nodded. "Tell me."

"I've seen him look at you. He's afraid of you. Even on the plane coming over here. I could see it then, too."

"You don't mean worried? Nervous?"

"I could be wrong."

"But you don't think so."

Another shrug. "After three thousand arrests, I can tell worried from scared. Me, you make nervous. Him, you scare. The man knows something you don't."

"Thank you."

"Anyway"—Lesko buttoned his coat—"take care of yourself." He almost extended his hand, but brushed his hair back instead.

"You too, Lesko." Bannerman saw him to the door.

—15—

Irwin Kaplan could have done without the platform tennis. And he could have done without hearing how the game was invented for days like this. What was invented for days like this was the Sunday paper and an electric blanket. The weather was ridiculous to be out in, let alone play games in. There was no sky. Only a low frozen mist that soaked his clothes from one side as he sweated through them from the other. The surface was slick. Hagler had fallen twice. Clew, once.

If God was good, one of them would break a leg. Himself included. It would spare him, for a while at least, the discussion he'd been dreading for the ten days since the four of them sprinkled dirt on Palmer Reid's coffin.

Too late now, he thought. The match, in its third and final set, was almost over. Fuller and Hagler against himself and Clew. It could not be called the deciding set because Fuller, with or without a partner, could have blown them out anytime he chose. But he didn't care about winning. Not at paddle, anyway. What he wanted was for everyone to work up a good tired sweat because he had this theory. Maybe more of a superstition. He felt that life and death decisions should never be made by people who are too comfortable. You don't sit around a Palm Springs swimming pool, for example, and decide whether Jack the Ripper should be put back to work.

Another part of his theory, Kaplan knew, was that a hard game of paddle tended to clear the mind. Fast, aggressive, fought at close quarters, almost like hand-to-hand combat. Great for purging hostilities. Plenty of chances to smash a wet ball into the net man's face. Especially when the net man is Hagler, who you really don't like very much. But also Bart Fuller for not, as Kaplan had secretly hoped, slamming the door on Roger's brainstorm when he'd first brought it up.

Kaplan had come today hoping there was still that chance; Hagler hoped the opposite. They'd arrived at Fuller's house together. Hagler had collared him in the driveway, eager to show him his latest printout detailing the Ripper Effect that followed the sudden death of Palmer Reid. Reid's body had barely cooled before Hagler was at his computer asking it what would happen next. The computer thought about it for maybe ten seconds before producing a list of more than fifty people who would now either resign, retire, or otherwise run for cover. By the Friday following the funeral, half of them already had. A week later, most of the rest were gone as well. Hagler, he suspected, had helped things along by letting it leak that Reid might not have died of natural causes and that his private files, in any case, could not be found.

Roger Clew, thought Kaplan, should have been equally enthusiastic, if not over the death of a man he despised, then at least over the first real test, however unplanned, of the Ripper Effect. But he was not. He'd seemed distant. Distracted. Almost frightened. That was not like Roger, but it was, to some degree, understandable. Roger had built a career on the perception that he was the one man who enjoyed Paul Bannerman's trust and could control him. Take away that control and all bets are off concerning any further testing of the Ripper Effect.

Another possibility, of course, was that Roger had run a test of his own. That he had set something in motion that ended up getting Mama's Boy angry and Palmer Reid dead.

That would not have surprised Kaplan. And it might explain the haunted look he thought he saw in Roger Clew's eyes that morning, and a mind that was not on his game, which they were now one point from losing. Whatever demons he was carrying, three hard sets of paddle tennis were doing little to exorcize them.

The ball, a too-short lob by Hagler, arced lazily toward Irwin Kaplan. It was a gift. An easy winner. They'd go back to deuce. The hell with that, thought Kaplan. He stepped under it and slapped it out of bounds.

Barton Fuller frowned. His eyes accused Kaplan of a deliberate miss-hit. Kaplan ignored him. His own eyes, glancing toward Fuller's glassed-in porch and the coffee and rolls that awaited them there, said enough of this nonsense.

Fuller nodded. "Let's talk," he said.

"I will make three remarks," Barton Fuller said, pouring coffee, "and then I'm going to leave you while I shower."

A knot formed in Kaplan's stomach. Fuller was setting the agenda. But he was saying that he could not stay to discuss it. Which meant that Irwin Kaplan, unless he walked out with him, was about to be a party to a conspiracy.

"The first," said Fuller, who had just transformed himself from a paddle tennis buddy into the secretary of state, "is that I am entirely familiar with the circumstances leading up to and surrounding the death of Palmer Reid. Roger has briefed me. If either of you have anything to add, anything you think I should know, by all means tell me but do so individually and in private."

Kaplan glanced at Clew. He thought he reddened slightly.

"My second remark," the secretary continued, "is, for the record, unrelated to the first. Roger has been to Westport. You might ask him to tell you about his trip if he hasn't already."

He had. To hear Roger tell it, the trip was a bust. Apparently, however, he and Fuller had some new thoughts about it. Or Fuller had.

"The third remark is also unrelated." Fuller's face took on a pained expression meant to show how deeply he disliked the need to be coy. He looked at Kaplan and then, in turn, at Hagler. "I am keenly aware of the fact that you have two of the most thankless and most frustrating jobs in this entire administration. You are in a war that must, at times, seem unwinnable. But it must be fought, and it cannot be lost. Anything you need, any help I can give, is yours for the asking. No promising strategy should be overlooked, no weapon untested."

In the silence that followed this last, Fuller looked into the eyes of each man in turn, holding their gaze until he was satisfied that the message was understood. Kaplan and Hagler answered with nods. Clew looked at his watch.

"Mr. Fuller," Clew said, "if you're going to take your shower . . ."

Fuller hesitated.

"Sir," Clew told him, "we understand."

"Irwin?" Fuller turned to the balding DEA man. "Do you?"

Kaplan sipped from his mug. "You said we could talk? Privately?" He saw Roger Clew frown. Kaplan paid no attention.

"Any time. On any subject."

"Thank you for the game, sir."

Barton Fuller left the room.

Roger Clew waited until he heard footsteps on the floor above him. "Any questions about that?" he asked.

The two men shook their heads. It was clear enough. Fuller had, no mistaking it, given his blessing.

"If we're through tap-dancing"—Hagler buttered a roll—"let's talk about Westport. Do I gather that Bannerman's had a change of heart since you saw him?"

Clew shook his head. "No change. He just wants to be left alone."

"But he still owes you a favor. He acknowledged that." Hagler remained standing. It was his habit. A short man, although stocky, he tended to compensate for his height by standing while others sat or sitting while others stood.

Clew held his thumb and forefinger an inch apart, as Bannerman had. "Not a big one. Not as big as we'd like. Not yet."

"What does *not yet* mean?"

"Except for a quid pro quo on those drug warrants Irwin lifted, he doesn't feel that he owes us. Or needs us. I think he will soon. We just have to wait."

Hagler gestured toward the briefcase that held his printout. "I have five priority targets in there. All of them hot. You said you'd deliver Bannerman. I need him now."

"It's not that simple, Harry. The fact is, Bannerman's right. We need him more than he needs us. If we're patient, that will change."

Irwin Kaplan leaned forward. "May I ask why you think so?"

"Because regardless of Bannerman's wishes," Clew told him, "he's not going to be left alone. That honeymoon's over. Since Switzerland, we've had inquiries from the Swiss themselves, from Interpol, and four or five other intelligence services, some of whom had assumed Mama's Boy was dead. We've even picked up some coded traffic from a KGB agent in Bern. We haven't broken it but it's clearly about Bannerman because it uses the same designator for him that it's used in the past plus a geographical designator that seems to be Westport. If that's not enough, other people who now know about Westport include"—he ticked them off on his fingers—"your old friend Lesko"—he nodded to Kaplan—"at least four other New York cops, Susan Lesko— who is, incidentally, still on the payroll of the *New York Post* —plus almost everybody in Europe whose last name is Brugg."

"These inquiries you mentioned?" Kaplan asked. "What sort of inquiries?"

Clew spread his hands. "Has he gone back to work? Is he available? I tell them, 'No, he's retired,' but nobody believes it. Next they ask if it's true that he's taken over a whole Connecticut town and threatened to kill or maim any government operative who enters Westport uninvited. I told them that it is."

Kaplan frowned. "Was that smart, Roger?"

"Time will tell."

Kaplan didn't like this at all. Clew, he gathered, had as much as said that Bannerman was an outlaw under no government protection. "You might as well have told them to take their best shot."

"Listen," Roger shook his head sharply. "No matter what I tell them, they will assume that it's a half-truth at best. If I say, hands off, he's ours, they will assume that this administration has turned Westport, Connecticut, into a giant safe house for assassins. Wouldn't you?"

Kaplan shrugged. Hagler stared.

"Would you believe the truth?" he pressed. "That the United States government has tolerated the expropriation of property to which it has legal claim? That Bannerman, the famous Mama's Boy, has decided to create and police his own little world and that we cannot, except at the risk of serious bloodshed and national scandal, do a thing about it? Would you believe that any government could have a team like this, maybe the best in the world, living on its soil, armed and intact, and not be using it?"

"Roger"—Hagler was pacing—"why the hell are we here?"

"To be briefed. To understand the situation. To be ready to react if it changes."

"Bullshit." Hagler bit into his roll, "You've got a scheme going here, Roger. We want to hear about it."

"There's no scheme." He showed his palms. "I would simply suggest to you that if Bannerman's old friends know where he is, so do his enemies. Sooner or later, someone will try to hit him. When and if that happens, Bannerman will need our help."

"The Ripper Effect. Have you shown it to him?"

"No." Clew looked away.

"You're supposed to be so tight, why not?"

"The timing is wrong."

"Don't tell me about timing. While we're sitting here, there are people packing Semtex into portable radios. You're going to wait until a couple of more airliners drop on Scotland?"

"If that would get him to act, yes."

Hagler stared, then started to speak. Kaplan interrupted.

"When you have a problem," he said, his expression pained, "and you have a friend who can help, you go ask him. Explain to me why this is more complicated than that."

"We ask friends if we can borrow their ladders, Irwin," Clew said patiently. "We don't ask them to risk their lives. Nor will Bannerman ask his people to risk their lives for someone else's problem."

"It cuts no ice," Kaplan asked, "that he's an American, and that his country is under siege?"

"As a matter of fact, it does," Clew answered. "If this country's problems touch him, or anyone close to him, he will act. Go try to make a serious drug buy in Westport. Go hurt one of his neighbors."

"I see." Kaplan sighed.

"Do you?"

"Sure." He stood up and began gathering his belongings. "It's the new American dream," he said wearily. "Sorry about your problems, America, but you're history anyway. You've got an economy that is now more dependent on drug money than it is on foreign oil. You've got cities in which it's a statistical certainty that someone in every family will be the victim of a crime at least once a year and nearly all those crimes will be drug related. But I've got mine so screw everybody else. What I'm going to do is pick a nice whitebread community like Westport, draw a circle around it, and say, this is my world, there's the border, keep your problems on the other side of it or I'll kill you." He turned to face Hagler. "You sure you need someone like that?"

Hagler nodded. "I need him."

"What for? You could borrow picked men from any of a dozen federal agencies, to say nothing of the Delta Force or the Rangers. And you'd have men who'd follow orders."

"Lawful orders," Hagler corrected him. "And in writing. If we were talking lawful, we wouldn't need Bannerman."

Kaplan started to argue but Clew waved him off. "Irwin," he said patiently, "it's true that we have no shortage of Rambo types who are dying to be set loose. They're talented, well trained and very gung ho but there are three things wrong with them. First, if captured or otherwise identified as American service personnel, we would have to expect reprisals against our civilians. Second, take the weakest person in Bannerman's entire network and that person, guaranteed, has a hundred times the experience of the best operatives we could field. Third, our own people, no matter how carefully we pick them, will eventually burn out. Bannerman's won't. His people, each of them, are the one in a million who can do this kind of work without being destroyed by it. It takes years for people like these to develop. We don't have years."

"You also don't have Bannerman." Kaplan sat back. "And even if you did, so what? He's got maybe a dozen agents. That's a pinprick, no matter how good they are."

"They're a beginning. And they're a test. We've discussed all that."

"You also keep saying they're one in a million. And just now you as much as said our own people are useless. So what do you do with this test?"

"First things first, Irwin."

Kaplan turned to Hagler, spreading his arms. "Did I just ask an unreasonable question? Roger the dodger here insists he has nothing up his sleeve and now he wants us to believe there's nothing in his head either. Do we believe that, Harry?"

Hagler didn't answer.

"And do we believe that Roger is just going to sit back and wait for Bannerman to develop a social conscience or do we think he's going to give him a little push."

"Irwin—" Clew set down his mug.

"And do we think—is it just possible—that Roger has given him a little push already?"

Clew's face turned ashen.

"Deny it, Roger."

"I do deny it. It isn't true."

"Okay." Kaplan nodded. "Benefit of the doubt. Now deny that you know exactly how you intend to hook Bannerman, and keep him hooked, and how you hope to milk the shit out of the Ripper Effect after that."

"I deny that, too," he said evenly. "There is no such plan. There is no such hook. Not that I haven't tried to think of one."

"And the best you've come up with is wait and see."

"For the moment. Yes."

"Look at Harry." Kaplan gestured with his head toward

Hagler who was pacing the sun porch, his eyes, now and then, falling on his briefcase and lingering there. "Does he look like someone who's going to wait and see?"

Hagler froze.

"Yes," Clew answered. "Not for very long. But yes."

Kaplan held his gaze for a long moment. Then he looked up at the ceiling. The sound of the shower had stopped. Fuller, he assumed, was probably listening at this point. It would be hard not to. Unless he had a hell of a lot more faith in Roger than Kaplan could manage at this moment.

"The man said we could talk to him. Individually and in private."

"He didn't say you could compromise him. I'd rather you left that to me."

"Well. . . ." Kaplan pushed to his feet and retrieved his paddle racket from a wicker table near the porch door. "I'll tell what *I'd* rather. I'd rather go home, take a hot shower, then climb back into bed with my wife and the Sunday paper, let my kids and the dogs climb in with us, and start my Sunday morning all over again. That's what I'm going to do."

Clew started to speak. Kaplan stopped him. "There are two ways," he said, "that I'll talk about this again. One is with Bart Fuller. Off the record. Just him and me. The second is with Bannerman himself to see if—"

"You can't do that."

"Don't give me *can't*. He's in the goddamned phone book. Or I'll get Lesko to introduce us. We'll walk him down to the post office where I'll show him the flag and see if he still recognizes it. After that, if he still hasn't shot me, I'll ask him straight out what he thinks of your little computer game. And then, if he says it could work, I'll try getting him to give it a shot after he satisfies me that his killers are nicer than their killers."

"This conversation," Clew said coldly, "stays here. The three of us. You gave your word."

"The two of you," Kaplan corrected him. "If and when you decide to level with me, we'll take another head count."

Clew watched him leave. "Like you said," he muttered, "he's a pain in the ass."

"I never said he was stupid." Hagler stood close to his shoulder, his own voice kept low. "Is he right, Roger? Do you have something going?"

"Like what?"

"A way to move things along here."

"Patience, Harry. My immediate concern is getting Irwin locked in."

"You really think he'd go to Bannerman?"

"No. Not to Lesko either. He won't do anything that would compromise Fuller."

"As long as we're whispering, what do you have in mind? More drugs in his kids' lockers?"

Clew turned on him, glaring. "That better be a joke, Harry."

"Roger," Hagler closed one eye. "I've got six years in this job and not a single big win. I don't joke. And don't tell me to be patient."

"Tell me to my face. Do you think I'd set up that man's kids?"

"I think you'd do what works, Roger. So would I."

—16—

The last week of January. Westport.

Susan Lesko had gone home with her father.

He took her, by train and taxi, to her apartment on Manhattan's West Side. He had hoped to spend the night with her, that night at least, sleeping on her couch. She said no, firmly. She wanted the couch for herself. She did not tell him that.

The bruises on her face had faded, for the most part, to a pale yellow, and the cuts had almost healed. Her own doctor would remove the sutures. The predicted aftereffects of her cocaine overdose were now little more than light-headedness, an occasional nightmare, trouble recapturing certain memories, trouble dismissing others. She would be fine, she told her father. She needed time to be alone.

Susan stayed home three days. She took no calls, letting her machine screen all of them, returning those of her father only when he threatened to come and kick in her door unless he heard her voice saying that she was all right.

The call she'd been hoping for did not come. Not even a just-making-sure-you're-okay call left on her machine. It was just as well. For all that she rehearsed . . . fantasized . . . what she might say to him, she knew that she would remember none of it if the call should come. Her response would be cold, or angry, or bitter, or, worse, she might cry.

Her apartment was strange to her. It was as if another person had lived there before. The furnishings, photographs, even the clothing and cosmetics seemed to have meaning only to that other person, no longer to her.

Especially her bed. They had made love on it. Their first time. She had made love more joyfully, more hungrily, longer, more often, more generously than with all the boys and men who had touched her life taken together. She had pleased him there. He had pleased her. He had loved her. Deeply. Thoroughly. She was not wrong about that. It was in his words, in his touch, and in his eyes. Eyes that she had caused to come alive. Eyes that died again as he stood by her bed in a hospital in Davos. She had not seen him since, except in her memories. And in her dreams.

It was just as well, she told herself. Her father was right. She wasn't even twenty-five yet. She had her whole life to live. There would be other men. They would be closer to her age. They would live in the same world. By the time Paul Bannerman was twenty-five, as her father pointed out, he was already killing people.

She'd tried to argue that. "What about soldiers?" she asked. "Killing is what they're trained for from the time they're eighteen. They're ready and willing. *Semper fideliso.* What about street cops? What about Raymond 'the Terrible' Lesko who was no older than Paul when he threw a rapist down an elevator shaft, the story goes, or the four or the nine more men he shot depending on which of the other stories you believe? And don't say that's different."

"It is and it isn't," he answered. "You've grown up with cops. You've seen how cops, after a few years on the job, get so they can only talk to other cops. It's what happens when day in, day out, you only see people when they're at their worst. Even someone they stop for running a red light, decent guy, wife and kids, is all of a sudden insulting, he hates you for doing your job, and now and then he pulls a gun and blows a hole in you. Cops get so they can only talk about these things to each other. No one else could understand. No one else wants to know. Including their wives. What wife wants to hear that shit every night? So they talk about

new slipcovers, or what's on TV. They pretend. They wait
for the pension. Meanwhile, the cop starts seeing women on
the side. Lady cops. Hookers. Cop groupies. Women who
live in his world or at least he doesn't have to pretend with
them. At least there isn't this great big wall between them.
And in the end, most cop wives never make it to the pension
anyway. Except for the part the divorce court gives them."

"That's what happened to you and Mom?" she asked.
Although she knew the answer.

"Every story's different," he said, "and every story's the
same. The point is, you take what happens with cops, and
you multiply it by ten, and maybe you're still not even close
to what happens to people like that crowd up in Westport."

"I love him, Daddy," she said, very quietly.

He sat her down. Hugged her. "You want the truth? I
even like him. A little. The guy you think you love is Paul
Bannerman. Nice guy. You could do worse. But the guy you
can't live with, for a million reasons, is Mama's Boy."

She said nothing. She shuddered.

"I'll even give you this," Lesko said gently. "Maybe this
country needs people like him sometimes. Maybe, with everything that's going on in the world, I'm even a little sorry
he's trying to hang 'em up. But they'll never let him do it.
Not his friends, not his enemies. No one knows it better
than Bannerman. He knows he was kidding himself. Sooner
or later, it's going to hit the fan. I don't want you in the
middle of it when it does. To give the guy his due, Bannerman doesn't either."

"I'm a big girl," she said stubbornly. "I can take care of
my—" She bit her lip. An abrupt wave of her hand told her
father that he had no need to contradict her. The marks on
her face, the bandage that still covered her left eyebrow,
were proof enough.

He answered anyway. "I know," he told her, "that next
time you'd be more careful. It's not that simple. It's not like,
living in New York, you're careful where you walk at night
and who you let into your apartment. We're talking killers
here. On both sides. With them, in the time it takes you to
even to get nervous, someone would be dead. And if Bannerman has you to worry about, and it slows him down because
maybe he doesn't want you to see something that would

make you afraid of him, that someone could be him. It's a different world, Susan. And you can't live in it. I know what I'm talking about.

"I know you do." She squeezed his hand. And she knew that when he spoke of different worlds, and of different people, and of impossible loves, he was also talking about himself and a tiny elegant woman named Elena Brugg.

He'd said little after that. Nor did she argue. She wanted to say, but didn't, that sometimes people know things that aren't true. Or that shouldn't be true.

The three days passed. On Tuesday morning, Susan Lesko kept an appointment with her doctor. The stitches were removed. A ski accident, she told him. He said she was lucky, that there would be a scar but it would not be terribly noticeable. The Swiss surgeon knew his business. The hairline fracture of her cheekbone had knitted properly; it would leave a small lump under the skin that might shrink in time. The bruise over it, small but dark and clotted, would also fade eventually. In the meantime, makeup would cover it. He replaced the bandage on her brow. Keep it on for another day or two, he said. She stripped it off before she reached the street.

Her doctor's office was on Park Avenue near Thirty Eighth Street, a few blocks south of Grand Central Station. She walked toward the terminal, intending to pass through, to continue up Fifth or Madison for a while and enjoy the rare springlike temperature that had worked up from the Gulf overnight. But as she reached the station lobby, her eye fell upon Gate 25, just left of the escalators. She had used that gate many times in recent months, many weekends in Westport. Another train was boarding, going there again. She looked away, biting her lip. But slowly, almost unwillingly, she turned her head to stare up at the main Departures board. The Westport train, it said, would leave at 11:07. She checked her watch: 11:02. She bit harder.

It was foolish. She knew that. But there she was, at a quarter after twelve, standing near the Westport station, trying not to be noticed, watching local businesspeople walk into Mario's just across the street.

Billy McHugh would be at the bar. Molly Farrell would

be seating luncheon customers. One might be Paul. He took lunch there often.

The thing to do, of course, would be to walk back into the station, keep her head down, and wait for the next train back to New York. She knew that. The last thing she needed was to be caught standing there like a dummy if Paul Bannerman's car suddenly popped around the corner.

On the other hand, she was hungry. It had been days since she felt much like eating. Eight pounds lost since Davos, when two would have been plenty. Portions at Mario's were huge and they were good. And Molly, who had stayed with her in the hospital, talked to her, listened to her . . . was a friend. So was Billy. He'd been there as well, she heard. He'd always been kind to her.

Her father tried to tell her things about both of them. He meant well, she supposed, trying to make her feel well rid of them. And there was probably some truth to the stories. But not much. No one who spent ten minutes with Billy, let alone Molly, could believe that he would . . .

Never mind. It's too ridiculous.

Susan went in.

Billy saw her first, then Molly. Billy waved, a big grin, then held up a bottle of the Chablis that she liked. Molly ran over, took her by the shoulders, inspected her face, smiled her approval, then kissed her cheek and led her to the small window table that she had often shared with Paul.

See? They were glad to see her. They were friends.

Molly, after five minutes, went back toward the office. While there, Susan felt sure, she made a phone call. Susan saw that in the glance she threw at Billy as she returned and in the briefest flicker of sympathy that crossed her eyes as she stopped once more at the table before returning to her station at the door.

Susan ordered. She watched the street. Paul did not come.

So on Wednesday she took the train again. And on Thursday. And again on Friday.

On that Friday, Detective Lieutenant Harry Greenwald pulled his car into a metered space on Broadway near the corner of 181st Street and waited, his engine running, windows up. He was ten minutes early.

Greenwald was well off his beat, but he knew this neighborhood. He had grown up not far north of here, in the Inwood section. Right against Fort Tryon Park and in the shadow of The Cloisters.

Used to be nice, he thought ruefully. Trees on most of the streets. Window boxes with flowers. People mostly Irish and Jewish. Working stiffs. Kids grew up to be cops, firemen, postal workers. The Jews had all the stores. In the streets, always a touch football game or a stickball game going on. Not that much traffic. Cars waited until a play was over. Even so, the cops were supposed to break up the games. Confiscate the stickball bats. No big deal if they did. The kids would just go down the nearest basement and steal the super's broom. That's what crime in the streets was like in those days. That and throwing snowballs off roofs at people walking by and sneaking into the subway to go up to Baker Field on Saturdays. And sneak in there, too.

The Jews weren't that much on football, Greenwald remembered, even counting Sid Luckman and Sammy Baugh. But they were better at stickball and school-yard basketball. Hell, back before the war and a little after, the Jews were better at all the sports. Look at boxing. The only thing the Irish kids had on them was that they got new suits every year for Easter but even that was dumb because that time of the year you pay retail.

Greenwald smiled. It was nice.

Look at this shit now, he thought. No Irish, no Jews. Go find a tree that hasn't been poisoned to death by the air. Garbage in the streets. Graffiti sprayed on every building. And he could sit there an hour without ever seeing a single white face except on weekends when the cars from Jersey and Connecticut drive in to make a buy. Cocaine was the only white thing left here if you didn't count the new Reeboks on the feet of every kid with a beeper on his belt and a pocket full of crack vials.

Greenwald shook his head. Say any of this at home and his daughters call him a racist. He wouldn't have to say *nigger*. Or *spic*. All he has to say is *nonwhite* and it's like he's the Grand Dragon. Never mind that they live out in Port Jefferson where there isn't a black family within a half a mile. It's why he doesn't bother talking to them about it. What do they know?

Anyway it's not the black blacks. It's not the ones whose parents grew up in the city and who busted their asses to get someplace like the Jews did in the thirties and like the Irish did before that. You look at the blacks who are in pro sports or the blacks on the cops. They're mostly from the old-time families. What it is, mostly, is the Jamaicans and the Dominicans. For ten years now they've been coming by the planeload. They head right for the welfare office for something to tide them over until at least one member of the family can hook up with a drug gang. First thing they buy is those Reeboks. Then the beeper. Even kids who don't deal wear beepers so they get respect.

Next they buy a gun.

This isn't true? This is racist? Five Dominican gangs have divided up the entire West Side, Broadway to the river, from 133rd Street to 181st. The Jamaicans, the "posses," have St. Nicholas Avenue and are moving east and south with guns and crack. More than 500 shootings, counting misses, in the past year. Over a hundred didn't miss. Are there decent people here? Hardworking? Religious? Sure. You can spot them on their way to work, on their way back, and buying food or going to church. They're the ones with their heads down, moving fast, keeping their kids close until they can get home and lock the door. They try to keep their kids clean but sooner or later the kid has to go to some shit public school or go find some shit job. That's when he learns economics. What's better, kid? Two hundred bucks a week for pushing a broom or $1,500, part-time, pick your own hours, no heavy lifting.

He saw Wiggins coming. Skinny. All arms and legs. Crossing 181st, doing a roll, looked like he was floating, head bobbing to the sound from a Sony Walkman. Greenwald rolled down the sidewalk window and whistled. Wiggins made a show of innocent confusion. You talking to me? I ain't done nothin'. What do the man want with me? Greenwald flashed a badge. Yelled at him. Ordered him into the car.

To anyone watching, the thin black man was arguing, denying, occasionally flinching whenever Greenwald raised a hand. In fact, Detective Sergeant K. T. Wiggins, now back on undercover after helping to guard Susan Lesko, was handing an audiocassette tape to Harry Greenwald. Greenwald snapped it into the machine he held on his lap.

"The first voice," said Wiggins, holding a hand over the "play" button, "is a Jamaican called "Buster Bang." Real name: Nathaniel Weeks. He's a hitter . . . enjoys his work . . . for a Jamaican gang called the Jungle Posse. The second voice is Hector Manley, street name is "Dandy." Hector's garbage but he's quality garbage. Couple years of college, one year in a Catholic seminary, quit, became a goon for the Labor party, busted one head too many and had to split. Hector is with an elite offshoot called the Jungle Lites. The meeting is in his apartment. It was wired just two days ago when Hector got rousted by the DEA. Hector is worse than a hitter. Story is, the Jungle Lites were—"

"I know," said Greenwald. "Trained in Cuba. Urban guerrilla techniques. And this is about Westport?"

"If I was sure, I would have called Lesko myself. You listen. You tell me."

Greenwald pressed the button. Voices came on, melodic, singsong. One good thing about Jamaicans, thought Greenwald, is you can eavesdrop without needing a black guy to translate. They all sound like Harry Belafonte.

"Right here," said Wiggins. He turned the sound up.

". . . got to bang that dry cleaner man. Got to bang him soon."

"Not yet. I will speak with him first."

"He is hurting us, Dandy Man. The others see we do nothing, it makes them brave."

"On Saturday, I will go to see him. Do nothing until then."

"What about the Arab? Have you decided?"

[A pause.] "We are to meet next week. Wednesday."

"It's a lot of money, Dandy Man."

"It is also a lot that he asks."

"Forty cars? We can have them in a day. The drivers are no problem. We have brothers in Norwalk and in Bridgeport. We have it fucking surrounded, Dandy Man. Give me two days, three at most, and it will be done. We will be famous, you and me. No one will ever forget us."

"Certainly not the police." [Then, thoughtfully.] *"You would do this thing, Buster?"*

"Think of it, Dandy." [Voice excited, gleeful.] *"Forty cars, all at once. One big bang and there is no more town. Fourth of July, man, and we can watch it. There is a highway bridge where we can see it all. They will think it is the end of the world."*

[There was a sound. A door buzzer.]

"Have you spoken of this? To anyone?"

"Only you, Dandy Man. And the Arab."

"You will say nothing to these men. Nothing at all."

"But we do it?"

"It might be done. Yes. On Wednesday, I will decide."

Wiggins pressed the "stop" button. "That's it," he said. "There's another meeting but the tape runs out before it gets going."

Greenwald stopped writing. He'd been making notes on a pad. He brought his pen back up to the first item. "Who's the 'Dry Cleaner'?" he asked.

"That's not a street name. They're talking about Wesley Covington. Owns a Minute Man franchise on St. Nicholas Avenue up in the Heights, lives on 153rd Street. He's formed a block association to try to keep out the dealers. Has neighbors, volunteers, patrolling with bullhorns and walkie-talkies."

"They're taking on the Jamaicans with bullhorns?"

"They had softball bats. Local cops made them leave 'em home. Said they should use nine-one-one instead." Wiggins sniffed. "Show me a cop who'll answer a call on 153rd."

"And Buster Bang wants Covington hit."

"Buster always wants everybody hit. Hector's not a whole lot nicer but at least he tries to talk first. And right now he doesn't need Buster's kind of heat."

"Who's this 'Arab'?"

"No idea. Unless the DEA knows. And if they'll tell us."

"Why shouldn't they?"

"They don't even know we have this tape. We asked for something else. They sent this with it by mistake."

Greenwald was silent for a long moment. "Between Norwalk and Bridgeport, visible from a bridge. That could only be Westport. What's this forty cars?"

Wiggins shook his head.

Greenwald frowned. "Could we be talking an invasion here? Forty cars full of shooters all hitting Bannerman's town?"

Wiggins shrugged doubtfully. "Sounds more like forty bombs. But there's no way to ask Buster Bang. He got banged himself last night. Someone threw him off a roof. We could always ask Hector but all that does is make him bag it. Then maybe the Arab takes his business someplace else."

"Who did Buster? You heard any talk?"

"No, but it didn't seem to scare Hector. This morning, he's out making his rounds like nothing happened."

"This Arab," Greenwald returned to his pad. "That's another street name, right? We should have it in the computer."

"Or a real Arab. Lots of them around. They bring in most of the heroin and hash. Ask me, Hector got offered a supply deal, cut rates, in return for a favor."

"Which has to be a hit on Bannerman."

Wiggins spread his hands.

"But Lesko says Bannerman doesn't know from drugs. What would Hector have against him?"

"The question is what the Arab has against him. Hector might not know he exists. All Hector wants is to get rich and go back to Kingston. Hector, by the way, sees himself running for prime minister some day and being loved by all the people. That's after he kills everybody who remembers he used to crack skulls."

"Can I keep this?" Greenwald tapped his machine.

"Like I said, we got it by accident. I've never heard of it."

"You better go." Greenwald looked around. "Just bust out of the car. I'll chase you for half a block."

"No more than that. You'll come back, you won't have a radio. Anyway, then what?"

"You want to know?"

"Shit, yes. This is interesting."

"I'll talk to Lesko. In the meantime, don't walk with your head down. You never know who else is going to fall off a roof."

Friday. Half-past noon.

Molly picked up a menu and walked to Susan's table. She pulled out a chair and sat.

"Susan. This is getting a little dumb," Molly said, not unkindly.

"I know it is," she nodded.

"Why don't you go to his office and get it over with?"

"He knows I've been coming here, doesn't he?"

"Except for today, yes."

"I keep hoping he'll come and have this out. If I go over there I'll get mad, or say something stupid, or I'll start crying in front of his travel agents. I do better in restaurants."

"Speaking of which, what can I get you?"

"Just a salad, I guess." She took a breadstick from the basket and bit off an end. "Can I ask you something personal, Molly?"

"Sure."

"I've heard things about you. About all of you. Are they true?"

Molly looked into her eyes. She did not see a reporter there. Only a hurt young girl trying to understand Paul Bannerman through her. "I guess," she answered. "Probably."

"Then how do you stay like you are? I mean, with all of that."

"You grew up with policemen," Molly told her. "They start out being like anyone else. Some get mean. Some don't. We're not all that different."

"And like policemen, you're only comfortable with your own kind?"

"As a rule, that's true. Sad, sometimes. But true."

"You've never seen an exception."

Molly cocked her head toward the bar. "Billy here is thinking of proposing to his landlady. We're not sure he's ever really had a relationship with a woman before. We'll try to get him to go slowly. And we'll have to watch it carefully. Yes, Susan, we've seen exceptions. But we've seen some real disasters."

"Don't you think"—Susan touched her hand—"that I wish I could turn off what I feel and walk away from this? I see my father trying to do the same thing. I don't know if you've noticed, but he's in love. And it's with a woman who, two years ago, he'd have happily sent to prison."

"I could see it," Molly nodded. "He's struggling with it, just as you are."

"And as Paul is?"

"I think so."

"Then why doesn't he have the guts to come here and talk it through?"

"You said it. He's afraid to."

"Then, damn it"—Susan folded her arms—"I'm going to keep coming here until he does or until I've lost so much respect for him that I don't care whether he comes or not."

Molly rose to her feet. "I have to make a phone call," she said.

All women, Bannerman had long suspected, are crazy.

First there was Molly, on the phone, agreeing for the sake of argument that he was doing the right thing. Staying away. Making a clean break. Then in the same breath saying there's right and there's right. "Get over here," she said. "Talk to Susan. If you don't come settle this, *now,* I'll send Billy to drag you over." Bannerman could only sigh. He's right, but he's wrong. Women.

Then there was Susan.

She was hurt. And confused. He understood that. But she, if not Molly, had always been sensible. Once he explained, gently, but firmly, she would have to understand. Then he would walk her to the train, and that would be that.

"You're a pain in the ass, Bannerman. You know that?"

"Um . . . hello, Susan."

"It's about time. Sit."

He took a breath, struggling to recall what he'd intended to say. It did not help that Molly lurked within earshot, pretending not to listen, but exchanging smug little grins with Billy. *Glad you're having a nice time,* he growled inwardly.

He sat. He raised both hands in a gesture of peace, cleared his throat, and began the explanation, rehearsed in his mind, of why this could not possibly . . .

Look, Bannerman," she said through her teeth, "I've been *explained to* up, down, and sideways. My father says a nice girl like me doesn't belong with killers but he couldn't tell me why I belong with him. Molly likes us together but she's afraid I think you're Robin Hood. Carla Benedict says a candy ass like me would only be a distraction who would mope and moan every time you're ten minutes late for dinner and, besides, I'm probably not even a good lay."

"Carla said that?" Bannerman blinked.

"I read between the lines."

He tried regaining control. He tried taking her remarks, one at a time, and addressing them sensibly. At this, he thought he heard a moan from Molly.

"I've made a decision," Susan announced, interrupting his explanation of the difference between being a cop's daughter, well removed from the things he did on the job, and being in a relationship where there could be no such distance.

"I'm going to shoot somebody tonight," she told him.

Bannerman blinked.

"And then another one tomorrow night," she said. "Someone with six kids. And then a couple more every week after that until I get used to it. Until you say, 'Hey, maybe this kid's my kind of woman.' "

"Susan—"

"And you'll take me on that ski trip you still owe me, where you'll fall in love with me because I am, by God, a pretty damned good woman and then—"

He raised a hand. She took it and slammed it to the table.

"And *then*"—she leaned forward—"I'll dump you and let *you,* for a change, sit outside my building for five nights straight before *maybe* I let you come crawling back, you creep."

Paul glanced toward Molly as if for help. She had turned her back. Her shoulders were shaking. He would get her for this, he thought darkly.

But now his eyes were back on Susan. They rested on her cheek, still bruised. He wanted to reach across the table and touch it. To feel the long brown hair that flowed over her shoulders. To smell its freshness. To kiss the healing wound above her eye. It wasn't so bad. It made her, somehow, even more attractive than before. He wasn't sure why. Perhaps it was her lack of self-consciousness about it. The way she carried her head. Chin high. I am who I am. A scar doesn't matter.

His eyes drifted to the swell of her breasts. Over her shoulders and arms. Hands that had touched him, caressed him. How he had missed her. How he had wanted her. Not just her body. Her. To wake up with her. Come home to her. Ride bikes with her, go to movies, fix meals with her. Anything. Everything. Take walks with her . . .

"Let's get out of here," he said. "Let's go someplace where we can talk."

"About how it can't work?"

"About how to keep your father from beating up on me if he hears we're even thinking about it."

"Thinking about it can't hurt."

"No. Maybe it can't."

He drove her to the town beach. They had it almost to themselves. Just a few people walking their dogs. They talked, haltingly at first, and then somewhat more easily as the short winter day turned into evening. Together, they watched the sun go down. The temperature dropped. She shivered. He put an arm around her to keep her warm, then said he'd better take her to the train. "I'm not going home tonight," she said.

She stayed at his apartment. He made a light supper. They did not make love. They barely touched except for a single light kiss to her forehead after she fell asleep on his couch and he carried her to his bedroom. He took the couch for himself. He slept in his clothing. In the morning he found that she had covered him.

He prepared breakfast. They talked some more. Nothing of substance. Neither seemed willing to risk the fragile illusion that they were simply two ordinary people, having breakfast in their robes, enjoying an ordinary, lazy Saturday morning.

Susan showered first. He waited until he heard the water splashing, then went to the locked cabinet where he kept his telephone answering machine, his private line, its volume control at its lowest point. He opened the cabinet, and, adjusting the volume so that it was audible, just barely, pressed the "play" button. Reality returned with the sound of her father's voice. A message left on Friday evening. Leaving a New York number. Insisting that he call at once.

His first thought was that Lesko had learned that his daughter was there. He listened to the next message. Lesko again.

"Bannerman? You're there, right? Pick up the damned phone." He turned the volume back down. Some other time. Next message.

"Bannerman? Not that I want to ruin your weekend or anything but how about this? How about it looks like some-one wants to drive forty carloads of explosives into your happy little dreamworld up there and blow it all to shit? Does that get your attention?"

—17—

"Hey David."

No answer.

"Come on." Lesko whispered into hands cupped over his mouth. *"Talk to me."*

"About what?" came the response. "Lesko?"

The answer startled him. But it was Greenwald's voice, coming from the radio he was holding. He must have had his thumb on the button.

"Forget it," he said, embarrassed. "It's okay."

He was standing within a rack of finished dry cleaning, watching through plastic bags. Bannerman was five feet away, also hidden.

Lesko had played the tape for him, over the telephone, three times. Bannerman listened, then said he'd meet him in two hours. Lesko heard reluctance, resignation, in his voice. *Well, sorry to ruin your Saturday morning,* he thought, *but tough shit.*

Lesko could see the back of Wesley Covington's head and the front window beyond. St. Nicholas Avenue was almost dark. Covington's delivery truck sat at the curb. Greenwald was in it. Covington had sent his pressers home. One clerk remained, at Lesko's insistence. The place should look normal.

There was no way to be sure that Hector Manley would come. Except the man said Saturday. It didn't figure he'd show up on 153rd Street, not with all those bullhorns, so if he was coming at all it would have to be at the store, most likely at closing time.

"Lesko?" Greenwald's voice. "I see him."

"Where?"

"Across the street . . . watching. He's got a leg breaker with him. The Dandy Man's no midget but this guy's a house."

"Just don't let him see you. Let me know when he moves."

"He's moving. Here he comes."

Lesko could see them now. They appeared on the sidewalk, framed against the truck. The smaller one moved closer to the window. He stopped there in its light, staring through it. The big one, the house, caught the eye of a customer who was about to enter. He glared at her with barbully eyes. Stupid eyes. She turned away. Now his eyes met those of the girl at the counter. He motioned again with his head. "I'm not going," she said quietly to Covington.

"Please." He reached behind a partition and produced her coat. "I won't be long." He placed it over her shoulders.

"I'll go because you say," she told him. "Not pig face out there."

Gently, firmly, Covington guided her to the door. He kissed her hair, then eased her through it. He watched as she passed between the two men outside, wincing as she mouthed an obscenity toward the big one. He waited. Her footsteps receded. He turned the sign on his door so that the word *Closed* faced outward. He returned to his place behind the counter.

"Bannerman?" Lesko whispered loudly. "I'll handle this. Stay out of it."

"Fine with me," came the muffled answer.

"Mr. Covington?"

"I hear you."

"You okay?"

"A little nervous. I'm fine."

Lesko had already told him: "You see a gun, you drop. They just want to talk, you listen, but stay behind the counter with your back close to the conveyer. They say things to scare you, be scared. We don't want them wondering what makes you brave."

The door opened.

Hector Manley entered first, then the other. There was no question which was which. The leg breaker, close to 300 pounds of him, was dressed in a hooded sweatshirt of olive drab. Thick black boots laced over army fatigues. An inch-thick chain around his neck, not gold, stainless steel. He wore wraparound sunglasses with black plastic frames. Hector wore a trench coat of black leather, cut extralong in the style of Eastern Europe, a turtleneck sweater, white, the same voodoo sunglasses. Boots were gray. Cowboy boots. Looked like snake. Probably his mother, Lesko thought. But not a bad looking guy. Lesko could see where he got his name.

The man in leather did not speak. He waited, hands clasped in front of him, his eyes locked on those of Wesley Covington. The hooded one approached the counter, peering beyond it. Searching. Listening. The fingers of one huge hand brushed lightly over the top of the cash register. He looked at Hector. Hector nodded.

The cash register moved. It began to tilt. Very gradually. The big man added pressure. It crashed to the floor. Change rolled across linoleum. Still no one spoke.

The big man found the hook on which outgoing garments were hung. He ran his fingers along it. It began to bend. He tore it from the counter. Screws and splintered wood came with it. In a lazy, contemptuous backhand motion, he flung this hook toward Wesley Covington. It missed. It vanished into the hanging garments a foot away from Raymond Lesko. The screws, the torn wood, caught the plastic. It stayed there.

Hector Manley raised a hand, then lowered it slowly toward the pocket of his coat. He interrupted this motion to make a gesture that, it seemed, was intended to reassure the man behind the counter. He continued, into his pocket, and produced what appeared to be a small group of photographs. With these, he approached the counter. There he laid them out, one by one, facing Wesley Covington. There were four.

He touched a finger to the first one. The touch was light, almost gentle.

"Your wife?" he asked.

Covington did not answer.

"It will happen on the street," Manley told him.

Covington stared.

"The streets are dangerous. It will happen in full view of her friends. They will not save her." His voice was soft, his diction precise, his manner sorrowful. "There are some," he continued, "who will blame me for this sadness. They will say, 'Covington challenged the Dandy Man. He paid the price.' But in truth, Mr. Covington, you will have yourself to blame."

He pointed to the second photograph.

"Your little girl?"

Lesko should have seen it coming. He saw the muscles growing in Covington's back. He saw the hands balling into fists. But he had told Covington to do nothing. Say nothing. Make them push a little. Make them want to step behind the counter, put their hands on you, get them within reach. But the picture of his daughter was not a little push. Lesko heard what sounded like a dog. He almost looked around. But then he realized that the long low growl was coming from Covington. By the time he knew that, Covington's hands were across the counter. They were clawing at Manley. One found his lapel. The other his throat.

"Shit!" Lesko muttered. He braced himself.

Manley fought off Covington's lunge. A forearm knocked one hand away, an elbow the other, and with it he smashed the side of Covington's head. But Covington had gripped his coat again. With a great heave he pulled him forward, over the counter. Manley rolled and twisted free. The bigger man moved in.

"Heads up, asshole." Lesko tore through the plastic. One stride, one kick, caught Hector Manley in the throat. Manley rolled over, wide-eyed and gasping. Covington leapt on him. The clothing hook appeared in Lesko's right hand. He swung it from the floor toward the big man's crotch. It sank in there. He ripped it loose. The big man tried to scream but could not.

"You like to break things, fuck face?" Lesko hissed. "I'll show you breaking things."

"*Lesko? What's happening in there? Lesko?*" Greenwald's voice.

Lesko was too busy. Gripping the broken steel shaft, he rammed the clothing hook between the big man's teeth, snapping some. His cheek swelled impossibly. Lesko twisted the hook, setting it. The big man flailed at him with his legs and, with his hands, tried to seize the shaft. With a roar, Lesko hauled him to his feet, then, as with a gaffed tuna, swung him over his shoulder and sent him sprawling, gagging, into an open space between the racks of finished clothing. He tried to rise, reaching for the heavy chain he wore around his neck. Lesko moved toward him. His foot struck the broken cash register. He picked it up, grunting, and, from a shot-putter's stance, sent it crashing against the hooded head and shoulders. The big man fell as if axed.

Dimly, from the street outside, he heard the horn of a car. A long blast. Not far away. It was not stopping.

"*Lesko? I think there are more out here. I think that's Hector's car.*"

Lesko found the radio where he dropped it.

"Tell him to ignore the horn." Bannerman's voice. Calm, quiet.

"What?" He was breathing heavily.

"It's not a problem. Tell him to ignore it. Then drag the other one back here."

Confused, Lesko blinked, but he obeyed. He seized both Covington and Manley by their collars, pulled them apart, and threw Manley, bodily, into the pressing station behind the conveyers.

"*Lesko? I think there was a hit. I think there's a dead man across that horn.*"

"Tell him you know," said Bannerman.

"I know what?"

"That their driver is dead." Bannerman gestured toward one of the figures writhing on the floor. "He said it. The streets are dangerous."

The horn still blared. Another sound. Gunfire. From another direction.

"*Lesko? There's shooting out here. Automatic weapons. I see people diving into doorways.*"

"Tell him you know that too."

Lesko stared at Bannerman. But he pressed the button. "Harry?" he shouted. "It's okay."

"How long before a police response?" Bannerman asked.

"I don't know. Around here? Ten minutes."

"Then that's how much time we have."

The big man, his body twitching feebly, was tied wrists to ankles. A bloody foam bubbled from his nose and mouth. There was no need to gag him. Next, Bannerman tied the Jamaican known as Dandy. He, too, was bleeding from the mouth and wretching to clear his injured throat but he was conscious. His sunglasses clung crookedly to his face revealing one eye, moist with pain, fearful yet defiant. Bannerman forced a cloth between his teeth. Wesley Covington appeared with two canvas laundry bins, one inside the other. He separated them, lined them with plastic. With Lesko's help he lifted the big man into one of them, Hector Manley into the other.

Bannerman stepped back. He shook his head at the damage Lesko had done to two large men in so short a time.

"Any chance," he asked idly, "that you and Billy McHugh were separated at birth?"

"What?" Lesko gave Manley's bin a final kick.

"Never mind."

"Just hold the door, okay?" He seized the bin containing the big man and spun it toward the front.

Wesley Covington unlocked the rear of his delivery truck. With Lesko, he lifted one bin inside, then the other. He moved briskly, although unnerved by the horn that still blared up the street. Farther down, where the gunfire had been, sparks from a ruined electric sign spat eerily into the night. There were no pedestrians in view. Lesko looked at Bannerman, his expression a blend of awe and irritation.

"You did all this? Out here?"

Bannerman ignored the question. "Lesko, you ride up front with Mr. Greenwald. Mr. Covington? Please ride in the back with me."

The black man hesitated. "You men aren't cops, are you. This is no bust."

"It's better than that. Please get in, sir."

They were two blocks to the south, Harry Greenwald driving, when a flash of brilliant light seared through the glass of the rear door. Covington jumped. Bannerman put a hand on his shoulder. "Easy," he said. "It's not your store."

The horn, Covington realized, had gone silent. "It's that car?"

Bannerman nodded.

"Phosphorus, right?"

"You know it?"

"I was in Nam. Marine lieutenant."

Bannerman nodded again. He had assumed something like that.

Covington gestured toward the bins. "What are you going to do with these two?"

"They won't bother you again. Can you live with that?"

Covington understood. "I guess. Easy."

"The girl who wanted to stay with you . . . I'm sorry, I forgot her name."

"Lucy. She's family. She'll be home by now."

"She was very brave. It will be hard for her to wait. We'll take you there now."

"How much can I talk about this?"

"The story for the police is that these two came to see you. They heard their car horn. They ran out. You heard gunfire. You closed up shop and left. Otherwise, tell your own people whatever you like."

Lesko rapped on the paneling. "Here's One hundred fifty-third."

Covington moved toward the door. "Do I get my truck back?" he asked Bannerman.

"Tomorrow morning. You'll find it. Do you have an extra set of keys?"

"Yes."

"Be alone when you open it. I'll leave you a present."

Covington's eyes narrowed. He glanced toward the bins.

"Not them," Bannerman reassured him. "Something useful."

The truck slowed, then stopped. Covington hesitated. He

held out a hand. "Am I ever going to know who I'm thanking?"

Bannerman took it. "You're a good man, Mr. Covington."

They dropped Harry Greenwald where he had left his car. He seemed stunned. His collar was wet with perspiration. Yet he was reluctant to leave them.

"Fucking Lesko," he muttered. "That's your idea of asking a few questions?"

"Hey," Lesko snarled. "Who figured on the moose? Who figured the dry cleaner goes ape shit? Anyway we got their attention."

A car slowed to a stop a half-block behind them. It blinked its lights. A second car pulled up. It did the same. Greenwald's hand went to his hip.

"They're friends," Bannerman said. "We'd better go."

Greenwald shook his head. A machine gunner, a sniper, and a firebomber. Everyone should have such friends. "When do I hear?"

"Tomorrow."

"If Hector talks."

"Tomorrow," Bannerman repeated.

The truck swung east on the Cross Bronx Expressway, following the signs to I-95 and New England. One of the two cars moved ahead. The other stayed to their rear. Bannerman had asked Lesko to drive. He would remain in the back. It was time to begin that talk.

In the random wash of light from other vehicles, Bannerman reached into the bigger man's bin and pushed back his hood to reveal long hair worn in dreadlocks and an ear studded with several rubies. The man made no sound, no movement. Bannerman checked the pulse at his throat. Then he turned to Hector Manley and unknotted the cloth that gagged him.

"What's this one's name?" Bannerman asked.

No answer. A hard stare.

"I know it's not Buster," he said. "Because Buster Bang was thrown off a roof a few nights ago. Why do I think you did that, Mr. Manley?"

Still no answer.

Bannerman shrugged. He reached into the big man's bin and pulled loose a plastic garment bag. He knotted it at the shoulder, then pulled it over the big man's head. With the cloth that had been used to gag him, he secured the bag around his throat.

"What are you doing?" Hector rasped.

"If you won't talk to me," Bannerman said, his manner resigned, "we need some way to pass the time. We'll just sit here and watch him die."

The Jamaican turned away. He stared through the window.

"You're not cops," he said finally. "You're not friends of the cleaner man. What is this?"

Bannerman didn't answer. He reached to tuck a loose end of the plastic into the cloth that held it.

Hector kept looking through the glass. His eyes narrowed. "Are we going to Connecticut?"

"Yes."

"What town?"

"I think you know."

"Will you tell me . . . do you live there?"

"Yes. I do."

Hector Manley fell silent. He seemed to smile. Then, "This is pointless. Let him breathe."

"Explain, please."

"The way to change my mind about Westport is to do it with money."

Bannerman blinked. Then he understood. Hector had refused the job after all. "Bad guess, Hector. The Arab didn't send me. I'm the intended victim."

"Then it is all the more pointless." The man squirmed to face him. "I would not have done it."

"Who is 'the Arab?' "

"I don't know."

Bannerman stretched his arms. He sat back.

"What are you going to do with me?"

"Peel your face off."

"Peel . . ."

Bannerman closed his eyes.

"What are you talking about?" the Jamaican asked.

"It will be done on an operating table." Bannerman stifled a yawn. "Then you will be taken back to New York and released on the street where you live. You will have no face, no eyes, no tongue. Your friends will find you stumbling about, trying to scream. I need them to see you that way."

Hector tried to spit. His mouth was dry.

Neither man moved or spoke for several minutes. Bannerman appeared to doze. He waited, giving Hector Manley's imagination time to see himself groping from one parked car to another, hearing the screams of women, children running from him, older boys tearing at his pockets, taking his jewelry.

"I don't believe you," he said finally. ̄

"I know you don't. Get some rest."

"This, I take it, is to frighten me? To make me talk?"

"Talking won't save you. But you will talk. Trust me."

They were silent again. The truck reached the tolls at New Rochelle.

"I told the truth," Hector Manley said hoarsely. "I would not have done it."

Bannerman checked his watch in the light of the unmanned booth. "Done what, Mr. Manley?" he asked.

Hector bit his lip. "Car bombs. Scattered throughout Westport. Timed to go off all at once."

"Forty of them?"

"Yes."

"Where, exactly?"

"The Arab had a street map. He drew boxes on it, one where each car was to be left. Remove that plastic and I will show you those that I remember."

"Who is the Arab? Where do I find him?"

"I don't know. This is the truth."

"Very well." Bannerman lowered his chin.

"I was not interested because it was stupid," Hector Manley said, his voice more firm than before. "Think about what he asked. Forty stolen cars, driven by black men into a town where even one black man is noticed. The Arab is a fool. It could never be done."

"Buster Bang seemed to disagree."

"Buster was a greater fool."

"He didn't hear you say no."

"He did the last time we spoke."

"On that rooftop?"

The Jamaican tossed his head vaguely. "I told him not to speak of it. But he tried to find others who would do this. It had become a sickness with him."

"When and where, were you to see the Arab again?"

"I don't know. I've seen the man only twice. Each time he found me."

"Mr. Manley," Bannerman said patiently, "you're meeting him next Wednesday. Where? And what then?"

Manley seemed confused. Then his eyes widened as he remembered the conversation with Buster and he realized that it had been overheard. "That was a lie," he said. "I told Buster there was to be a third meeting only to keep him from doing what he did in any case. It is true that I would not have done what the Arab asked but I would have taken the payment he offered."

"What sort of payment?"

"The offer was heroin. Five kilos on agreement. Fifty more when the cars were in place. After that, a guaranteed supply for two years at twenty percent below the market rate."

"How much is that?"

"It depends. Many millions."

"This did not tempt you?"

"I would have taken the five kilos. I might have taken the next fifty as well, and then I would have had to kill him. But I would not have done this thing in Westport."

Bannerman did not speak.

"Is Ruby dead?"

Bannerman raised his head. The earrings. Now he remembered a ruby ring as well. *Ruby.* He reached into the other bin, his fingers finding the big man's throat. "Yes. He is."

Hector Manley made a sound through his teeth. He turned away. "Will you tell me your name?" he asked.

"It's Bannerman."

The Jamaican mouthed it, frowning. He shook his head. "What is your real name?"

Bannerman understood. He smiled. "It's not a street

name. That's it. Paul Bannerman. Some people know me as Mama's Boy."

The Jamaican mouthed this as well. He shook his head. If it had meaning to him, he gave no sign. If anything, Bannerman thought, he seemed to be wondering why anyone would choose such a name.

"Hey," Lesko rapped against the panel. "Here's Westport. Where to now?"

"To the clinic. You know the way."

"Then what?"

"Um . . ." Bannerman winced. "Actually, we have to talk about that. I have a dinner date in one hour. Someone you know."

A long silence. "We'll talk, all right." Another silence. "You prick."

The truck swung onto the exit ramp.

Manley was staring at him. "A clinic?"

"And an operating table. I believe I mentioned it."

"For the last time"—the Jamaican's mouth went dry again—"I told the truth."

"So did I."

—18—

Two in the Morning. Zürich.

Urs Brugg groped for the telephone that chirped at his bedside. He brought it to his chest. Before lifting the receiver he made note of the line on which the call was coming. It was the line that had a scrambling device. He touched a button on his bed and his upper body began to rise. He lifted the receiver.

"Urs?"

"Yes, Leo." He rubbed his face. "Good morning."

"You said at any hour," the KGB Chief of Bern reminded him.

Urs Brugg grunted, acknowledging the literal truth of it. It was a truth, however, that he had considered open to reasonable interpretation.

"We've located them, Urs. The three of them."

He turned on one elbow. "The ones who—"

"Killed Josef, yes. And shot Elena."

"Where are they?"

"They have gone to Spain. Apparently in search of new employment. It seems they have mentioned the killing of Dr. Russo among their credentials even though his death was not intended. Inquiries were made to verify their claims. This is how we learned who they are."

"Where in Spain, Leo? What are their names?"

"Urs . . . this is not the way. If you like, my people will deal with them. They will bring you proof. It will be finished."

Urs Brugg shook his head. "I am already more in debt to the KGB than is comfortable for me."

"Not the KGB," the other man said. "This is Leo. Your friend. And there is no debt."

A brief pause. Long enough to convey skepticism. Not so long as to be impolite. "Leo, where are these men?"

"Two are men. Their driver was a woman."

"Their names?" Urs Brugg switched on his reading light.

The KGB man gave them. He read, from notes, what was known of the three. The leader was British. Educated, well spoken, fetish for cleanliness, sexually active, extremely so, although he is said to despise women. Second man, rarely speaks, Algerian but travels on a French passport. The woman, a German, is a known prostitute and drug addict. Between assignments, sells herself to keep them in funds. Otherwise, it appears, one of her duties is to find girls, preferably students, backpackers, for the Englishman. He likes to bathe them, then rape them.

Urs Brugg scribbled quickly. He looked at his notepad as if it were soiled.

"Their address, Leo?"

"It's not a good place for this, Urs. They are in Marbella, living in a rented house not far from the beach."

"I know Marbella."

"Then you know how easily it can be sealed. Getting men in will be one thing, getting them out quite another. My people, on the other hand, are already in place."

"Leo, your friend asks you . . . do not interfere."

"Friends give advice, Urs. Either let me help you or give this to Mama's Boy."

"I am sure, as it happens, that he will insist on it. But I am grateful to you, Leo."

"If he does not . . ."

"He will. I know the man." Urs Brugg flipped to a fresh

page of his tablet. "Now," he asked firmly, "where, precisely, is this house?"

Bannerman had called Susan from the clinic. He was leaving now, he told her. He would be home in ten minutes.

As he drove past the gatehouse and approached his unit, he could see sparks from his chimney, burning fragments of newspaper, spiraling into the night sky, evidence of a fire freshly built.

He could see her in his mind. Kneeling before the fireplace, poking at the logs, helping their blaze to settle into gentler flames. She'd have put music on. Something mellow. Vivaldi or Brahms. And she'd have opened a bottle of wine. It would be waiting in a ceramic cooler. Dinner, she'd told him, was in the oven.

Never so much as then had he realized how he'd missed her. These past three weeks, since Switzerland, he had come to dread driving home at the end of a day. He would watch other cars as they turned into driveways of homes that were warm and welcoming. A few still had Christmas wreaths on their doors. He could see people through the windows. He could smell their evening meals. More than once he had reached his gatehouse and then turned back. To Mario's. His office. A movie. Anything to avoid the cold and lifeless cave his home had become since Susan had last spent the night with him.

But she was there now. They'd been together only since yesterday and already it had begun to seem that she belonged there.

He remembered her expression, that morning, as he left her, having lied to her again. He had an appointment in New York, he'd told her, that he could not reschedule, much as he wanted to spend the day with her. She was disappointed, but fully trusting. He asked her to stay, wait for him. He would call Avis so that she'd have a car; he knew that there were things . . . clothing, cosmetics, that she'd need to pick up.

He'd seen her face throughout the day, or imagined it. He'd seen her as he drove to his office where he returned the calls her father had left on his machine. Messages that he'd erased as she showered. He'd felt her presence as he consulted with Anton, and, soon thereafter, as he enlisted the help of Glenn Cook, his silent marksman, of Molly Farrell, his bomber, and of John Waldo, his machine gunner, then gave them their instructions.

He saw her again, in the evening, in the darkness of Wesley Covington's delivery truck. He saw her body. Dead. Those flawless legs. Long and strong. Blown off at the thighs. Her chest crushed. Recognized her only by her hair and by the rings on her fingers because her face was shredded and torn by flying glass and jagged bits of sheet metal from one of forty exploding cars. It was that vision of her that told him what he would do to this man known as the Arab. And to all those like him.

But tonight . . .

Tonight there was the fire, the wine, and the music. Dinner on the floor. He would try to tell her all the things that he'd never quite learned how to say to a woman. Perhaps had never felt. How the mere touch of her hand meant more to him than all the joys of his life put together. More than all the birthdays and Christmas mornings and victories and cheers. But he would go slowly. Take Molly's advice. Not push it. Although he wished that Molly would stop treating him like a teenager on his first date. He wasn't so dumb about women. Or about their needs. What Susan wants is what any woman wants. Someone to care about, to share herself with, a home, feeling safe . . . loved. Interests of her own. Children, a career, maybe both. He could add, he supposed, not being lied to. But . . .

. . . one day at a time.

He knocked on his door. Three short raps, then two. He reached for his keys. He wished he'd thought to bring flowers.

Hector Manley, eyes bulging, teeth snapping, lay strapped to an operating table in the basement surgery of the Greenfield Hill Clinic. He was naked.

Around him, ignoring him, were two men and a woman dressed and masked in surgical greens. Outside, in the corridor, Lesko watched through a round glass plate in the operating room door. One hand had formed a fist. He smashed it, rhythmically, into the palm of the other. He had stood this about as long as he was going to.

"Talk to me!!" the Jamaican screamed. "Bannermannn . . ."

One of the men, a male nurse, sorted instruments. He held up a small saw for cutting bone, looking questioningly at the surgeon whose back was to Lesko. The surgeon nodded. The Jamaican screamed again.

The surgeon returned to his work. With a swab dipped in iodine, he painted lines on Hector Manley's face where the incisions were to be made. Under the chin, behind the ears, two inches beyond the hairline. He stepped aside. The female nurse, holding a camera, took photographs from several angles. Manley looked beseechingly into the eyes of the nurse. She gave no response. She took more pictures. Manley looked at the surgeon, blinking, then turned his head from him. There was something there, Lesko couldn't see what, that frightened him as much as the instruments, that horrified him as much as the chilling detachment with which they went about their preparations.

"Enough of this shit," muttered Lesko. He raised a hand to the door.

"Mr. Lesko. Please."

The voice came from his right. He turned. Anton Zivic, blue business suit, immaculately groomed, had been watching him.

Lesko's hand remained on the door. "I'm not going to let you do this," he said.

"Do what, Mr. Lesko?" The former GRU colonel approached him. He peered through the glass.

"Carve the guy's face off." With his right hand, Lesko pulled back his coat to show the police special at his hip. "That doctor picks up that scalpel, I'm taking the Jamaican back to New York. You want answers, I'll get them my way."

Zivic made a face. "Relax Mr. Lesko. And please keep your voice down."

"Relax, my ass." He moved forward. Zivic raised a hand.

"It's theater, Mr. Lesko. Mr. Manley has not yet been harmed. If you do not interfere, there will probably be no need."

"Theater," Lesko repeated blankly.

Zivic smiled. Sympathetically. He gestured toward the masked and gowned figure with the iodine swab. "That man is no surgeon. I should think you would have recognized him by now."

Lesko looked again. The man had rounded the table to the side where the instruments were laid out. Manley's eyes, wide and blinking, followed him. Lesko got his first good look. It was Loftus. Behind the mask, a plastic bridge crisscrossed with tape covered his broken nose. His cheekbone, also fractured, bulged to one side. One eye was still discolored. A rod from the device that wired his teeth had poked a hole through the mask. Now Lesko understood why the sight of him had so terrified the Jamaican. Better to look up and see Dracula standing over you.

"He was here anyway," Zivic explained. "Convalescing. He complained of having little to do. I asked him if he'd like to try his hand at playing the part of a maniac."

Lesko shook his head slowly. If Loftus had fooled him, he could only imagine what was passing through the mind of Hector Manley. Still, he was not sure about this at all.

"All that talk in the truck coming up here, that was all bluff?"

"Essentially. Yes."

"When you say *essentially,* what's left over?"

The smile faded. "It was a bluff, Mr. Lesko," he said, "but only if it isn't called. One way or the other, that man is going to tell us what we need to know."

Lesko twisted his lip. "And if he doesn't?"

"He will."

"So you were serious. You'd do what Bannerman said. With his face."

"If we were entirely serious, Mr. Lesko, we would not be using actors. We have someone who can do that. She would be in there now. But it will not come to that."

Lesko blinked at the word *she.* Figured to be Carla. He would never forget, on that hill in Davos, how she was all set to core old Lurene's eye like a fucking apple. Her words. Or maybe it was the other one, Janet. Doesn't talk. Just knits. Looks like her idea of a good time is to microwave live puppies.

"I can see why you and Bannerman get along," he said. "You're both pricks."

Zivic looked up at him, his expression cool. "We can't all have your degree of delicacy, Mr. Lesko."

"Yeah, well, you don't see me doing shit like this. You also don't see me wrapping plastic around some poor slob's face and watching him die just to get a conversation going."

"Mr. Lesko . . ."

"And I'll tell you something else." Lesko poked a finger at him. "My daughter's with Bannerman now. They're having a nice dinner someplace, right?"

"Someplace," Zivic nodded.

"First chance I get, I'm going to tell her about tonight. I'll tell her so next time she sees a red cabbage at the supermarket, all wrapped up nice, she should think of the guy named Ruby and never forget who—"

"Have you examined the body, Mr. Lesko?"

"I saw all I—"

"You killed him. Not Paul. Tell your daughter that."

Lesko stared. "Bullshit."

"Hitting a man with an eighty-pound cash register, Mr. Lesko, does damage. You broke the man's neck. You'll also find that he has a pint or two of blood in his lungs from your ministrations with that clothing hook. It's only a question of what killed him first. Paul found no heartbeat by the time he sought to salvage a psychological advantage from the situation as you left it."

Lesko reddened. "Even if I believed that—which I don't—"

"Please go home, Mr. Lesko. You are becoming tiresome."

"—from what I could hear," Lesko continued, "once the guy started talking, Bannerman couldn't shut him up."

"Take the truck if you wish. Although Mr. Covington would like it back in the morning. There will be a package in it. Please treat it carefully."

"So what's the point?" Lesko pressed. "If the guy wants to talk, let him talk. Or do you drag it out because you like it?"

"In a few minutes," Zivic said patiently, "I will open that door. I will tell Mr. Loftus that he is needed elsewhere to

treat a gunshot wound. Mr. Manley will be left alone for a
few hours, strapped to that table, to consider his future.
When I decide he's ready, he and I will have a talk. If it is
satisfactory, it is possible that he will, in fact, have some sort
of future."

Lesko straightened. "I think I'll stick around."

"To what purpose?"

"To make sure you—" He stopped himself. "To hear
what he says."

"Then understand me, Mr. Lesko. That man in there
knows the uses of terror as well as we do. He was trained in
it, in Cuba. I will want to know what he has learned and
how he is expected to apply it. But above all, if he is to
survive his visit with us, which is possible although not
likely, he will tell me everything he knows, or thinks, or can
intelligently guess about this plan to bring car bombs to
Westport. Have you ever seen the effect of such a bomb, Mr.
Lesko?"

He didn't answer.

"I have," Zivic told him. "So has Paul. Twice in Beirut.
Once in Rome. The least destructive of these killed fourteen
people and maimed three times that number. If one bomb
does that, Mr. Lesko, what might forty do?"

Still no answer. But he could see it. He remembered the
Marine barracks in Lebanon. More than 200 dead. A whole
building down on top of them. He knew what one bomb
could do. Let alone forty. To a town that Susan, damn her
anyway, doesn't have the sense to stay out of.

"Then considering the stakes, Mr. Lesko, you will understand when I tell you this. If you interfere, trust me, you will
be shot."

Something was wrong. There was Susan. She was by the
fire, kneeling, pouring wine into two glasses. The music was
playing. She'd chosen Vivaldi. *The Four Seasons.* Candles
were burning on the mantelpiece. She wore a blouse, it
looked like silk, white, billowing sleeves, the top three buttons open. He could see that she wore nothing underneath.

Everything, except the new blouse, which she must have
bought that day, was as he'd envisioned it. All except for her

eyes. The smile was there. A bit self-conscious perhaps. Perhaps more than a bit.

Bannerman draped his coat across a chair. He paused to study her, admire her, letting it settle on him that she was really there, that she'd stayed, and that, in the light of the fire she was so thoroughly, heartbreakingly lovely that her presence seemed a dream. He crossed to her, kissed her lightly on upturned lips, lingered a moment, touched her hair, then lowered himself to the thickly piled carpet facing her. She handed him a glass. "Cheers," she said and sipped. She lowered her eyes.

"You know what?" she asked.

"You're very beautiful," he said. "What?"

She smiled, made a face. "Never mind."

"Tell me."

She appeared to be debating whether or not speak, perhaps wishing she'd said nothing at all. She rose up off her heels. Setting down her glass, she reached for him, her fingers sliding through the hair at his temples, to the back of his neck. She pulled him closer. Her lips parted. She kissed him, hungrily, her tongue searching, her body writhing against his. Now her lips found his cheeks, his eyes, his forehead, then his mouth again. At last, she sat back. He took a deep, shuddering breath.

"That's how you kiss a woman," she said. "Pecks are for grandmothers with bad breath."

A silent groan. Bannerman thought of Molly. He could see her grinning, applauding.

"Grandmothers," he repeated.

She nodded. She touched a finger to a place between her breasts. "Then you reach for this button. But you do it slowly. And not from there."

Bannerman closed one eye. Now he could feel Molly in the room. She was holding a clipboard. Making notes. Grading him. "Listen," he said. "How about if I go out and come in again?"

"It won't help." She gestured, taking in their setting. "This is kind of . . . I don't know."

"I think it's very romantic, what you've done here."

"I think it's nice," she twisted her lip. "But it's corny."

"Corny," he said blankly.

"Romantic would have been last night, when I came in to cover you, if you were only pretending to be asleep and you reached up and pulled me down with you. I was naked, by the way."

Bannerman felt his color rising. Molly made three big checkmarks on her clipboard, then tilted her head smugly.

"Or"—Susan cocked her head as well—"romantic would have been me waking up this morning to the touch of your fingers lightly running up and down my back, down over my hips, me feeling your chin, not too rough, just a nice masculine little stubble against my shoulder, feeling you start to swell against my thigh. I was naked all night, too."

Bannerman glanced, involuntarily, toward his bedroom.

"Couldn't help it," she said. "Had to rinse out my things."

"Um . . . Susan . . ." Suddenly he couldn't think what to do with his hands.

"I know." She wagged a finger. "Shouldn't rush things. One day at a time."

He couldn't think what to do with words, either.

"Vivaldi's okay," she said, her nose wrinkling. "But I was hoping you'd have Ravel's *Bolero.* You don't happen to keep a copy stashed for your less-fragile houseguests, do you?"

He blinked.

"Never mind." He didn't get it, she realized. *Ten?* The movie? Bo Derek? Never mind. Probably no use asking about leather and chains and stuff either.

Not that he didn't know how to be sexy. Usually, he was wonderful. So patient. And giving. He could make you believe you were the most terrific, the most exciting, the most beautiful woman in the world. And the best lover. Although the first time, she remembered, it took him forever to work up to it. Truth is, it was her idea. She'd practically raped him. Granted, she now realized why he'd been dragging his feet. He was being Mama's Boy then. Trying to see what this nosey reporter, this kid, might have learned about Westport. Well . . . this *kid* may not have been a nympho but she didn't just come out of a convent either. Or out of a David Niven movie. She didn't need wine, candlelight, and elevator music every time either one of them wanted a roll in the sack.

"Don't you ever want to just jump on my bones? A good, happy, rip-roaring, spontaneous screw?"

He cleared his throat. "The truth? Just about all the time." He glanced past her shoulder. There was a wing chair, red leather, behind her. He saw Molly Farrell in it. She sat cross-legged, chin resting on two fists, enjoying herself thoroughly.

"How about now?"

"Well . . . yes. Sure," was all he managed.

She seemed to consider it. She shook her head. "The mood's all wrong."

Bannerman threw up his hands. He glared, murderously, in the direction of the wing chair. Susan turned.

"What do you keep looking at?" she asked.

"Nothing. Um . . . nothing."

Her eyes narrowed. "You're not, by chance, recording this, are you?"

"Are you kidding?" he asked, incredulous. "Who would I let hear it?"

"Just asking." She sipped her wine. A drop fell on her sleeve. She brushed it off. "Do you like this blouse?"

"It's very, um . . . sexy."

"I bought some other things. Do you want to see?"

He reached for the loose fabric, fingering it lightly. "How about later?"

"No." That look again. "I want to show you."

She stepped into the bedroom and returned with several packages. All showed the names of local merchants except one, a plain brown bag, folded over. Susan put this to one side. She opened a bag from Ed Mitchell's, a clothing store for men. "I bought you a shirt," she said. "It'll look great on you. You need more color."

She produced a shirt with a Burberrys label, long sleeved, button-down, casual. It was a handsome forest green with yellow stripes set wide apart. Bannerman took it in his hands. For several moments he held it, examining it as if it were fragile. He did not speak.

"Do you like it?"

"Very much." His expression grew soft. Far away.

He seemed, to Susan, genuinely touched. So much like

her father when she brought him a gift for no special reason. "It's just a shirt," she said.

"It's a beautiful shirt. Thank you."

She reached into another bag. "I bought myself another top. On sale." This one was green, a lighter shade than his, a very wide neck. "Want to see it on?"

"Sure."

She set it down, then tugged her white silken blouse loose at the waist. She pulled it over her head.

"I didn't mean—" He stopped.

"Would you rather I did this inside?" She crossed one arm over her breasts, her free hand holding the green top.

Bannerman's head moved indecisively.

She lowered the arm, unfolded the new top, taking her time. Her movements seemed natural, unforced, thoroughly unself-conscious. Yet Bannerman began to have a feeling that they were also entirely deliberate. That she knew perfectly well the effect that her unabashed nakedness would have on him and was pretending to be oblivious to it. That and the shirt. He could not remember the last time that a woman, not of his world, had brought him a gift. But these were fleeting thoughts. Wispy. Nothing he could grasp and hold or seize control of.

Control. The word brought a rueful smile. The last thing he controlled in the past half hour was the wheel of his car.

Raising her arms, she slipped into the pale green top. She shook out her hair. The green went well with it. The neck, very loose, extended to the edge of one shoulder. A touch, the smallest tug, would have left the shoulder bare down to the top of one breast. The effect was, in its way, more erotic than her nudity.

"It's . . ." He swallowed.

"Sexy?"

"And then some."

"Which one do you like better? Want to see the other one on again?"

"Susan"—he brought both hands to his eyes, covering them—"Why are you doing this to me?"

She looked at the fire, took a breath. "I bought one other thing."

He nodded. "Let's see it."

"Don't peek, okay?"

"I promise."

She reached for the folded paper bag, opened it, and slid it's contents onto the rug between them. It made a *thunk*. "You can look now," she said.

His eyes followed the sound. They found it and blinked. He was looking at a pistol, flecked with tiny pits of rust, the bluing well worn. He picked it up. Colt—Super .38 Automatic, it said on the barrel. It was at least thirty years old.

"Where did you get this?" he asked, frowning.

"I saw an ad. It was sort of an impulse."

"It was also a crime. You can't just walk in and buy a gun in Connecticut."

"I guess the man didn't know that. Will you teach me to shoot it?"

"Susan . . . what for?"

"Because I'm going to stay with you. Because I want to be someone you can count on."

"To do what? Shoot people?"

"If they tried to hurt you. Yes."

Bannerman touched his temple as if a pain had begun there.

"Or to hurt me," she added.

"No one will hurt you," he said earnestly. "No one will ever try that again."

"You, then. Will you teach me?"

"Absolutely not. You'd end up shooting yourself. Or some passerby."

Her eyes flashed. "That's patronizing, Bannerman. Knock it off."

"It is not," he said firmly. "Learning how to shoot takes hours. Learning when to shoot takes years. Being able to shoot . . . maybe never."

"I'd have a pretty good teacher."

"Wrong again. I'm average at best. The worst shot on the Westport police force is probably better than I am."

"I don't believe you."

He spread his hands. "Your father never taught you about handguns?"

"Just never to touch his."

"Then ask him, if you won't believe me. He'll probably

tell you that when you're close enough to use a pistol you'd usually be just as well off with an ax except that the handgun makes lots of noise while you're missing and it makes the man you're shooting at want to run and hide. You've seen too much television, Susan."

"Watch it."

He rose to his feet. He began pacing. "On television, shootings are neat and clean. One shot and the bad guy drops. You never see—"

"I'm a reporter, Paul," she said evenly. "I've seen people die."

He stopped. "What people?" he asked doubtfully.

"At crime scenes. In emergency rooms. Shooting and stabbing victims. Car crash victims. I've been there when their bowels let go. When they swallowed their tongues. I've seen rape victims. And their rapists. I've seen two of them, in a police station, laughing about what they'd done. If I had a gun that day—"

Bannerman shook his head abruptly.

"I keep trying to tell you, Paul. You didn't invent me."

He said nothing.

"Do you love me?"

He hesitated. "Yes."

"But for who I am."

"For who you are," he nodded. "Not for trying to be more like me. I can't stand the thought of you with a gun."

She did not answer. Neither spoke for several moments.

"Want to see my boobs again?" she asked.

His head snapped up.

"Just trying to ease the tension."

Bannerman's hands slapped against his cheeks. *What does it take?* he asked himself. What does it take for one single conversation with Susan Lesko to go his way for more than a few seconds at a time?

"Come here," she said. She moved the packages aside. And the pistol. She covered it with the new green top.

An hour had passed.

The fire had dropped to a whisper. They lay on pillows, under a quilt. She had sent him to get them. Afterward.

They lay facing each other. He on one elbow, touching her, exploring her, his eyes filled with . . . she wasn't sure.

Wonder, perhaps. A sense of discovery. They had made love before, many times, but it seemed that they were different people then.

He made love differently as well. Hard to say how, exactly. It was more . . . respectful. More . . . admiring. Or just more.

And so gently. She reached her fingertips to his eyes. They were gray when in shadow, green when he faced the fire. Those eyes. They'd seen so much. And yet they could still be tender. They could become flustered. They could blush.

"Would you promise me something?" she asked him.

"I'll try," he said.

"Stick around here. Don't take any trips. Not for a while."

"I wasn't planning any." A short pause. "Like where?" he asked.

"Like to Europe. No unfinished business. What happened over there, I'd like you to just let it lie for now."

Bannerman frowned. His mind drifted to his answering machine. He had locked it back in the cabinet. Had he forgotten to turn the volume down?

"Susan," he asked, "have I had a call?"

She nodded. "From your office. A half hour before you called. I thought it might have been you."

"What was the message?"

"That someone was trying to reach you. He had the same last name as Elena."

"Urs Brugg."

"I guess. It's not about Elena. Part of the message said she was doing well. But he wants you to call. He said it's urgent."

Those eyes, she thought. Those beautiful eyes. They were flat now. Lifeless. As if a switch had been thrown. But only for a moment. Here was that gentleness again.

"Will you promise?" she asked.

"It's probably nothing."

"Come on, Bannerman."

"Okay," he nodded. "How about if I promise that I won't do anything foolish, or dangerous, or anything that would keep me away from you one minute longer than it must.

And that includes not even going to New York again if I can help it."

"How about," she closed one eye, "if you don't do anything at all, except be with me, for a solid week. I'll go rip out the phone. Also the one you think I don't know about."

He grimaced as if stung. But privately, he was pleased. "I'd like that." He said, bringing her fingers to his lips. "I want that. But you know I can't. Don't you."

"Obligations?"

He nodded.

She said nothing.

"I appreciate that," he said.

"What?"

"You not asking, what about my obligations to you?"

"Oh yeah. Right. What about them, Bannerman?"

Bannerman groaned inwardly. Another checkmark.

"It's okay." She patted his rump. "Go make your call."

"Maybe tomorrow."

"He said it was urgent."

"He's not here with you. I am. And there's nothing in the world I'd rather be doing. No place I'd rather be."

He kissed her. Lightly. Tenderly. His lips tasting her.

"Which reminds me," she said, trembling, "I made spaghetti."

He kissed her again.

"But no garlic bread. You mind?"

"It doesn't matter," he murmured. "All I'll taste is you."

Oh, brother.

All I'll taste is you.

Silver-tongued devil.

But she liked it. Good move, Bannerman.

Now they'll have their dinner. Another bottle of wine. No garlic bread, so they can sleep, face-to-face, without curling each other's hair.

Back to the fire. A couple of fresh logs. They'll make love again there. Then sometime later he'll carry her into the bedroom, stroke her back until she falls asleep, make love again in the morning, maybe shower together.

And then he'll go to his office. Maybe he'll call Urs Brugg from there. Probably not. Because the way to bet is that as soon as she's asleep he will quietly slip out of bed and close the door behind him.

She won't ask if he did that, she decided.

She won't make him lie to her.

—*19*—

In the communications center of the Soviet Embassy in Bern, Colonel Leonid Belkin stood at the shoulder of a younger man, burly, twice his size, watching as a series of cryptic English phrases scrolled up the computer screen.

"Stop there, Yuri," he said.

The screen read:

```
ENMITY: BANNERMAN/POSSE        100.0
ENMITY: BANNERMAN/JIBRIL       100.0
ENMITY: BANNERMAN/TRE GROUP      0.6
```

"What might that mean?" he asked.

"It is . . . an assessment of some kind."

"Have those names appeared before this?" he asked.

The younger man shook his head. "On these disks? Only Bannerman. But perhaps on the others."

"What of those letters? *T R E*."

"Ah, yes. They refer to 'the Ripper Effect.' That is the designator for this program."

"Who is Ripper?"

"A code name, I think."

"Of Roger Clew?"

Yuri Rykov shrugged. "Clew's diplomatic code name is Dancer. The only Ripper I find is a nineteenth-century English maniac who . . ."

Speculation. Belkin lost interest. He gestured accordingly. "This list," he peered at the screen, frowning, "it is obviously an assessment. But of what? And in what context?"

"It gives no context. There is only these three lines. They were transmitted to Clew last night, by modem, by that man." He pointed to a file photograph clipped to one of the dossiers at his side. The face was that of Harold C. Hagler.

Rykov sat back, tapping his forehead as if to set his brain in motion. Abruptly, he rolled his chair to another machine and, in seconds, had called up a file. The word *Jibril* appeared in bold face. There were several listings under it.

"Arabs," he said, pleased with himself. "Syrians, specifically. There is your connection with Mr. Hagler. Freedom fighters."

"They are terrorists, Yuri, dogma notwithstanding. Try the other name. 'Posse.' "

The younger man's fingers flew across the keys. It was a sight that never failed to impress Leo Belkin. Such big hands. They had squeezed triggers. They had crushed throats. And yet they could play this machine with the touch of a Rachmaninoff.

"Nothing." Rykov grunted. "No file."

Although not always with the same result, Belkin sighed. "Can you not ask this Ripper program?"

Yuri tossed his hands. "Without their commands, we cannot access evaluative functions. We can only read what they send by modem."

Belkin motioned him back to the other machine. "If this is an assessment," he gestured toward the screen, "it probably refers to the consequences of a specific activity. Might that activity involve this business in Spain?"

"I find no reference to Spain. No match of any kind. Ask my opinion, I will say that the two are unrelated."

"Might it interfere, then?"

"I may guess?"

Belkin nodded.

"A prediction of enmity, if one hundred percent certain,

would seem to require a first priority. Those three in Spain are insects. They can be squashed at any time."

"And yet Bannerman has promised my friend Urs that he will see to them at once."

"If he is not distracted by new enemies."

Leo Belkin folded his arms, bringing one hand to his mouth. "I need him there, Yuri," he said quietly. "I need him in Europe, I need him vulnerable, and I need no distraction that would cause him to send others in his place."

The younger man said nothing.

"Hagler. Clew. They are up to something. Whatever it is, we must assume that it is not in our interest."

Rykov motioned to his attaché case. A chain and handcuff dangled from it. "We have only begun to review these disks. There are twelve others. Also more than nine hours of voice tapes."

"Teach me, Yuri. Then go back to Washington. Go today."

"To sit with earphones? We have reliable people who can—"

"I want you to create a distraction of your own." Belkin placed his finger on one of the dossiers. "This man."

"If . . . that is your wish."

"Yuri. . . ." Belkin squeezed his shoulder.

"This word *distraction*. It is not a euphemism."

The large man let out a breath. "It is good you told me."

"Hey. Lesko. Rise and shine."

Lesko's body twitched. He snorted. But still he slept.

"Let's go, will ya? We got roll call."

He heard a slamming of cabinets from his kitchen. Katz. Any second now he'd start bitching about— *"What a fucking pig sty. Don't you ever wash out cups?"* Lesko opened one eye. Then closed it.

"Come on. I got prune Danish. We'll pick up some coffee on the way."

Lesko tried to pull the covers over his face. But they felt wrong. And the sheet beneath him felt like leather. And out in the kitchen, Katz sounded like he was dragging furniture across the floor.

He opened one eye again. Shit. Where's this? He raised his head and blinked until it cleared.

He remembered now. Westport, not Queens. Greenfield Hill. A couch in the staff lounge. It *was* leather. The blanket was his topcoat. There was no Katz, coming in, like always, to pick him up. But he could still hear him. The slamming and dragging. Lesko rubbed his face, hard.

The racket was coming from outside. He crossed to a window that looked out on the parking lot in the rear of this former Victorian mansion. Covington's delivery truck was still there. Bannerman's blue sedan was next to it. Lesko looked at his watch and cursed. Almost ten o'clock.

Now he saw what was making the noise. A man in an orderly's uniform came into view. He was dragging two laundry bins. Their plastic wheels clattered over the macadam. He stopped at the rear of the truck, opened the door, and lifted one of the bins inside. It was empty. The other contained the sheets and blankets they'd borrowed from Covington's. They had been washed of blood stains and folded. Another man appeared. Lesko recognized the slender build and blond hair of Glenn Cook. Guy who ran the local ski shop. Bannerman's long-distance shooter. He was carrying a case that was about four feet long, a foot wide. The first man lifted the folded blankets. Cook placed the case inside the bin, then covered it. That, Lesko assumed, was the present that Bannerman had promised Wesley Covington. He could guess what it was.

"Hey. David?" he called softly.

No answer. Just a feeling.

"Are you back?"

Still nothing.

"I could use you, you putz," he said aloud. Then he felt stupid. He picked up his topcoat and hurried from the room.

Making his way to the basement, Lesko stopped first at the door to the operating room. The Jamaican was gone. He tried several other doors including that of a second surgery where the body of the other Jamaican, Ruby, had been kept. He was gone as well. Nothing left to show that he'd been there but Lesko could see him in his mind. His jaw shattered. Neck broken, no question. No blue lips or any of the

other physical signs of asphyxiation. The Russian had told
the truth. Bannerman had not suffocated him. Which still
didn't say he wouldn't have, Lesko told himself, if the cash
register hadn't killed him first.

Okay. So it wasn't just the cash register. It was still an
accident. Mostly.

Lesko returned to the stairwell and climbed toward the
main entrance hall where the clinic had its administrative
offices. He stopped at a pair of mahogany doors that had
once opened onto a parlor. He heard voices inside. Bannerman and the Russian. He thought he heard the name Urs
Brugg. He leaned closer. There was only silence.

"You may join us, Mr. Lesko." Zivic's voice. Lesko
grunted and turned the knob.

They were seated at a coffee table. A large map lay open
on it. On one wall, Lesko saw a bank of television monitors.
One screen showed the basement corridor. Another showed
the main entrance hall outside. They'd been watching him,
he realized, since he'd climbed off the couch. He hoped they
hadn't heard him too. Goddamned Katz.

Lesko offered no greeting. He didn't even look at Bannerman. "Where's Manley?" he asked Zivic.

"Unharmed and resting, Mr. Lesko. But probably not
asleep." Zivic gestured toward the monitors. "He is behind
one of those doors you've been rattling."

Zivic looked fresh and clean. Different suit. Same with
Bannerman. Lesko felt like a pile of Covington's laundry.
His mouth tasted like a crotch.

"Did he talk?" he asked.

Zivic glanced toward Bannerman who shrugged and nodded. Zivic reached for the map and rotated it toward Lesko.
"He did indeed."

Lesko picked up the map, a street map of Westport, and
studied it. It was covered with small rectangles, drawn with
a Magic Marker. The rectangles, he knew at once, repre-
sented cars. Cars with bombs. He was stunned. He had
never quite believed it before. But there it was.

There were eight rectangles within the two city blocks of
Main Street alone. Five more on Railroad Avenue between
Mario's restaurant and the commuter station across from it.
Two at the Compo Shopping Plaza where Bannerman had

his office. Two more at his condo complex. One at the town library, one at each of seven Westport schools, two each at the police and fire departments. The rest were scattered around Westport but not at random. Someone, probably Zivic, had written penciled notes near their locations.

"These here." Lesko pointed. "These are where you guys live?"

"Some." Zivic nodded. "Others are at main access roads, presumably to block the arrival of emergency equipment from other towns. A few more appear to be at gasoline stations."

"Somebody really scouted this town," Lesko said, frowning. "The Arab guy?"

"Or whoever," Zivic answered.

Lesko's frown deepened. "Not a local, though. Not someone who lives here. Not someone who ever tried to find a parking space on Main Street."

"Bravo," said Zivic. He glanced once more toward Bannerman who still had not spoken. There was a hint of I-told-you-so in Zivic's manner. "Please finish your thought, Mr. Lesko."

"I mean"—Lesko waved the map disdainfully—"the plan is perfect, right? All it needs is forty cars, forty black junkies who think they can pass for white, and forty accomplices from Westport who will save exactly the right parking spaces for them at exactly the right time. Piece of cake." Lesko spat.

"Then you agree with Mr. Manley."

"That it's a load of crap? Yeah."

"Mr. Manley, by the way, remembered a few more things about the Arab. It seems that he represents, or so he claims, an organization called the Popular Front for the Liberation of Palestine—General Command. That is the group, financed largely by Iran and Libya, that is believed to be responsible for the bombing of the Pan Am flight over Lockerbie, Scotland. The Arab as much as admitted it. He suggested to Mr. Manley that they are brothers under the skin, so to speak, sharing a common cause against all who would oppress them and deny them what is theirs by right."

Lesko snorted.

"You seem skeptical."

"No one guy can be so dumb." Lesko curled his lip. "He comes in with the worst possible plan, tries to recruit the worst possible people to do it, he practically hands out business cards and he tries to tell a drug dealer and killer like Hector Manley that if money won't get him interested, how about social justice."

"But if he's not so dumb"—Bannerman leaned forward—"what then?"

"Fuck you, by the way."

Bannerman ignored this last. "What then, Lesko? What else could he be doing?"

"Two things." Lesko considered. "No, three. One is to tie you up in Westport, checking parked cars, now and then grabbing some poor son of a bitch who happens to be black and driving through town and strapping him to that table downstairs. Two is to get you to make dogmeat out of Hector's posse for even thinking about this."

"And the third?"

"Go kill some Arabs."

Bannerman and Zivic exchanged looks. From their expressions, Lesko thought, they'd reached the same conclusions.

"How does Urs Brugg figure in this?" he asked.

Bannerman's face showed nothing. He had seen Lesko's ear at the door, too late, but it had only been for a moment.

"It's another matter," he said. "No connection."

"It's connected with me. Elena's okay, isn't she?"

"She's mending. She's fine."

"You going over, by chance?" His manner softened. "You going to see her?"

"I won't see her, no."

"Then what's with her uncle?"

Bannerman sat back. "Lesko, you'll understand, won't you, if I don't share my every thought with you."

"You're sharing too goddamned much already."

Bannerman gestured vaguely toward the map, signaling a return to the subject at hand.

"Anton said that you might return Mr. Covington's truck. It's on your way."

"I might. What's that package in the laundry bin?"

"It's a sniper rifle. Silenced. A night-vision scope. It will help him keep One hundred and fifty-third Street clear for six hundred yards in either direction. There are also four phosphorus grenades. Don't get stopped for speeding."

Lesko had guessed it. Pretty much. A thoughtful guy, Bannerman. Most guys would only refill the gas tank. Bannerman gives him a way to put a bullet up a dealer's ass from three blocks away or to cauterize a crack house. But what the hell, he thought. His pleasure. "I'll take it."

"Just park it somewhere in Manhattan. Call him and say where it is."

"What do I say about Hector and Ruby?"

"No one will see Ruby again. I haven't made up my mind about Hector. He'll be with us here for a while but please don't tell that to Covington or Detective Greenwald. I don't want anyone to know he's still alive. You can assure Covington, however, that Hector will not bother him again. I'll call him myself before long."

"No carving? Hector's face, I mean."

"There's probably no need."

"No need," Lesko repeated, shaking his head. "Bannerman," he asked, "do you begin to see why your average father doesn't want his only daughter hanging around with you?"

"As a matter of fact, I do. But she's safest here. You're welcome to stay yourself until we get this sorted out. I need to be away for a few days. You can keep her company."

Lesko saw Zivic's jaw tighten at the mention of Bannerman taking a trip. He had the impression that they'd argued about it.

"This is about Urs Brugg?"

Bannerman gestured dismissively.

"Hey," Lesko snapped. "I know how to use a phone too. Why don't I call him right now and ask him?"

Bannerman tried a shrug of indifference. But Lesko was watching Zivic.

"Suit yourself," he said. He scanned the room for a telephone, crossed to it, and dialed an outside line. An operator came on. He asked for directory assistance, Zürich, Switzerland. He could hear Zivic whispering. Bannerman sighing. Lesko gave the name.

"Put the phone down," Bannerman said wearily. "Please."

Lesko did not. "I'm listening."

"It's a personal matter. It's the men who murdered Dr. Russo. Urs Brugg knows where they are."

Lesko stared. An operator was telling him that the number was unlisted. He barely heard. He replaced the handset.

"Where?" he asked.

"As I said, it's personal. With me and with Urs Brugg. It's none of your affair."

"Like hell it isn't. Elena . . . she's—"

"Elena," Bannerman reminded him, "is someone you went to see exactly once after she was shot and haven't spoken to since. You have no claim on this. If you ever had one, you've lost it."

Lesko wanted to hit him. He held his temper. "I'm going with you."

"No."

"Then I'll go myself. I still got that passport."

"Go where, Lesko? Pick a country."

"Elena will tell me."

"No, Lesko." Bannerman shook his head. "She won't. Nor will Urs Brugg. Because they both know that you'll get yourself killed and some of us along with you. We've had this conversation before."

Lesko looked to Zivic as if for help. He saw none. "You didn't shut me out then," he said, hating that Bannerman held all the cards. "What makes this different?"

"You had a claim then. Susan. You don't now."

Lesko looked away. "I tried to call," he said, his voice softening. "I didn't know what to say. I felt stupid. I hung up."

Bannerman said nothing.

There was a carved marble fireplace in the room. A framed mirror hung above it. Lesko saw himself there. Hair disheveled. Two days' worth of stubble. Clothing a mess.

"What could I say to her," he muttered.

It was not a question. Bannerman did not try to answer.

"It's more than that, isn't it?" Lesko turned his head. "It's my daughter."

"There's that," Bannerman acknowledged. "If you come

home in a box I don't want to have to tell her how I allowed
it to happen. I'm also not sure that I want you covering my
back. Your heart might not be in it."

Lesko looked as if he'd been slapped. "You think
I'd . . ."

"Hesitate." Bannerman chose the word for him. "You
might not mean to."

"Bullshit."

"That's not all," Bannerman said quietly. "You've got
into the habit of judging me. Second-guessing me. That not
only makes you tiresome, Lesko, it makes you dangerous.
There will come a time when I need to act and you *will*
hesitate. You *will* get in the way."

Zivic squirmed. He didn't like this. It was not like Paul
to give reasons. Certainly not so many. To do so is to in-
vite rebuttal . . . reassurances. Was this simply to berate
Lesko? To match insult with insult? Zivic did not think so.
There was, he knew, no meanness in the man.

But there was surely stubbornness. To insist on going to
Spain. Alone if he must. With help, provided they volunteer.
Which, of course, they will. All of them. To go, even though
mindful of the curious fact that on one day he had no active
enemies and on the next . . . hundreds.

Zivic ticked them off in his mind. A Jamaican drug gang,
extraordinarily violent, armed and trained by Cubans. The
drug gang's allies, its sources, perhaps even the Cubans
themselves. An outlaw faction of the PLO, the most dangerous, the most implacable of them all. And now, very conve-
niently, the assassination team engaged by the late Palmer
Reid whose current whereabouts are discovered by, of all
people, the KGB.

If ever there were a time to hang back, to force the enemy
to show his hand, to seize that hand and see who or what is
on the other end of it, that time would be now. But Paul will
hear none of it. *"Never let an enemy pick the time,"* he says.
*"Never let him rest." How often we've heard that. The ques-
tion is, however, how many others have heard it as well?*

". . . never let a partner down in my life." Lesko was
arguing. "That's twenty-five years, Bannerman. Don't fucking tell me—"

"I don't need you."

"Yeah, well I need *this*. I go or you don't. I pick up that phone again and I'll have fifty cops watching the airports and they'll bust you for anything they can—"

"All right." Bannerman raised a hand. "I'll think about it."

"I'll wait." Lesko folded his arms.

Bannerman's eyes turned cold. "Behave yourself, Lesko."

"Look, you want me to say I'm sorry about giving you so much crap? I'm sorry. You want me to say I like you? I'll say it. I might even mean it a little. If there wasn't any Susan, if she didn't figure in this—"

"Will you do as I say?"

Lesko stopped. "Yeah."

"No arguments?"

"Call them suggestions."

"You're sure."

"Try me."

"Fine. Go see Elena. Leave tonight. Do that first."

Lesko blinked.

"Stop at my office on your way out of Westport. I'll call them. They'll book your flight. But do not tell Elena you're coming. Just go. I'll contact you through Urs Brugg in a day or two."

"What's"—he turned visibly pale—"What's the point?"

"To get her settled in your mind, one way or the other. You won't be useful to me until you do."

"I don't believe this."

"Is that an argument?"

"It's a suggestion," he said, his color rising again. "You want another one? Go f—"

"Make your choice, Lesko." Bannerman sat back.

They watched him leave, slamming the door behind him. Zivic winced at the single shouted obscenity that echoed through the center hall and again at the tortured grinding of Wesley Covington's gears. Then silence. He said nothing for several moments. Finally, he threw up in hands.

"I myself do not believe this," he said to Bannerman.

"What part?" A look of innocence.

"Are you going on a mission or are you matchmaking?" Bannerman tried to shrug off the question. Zivic would not let him. "Okay," he said finally, his manner a trifle sheepish. "No one else seems to have much control over Lesko. Elena might keep him out of trouble."

"And out of your way?"

"That would be nice."

"Let me test my grasp of your scheme," Zivic said wryly. "Lesko sees his born-again drug queen. He meets the family. They do not run screaming from the room. Perhaps he is now not so anxious to dash off to Spain."

"It was more of an improvisation. But yes. That's the idea."

"Perhaps he will even stay with Elena. Live happily ever after in Zürich while you and Susan live here in blessed relief from his constant disapproval."

Bannerman smiled. "God should be so good."

"God should also not be such a practical joker. But he is."

"What do you mean?"

"A man such as Lesko could never live in Zürich as a princeling of the Bruggs. A woman such as Elena does not become a hausfrau in Queens. A compromise is Westport."

The thought of Lesko as a permanent neighbor brought a glaze to Bannerman's eyes.

"Anton?"

"Yes."

"What stake might the KGB have in this?"

"My guess? Nothing sinister. The Bruggs are useful people to know. Even more so to have them in ones' debt."

"They'll know I'm coming. They'll be watching."

"As interested observers. Colonel Belkin knows that he has more to lose than to gain if he interferes."

"You know the man. What is he like?"

"A good mind. Pragmatic, not at all doctrinaire. Not even especially political, but a Russian first and last."

"Any chance he'd try to take me and then trade me for you?"

Zivic smiled. "If not before, why now? Besides, I am old news, especially since Gorbachev. And you are presumed to be under the protection of the State Department. But what could protect their people here if our friend Billy McHugh should vanish into the night and begin passing amongst them."

Bannerman nodded slowly, thoughtfully. "Could it be chance that so much seems to be happening at one time?"

"An epigram comes to mind: When it rains, it pours."

"You think it's coincidence."

"I think you know perfectly well what it is. Even Lesko knows."

"A setup?" Bannerman made a face. "No. Certainly not all of it. Too many ways for it to backfire."

"Not all of it taken together," Zivic agreed. "But break it down into its parts. Put Urs Brugg aside for the moment. What are you left with?"

"This car bomb business?" A sigh. A hint of sadness. "I know. It sounds like Roger, doesn't it."

Zivic nodded. "The tape of a Drug Enforcement Administration wiretap just happens, *accidentally,* to fall into the hands of—"

"One of the four New York cops." Bannerman finished his thought. "Four out of thirty thousand, who were brought up here by Lesko, who were seen by Roger Clew, and whose names he could easily have learned."

"His motive?"

"Lesko said it. Make us think we're under massive attack. Put us back to work killing drug dealers and terrorists. That wouldn't surprise me as far as it goes. The problem with it is that this plan, for Roger, is so transparent."

"Unlike, for example," Zivic asked, "his causing Palmer Reid to wonder about your recent visit to Switzerland?"

Bannerman said nothing. He appeared not to have heard.

Zivic understood. Paul, he knew, had not asked Roger Clew about the telephone call, cited by Palmer Reid, that had probably, ultimately, led to at least six deaths with more to come. He had chosen not to believe it. Or to believe that the call, if made, was innocent, although careless in the extreme. Or, at worst, that Roger's intention was merely to nettle Reid, never dreaming that an act of mischief could go so terribly out of control. This last would certainly explain why Roger's famously dormant sweat glands have so recently begun to function. Further than that, Zivic realized,

Paul was unwilling to go. Not without evidence. Anything more could not be forgiven. Nor could it be overlooked.

"The other problem with it," Bannerman said, as if he'd been lost in thought, "is one of scale. How could Roger seriously think that a dozen or so of us could make an important dent in so many of them?"

"He told you, did he not," Zivic asked, "that he was working on something that would—"

"Knock my socks off," Bannerman nodded. "But I've heard him say that about his recipe for chili."

Zivic said nothing.

Bannerman rose to his feet. "I know," he said softly, not looking at Zivic.

I know you know, thought his friend.

Bannerman stepped to the bank of monitors and threw a switch. Hector Manley appeared on one of the screens. He sat on a bed, cross-legged, dressed only in a hospital gown, staring back into the camera lens. A chain, coated with white plastic, ran from his right ankle to a bolt in the far wall.

"You'll find no more answers there, Paul," Zivic said gently. "The man is wrung dry."

"Take good care of him, Anton." Bannerman flicked off the screen.

Bannerman punched out the numbers that released the electric lock to the room in which Manley was held. He stepped inside, leaving the door ajar. He had brought a chair with him. He placed it, deliberately, well within the range of movement permitted by the chain. He straddled it, the slats facing Manley, his arms folded across the back.

"Have you been fed?" Bannerman asked

Manley nodded. He did not look up.

Except for the metal bed, bolted to the floor, a sink and a toilet with no lid, the room was bare. "You'll get some furniture this morning. A comfortable chair. A lamp. A radio. If you'd like some books or magazines, tell the men who bring them what you prefer."

Manley's expression had been sullen, subdued, a man without hope. A flicker of it, only that, now appeared in his eyes.

"When will I be killed?" he asked.

"You'll be here for several days. I'll decide after that. In the meantime, no one is going to hurt you."

"No . . . operation?"

"You didn't force my hand. I'm glad that you didn't."

The Jamaican seemed to wilt. He closed his eyes. "How," he asked hesitantly, "might I *not* be killed?"

"I'll decide whether you are a danger to me or not. But I'm afraid you're definitely a danger to Mr. Covington and his family."

Manley considered this for several moments. "If you want the truth," he said, "I respect the man. But he challenged me. Many people know it. If I return, I will be a danger to him as he will be to me." He looked up. "I could have lied to you, Bannerman. But you would have known it."

"No chance of reaching some sort of truce?"

Manley stared at him curiously. "If there is a point to it, I will try to think of a way."

"Let me know what you come up with."

The Jamaican nodded slowly. He straightened his legs, easing them onto the white tile floor. "Who are you, Mr. Bannerman?"

"You claim you were never told? By the Arab?"

"Never."

"Or by the Cubans?"

The question seemed to surprise him. "How are they involved in this?"

"You take direction from them, don't you?"

Manley shook his head. "Not at all."

"Were you not trained in Cuba?"

"In urban guerrilla tactics, yes. And in Marxist theory. The evils of the capitalist system. But we were also trained in the distribution and sale of cocaine. Sitting through all that political nonsense was the price we paid for what was useful."

"Then what did they get in return?"

"American dollars. Hard currency," he answered. "Cuba is a conduit from the suppliers in Colombia. They also, of course, cherish the hope that the blacks of your rotting inner cities will rise in revolution. We are expected to organize them. We will not. We will take what we can and run as fast as the rest." Manley looked at him curiously. "How is it you don't know this?"

"Know what?"

"About drugs. About me."

"I have no interest in the drug trade. Except when it affects me. And except that I detest the people who use them."

"Then we have something in common."

Bannerman raised an eyebrow.

"It's true," Manley assured him. "Drug use is forbidden to anyone who works for me. Break that rule and you will be stretched across the hood of a car as a quarter-inch hole is drilled through your knee."

Bannerman pursed his lips. He found that interesting. "An electric drill?" he asked. "Not a bullet?"

"Progress, Mr. Bannerman. It is a refinement developed by the Belfast Irish, not by me. It is slower, more terrible to endure but"—Manley hesitated; his hands dropped to his own knees as if to protect them.

"I wouldn't dream of it," Bannerman shook his head. "Please go on."

The Jamaican made a gesture that said there was little to add. "Only that, terrible as it is, there is a certain practicality to it. The damage is far more easily repaired than that done by a bullet. Those so punished eventually walk more or less normally, much the wiser for their experience." Manley looked at his hands. "Mr. Bannerman?"

"Yes?"

"Will you ever tell me who you are?"

"It's too long a story."

"It seems that I have time."

"I'm afraid I don't." Bannerman rose from the chair. "But you might say that I am to Westport what Mr. Covington is to One hundred fifty-third Street."

A rueful smile. "Mr. Covington does not leave the bodies of dealers in the trunks of cars just outside his borders. There have been such stories about Westport. This was you?"

"Among others. Yes."

"And you are left in peace? The authorities do not trouble you?"

"On the whole, no."

"This town. Westport." He did something with his face to show that he was aware of the absurdity of what he was about to ask. "Can a black man buy a home here?"

"Certainly. It's the law."

"But there is also, I take it, Bannerman's law."

"Bannerman's law says you might want to find another line of work first."

"If I live that long."

"There's that. Yes." Bannerman reached for the chair. He turned to leave.

"May I ask you something? An observation?"

Bannerman waited.

"This is not personal with you. You do not despise me."

"For selling drugs, you mean?"

"Yes."

"Not especially. You don't force them on anyone."

"How then," the Jamaican asked, "can you condemn me for defending what is mine? Are you and I so different, Mr. Bannerman?"

"But you're not defending. You're attacking. Wesley Covington wants no part of what is yours. That's where we separate, Mr. Manley, and that's what will kill you. All Covington wants is to be left in peace."

"Which, I take it," Manley said, "is all that Paul Bannerman wants?"

"That's all. Yes."

"Who would believe that, Mr. Bannerman?"

"Try, Mr. Manley." He closed the door behind him.

—20—

Lesko was fighting sleep. Which was aggravating. Also dumb.

The whole idea was to sleep all the way to Zürich. Which is why he popped a shot of Nyquil as soon as he strapped into his seat. Then two glasses of champagne, which you get, he assumed, so you'll feel less stupid about paying three times as much for a first-class ticket. Not that he paid. Bannerman did. Probably gets them free.

Then two vodka tonics before dinner. Which comes with wine. By the bottle. Then some cognac afterward, which by this time you're spilling down your shirt. Because you're nodding off. Which he'd already done twice. Which would have been okay except he was also dreaming. The first dream has Elena in it. She doesn't even know him. He goes and knocks on her door and says how glad he is to see her and she looks at him funny—like she's trying to place him—and then she sort of remembers but she really couldn't give a shit so she says take a walk and she closes the door.

Next came Katz. Saying I told you so.

"I mean," says Katz, *"would you want to see you again?*

*Back in the hospital was one thing. She was all doped up.
Hitler could have walked in and she'd say how's it going,
heard you were dead.*

*"You're also a putz, Lesko. Bannerman says go and you go.
You know why? You think he gives a good goddamn about
you making it with Elena? And he's not going to call you
from wherever those shooters are, either. Because, for one
thing, he knows that after Elena dusts you off you're not
going to be interested anymore anyhow. Meanwhile he gets
you out of his hair. What do you think he's doing right now?
Packing? Bullshit. He's back there screwing your daughter's
brains out, that's what he's—"*

Lesko had swiped at him. Head snapping up. Brandy
glass sent flying. Flight attendant came running. It's okay.
Sorry. Just a dream. No harm done.

Except Lesko didn't want to sleep any more. Almost five
hours to go. He didn't want to spend them seeing Elena's
face, looking at him like he's a turd on the sidewalk, slamming her front door on him. And he sure didn't want to
spend even five minutes of it taking any more crap from
Katz. You'd think a first-class plane ticket would keep out
the riffraff. The only first class Katz ever saw was when he
made PFC.

Maybe the movie would keep him awake. He doubted it.
It was an old one. *Field of Dreams*. About this farmer who
builds a baseball diamond in his cornfield and a bunch of
dead ballplayers show up to play on it. *That's all I need,*
Lesko thought. *More ghosts.* He couldn't watch it anyway.
The Nyquil. Just a lot of colors swimming around and his
eyes getting heavy.

"Hey, Lesko?"

"Leave me alone," he murmured.

"Are you really gonna do this?"

"I'm warning you, David—"

"Just tell me."

*"One more word about Susan and you're going out that
window."*

"What? What'd I say?"

"About her and—" He chewed his lip.

*"About her with Bannerman? Hey, dummy. That wasn't
me. It was you."*

"It was you," Lesko snarled. *"Just before."*

"No way. I just got here. But I heard it."

Lesko's head jerked. *"What do you mean, you just got here? From where?"*

"I don't know. I never remember."

"You weren't here an hour ago? Before the movie?"

"I got a flash for you, Lesko. There's a whole lot of times when you think I said something and I didn't. It's you. I don't talk about Susan that way. You shouldn't either."

Lesko showed his teeth. But he kept them clenched.

"And anyhow it's none of your business. She's all grown up. It's her life."

"That's your idea of a life? With a guy like Bannerman?"

"You with Elena is better? At least Bannerman didn't kill your partner. What kind of loyalty is that?"

"Things change, David."

"Not that much."

"She's different now. She's clean. And you're dead. These are fairly big changes."

Katz glowered but said nothing. He turned his face away. Which at least, thought Lesko, was back in one piece. If the schmuck was going to keep showing up, Lesko supposed, it was better he looked more presentable than when his brains were running down the inside of his windshield.

"Wait a second," Lesko's chin bobbed up. *"If that wasn't you before, how do I know this is you now?"*

"You listen, that's how. If what you hear is really shitty, you know it's you."

Lesko ignored this last. *"Was that you this morning?"*

"When?"

"You came in with Danish. Like you used to."

"Oh, yeah. I got mixed up."

"Why? What were you doing there?"

"I'm your partner. Remember?"

"You're not my partner. You're dead. And if you weren't dead you'd be up in Sing Sing right now getting corn-holed by everyone you ever busted up there because you were a fucking thief."

Lesko heard a sound from the window seat. Like a catch in the throat. He turned. Katz's face was lit by the screen. Tears welled in his eyes.

"Oh, Chri—Now what?"

"You're such a prick, Lesko." Katz hid his face.

A loud sigh. *"David,"* he shifted uncomfortably. *"Okay, I'm sorry."*

No answer.

"What do you want from me? Just tell me."

"I want us to be partners. Like before."

"David—you're dead."

"You keep saying that."

"David, this is crazy," said Lesko, not unkindly. *"Maybe it's me who's nuts. I'm sitting here talking to you. I know you're not there. I know you're not real—"*

"Sir?" A woman's voice. Distant.

"So? Then what difference does it make?"

"Sir? Mr. Lesko?" It was closer. He felt a hand on his shoulder.

"Lesko?" Katz's voice was fading. *"What could it hurt?"*

Lesko lifted his head. The stewardess. Leaning close. Kneeling. Another woman, two rows forward, turning and glowering at him, fingers to her lips, shushing him.

"Huh? What?" he blinked.

"You were talking in your sleep."

"Right. Yeah. I'm sorry."

"Can I get you anything?" she asked. "How about some coffee."

"No—Yeah. Coffee's fine."

"Right away." She walked briskly toward the galley.

Lesko rubbed his eyes. He glanced at the window seat. Then up to the screen. *Field of Dreams.* Shoeless Joe Jackson walking off the field. Into the dense corn. Back to where he came from. Fading into it. The cornstalks never moved. And the window seat was empty.

"God damn you, David," he whispered. *But maybe you're right. What could it hurt? And maybe you're also all I got.*

Bannerman had decided on a team of five. It would mean, he realized, leaving Westport thinly defended but, with luck, most would be back before their absence could be noticed.

He and Billy would travel as a unit. They would fly to Lisbon, from there to Malaga. That would leave them less than an hour by car from Marbella. Carla Benedict would head the second unit, arriving by a different route. She would fly to Madrid, connect at Seville, then make her way south by train.

He'd chosen Carla reluctantly. She was good, no question, she was fluent in Spanish, and her appearance was such that she would blend nicely among the fading showgirls and minor actresses that were drawn in great numbers to the resort towns of the Mediterranean. But Carla liked to improvise—sometimes to good effect, as when she gambled on intercepting Lurene Carmody, but just as often to bad effect, as when her gamble left Gary Russo in a situation for which he was not trained. That was the other thing. Russo. This was personal with Carla. She would want to be the one to avenge him. If she saw the opportunity she would strike, regardless of her assigned role, regardless of the plan. Bannerman had shared his concern with her. She had promised to behave. Be a team player. And she had begged for the chance. Bannerman had relented. But now, her team already there—they had left even before Lesko—Bannerman's misgivings still nagged at him. Asking Carla to be patient was like asking a cat to ignore a crippled bird.

The third unit, their backup, was John Waldo. Waldo worked best alone. His job was to arrange alternate escape routes, cover their retreat, create diversions if necessary, and to acquire weapons, which should be waiting for him by the time he and Billy arrived.

Would be waiting, Bannerman corrected himself. John never missed. Goes in, does his job, disappears. No one ever remembers seeing him. Like a ghost compared to . . . what had Susan called her? Oh, yes. Calamity Carla.

Susan.

She had taken it well. That he must suddenly take a trip. Two days, three at the most. She'd asked no questions. She seemed to know that he was waiting to see if she would. But except for an awkward silence here and there, a staring into space, they had passed the evening as any other couple might. A quiet dinner. A walk, afterward, down to the water's edge. The stars were bright. She taught him the names of some. She pointed to Regulus in the southwestern sky. It was in her sign, she told him. She was a Leo. His sign, Aquarius, was opposite, far away. Somewhere down by Peg-

asus. It could be seen, she said, only when her sign could
not. Then, as if this had meaning to her, came the longest of
the silences. They walked back from the beach, they held
each other, and, once again, they made love through the
night. There would be time enough to sleep during the flight
to Lisbon.

He'd found himself wanting to tell her where he was going. Even why. To let her know that he trusted her. But
there were the others to think about. He had no right to
trust her with their lives. She assumed, he felt sure, that he
was off to Zürich. That phone call from Urs Brugg. Better
to leave it at that. But she hadn't even asked that much. She
asked only, that morning, that he call her if he could. Talk
about the weather. Anything at all. Just so she'd hear his
voice. He said he would try.

"You thinking about Susan?" Billy touched his arm.

Bannerman straightened. He'd been staring through the
window at the cloud cover five miles below them.

Billy pointed to the surface of Bannerman's tray table.
There were a series of *S*'s on it, traced with Bannerman's
finger using the condensation from his cold drink. Bannerman had not realized he was doing it. He nodded. "Among
other things."

"I do that too," the bigger man told him. "I write *Angela*
a lot."

Angela DiBiasi. His landlady.

"Sometimes I write . . . *Mr. and Mrs. William Mc-
Hugh.* Just to see how it looks. You ever do that?"

Embarrassed, Bannerman wiped the letters away. "No.
Not lately." Not since he was fifteen. He folded his napkin.
"What did you tell her, by the way, about this trip?"

"She knows you get free tickets to places. And you're my
friend. Sometimes you take me with you, that's all."

"Would you ever tell her about your life? What you've
done?"

"Like what?"

Bannerman glanced meaningfully at the heads of a couple
in the seats in front of them. "Like . . . um . . . what you
do."

Billy understood. "What good would that be?" he asked.

"I don't know." He wished he hadn't brought it up. "I've

never been . . . with someone . . . this long before. I don't think I'm very good at it yet."

"I never been with someone at all, not counting hookers. And not counting your mom."

Bannerman said nothing. Billy gasped. He brought a hand to his mouth. "I didn't mean—"

"I know what you meant," Bannerman said gently.

Billy was silent for a long moment. "She used to teach me things. Nice things. Did you know that?"

"You told me."

"A lot of people . . . they were afraid of me. Because of things they heard. But not Cassie."

"I know."

"She was trying to teach me about art. All kinds. Paintings and statues."

Bannerman remembered. The first time he'd ever set eyes on Billy was that day in Vienna when he'd gone to see the blackened remains of the house on Gruenstrasse where his mother and two men were murdered. Billy was there. Covered in soot to his knees and elbows. His clothing soaked through from a steady rain. Eyes moist, yet cold and dead. Holding a charred art book he had found under a collapsed section of roof. She had bought it for him. He had left it with her so he would not lose it. Or get it dirty. He still had that book, Bannerman knew. But before the pages had fully dried, eight men were dead. Five by Billy. Two by himself. One a suicide. It might have been more had not the Americans sent Roger Clew, a reluctant innocent, to negotiate a peace.

"You remember that day I first saw you?" Billy asked. "One look at your face, one word out of your mouth, I knew who you were."

"I was just thinking about that myself."

"Lot of people came by from the cemetery. She had a lot of friends. But with me, she was special."

Bannerman had not seen anyone else. Perhaps a passing car or two. "How long had you been there?"

"I don't know. Couple of days."

"In the rain?"

Billy shrugged. "No place else to go. Till you came."

"But these friends . . . no one tried to . . . ?"

"They were scared, I think. I wasn't in a good mood. But Johnny Waldo brought me a dry coat. I ruined it on him."

Bannerman grunted. A month or so later, Waldo drove up next to the car of an American agent who was involved in the killing and put a bullet through his head. As Billy said, his mother had a lot of friends.

Billy was still talking. Mentioning others who came to Gruenstrasse. Some names were familiar, others not. Some were long dead. Through his own drifting thoughts, Bannerman thought he heard the name of Roger Clew. That couldn't have been. The better part of a year had passed before Clew had even—

"Did you say Roger? He was there?"

"Uh-uh." Billy shook his head.

Bannerman rubbed his eyes. Roger was too much on his mind of late.

"I said his boss. Guy Clew works for."

"Bart Fuller?"

Billy nodded. "Clew worked for him back then too. But mostly all he did was go to trade shows for the State Department. He was nothin' until they got him to—"

Bannerman interrupted him. He knew all that. "What about Fuller? You're saying he was at the burial?"

"And then the house. Yeah."

"What connection did he have with my mother?"

The bigger man frowned. He seemed uncomfortable with the subject. He tossed one hand to show that it had no significance.

"Billy," Bannerman turned in his seat. "Don't you think this is something I should have known about?"

"It was private. With Cassie. It was none of your business."

Bannerman blinked. "Are you saying they were lovers? My mother and Bart Fuller?"

"Not like you think."

"How many ways are there, Billy?"

"He just liked being with her. Nothing ever happened. Your Mom told me so. Also I followed them a couple of times, just to make sure she wasn't being set up or anything. They took walks, mostly. You know how you can hold a woman up so high you're even afraid to hold her hand? He was like that."

"Did you ever speak to my mother about him?"

"I told her I followed them. She wasn't mad."

"What did she say about him?"

"She liked him. But he was married. And neither one of them wanted to screw that up. I'm trying to tell you, it was nothing. It was . . . there's a word."

"Platonic? An infatuation?"

"Both of those. Yeah."

"Did you talk to him after the funeral?"

"I never talked to him. Well . . . once, maybe. I'm not sure."

"Tell me about the *maybe.*"

Billy hesitated. "Remember we went to Paris to line up Carla and Doc Russo? It was like two weeks after she died. Anyway, this guy calls me at the hotel to tell me to check my box. He says there's a list of names. He says the first name on the list is this Austrian cop and he's the most scared. I should start with him."

Bannerman remembered. It had never occurred to him to ask Billy how he'd found these people. Billy was the professional then. He was a babe in the woods. It was enough that the first man had talked and confirmed the other names on Billy's list, before Billy cut his throat and burned his own house down around him.

"And the man who called," Bannerman said quietly, "you think that was Barton Fuller."

"I didn't know his voice. I only thought so."

"Why?"

Billy shrugged. "It just figured. I knew he worked in Paris and it sounded like a local call. He also called your mom "Cassie." Everyone else called her "Mama." And he sounded all torn up. He sounded like he wanted to kill them all himself."

"But if he was not involved, how could he have known all those names?"

"I don't know. He knew them."

"Could it be," Bannerman pressed, "that he was part of it? That he knew about the raid but didn't realize they intended to kill her? And had . . . I don't know . . . an attack of conscience afterward?"

"We got them all. You talked to a couple of them. They would have given us their own mothers by the time the Doc got through with them."

Bannerman nodded slowly. Yes. They would have.

The story, as it was ultimately pieced together, began with what should have been a fairly routine operation. A KGB agent had been turned by Cassie Bannerman. He was left in place, in Budapest, but he was about to be exposed. She sent another agent, a Hungarian national, to bring him out, spiriting him up the Danube to Vienna. The KGB wanted him back or they wanted him dead. They offered to release two imprisoned American agents in trade. Cassie refused. The KGB went to her superiors, this time sweetening the offer with cash. They accepted it and were recorded doing so by the KGB. The Russians now had them. They insisted on the verifiable death of not only the KGB defector but of Cassie Bannerman as well.

The Americans knew of, and occasionally employed, three Viennese who were former members of Heydrich's Einsatzgruppen—killing squads—during the war and had since built new careers as policemen with the help of forged identity papers. They were given the job. They, in turn, hired the two German gunmen, kept escape routes open and created a diversion.

The Americans, as one of them later insisted, weeping, had not wanted Cassie Bannerman's death. KGB blackmail or no, he had even tried to lure her away from 16 Gruenstrasse. But something, perhaps that, had made her suspicious. She would not leave the defecting Russian or the agent who had brought him over. She was in the act of finding a new place to hide them and the Americans realized that they could wait no longer. Nor could they save her.

"Is it possible," Bannerman asked, drumming his fingers on the tray table, "that Fuller had been warned to keep his distance from Gruenstrasse? I mean, if you knew he was seeing my mother, they must have known it too."

"I told you," Billy was trying to doze, "I don't even know it was him."

"But it would make sense. They couldn't risk letting an

American consul get killed. After it happened, he realized why they wanted to keep him away."

"Maybe."

"And he had to know that you were close to her. Why else would he have picked you to call?"

Billy took a breath. "Like I said—"

"I know. You don't know who it was. But weren't you curious?"

McHugh looked at him. "You don't think I would have dusted him if I thought he was part of it? I mean, even thought it?"

"How could you be sure he wasn't?"

"Like I said," he answered patiently, "no one fingered him. No one even mentioned him. They would have."

"You've seen him on television a dozen times since then. What about his voice? Was it familiar?"

Billy grumbled. "You know what you sound like?"

Bannerman waited.

"You sound like that kid I picked up sixteen, seventeen years ago. You wanted all the answers. You wanted everything neat. It doesn't ever come that way. You go with what you got."

Bannerman sat back. He stared through the window. There would be time enough, he thought, to ask Barton Fuller. Perhaps he'd see the answer in his eyes.

Not that it mattered, necessarily. After all these years. Except that it might explain a few things. Such as why Palmer Reid never tried harder than he did to retake Westport. Fuller might well have blocked him. But why? Out of sentiment for Cassie Bannerman? Somehow he doubted that.

Whatever the answer, and if it was indeed Fuller who made that call, Bannerman would need to rethink his assessment of the man. He'd always respected him, certainly. Even liked him. Perhaps seeing in him some of the qualities his mother must have seen. But he'd never thought of Fuller as the sort of man who could mark other men for death.

"Hey." Billy nudged him.

"Hmm?"

"Forget Fuller. Get some sleep."

"Sure."

He might have done it out of emotion . . . bereavement
. . . hatred. Bannerman could understand that. It was how
he himself had begun. And look where it led. Each time, it
became easier. More impersonal.

"You hear me?" Billy said.

"Yeah."

"Get some sleep."

He wondered if it had become easier for Barton Fuller as
well.

Bannerman closed his eyes.

—21—

"David?" whispered Lesko.

No answer.

This is so goddamned dumb.

His plane had landed before seven. The sun was no more than a grayish glow to the east. He'd passed through immigration without incident, looking beyond the glass booths to the place where Elena had been waiting the last time he came. There was no one. Just the backs of other passengers following the signs to baggage claim and customs. He had nothing to claim, nothing to declare. Just the clothes on his back and the small overnight bag he'd carried on board.

He passed through a knot of waiting relatives, scanning their faces out of habit. No one looked at him.

He paused at a bank of public telephones. Too early to call. He didn't know what he'd say to her anyway. Or whether he'd even make the call. But the phones reminded him that he needed to change dollars into Swiss francs.

Near the currency exchange he saw signs, in English, pointing to a train that ran directly to downtown Zürich. He followed them. It would kill some time.

But only ten minutes' worth. He found himself in a cavernous main terminal, track announcements blaring in German, in the middle of rush hour, clusters of vacationers pushing baggage carts with ski bags through the crowd. He found a coffee shop. He used its bathroom to wipe some of the shine from his face and to brush his teeth. He sat down with a pot of coffee. He wished he had something to read.

"Can you think of anything else?" He heard Katz's voice in his head. He ignored it.

"I mean, maybe you could take a bus tour. That'll take care of the morning."

"Leave me alone," he muttered.

"Then there's lunch. Maybe after that a museum until whatever time the bars open around here and you can get sloshed enough to go ring her doorbell."

"David . . ." He chewed his lip. Never mind. He wasn't even sure it was Katz. Not wide awake. It was probably himself. All 240 pounds of him. Needing a shave. Probably stinks. Wondering if she'll even open the door when she sees him. But Katz, or whoever, was right. Either get it over with or climb back on the train. With a sigh, he pushed to his feet.

"Elena?"

No. Another woman's voice. Speaking German. Probably a maid. He said his name. She said "Jah, something, something, bitte" and was gone. Too late to hang up. He waited.

"Lesko?"

His stomach flipped.

"Lesko, is it you?"

"Yeah. It's me. How are you, Elena?"

"It is—it is good to hear your voice. You are well?"

"I'm fine. And you?" *Schmuck. You just asked her that.*

"I have been thinking about you."

His stomach turned again. "I would have called. Things got a little busy back home."

"Back home?"

"Where I live." He squeezed his eyes shut. "Back in the states."

"Lesko, where are you now?" She seemed alarmed. "You are not in Spain."

"Spain?" Why would he be in Spain. Then he understood.
"No. No, I'm not."

"Where are you, Lesko? This minute."

"I'm here. Zürich. I wondered . . . maybe we could get
some lunch."

She gasped. "Where, precisely?"

He told her.

"I will come for you," she said. "Ten minutes."

On the sidewalk outside his apartment building on Ver-
mont Avenue, not far from the White House, Harry Hagler
watched as a tow truck dragged the last of four badly damaged automobiles up the ramp from his basement garage.
This one was charred. All its windows shattered. Several
dents and scars made by flying metal. Hagler held a rolled-
up newspaper in one hand. He slammed it against his open
palm.

His own car was still down there. What was left of it.
Being picked over by a crew from the FBI forensics labora-
tory. A bomb had done it, no question. Radio controlled.
Fragments of the receiver had already been identified, although not its type or origin. It had gone off midmorning,
probably accidentally, triggered by someone's inadvertent
use of the radio frequency chosen by whoever had planted it.
The timing of the blast had been fortunate. No injuries. No
one had been in the garage. The assassin had intended, the
FBI assumed, to wait for Hagler to drive out, follow him in
another car, and detonate the charge at a predetermined
time and place.

But, if so, the killing had been carelessly planned. Hagler
rarely used that car because he seldom left the District except by air. It had collected two weeks' worth of light basement dust since it was last driven. A professional should
have noticed that, thought the federal agent in charge.

Hagler turned away. He walked northward along Ver-
mont Avenue to the intersection of L Street where a Lincoln
Town Car waited at the curb, its engine running. Roger
Clew's chauffeur climbed from the car as he approached and
stepped to a nearby doorway, arms folded. Hagler entered
the Lincoln.

"Well?" he asked Roger Clew.

"I've tried all over Westport. I don't think he's there."

"Of course, he's not there, for Christ's sake. He's down here."

"We don't know that."

Hagler hooked a thumb back in the direction of his building. "That was a bomb, Roger. A car bomb. You don't see a hint in there someplace?"

"Terrorists plant bombs, too, Harry. And some of them don't like you."

"You mean Jibril? He's got a whole school for how to blow people up. He wouldn't have missed."

"Neither would Bannerman." Unless he meant to. "Anyway, why would he single you out? As far as I know, he's probably never heard of you unless you left a trail up there."

"I didn't." Not to me.

Hagler began to unfurl the newspaper he was carrying. He stopped abruptly. It had suddenly occurred to him that he was in another car. Eyes widening, he jabbed a finger toward the floor.

"It's clean," Clew assured him. "So is Kaplan's."

"You talked to him? What does he say about this?"

Clew shook his head. "He wouldn't take my call. He's been ducking me for two weeks. He won't even meet me at Fuller's house."

Hagler fell silent. Through Clew's window he saw the tow truck, dragging the car with the blown out windows, heading up toward Thomas Circle, leaving a sprinkling of glass each time it hit a bump.

That bomb, he thought.

For it to go off, accidentally, someone has to *happen* to be transmitting on that frequency—odds maybe 500 to 1 against—and they must *happen* to be passing the garage entrance at the time so a strong enough signal can get in and at a time when there *happens* to be no one else in the garage, not even the security guard who works there.

"Okay," he said quietly. "It was a message. Bannerman has to be on to us."

Not us, damn you. You. "How, Harry?" he asked wearily.

"Maybe he's got us wired."

"We're swept three times a week, Harry. All of us. There's no wire."

"Then maybe the Jamaican. Maybe he sold us out."

"Harry . . . does he know who we are?"

"No. He couldn't."

"Does he know who Bannerman is?"

"No."

"Then it's not the Jamaican."

Hagler fell silent again for several moments. Then, "Do you read *The New York Times,* Roger?" He indicated the newspaper he was holding, now opened to the "Metropolitan" section.

Clew's eye dropped to the page. It followed Hagler's finger to a two-column article. Its headline: "Five Die In Drug War." Clew snatched it from him.

The report chronicled a weekend of violence on Manhattan's Upper West Side. A bombing and a machine gunning on Saturday evening, thought to be an encounter between rival factions. One dead. Fire bombed in his car. Burned beyond recognition. Then, on Sunday, four more street killings in three separate incidents. Two of the dead were members of a Jamaican drug gang known as the Jungle Posse. The other two, members of a rival Dominican gang. A photo was shown of the man who led the Jamaicans. The police were seeking him for questioning. Clew read the caption under the photo. He wilted visibly. The caption identified Hector "Dandy" Manley.

"Did you notice," Hagler asked quietly, "that another car got bombed?"

Clew couldn't speak.

"The charred body. Unidentified. What'll you bet it's Manley?"

Still nothing.

"While I've got your attention"—Hagler closed one eye—"let me ask you another question. Could Bannerman have gotten his hands on one of our computers?"

"No. No way."

"This doesn't look to you like the Ripper Effect put to work? First he cooks Manley, then he sits back as the Jamaicans and the Dominicans run around killing each other? Not to mention blasting my car by way of a thank-you note."

"No," Clew said firmly. "There's no way he could have it."

"Yes, there is, Roger. From Irwin."

Clew stared. Then he shook his head. "You know him better than that."

"Maybe. But if he did, I'll blow his fucking head off."

Clew sat back, hugging himself. Asking himself. Is it possible? And if Bannerman did have the program, look what else he was doing with it. Setting them against each other just like the drug gangs. Making them paranoid.

"I'll go see him," he whispered. "Today. I'll go to Westport."

"And what? Ask him? You can't even find him."

"Let me think, Harry."

"You walk in there, with all this, you better damned well bring some backup."

"That's the *worst* thing I could do," he snapped.

Or maybe it isn't. *Wouldn't I do that,* Clew wondered, *if I were worried about him? If I'd tried to reach him and couldn't? If I'd heard about a plot to bomb Westport?*

Maybe.

And maybe I just go. Find him. Feel him out. Look into his eyes. Then, if there's nothing there, play it by ear. Maybe give him the Jibrils after all. Or maybe give him Harry Hagler. Damn you, Harry.

"I'll make one more call," he said. Maybe two. Maybe he'd try Lesko first. See what he knows, if anything.

"Don't just call. Go."

"Harry," Clew hissed. "I'll handle it."

Damn you.

The messages on Paul's machine, which he no longer locked away, were all from Roger Clew. He left no name but Susan knew his voice. It was the man from the State Department who had brought her from Switzerland. Except he was calmer then. A bit nervous but in control. Now he was breathing deeply. Swallowing often.

"Listen . . . Paul," went the first message. *"We have to talk. Did you . . . ? Never mind. Just call me."* Click.

The message had been recorded shortly after noon. A second message, apparently, followed a call to Paul's office.

Clew seemed to have learned that he had gone someplace. He had also tried to reach Anton Zivic. For some reason, Zivic's absence from his Main Street shop was cause for concern.

"Where is everybody?" he asked. *"What the hell's going on?"*

Between the second and third calls he had obviously tried to reach her father. He was now even more upset. But there was something different about his voice. It had, she thought, a certain coldness to it.

"Something is happening," he said into the machine. *"I can't tell you over the phone but it's big and it involves a major threat to the security of your base. If I can't reach you, if I can't even reach Lesko for Christ's sake, if you're unable to reach me, I may have to move some people in there for your own good."*

Paul's base?

That, she assumed, could only mean Westport. But what major threat? And—good question—where was everybody. And what's this about moving people into Westport? Who? The Green Berets?

She punched out her father's number in Queens. No answer. Another machine. On an impulse, she called Paul's office, identifying herself.

"Did Paul leave word where he could be reached?"

Sorry, she was told. Not authorized to say. But she might try asking Mr. Zivic.

"But isn't he with them?"

A short pause. "No, he isn't."

"Well, I know that they've gone back to Switzerland. Paul and my father. Are you telling me there's no way to get a message to them there?"

Another pause. "Your father is in Zürich. But we have no hotel for him."

"My father, you said. But not Paul?"

"Miss Lesko . . . you'll really have to talk to Mr. Zivic. You might try him at the Greenfield Hill Clinic."

Susan replaced the phone.

Damn.

Her father in Zürich. No hotel. Apparently without Paul. Which might mean that he's gone to see Elena. Which is fine except why the urgency? He's probably traveling on that same fake passport. And what did this have to do with Urs Brugg's urgent message to Paul? *We'll assume,* she decided, *that Elena is not pregnant and that my father is not being summoned to do the honorable thing. And we'll grant that my father did not need Paul as chaperone. So where is Paul?*

She could, she supposed, ask Anton Zivic. Nice man. Seems second only to Paul in this Westport thing. But she didn't really know him. What about Molly?

Wait a minute, she decided. *First let's see who else is gone around here.* She found a phone book and flipped to the number of the Westport Library where Carla Benedict worked as a researcher. She dialed it, asking for Carla, planning to hang up if she came to the phone. But Carla wasn't there. Took a few days off. Probably back later in the week. One down, three to go.

She dialed Mario's. Asked for Billy. Same story. Two down.

"And Molly's away too?" she asked.

"No," the relief bartender told her. "She's here. Want to talk to her?"

Susan hesitated. "Thanks. No. I'll just come over."

Molly's presence, business as usual, surprised Susan as much as it gratified her. But there was no reason, she supposed, to assume that Paul would always travel with the same group of—specialists?—whatever—just because these three, plus that doctor they lost, were with him in Switzerland. She slipped into her coat, feeling for the car keys in her pocket. Her eye fell on the leather reclining chair near Paul's fireplace. She went to it, knelt, and reached beneath it. Her fingertips found the automatic pistol that he had slid under that chair two nights before. She'd half-expected Paul to have taken it down to the shore and thrown it far out into Long Island Sound. He hadn't. Must have had other things on his mind. She slipped it into her purse, down to the bottom, covering it with her wallet and two packets of tissues. She didn't know why. Yes, she did. It was because of all the phone calls, all the mystery, the hints of imminent violence. And because she was alone. And because she was damned if she was going to become a victim again.

* * *

They had barely spoken. Elena's car, a new Mercedes, wound silently up narrow streets following signs that read "Zurichsberg." It was to Zürich, Lesko guessed, what Greenwich, Connecticut, was to New York except closer to town. It was where the rich people lived. Big houses. Many hidden behind walls or thick evergreens. He wondered if anyone there, in their whole lives, had ever cooked their own dinner or carried out a load of garbage. This was a mistake. He didn't belong here.

A chauffeur drove the car. A real one. Not a bodyguard. But Lesko had seen the second car, two men in it, that had pulled up fifty feet behind the Mercedes and stayed at that distance as it climbed the hill. He'd tensed when he saw it. But the chauffeur, holding the door for him, followed his stare and nodded a reassurance. He urged Lesko to enter quickly.

She was in the backseat. Her eyes shining, her lips moving. She seemed to be trying different words but all that came out was, "Hello, Lesko."

Nor could he reply at first. She seemed even smaller than he remembered her. More vulnerable. She was wearing a dressing gown of some sort, loose fitting, Oriental. A dark fur had been draped over her shoulders. She could not use the sleeves because both arms were in slings. The left arm, shattered by gunfire, was encased in plaster. Metal screws protruded from the cast. The right arm rested on a lighter sling that kept pressure off her shoulder. Where her gown opened at the throat he could see the edge of a bandage. He had almost forgotten how badly she'd been hurt.

"You shouldn't be out," he scolded her gently. "I could have grabbed a taxi."

"I'm fine," she told him. "There is no more pain."

Lesko knew she was lying. He knew what bullets did. And what they felt like.

The Mercedes climbed higher, past homes that became increasingly elegant and grounds more spacious as they drove. Lesko tried to imagine the house Elena would have chosen. The driver slowed and reached to press a button. Just ahead, on the left, a heavy gate swung open. Its ironwork had been covered with metal plates to obstruct the view within. The Mercedes entered. The chase car stayed at the curb outside.

There was a circular driveway, not so big, space for five or six cars at most. It led to a house that seemed more French than Swiss. A château. Sort of a salmon color trimmed in white stone that looked as if it had recently been sand-blasted. The house was substantial but not huge. Not much land around it either. But what it had was richly landscaped with shrubs and rock gardens and an occasional bronze sculpture. The gate closed behind them. A woman stood waiting at the front door. She wore a nurse's uniform, her expression a mixture of exasperation and concern. Ignoring Lesko, she hurried to Elena's side of the Mercedes and helped her out of the car.

Inside, lots of marble. More sculpture. A main hallway with a curved stairway straight ahead and double doors on each side. The nurse opened one of these. It was the living room, Lesko guessed. Or the library. Many books lined the walls, some behind glass. There was a fireplace, freshly lit and blazing. Two plush chairs faced each other in front of it. There was a wheelchair next to one of them. The nurse tried to force Elena into it. She shook her head impatiently, stepped past the nurse and eased herself into one of the chairs. She beckoned the nurse closer, whispered something to her. More exasperation, a rolling of the eyes, but whatever Elena said to her, the nurse seemed to throw in the sponge. Elena patted her hand. "Danke," she added. The nurse took her fur and left the room.

"The nurse knows it too," Lesko told her. "Going out was dumb."

He stood facing the fire. He could not look at her because she was staring at him, her eyes alive with pleasure. It embarrassed him.

"It has been three weeks," she said. "I have indulged myself enough."

"Yeah, well," he admonished her, "it's going to be more like three months. That's not a skin rash you got there."

"Sit, Lesko," she said. "Please."

He hesitated.

"Must I tell you that it hurts to look up at you?"

He took the chair opposite.

Elena eased her right arm out of the light canvas sling. She winced, then tried to disguise it with a smile. Lesko leaned forward as if to rise but she waved him off with a motion of her fingers.

"If I ask you why you came, Lesko," she said, her breath catching, "what will you say? That you were passing through?"

Lesko made a face. He would have. "Truth is," he told her, "I came to see you. I been thinking about you."

"Nice thoughts?"

"Yeah. Mostly."

The qualifier caused her to drop her eyes. Lesko saw it.

"Not mostly," he said. "All of them."

A shy smile. Her fingernails picked idly at the stitching of her gown. "Will you tell me some of them?" she asked.

"Just"—he shifted uncomfortably—"Just thoughts."

"Tell me." She kept her eyes down. "Please?"

Lesko felt his color rising. He could not tell her of the times when he'd imagined himself holding her in his arms. Her face against his chest. Now and then he'd bring a hand to her cheek. Sometimes he would kiss her. Never on the lips. Just the forehead. A couple of times, back home, lying in bed at four in the morning, he'd imagined that she was there with him. But he had not imagined her there on purpose. It was a dream. The half-awake kind. Like when David Katz comes. Nor were they doing anything. She wasn't naked. She was just there.

"I thought," he said with effort, "about how brave you are. And how bad I feel that you got hurt. And . . . I don't know. Lots of things."

She waited.

"And how you're so beautiful," he said hoarsely.

She smiled. "I am not. But thank you."

"Don't argue."

Her eyes fell again. "I dream of you sometimes."

Lesko blinked, startled.

"In my dreams," she said slowly, "you have forgiven me."

He let out a breath. "I told you before. We're square. Forget that part."

There was a knock at the door. The nurse entered. Lesko

did not know whether he was annoyed or relieved. She brought a tray of coffee, which she set down at Elena's right hand. She stepped back into the hall and returned with a rectangular object that was covered with a cloth. She set this down as well and walked from the room. Elena tried to pour. The arm had no strength. Lesko crossed to the tray. He dropped to one knee and did it for her. His hand was shaking. He cursed himself.

"Do I make you ill at ease?" she asked.

"How do you like your coffee?"

"Black. Please answer. Do I?"

"I guess. A little."

"Why?"

"Because you make me crazy sometimes, that's why."

"Have you ever wanted to make love to me?"

Lesko needed both hands for his cup. "See that?" he said. "That's what I mean."

"It is an honest question. I have certainly thought of you in that way."

He had to put it down.

"Furthermore"—she forced firmness into her voice—"I have asked you to come visit me, even live here with me, as long as you like. I think this invitation deserves the courtesy of a reply."

"Will you"—Lesko rubbed his face—"Will you please stop?"

"You Americans have an expression. Cards on the table."

"Yeah, well, we have one about beating around the bush, too. It's also a custom."

"And that opposites attract."

"But not oil and water."

She became subdued. "That is how you see us?"

"Elena." He softened his voice into a reasoning tone. "Will you look at me? Take a real good look."

"I have looked. You wish for proof?" She reached for the object the nurse had set by her chair. She tugged at the cloth that covered it. Lesko could see that it was a painting, framed. He moved to help her with it.

He sat back, stunned.

It was him. Ten years younger. Thirty years less angry. But the face was still hard. And yet . . . contented. There were mountains in the background but they were low. It gave the feeling that he was standing on the highest peak, looking off in the distance, liking what he saw. When he could speak, he asked, "Who did this?"

"I did."

"What, personally? You painted this?"

"From memory." She wrinkled her nose. "Now I see the mistakes. But that is you, Lesko."

"I wish."

"You see? You think you are unattractive. You are not." Lesko grunted.

"Your manner is coarse, Lesko, but your features are not. You are an intimidating presence but I think much of this is deliberate. In any case, it no longer works with me because I have seen great tenderness in you. And integrity. And strength. You are a man. In my life I have met only one other like you. Perhaps two." *Urs Brugg was one,* she said in her mind. *Paul Bannerman, perhaps, the other.*

Lesko's color rose again. The last people who said anything like this to him, besides Susan, were the hookers when he was working vice. And that was because they knew he'd never hit on them for sex or money for not busting them.

He cleared his throat. "I . . . admire you too."

A hesitant smile. "You feel more than that, I think."

His color deepened.

"Cards on the table, Lesko," she said.

Lesko groaned inwardly. She was about to make him crazy again. But at least she was plowing straight ahead. Which was more his style. If she'd tried any of that feminine wiles shit he knew he'd be a puddle by now.

"You want cards?" He set the portrait down carefully. "Try these. My whole pension plus what I make on the side probably couldn't buy one of those statues you leave out in the rain. You pick up a new Mercedes every time your old one gets a window shot out and I run around by subway. Start hanging out with me and you've had your last invitation to anything fancier than awards night at the bowling alley."

She held his gaze, not amused. She gestured vaguely at her surroundings. "If I had none of this, what then?"

"The point is, you have it. I don't."

"Very well." She raised her chin. "I will leave the money here. You will bring me home with you. You will take care of me."

Lesko pushed to his feet, stepping behind his chair as if to keep it between them. He didn't believe this. Not in his dumbest daydreams, not even at four in the morning would he—"Look." He winced. "Could we change the subject for a minute? Where's Bannerman?"

"No, we cannot. I have dealt you a queen. You will please cover it."

"Let me get this straight," he said, fingers to his temples. "You'd give up all of this. Just to be with me."

"Certainly not. It would be here for our visits."

"Just checking." He made a face. "And how long would you expect this to last?"

"Until you hurt me."

"So we're not talking marriage here."

She shrugged. "We can marry. If you wish. But I would like a child in any case. You seem to do that well."

The room tilted. Lesko held fast to the chair. Through a soft mist, layers of gauze, he could see Elena rising toward him, eyes moist, lips tight as if she were trying not to let him see her laugh, guiding him back to his chair. Now she was kneeling, her good arm resting on his thigh. She was talking to him. He heard only fragments. Like *Poor Lesko.* And from time to time she would grin broadly as if recalling something funny. *I know how this must seem to you. To me as well. I had no idea that I would say such things.*

Here was this woman who, two years ago, had calmly tried to bargain for her life and now, in this dream, she was back and she wanted him to take her home and give her babies—*Poor Lesko*—which meant that she would actually have to be in bed with him, not make-believe like in the other dream, and he would have to try not to roll over and crush her some night like he heard pigs do with their young. *It is not a requirement.* She's still on babies. *Perhaps it is foolish.* Then about how she's forty-six years old but other women that age have had healthy . . . *but your wishes must be considered as well* . . . and he had time to shower and take a nap before lunch and then they could discuss these matters with clearer heads . . . *I will ask Uncle Urs to dinner. He wants so much to meet you.*

Lesko barely heard. This could not be happening. His fingers traced lightly over the back of her hand as if to see if she were real. They floated up against her cheek with a will of their own and they felt the texture of her hair. It was shorter now. And lighter. Kind of halfway blond. It was like that last time, too, he remembered dimly. Maybe he should say he likes it.

The fingers moved on. They brushed downward near her lips, which turned, and, with a soft kiss, welcomed them. They moved on to her shoulder, the injured one, barely touching it, his brain playing a scene in which men were shooting at her and he saw himself plunging toward them, he heard his own voice in a bellow of rage and his hands were seizing them, tearing away their weapons, snapping the bones of their arms and hearing their shrieks. But another hand was there now, taking his, gently, guiding it once more to her lips and then downward against her breast where it could feel the beating of her heart.

Somehow, he had slid from his chair. His body, sapped of strength or will, had melted to the floor beside her. It enveloped her. His hands, searching for a way to hold her that would cause no pain, touched her in places, a hip, a thigh, that should have been forbidden to them. *Such a rough man, Lesko . . . Such a gentle man.* They found the firm flesh of her back and they made it shudder. Her face turned upward toward his. He saw that tears had welled in her eyes and were spilling to the corners of her mouth. He asked what's wrong, he thought. Was he hurting her? Perhaps he didn't ask. There was no answer save the light of a hundred diamonds dancing in her eyes and on her cheeks. He saw in those eyes . . . he didn't know what. So many different emotions, each coming fast on the other. Another man might have taken them together and called them love but Lesko could not. To be loved, a man like himself, by a woman such as this, it was not possible. Affection, perhaps. Born of gratitude, or need. And the tears were more likely born of relief, purging her soul of a spell she had somehow cast on herself, washing away the torrent of unwanted emotions with which it had betrayed her for so long.

Lesko could not articulate such thoughts. He could only feel them. He could only let them settle in his own heart and simmer there until his brain and his instincts began to function once more and remind him that this was ridiculous. It could not work. Not for long. Perhaps for a year. Perhaps only a month. It might not even last the night.

But here it was. For whatever reason. And better than any dream.

And he would take it.

Late afternoon. Westport.

"Molly"—Susan leaned across Paul's regular table at Mario's; her voice was low but firm—"I want to know what's happening here."

She had told her of the calls from Roger Clew. Of her attempts to locate Paul and her father. Of her knowledge that at least two of the others, probably more, had suddenly left Westport and were almost certainly en route to Europe.

Paul's friend, her friend, had listened attentively, showing no sign of alarm. But Susan saw a light in her eyes, which she had not seen before. Molly reached for her hand and squeezed it.

"As for your father," she answered, not hesitating at all, "you're right. He's gone to sort himself out with Elena once and for all. He's in no danger."

"But Paul is?"

She waved the question to one side. "As for Roger Clew, you're sure he said that? That he'd send people into Westport?"

"It's still on the machine," Susan told her. "Go listen for yourself."

"Give me a second."

Molly walked from the table to the bar where she reached for a phone and tapped out two different series of numbers with a pause in between. She listened without speaking. Susan realized that she'd memorized Paul's remote access number and was now listening to the voice of Roger Clew. Molly met Susan's gaze and gave her a nod of acknowledgment. She broke the connection, held up one finger, then dialed another number. Susan watched her lips. They pronounced the name of Anton Zivic, then waited.

Now she was speaking to him. Susan could not hear but she could pick out other names. *Roger,* spoken with a frown. *Paul,* spoken with . . . at least not with concern. Even a smile here and there. Then her own name. Molly was looking at her. Her eyes, thought Susan, kept flicking down to her purse, which sat on the table at her elbow. Molly was listening, nodding, and agreeing. She replaced the phone and stepped from behind the bar.

"That was Anton?" Susan asked, more an observation than a question.

"Yes. And I called Paul's machine."

"I saw. Are you going to tell me?"

"About Paul? You know I can't. If it helps, even our own people don't know where he is. Just Anton and myself because we need to."

"Can you tell me if he's in danger?"

Molly seemed as if she were going to say one thing but chose another. "No more than usual," she said.

"You were about to say something else."

Molly brushed her hair from one cheek. "I was about to lecture you."

"I know," she nodded. "Get used to it, Susan. If you can't stand the heat, go find yourself a yuppie."

"Not exactly," Molly smiled, "but close enough." She gestured with her thumb toward Susan's purse. "What's the gun for?"

"How did you know?"

Molly didn't answer. Susan turned her head toward Mario's single front door. Metal detectors, she assumed. Now she understood why several heads had snapped up when she entered. And why one of the ceiling lights had suddenly begun to blink. She could probably make that happen all over Westport.

"Susan," Molly repeated. "Why the gun?"

"Just trying to fit in."

"Do you know how to use it?"

"I asked Paul to teach me. He said he's not very good. Is that true?"

Another smile. A rocking motion of the hand. Molly

chose not to elaborate. "Challenge Paul to a contest shooting at tin cans," she might have said, "and you might very well beat him. Come at him with a gun, let him see you coming or miss with your first shot, and he will surely kill you."

"Please don't carry that," she dropped her voice, "anywhere in Westport until I tell you that all of us know you by sight. And until then, never, ever, reach into your purse while there's a weapon in it."

"Especially if I see a blinking light?"

Molly hesitated, then grinned approvingly. "Especially then. Yes." She tapped the table to signal a change of subject. "I hope you trust me," she said, "because I'm about to ask you to do something. You can't say no."

"Give you the gun?"

She shook her head. "Fly to Zürich. This evening. You'll have your travel documents within the hour. Travel light. Join your father at Elena's house. Stay there until Paul contacts you."

Susan frowned. "This is about Roger Clew?"

"Yes."

"Getting little Susan out of the way in case there's trouble?" She straightened. "I'd rather stay and help. Sooner or later, you're going to have to find out what I'm made of."

"What you're made of"—Molly put a hand on her arm—"is old Raymond 'the Terrible.'" She meant it as a compliment. "But we're not staying either, exactly. We'll have faded away by the time you board your flight. There will be nobody for Roger Clew to find. We don't want him finding you."

"That's all you'll do? Just run?"

"I didn't say that."

"Then what happens when he gets here and finds nobody home?"

"We'll have found him," she said.

— 22 —

Urs Brugg could not help himself. He was staring at Lesko. Less blatantly, he hoped, than young Willem had. And without tittering, certainly, as had three more of his nephews plus two of their wives who had insisted on escorting him the short distance between his own home and Elena's. Add to these his driver and his bodyguard who also wanted see this man. In all, his escort was redundant by a factor of eight.

But he could not blame them. Their curiosity was no greater than his own. And the cousins and their wives had stayed only long enough to be introduced to the notorious Lesko.

Raymond 'the Terrible' Lesko.

Lesko, the lumbering American giant had managed to turn the formidable Elena Brugg into a schoolgirl romantic.

There was Elena. Alternately blushing and blathering. Confusing the names of her cousins. Dropping things in her kitchen from which she flitted back and forth assessing the progress of the meal she had insisted on helping to prepare. Trying to serve aperitifs with one weakened arm, spilling much of what she poured. Lesko rushing to assist. Spilling even more. Elena giggling. Who, Urs Brugg wondered, had ever heard Elena giggle?

But now, alone at last. The relatives were gone. His bodyguard and driver had joined Elena's outside the gate. The only remaining upheaval, thought Urs Brugg, would be Elena's cook expelling her bodily from the kitchen if she did not promise to calm herself, leave the lids of pots alone, and keep her hands off the china, which had begun the day as a service for twelve but could now fully accommodate only ten.

Lesko sat before him. Stiffly. Hors d'oeuvres—an assortment of cheeses and meats—sat untouched on a tray before him. Twice, Urs Brugg had seen him reach, only to withdraw his hand, lest, thought Brugg, he partake of it incorrectly. Urs Brugg wheeled closer and helped himself, using his fingers. Lesko watched, gratefully, then did the same.

"I have looked forward to this meeting," said Urs Brugg pleasantly. "Although I confess I did not foresee this circumstance."

"I sure as h—" Lesko stopped himself. "I didn't either."

The older man glanced in the direction of the kitchen. "I have never seen Elena like this. It is a remarkable change."

Lesko could only nod. He had never seen anyone like this. Not toward him. Not even his ex-wife. Fussing over him. Flattering him. Touching him every time he came within reach. All defenses down. The gates wide open.

"There is something within her . . . some need"—Urs Brugg seemed to be struggling with this—"that could be fulfilled only by you. I have known this for some time. Perhaps I understand it. Perhaps I do not. I am delighted, of course, to see her so happy, but—"

"You don't want to see her get hurt."

"Just so, yes."

"I couldn't hurt her. Not ever."

Urs Brugg raised his glass, saluting Lesko with it. He sipped. He seemed relieved that this one subject, at least, had been successfully raised and disposed of.

Lesko was no less relieved. A part of him would have bet his pension that Urs Brugg's first words to him would have ranged somewhere between "How much will you take to get out of the country and never come back?" and "Where do you get off, you mountain of shit, thinking you belong in the same world with her, let alone the same bed?"

"May I speak frankly, Mr. Lesko? Man to man?"

Lesko nodded. *Here it comes,* he thought.

Urs Brugg squirmed in his seat. "It is a subject best brought up by her mother or father. It seems I will have to do in their place."

Lesko stared blankly.

"Would it surprise you to know," Urs Brugg asked, choosing his words carefully, "that Elena has had very little experience of an intimate nature?"

What the hell is this? he wondered. His cheeks became warm. "I—ah—never thought about that, exactly," he answered. "But I guess it would, yes."

"It is not so hard to understand. To love, and to be loved unselfishly in return, is a rare thing for a woman of wealth and power."

"I guess." He was about to say that he'd never thought about that either. But he had. He'd imagined her with millionaires, big-shot politicians, society guys. Not just in her past. In her future as well. He imagined them laughing at him.

"The first casualty of wealth, Mr. Lesko, and certainly of power, is trust in the motives of one's friends."

Lesko darkened, this time in anger. "She has nothing I want," he said quietly. "Neither do you."

Urs Brugg raised his hands. "I did not mean you. If I know nothing else about you, Mr. Lesko, I know that. In my clumsy way, I was leading up to what you have that Elena wants."

"Which is zero. Or close to it."

Urs Brugg sat back, frowning. "Is it possible, Mr. Lesko," he asked, "that you do indeed have such a low opinion of yourself?"

"Not in most ways. No."

"But in terms of what Elena sees in you—the answer is yes?"

Lesko hesitated. Then he nodded.

"You place no value on courage? Loyalty? Strength of character?"

"In a friend? I place a lot of value. But this isn't about friendship. This is about taking care of somebody who's used to more than I can give her."

"What she is used to," Urs Brugg corrected him, "is loneliness. What she is used to is having no man, other than family, of whom she can be proud."

"You're saying you approve of this?"

"With reservations, to be sure. But yes." Once more, Urs Brugg glanced in the direction of the kitchen. He moved his chair closer. "Will you listen to a proposition, Mr. Lesko?"

"I won't take your money."

Brugg's expression hardened. "I am not about to bribe you. Do not insult me."

"Then I'm sorry. Go ahead."

"Will you take me at my word that I would have made this offer regardless of what has happened today between yourself and Elena? And that the offer will stand regardless of what happens in the future?"

"Okay. Yes."

Urs Brugg lowered his eyes. He fingered the armrest of his wheelchair as he considered the best way to begin. "Behind the main railroad station—you were there this morning—there is a park called the Platzspitz. Did you happen to see it?"

Lesko shook his head.

"That park, sad to say, is Zürich's drug bazaar. Heroin and cocaine are sold openly under the supervision of the Swiss health authorities. They provide clean tablespoons for the heating of drug solutions and they dispense some six thousand clean syringes every day. The intent is to help control the spread of AIDS."

Lesko said nothing.

"Six thousand syringes," Urs Brugg repeated, "for the nearly twenty thousand addicts who infest this city. Do these numbers not startle you, Mr. Lesko?"

"Not especially." He could name New York *neighborhoods* that had twice that many. As for controlling AIDS among junkies, his attitude would basically be why screw up a good thing if only the junkies kept it in the family. And the subject of drugs, he found, depressed him. Somehow he had gotten it into his head that the Swiss were basically too smart for that shit. "This Platzspitz," he asked, "your Swiss cops don't bother it?"

"Their position is that they would prefer not to waste their energies going after the ordinary drug user. They want the dealers. In the meantime, Switzerland is very likely to become the first European nation to decriminalize the use and possession of small amounts of narcotics."

Lesko sniffed. *That's got to be great for tourism,* he thought. *Half the junkies in Europe will be here within a week.*

Brugg raised a hand to signal the interjection of another thought. "I am an—admirer—of your friend, Mr. Bannerman."

Lesko had been waiting to get to that subject. Like, where is he? But he did not interrupt.

"Zürich is to me," Urs Brugg lowered his voice, "what Westport is to Paul Bannerman. I flatter myself that what he is to Westport, I am, in some measure, to Zürich."

Lesko waited.

"You have seen what has happened to New York. It is a rotting, angry place where the rich live in bunkers and all others live in fear. It is drugs that have done this. In a few years, if nothing is done, every city in Europe will have followed that path."

Lesko realized that. He knew the figures. They said that seventy tons of cocaine, just cocaine, were shipped into Europe last year. Up from fifty tons the year before. Most of it coming in through Spain. The Colombians had turned their attention to Europe because that's where the money is. A kilo of cocaine goes for three or four times as much in Europe as it does in New York.

But the real problem is what happens when supply outpaces demand and those prices drop. In the last two years they'd gone from about $55 thousand per kilo to between $25 and $30. When it gets down to the $8 to $13 range, as it has in New York, it's cheap enough to be worth turning into crack. And crack is a disaster. Eighty percent addictive compared to only 10 or 15 percent for cocaine in powder form. And addiction comes not in months or years but in days. Creating thousands of new street criminals every year in every city. It was going to happen. Nothing could stop it. Zürich had maybe five . . . six years before it was just as unlivable as New York.

"And you want to save Europe?" Lesko asked, without sarcasm.

"Not Europe. Only Zürich. My home."

"You and who else?"

"My family. A few friends. You, perhaps."

"What about your cops?"

"Some of them as well. A select few."

"What do you think I can do for you, exactly?"

"Teach us how to hurt them. These are the same people who destroyed New York. You know them. How they operate. How they think. I wish to retain your services, Mr. Lesko. What I ask is not so far removed from your present position. You are, I understand, a security consultant for the Beckwith Hotel chain in New York."

"What the Beckwith chain hired," Lesko pointed out, "was a retired cop who knows about sneak thieves and hookers. They don't want anybody hurt. I think you do."

"If that's what is needed, yes."

Lesko shook his head. "You don't want me. I'm not a killer. For that, you want Bannerman."

"I am aware of the difference between you and Mr. Bannerman, although I think it is not so great as you choose to believe."

"Then why did you tell him and not me about those three who shot Elena?"

"For her sake. For your safety."

"She's your niece, not his. The driver was your nephew, not his. Why did you send Bannerman?"

"One does not *send* Mama's Boy. But I knew he would go. Dr. Russo was his friend, not mine."

"So why wouldn't you ask him to do this other thing? Cleaning up Zürich. For that matter, why wouldn't you ask Elena? She knows how they work better than I do."

Urs Brugg ignored the question about Elena. "Because Paul Bannerman, by all accounts, is in no way sympathetic to the plight of the cities. His feeling is that any populace that has a drug problem has probably deserved it. He may have a point."

"I might even agree with him."

The real problem, Lesko had long since concluded, was not with the suppliers. It was with the public. Try lighting up a cigarette in a public place these days and people will give you all kinds of crap. Light up a joint at a party and these same people won't say a word. The cabdriver who won't let you smoke in his taxi will take you to a street corner where you can buy crack. The disco that's plastered with no-smoking signs has washrooms that are fucking supermarkets for cocaine and amphetamines.

Lesko had no patience at all with militant antismokers. He saw them as bullies. And gutless. They were the kind who only took up negative causes. Nice, safe causes. And only when they were in a nice, safe majority: "I don't do this, so you shouldn't either. And while we're at it, let's take *Playboy* magazine, which I don't read either, off the stands."

Take all that energy, all that bitching over some poor stiff who wants a cigarette with his coffee and turn it against the people who use recreational drugs, and at the very least you'll see the occasional user staying away from drugs because they're no longer worth the aggravation.

Look at Japan. Hardly any problem there with drugs. You know why? Two reasons. Get caught using them and you go to jail. Read up on Japanese prisons and you'll see why nobody wants to go there. Your cell has a cot and a toilet and that's it. No TV, no centerfolds on the wall, no nothing. Also no noise. No talking. Silence strictly enforced. If you happen to know another convict there, you never get near him. Make a new friend and you get separated. Compare that to Attica or Sing Sing where getting a sentence of three to five really means you spend eight months or so visiting with your old friends from the neighborhood until you're all back on the street. But Japan's jails are not even the biggest reason why they don't have a drug problem. The biggest is the Japs themselves. They won't tolerate drug use. They think it's not just illegal, it's wrong and it's stupid. Try snorting a line in front of a Japanese. You'll get your face slapped and then knocked on your ass and you'll sit there until the meat wagon comes to haul you away. Americans won't do that. They're afraid they'll get sued, which they might. They're afraid the cop who comes to get the user will also bust them for assault, which he might. So nobody sticks his neck out. Instead they yell at smokers.

"Mr. Lesko?"

"Hmm?" His mind had wandered.

"I have set aside a rather large sum of money. If you will help me in this, it is yours to draw on as you see fit. If you will not, I will proceed without you."

"I asked if you talked to Elena. You didn't answer."

"The fact is"—another glance toward the kitchen—"this was her idea."

"What was?" Lesko asked. "Hammering your local drug dealers or getting me involved?"

"Both."

"If that's true, why do you keep looking to see if she's listening?"

"Because she might have changed her mind. Her desire to follow Mr. Bannerman's Westport example is just as strong as mine. That much will surely remain. Her suggestion that I recruit you, while sensible enough in itself, may have been rooted in a desire to lure you back to Zürich. But now, you see, you've come of your own accord. I think she will now ask that I not involve you, just as she asked that I not tell you where those assassins can be found."

"Wait a second." Lesko raised a hand. "Let's take that piece by piece. You're telling me that Elena's in this Zürich thing no matter what?"

"Unless you dissuade her. My hope is that you will join her."

Brugg watched Lesko carefully, assessing his reaction to this last. He saw surprise. Some vexation. A modicum of disappointment. For the past several hours, Lesko had no doubt been thinking of Elena in terms of domesticity. Walks in the park. Introducing her to his friends. But Elena, although she certainly had changed in many ways, was still Elena. A strong woman. Tough-minded. Ruthless when she had to be. As she herself admitted, she had not yet attained sainthood. He continued to watch Lesko. Now a new reaction appeared. The beginnings of a smile. It confused Urs

Brugg at first. But then he knew, even before Lesko spoke, what he was feeling.

"She's really something, isn't she?" Lesko mused, the smile widening.

It was pride.

—23—

Bannerman's connecting flight, Lisbon to Malaga, landed shortly after ten that evening. The night sky was clear, the moon full and so bright that Bannerman had been able to make out the silvery wakes of cargo ships sailing the Mediterranean. Even, in the distance, the lights of the African coast.

From the airport at Malaga, where Bannerman rented a large and powerful BMW, he and Billy proceeded to the old Cádiz road, traveling west in the direction of Marbella.

Bannerman knew the way. He'd taken this road several times during his years in Europe. When first he saw it, not long after his mother's death, it was only two lanes wide. It followed the coastline, never more than a quarter mile from the sea. Modern hotels had just begun to appear. High-rises were few. The countryside, in large measure, still clung to its Andalusian character although it was clear that it would be a losing battle.

Now the road, four lanes in places, being widened to six in others, passed an almost unbroken chain of beachfront hotels and apartments from Torremolinos to Fuengirola. Bannerman hated to see that. Miami Beach on steroids.

Crowded April through September with overweight German tourists and hopeful American secretaries.

Marbella, some thirty kilometers farther to the west and, its offspring, the marina at Puerto Banus, looked into its own future and enacted laws limiting the erection of high-rises before more damage could be done. The result was that those places now expanded horizontally rather than vertically. The hills, once cooled by forests of pine and ash, were now covered with whitewashed condominiums. Half as many more were under construction. The architectural styles were only vaguely Spanish or Moorish. The place had little to do with Spain or with its culture. It had to do with money.

Drug money, certainly. Arms dealer money. Oil money. King Fahd of Saudi Arabia had built a walled palace there. Even a mosque. The streets, in season, were filled with Bentleys and Rolls-Royces. Swarthy little men from Lebanon and Kuwait walked with tall fashion models who spoke French or with prostitutes who spoke with British accents. Smug, uncouth-looking Americans, dressed by Benetton and Gucci, Rolex watches on their wrists, brittle hard-eyed women on their arms, strutted along the breakwater or held court in one of its open-faced restaurants. Many came by yacht, some nearly the size of destroyers, some nearly as well armed.

But Marbella was not now in season. There would be no throngs of tourists, no noise, no confusion. In one sense, thought Bannerman, that was good. In another, it was not. He would have preferred a crowd. Traffic jams. Even more, he would have preferred a different place. A large city. Marbella was too much like Klosters in that it had only one road leading in or out, the coast road to Cádiz, plus a second that ran north into the mountains and was, therefore, of no value. There was no airstrip. Escape by sea was a possibility. A night run by fast boat down the coast, then across the Straits of Gibraltar to Morocco. That would, Bannerman guessed, be among the choices that John Waldo was exploring. But if all went well, there would be no need to escape or hide. He and Billy would leave as they came, leaving a trail no one could miss.

To that end, he had reserved a suite at the Puente Ro-

mano, one of the more visible of Marbella's hotels. Its
grounds, stretching from the main road to the water's edge,
were laid out as a miniature village, lushly landscaped with
tropical plantings, waterfalls, and running pools. Its centerpiece was an old Roman bridge from which it took its name.
Billy was less than comfortable with Bannerman's choice.
Left to himself, he would have broken into a vacant house
or even slept in his car for the sake of anonymity. But anonymity, Bannerman reminded him, was not the point this
time. And if they were going to draw attention at all, it was
better to know that now.

He had signaled a left turn, the Puente Romano just
ahead. In the lights of the lobby entrance he could see the
hotel's airport shuttle bus, recently arrived, unloading passengers and baggage. Beyond it were two cars, their trunks
open. A small knot of people, four men and a woman, stood
exchanging greetings. Bannerman hesitated. Billy tapped his
arm.

"How about we drive a little more," he said.

Bannerman nodded. He flipped off the signal.

"Up ahead"—Billy had his finger on a map—"take the
next right."

"The house?" The address Urs Brugg had given.

"Yeah. Let's just see."

He continued on, no more than a hundred yards, then
turned. The car began climbing a shallow grade lined on
either side with small white villas, modest by the standards
of Marbella. Most were vacation or retirement homes,
owned largely by British pensioners, built when land was
cheap. All but a few were shuttered for the winter season
although the temperature, even now, was well into the sev-
enties and flowers bloomed everywhere. Every villa seemed
to have a swimming pool. Some were covered with tarpau-
lins, others reflected the stars.

"Up to your left," Billy said. "I think that's them."

Bannerman saw. A two-story house. A terrace of wrought
iron running the width of the upper floor. Two figures on it,
clearly visible by moonlight. One of them, a man, light hair,
was seated. The other, a woman, stood close to the railing.
A pair of binoculars hung from her neck. Bannerman main-
tained his speed. The hill climbed more sharply here, then

curved to the left. He saw their car. It was a van, a camper, parked facing out, garage door open. More wrought iron covered every window.

"Is there another way down?" he asked.

Billy shook his head. "It dead ends against the mountain." He pointed. "See that house that's lit up? Stop there, I'll climb in the back."

Bannerman understood. Make it look as if he's giving someone a ride home. No good stopping at a darkened house. Anyone watching from the house down below would wonder why no lights went on.

He stopped. Billy struggled into the backseat. Once there, he opened the rear door and slammed it shut. One person, one door slam. He squeezed down into the well.

"What's it look like from here?" Billy asked.

"The approach from the north isn't bad. Reasonable cover. Not good at all from the south. That house has a clear view of the entire road and a quarter mile of the coast road in each direction. Also the main entrance of the Puente Romano."

Bannerman passed the house a second time, now to his right. From the corner of his eye he could see that the man had moved. He was standing now, arms raised, elbows out. Bannerman knew that he had taken the binoculars from the woman. Bannerman kept his eyes on the road. He passed two more houses, both shuttered, swimming pools in back, one of them surrounded by a six-foot hedge, which gave it a measure of privacy, but the pool itself sat in full view of that terrace.

Bannerman reached the stop sign at the coast road. Billy stayed low. "Don't go to the hotel yet," he said.

"I'm not." He swung the BMW to the right, heading in the direction of Puerto Banus. "Billy? What do you think?"

"Something's funny here."

"Can you say what? Other than that bunch at the Puente Romano?" He knew why Billy had stopped him from turning in. And why he himself had hesitated. Too many for February. Especially arriving all at once, late at night, on a Monday.

"I knew one of those guys. Way back, he did a couple of

jobs for your mother. Guy he was shaking hands with, I think I know him, too."

Bannerman chewed his lip. "And suddenly they're here in Marbella. Off-season."

"Yeah."

"You don't suppose they could be here for us?"

"Wide open like that? Besides, they'd never take a contract on Mama's Boy."

"Then why else are they here?"

"I don't know. We could ask."

"First let's see who else is in town."

A part of Lesko wished that Urs Brugg's proposition had never been made. All he wanted to do was be with Elena, get to know her, see if they really had a chance. Zürich was Zürich's problem.

Elena, the way she talked, was ready to walk away from it. Go to New York with him. But he knew that wouldn't last. Home is home. Blood is blood.

Then there was the question of money. Elena said she'd leave hers behind, live on his income. When she said it, she meant it. She'd give it a decent shot. But that wouldn't last either. Picture Elena standing in a supermarket line in Queens, or waiting at a Laundromat or sharing a pizza in front of the television set.

Her uncle, Lesko realized, couldn't picture it either. But he swore, and Lesko wanted to believe him, that he would have made this offer no matter what. He was also talking serious bucks: $1,000 a day plus expenses, a car and driver, and a minimum six-month commitment. After that, Lesko could sign a longer term contract or he could pick up his marbles.

The amount staggered Lesko. In six months he'd make more than he'd get from the Beckwith Hotels in six years. And Urs Brugg, once again, took pains to assure him that this was no gift. A thousand a day, he said, was actually close to the average for a consultancy. Less than the retainer he paid his lawyer. But a good deal more satisfying.

It would mean spending much of his time in Zürich. And elsewhere in Europe. He was quickly becoming more comfortable here. In two trips, so far, he'd hardly run into anyone who didn't speak English, drink Cokes, or eat at MacDonald's. It would mean being with Elena in her own world, buying a little more time against the day when she looked around her and looked at him and wondered what the hell she was doing.

Why not, he thought? In for a penny, in for a pound. But first—

"Let's talk about Spain," Lesko said.

Urs Brugg raised one eyebrow. "Elena told you?"

"More or less. Those shooters. Where are they, exactly?"

"That situation is in good hands, Mr. Lesko."

"I want it in my hands. Bannerman wouldn't tell me because he said I had no stake. When he said it, maybe he was right. He isn't now."

"Trust me on this. You can only interfere."

"You want me to do that other thing because it's important to you. This is important to me."

"The Zürich situation falls within your area of expertise," Urs Brugg said quietly, firmly. "The Spanish situation falls within Mr. Bannerman's. What would you do there? Give those murderers a good thrashing? I suspect that Mr. Bannerman has something more in mind."

"As it happens, so do I."

"What you have in mind is avenging Elena's pain. It is personal with you. It is not personal with me, or with Mr. Bannerman, or, in fact, with Elena."

Lesko blinked. "Bannerman's going to kill them but we shouldn't think there are any hard feelings?"

Urs Brugg had to smile. American humor. Good. He will make Elena laugh

"It is a question, not of vengeance," he explained, "but of credibility. Normally, neither Bannerman nor myself would feel the need to track down a mere hireling. But once it became known that we had their names and knew where they could be found, we were left with no choice. Inaction would be perceived as weakness. A demonstration became necessary."

Lesko had heard Bannerman say that. Don't bother with shooters. Dime a dozen. Go for whoever hands out the dimes. But Lesko did not share that view. You don't let

killers walk. Even when it's not personal. Which this is.
Wait a second—

"Two questions." He leaned forward. "This job you want
me to do in Zürich. If I'm working for you, and if inaction is
weakness, what about my own credibility?"

"My credibility is yours. It will not be a problem. But the
simple truth is that I do not want you risking your life, at
this point, for so little purpose." He gestured toward the
kitchen. "I would never hear the end of it."

"Second question," Lesko said. "Those three names and
their address. Bannerman didn't have them. You gave them
to him. Why didn't you just take care of this yourself?"

Something happened in the older man's eyes. A hesitation. His lips had begun to move, as if searching for a plausi-
ble reply, when the telephone chirped. He made no move to
answer it but he seemed relieved by the distraction of the
sound. The chirping ended abruptly. It was picked up elsewhere.

Lesko saw the reaction. It surprised him. He hadn't
thought it was that big deal of a question. He decided to
press a little.

"It's not just because Bannerman's a pro," Lesko said.
"You can hire all the shooters you need. That's not counting
all your various nephews who carry Uzis under their raincoats. Why drag Bannerman all the way over to Spain?"

"He has, in your phrase, a stake in this. He lost one of his
own."

"So? You could have done him a favor. What are friends
for, right?"

There was no answer. Just a sucking in of breath and the
beginnings of a glare. The strained patience of a rich and
powerful man who was not accustomed to having his actions challenged. But those eyes. Lesko knew he had something. He did not know what. He could not back off.

"By any chance," Lesko asked quietly, "could Bannerman be walking into something he doesn't know about?"

"Such as what?" Brugg frowned, now annoyed. "A trap,
Mr. Lesko?"

"Such as. Yeah."

Another breath. "I value Mr. Bannerman more than you
know. I also like the man. The answer is no."

"What was the word you used? A *demonstration*. For whose benefit?"

A knock at the door. Lesko heard it open behind him. He kept his attention on Elena's uncle.

"That telephone call"—Elena's voice—"it was Mr. Anton Zivic."

Zivic. Westport. Susan. Lesko felt a chill. He rose, turning. But he saw no alarm in her expression. "Everything's okay there?"

An uncertain shake of her head. "Mr. Zivic said that there might be certain difficulties in Westport. Nothing serious, but he felt that it would be best to remove Susan. He took the liberty of sending her here, to this house. She is en route now. She will arrive in the morning. I told him that she is most welcome."

"What difficulties?" Lesko asked.

"He did not elaborate. You just came from there. You have no idea?"

Lesko shook his head. Unless it was that crap about the car bombs. Maybe Hector Manley's posse came looking for him. He doubted it. No use mentioning it.

"It is good she's coming." Elena smiled. "I have much to learn from her about her father."

"Sure. Get acquainted." He shuffled his feet. "That would be nice."

"Well." She shrugged, beaming at him, her expression untroubled, content. "Are you two enjoying your chat?"

"Very much," Lesko answered. He turned toward Urs Brugg. He was the kindly uncle again. Smiling affectionately, nodding.

"Dinner is in five minutes," she said. With a wave of her fingers, a last glance at Lesko, she stepped from the room.

Urs Brugg watched her go. "Your daughter," he said. "I look forward to meeting her as well."

Lesko gave him a look. Not unpleasant. Simply to let him know that Lesko knew that he was seizing on a convenient change of subject. "This thing in Spain," he said, "we don't want to talk about that at dinner, do we?"

"For Elena's sake, no."

"I'm going down there. First thing tomorrow. I'm not

going to wait for Bannerman to call. I want you to help me do it, and I want a gun."

A weary sigh. "For what purpose, Mr. Lesko?"

"I want to believe you're being straight with me," Lesko told him, "so I will. Maybe I even like that son of a bitch too. For *Susan's* sake, I'm going to keep an eye on him."

"He does not need you, Mr. Lesko. Truly, he does not."

"So he keeps telling me." Lesko looked at his watch. "Two minutes until dinner, Mr. Brugg."

—24—

The BMW covered the distance, Marbella to Puerto Banus, in less than five minutes. Bannerman kept one eye on his rearview mirror. There were two cars well behind him. When he turned off the Cádiz road, both kept going. He shut off his lights and watched them. One sped on. The other was slowing. It made a U-turn. He continued forward.

The town, if it could be called that, was little more than a warren of buildings, all housing shops and restaurants, that stretched in a wide arc around the harbor. Access to the waterfront by automobile required a pass, available only to those who had boats there. He would need to park the car outside, leaving it unattended. Ahead of him, near one of the pedestrian passages to the waterfront, he saw the lights of a discotheque. A dozen or so young people lounged on the sidewalk outside. He stopped near the disco. Billy got out and promptly vanished into the passage. Bannerman approached two teenage girls. They were chatting idly, sharing a cigarette. Tearing a $100 bill in half, he asked that they finish their conversation in the backseat of the BMW, watching it for him. He offered one of the halves. They would get the other when he returned. They looked at him, not quite masking that special contempt in which young Europeans hold the indecently rich. They took it nonetheless.

He entered the warren. There was no direct route, he knew, to the marina. One had to climb up and down steps, pass through tunnels, make several turns along the narrow streets. He proceeded, his pace casual.

Part way in, he passed a darkened service alley, sensing a shape there which he presumed to be Billy. He walked on, never glancing behind him. Soon, the masts of yachts came into view. He reached the waterfront. It resembled a boardwalk, except that it was concrete, lined with open air restaurants. He approached the best known of these, Don Leone. It was nearly empty. Only one young couple in T-shirts bearing the name of their boat. The woman held a sleeping infant. Bannerman chose a table nearest the water and asked for a wine list.

He had made his selection by the time Billy appeared. Billy took a seat, saying nothing. He appeared puzzled.

"What is it?" Bannerman asked.

Billy hesitated. "You remember Kurt Weiss? Skinny guy? Used to race cars?"

Bannerman nodded. They'd used him on occasion, once for surveillance and twice as a driver. Bannerman had not seen him in five years. Last heard of, he was working for an arms dealer named Grassi. "You saw him?"

"I think so. I'm not sure."

"Tailing me?"

"No. But maybe some other guys were. I'm not sure about that either."

"What did you see?"

"A guy's walking along, same direction as you. You turn, he keeps going. But then another guy is walking along, same direction as you. You turn again, same thing happens."

Bannerman shrugged. "It might be nothing."

"Yeah, but if that was a tail, that many guys, add to them that car that turned around, it means they must have this place covered like a rug."

"KGB?"

Billy made a face. "Them we expected. This feels, I don't know, like something else."

A man strolled by. Abruptly, Billy turned in his chair, staring hard at him. The man never looked back. But his cheek was twitching under Billy's gaze. He walked on.

"There's another one," Billy said.

Bannerman had to agree. An innocent passerby would have glanced at Billy, if only involuntarily.

"You know what I think?" Billy leaned closer.

Bannerman waited.

"We should split an order of paella. You should eat some, get back in the car, and get out of Spain. You've been seen. You made your point. Leave me here, I'll hook up with Johnny Waldo, and we'll be in and out of that house before you're two hours away."

Bannerman shook his head. "I want you with me. Let's leave the plan as it is and see what develops."

"The plan," Billy argued, "was before we saw those two sitting out in the open like they didn't have a care in the world. They were even backlit, the way the moon bounced off the glass behind them.

That had surprised Bannerman as well. It bordered on suicidal. But even professionals relax at times. And it did not have the look of a baited trap. The bait would have been just as effective if they showed movement behind drawn blinds without the risk of being picked off from below. Glenn Cook, with a night scope, could have finished them with two bullets in as many seconds from the roof of the Puente Romano.

"I should have stayed up on that hill," Billy brooded. "I'd have left them in their chairs. By the time they started to stink we'd all be home in bed."

"Or you'd be dead. We didn't see the other shooter. He could have been covering us. And this whole thing could have been staged."

Billy waved for the waiter. "There's a lot of that going around lately, isn't there."

"It does seem that way."

"Now it's Urs Brugg?"

"I hope not. But maybe."

The waiter came. He took their order, nodding approvingly at Paul's choice of a fino to start and a vintage rioja with their paella. He returned with the sherry two minutes later.

"Señor Bannerman," he said as he set down one glass. "Señor McHugh," he said, as he set down the other.

Billy's eyes became hooded. Bannerman smiled an acknowledgment. The waiter seemed pleased with himself.

"It is my honor to tell you"—the waiter dropped his voice, his tone at once confidential and respectful—"that Señor Grassi sends his compliments and insists that your meal be charged to his account."

"That's very nice of him." Bannerman nodded politely. "Did he say, by chance, how we might return the favor?"

The waiter beamed. "He says that you must not hurry your meal, but, if you are so inclined, perhaps you might join him for a nightcap at his hotel."

"Which is, I take it, the Puente Romano?"

"In the bar, sir. Yes."

"We'll be delighted."

At the reception desk of the Puente Romano, Bannerman collected his room key and asked that their bags, his own and Billy's, be sent to their suite. The keys to the BMW had been left with the doorman. He would park it. Sometime before dawn, John Waldo would crawl beneath it. He would tape two automatic pistols to the forward edge of the gas tank. While there he would check for explosives and voice transmitters. He would open the trunk, let the air out of the spare tire, and place two more weapons plus extra clips inside it. Through the night, he would be somewhere nearby. Neither Bannerman nor Billy would ever see him. Nor would any man or woman who threatened their safety.

Three messages awaited him. The first, a reminder from Ronaldo Grassi. The second, *"Call Anton—clinic."* The third, a telex from Urs Brugg dated two hours earlier. It read, *Arriving tomorrow, noon latest, with Lesko. Could not be helped. Susan arriving Zürich same morning per Anton Zivic.*

Bannerman stared at this last. "You won't believe this," he muttered to Billy.

"You won't believe *this*," Billy answered, looking toward the bar. "I see Grassi. Also almost everyone else."

Bannerman turned toward the bar. The first thing he noticed was the crowd. Hard to see how many because the bar was nearly as tropically lush as the grounds outside. Every table seemed occupied. Many faces, all turning toward him. Some saluting as they caught his eye. Some holding thumbs up. He recognized nearly all of them. In the center, seated in a peacock rattan chair, was the arms dealer, Grassi, a beefy, coarse-looking man, gold ascot, blue blazer, hands raised as if he were about to applaud. He did applaud. The others joined him.

Billy shrugged. "You wanted to be seen? You're seen."

Bannerman, his expression glazed, moved toward the bar. Billy stayed at his shoulder, his own eyes dancing from table to table, reciting the names of men and women he recognized.

Bannerman listened, gathering himself. He knew all but a few of the faces, most of the names. For whatever reason, they had assembled here from all over Europe. A few Americans. Expatriates. Several Germans, French, and Danes. Two Israelis, both female, one of whom had been Molly Farrell's instructor in explosive techniques. They were, with a few exceptions, contract agents, working for one Western government or the other, usually for several, occasionally for a Warsaw Pact country depending on the nature of the job. Among the exceptions were two Englishmen, formerly SAS commandos. Last he'd heard, they were bodyguards retained by the royal family. Good men. Dull job. Another exception was Grassi: Italian born and Brooklyn raised, he had moved back to Rome. A dealer. Weapons, spot market oil, laundered cash, possibly drugs although he denied it. Mob connected, but his own man. A high roller, lived well, also lived long because he was known to keep his word. Provided work, at one time or another, for half the people in the room. So had Bannerman.

Bannerman worked his way toward him, taking outstretched hands as he went, exchanging greetings. Only a few greeted Billy other than with silent nods. Most were afraid of him. Some had seen him work. The rest had heard the stories.

Seated at Grassi's table, following his progress, was Kurt Weiss. Billy had been right. He was probably Grassi's driver

now and one of his bodyguards. A second man, younger,
late twenties but almost totally bald, a neck wider than his
head, had not taken his eyes from Billy. In his expression
Bannerman saw . . . he was not sure. Interest, certainly.
No fear. A hint of envy. Perhaps a challenge. He made a
mental note to keep himself between them. All three rose to
their feet. Grassi made the introductions. The younger
man's name was Tucker. American. Southern accent. Another bodyguard. Surly. Said little. Bannerman asked Kurt
Weiss about his wife and son. They were well, living near
Salzburg. Weiss grinned broadly, flattered that Mama's Boy
remembered. Tucker all the while stared at Billy.

"Do you think, Mr. Grassi," Bannerman asked pleasantly, "that we might take a walk?"

The dealer beamed, pleased with himself. "*Mr.* Grassi,"
he repeated for the benefit of the man named Tucker. "Did I
tell you? Always polite. Always a class guy."

"And usually discreet," Bannerman added. "Can we talk,
please. Alone."

Grassi picked up a bottle of cognac and poured a waiting
glass for Bannerman, another for Billy. "Whatever you
like," he said, "but I don't know what I can tell you that
everyone here doesn't know already."

"Such as?"

"That you're here to pop those three turkeys up the hill.
We're all here to catch your act."

Billy groaned disgustedly. Bannerman took a seat. He
picked up his glass, swirling its contents as he scanned the
room. Grinning faces everywhere. A girl he'd known in college had once thrown a surprise birthday party for him. His
first and last. This made him think of it. All that was lacking
was a cake. He closed his eyes, rubbing them. "You're going
to help me to understand this, aren't you, Mr. Grassi."

He said it patiently, without menace. But he knew that
the answer would probably not come quickly. Grassi was
having too good a time, amused at his discomfort. He'd been
drinking, his face glowed from it, but he was not drunk.
Merely expansive. Bannerman, his eyes speaking for him,
told Grassi that he was less than pleased.

"Hey look," Grassi said, winding down, "I never saw

anything like this either. What's the harm if I enjoy it a little?"

"Well," Bannerman answered reasonably, "the word *un-confidential* comes to mind."

"Yeah, but you're among friends. You know who located those three, don't you? The KGB up in Bern."

"Leo Belkin. I know."

"That didn't make you wonder a little why they'd care? And whether they'd be down here waiting for you?"

"It did."

"So it figures you planned for it. Forget them. Except for Belkin, we told them to get lost."

"How did you come to be here?"

"Urs Brugg. We go back a ways. He called in a favor."

Bannerman waited.

"Belkin's a friend of his," Grassi explained. "He even offered to nail those three himself but Brugg didn't want to owe him that big a favor and, besides, he says he promised them to you because of Doc Russo."

He had not, but Bannerman nodded. "Go on."

"Anyway, friend or not, with the KGB you never know so Brugg asked me to keep an eye on things. Also to make sure the hitters stuck around until you got here."

"How did you do that?"

"Easy." A smug grin. "I hired them. Sent Kurt, here, over with some money. Told them to sit tight until I tell them what the job is."

Grassi reached inside his jacket. He produced a small stack of photographs, which he dealt out like playing cards in front of Bannerman, making three piles. He held up the last of these to show that it had information written on the back in longhand.

"News you can use," he said. "Background stuff. What jobs they did, references, how they like to work, how they're armed right now. Ask me, Reid scraped the bottom of the barrel for these three. Word is you iced him for it. Word is Molly Farrell rigged his phones."

Bannerman grunted. He leaned over the photographs.

"Lady from Mossad"—Grassi gestured with his thumb—"hasn't stopped bragging about her."

The photographs were recent. Marbella backgrounds. All

taken from a distance but with excellent detail. Two each were head and shoulder shots. One showed them all together, full length, walking up a dock from a large motor yacht that, Bannerman supposed, belonged to Grassi.

He was glad to have them. He'd had only physical descriptions and capsule profiles, third hand. But he did not linger over them. Better not to show that he was less than prepared. Enough that the descriptions were accurate. The Englishman, their leader, was one Martin Thomas Selly. Blond hair, worn long, combed back, receding chin, features vaguely aristocratic. Rejected by Sandhurst after psychological testing but claims to have graduated. Joined the South African Security Forces, deserted to avoid court martial on unspecified morals charges. The shorter man, Algerian, named Amal Hamsho, peasant face, crooked teeth, hooked nose, looked rather like one of the camels with which he was probably raised. The woman, Erna Katerina Dietz, born in Danzig but had a West German passport, bad skin, stretched tight, expressionless eyes dulled by drugs, a prostitute, $20 tops, probably how she met Amal. Altogether an unlikely trio. The Englishman must have scraped the barrel as well.

"Watch out for the Brit, by the way." Grassi pointed. "Kurt thinks he's nuts."

So is all this, thought Bannerman. Or is it?

"That explains you." Bannerman cocked his head toward the other tables. "Why is everyone else here?"

"Brugg suggested I call a few, mostly to keep the KGB honest, distract the Spanish cops, things like that. Kurt, here, gave me a list of people he thought you'd trust. What nobody figured on was that they'd each call three or four more. You were a popular guy, Paul."

"It is because," Kurt Weiss added, "he took care of his own." He smiled at Paul. "It's why, when you called, we always came. It's why we do not forget."

Tucker sniffed.

Weiss's smile faded. He looked at Grassi. Grassi only shrugged.

Bannerman remembered something about him. He liked to watch fights. He liked to stage them. There was something else Bannerman wondered about.

"Why the bodyguards, Mr. Grassi? Here of all places."

A look of innocence. "Kurt is my driver. Also my friend."

"I meant this one. The one with bad manners."

The younger man leaned toward him. "I've got a name," he said. "It's *Mr.* Tucker."

The nearest tables went quiet. Billy seemed to be dozing. Grassi put a hand on Tucker's arm.

"B. J. Tucker," he said to Bannerman. "Football player, Atlanta Falcons, two seasons, then he hit a coach. Philadelphia Eagles, two seasons, until he failed his third urine test. Then a felony warrant for beating up two cops who stopped his car. That was worth three to five. He jumped bail, blew the country, showed up in Rome a few weeks ago looking for work. You might call this a tryout."

Bannerman shook his head, but said nothing.

Grassi squeezed the arm, gesturing with his free hand toward the bar in general. "This is your competition," he said to Tucker. "What do you think?"

Tucker sneered. "Old men. Women. Couple of faggots. Has-beens. I could pick tougher people out of any truck stop in Georgia." He raised his chin toward Billy. "This is the one who's such a bad ass? He can't even stay awake."

Bannerman leaned closer to Ronny Grassi. "Don't do this," he said quietly. He pushed back his chair, not bothering to pick up the photographs. "Anyway, it's late and there are a few more people here I'd like to say hello to."

"Wait a second." Tucker straightened. "Don't do what?"

Bannerman looked at him. "You think he's testing you. He's not. He already knows that you're mean, that you're a bully, and that you're stupid. What he's doing is getting rid of you." He turned to Grassi. "Is that about right?"

Grassi tossed his head. "I wasn't sure about stupid."

Tucker froze, turning crimson. His eyes flicked between Bannerman and Grassi as if deciding which one to hit first. He lunged at both, one hand seizing Grassi's ascot, the other aimed at Bannerman's necktie. Bannerman slipped it, then shoved the outstretched arm toward Billy who was already rising, fully alert, no expression, eyes dead. Billy caught the hand in flight. He snapped the thumb. Tucker squealed.

Billy released him. He sat back down. Bannerman made two quick signals. In response, several figures moved at once to the lobby entrance, sealing it with their bodies. Others gathered around waiters and bartenders, turning them, blocking their view.

Clutching his hand, gasping, Tucker stared at him, first in disbelief, then in rage. He exploded. Snarling, he whipped his forearm toward Bannerman's face. Again, Bannerman ducked, toppling backward over his chair and rolling into a crouch. Grassi had scrambled away. Billy remained seated, arms folded, within Tucker's reach. Tucker roared. He lunged again, grasping Billy's lapels, heaving him to his feet. He cocked a knee, aimed at Billy's crotch. It was never thrown. Just in time, he felt a hard coldness beneath his chin. A knife, a broken glass, he didn't know which. He'd seen nothing in Billy's hands. He went rigid. Then, still gripping Billy, afraid to release him, afraid not to, he felt himself being eased backward against the edge of the table, and then across it. He was looking up now, hearing no sound, feeling Billy's breath against his face, seeing those dead eyes, the hardness still at his throat. But it was moving now. He felt it tracing upward, over his cheek, pausing at the corner of his eye. *No. No . . . no, don't!* But it was moving again, away from his eye, down his cheek toward the table's surface. He felt a tug against his ear. And a wetness. Eyes wide with fear, he tried to speak. Billy shushed him.

"This is my good suit," Billy said quietly, his face an inch from Tucker's. "Would you let go now?"

Tucker nodded, blinking. He opened his hands. They'd gone stiff.

"You want to stand up now? Nice and slow."

Tucker nodded again. Billy eased backward, off the table, guiding him. They were standing once more. Tucker tried to raise a hand to his ear but Billy frowned and shook his head. Tucker dropped the hand. The hard edge traced downward across his chest, pausing at his heart, then farther, below his waist. Billy released him, holding him only with his eyes.

"Look down," Billy said.

Tucker obeyed. He saw the knife. It had a wide curving blade in the shape of a bird's wing. A skinning knife. Beyond it, at his feet, were the buttons of his shirt. Tucker had felt nothing.

Billy's free hand groped for something on the table's surface. He found it. He brought it slowly up to Tucker's face. It was small and pink and smeared with blood. Billy waited until he saw in Tucker's eyes that he knew what it must be. Then he brought it to his own mouth. He chewed it, deliberately, slowly, and swallowed. Tucker's stomach bucked, his chest heaved. Billy forced him to his knees and stepped back.

A bar towel, tossed from the crowd, struck the side of Tucker's head. He seized it, pressing it against the stub of his ear. He knelt there, keening, his body rocking, hands over both ears now and his eyes shut tight as if to shut out the pain and the humiliation. A woman, one of the Israeli's, came forward with some napkins and a bottle of Perrier. She used these to wipe the blood from the table. Kurt Weiss wiped the floor. Ronny Grassi, his color only now returning, waved two men forward and gave them instructions. They nodded, then took the football player by the arms and led him toward a fire exit. He resisted, but only until one of them whispered into his remaining ear. The three left quickly. The sound level of the room picked up, many conversations punctuated by low whistles and nervous laughter. Another Billy McHugh story, thought Bannerman. Within a week it would be told all over Europe. Bannerman approached Ronny Grassi.

"Did you enjoy yourself?" he asked quietly.

Grassi had removed his ascot. With it, he dabbed at his own blood where Tucker's fingernails had gouged his neck. "I know." Grassi held up a hand. He did not want to hear Bannerman say it. "I figured he'd stomp out, tail between his legs. Who'd have figured he'd take on Billy, right here, with this crowd?"

"But you won't do this again, will you," he hissed. "Not ever."

Grassi looked at Billy. He was at Bannerman's side, waiting, Bannerman's hand on his shoulder. Bannerman, he realized, needed only to apply pressure to ease the bigger man forward. "No," he whispered. "Not ever."

"What will be done with Tucker?" Bannerman asked.

Grassi gestured in the direction of the marina. "They took him to my boat. My first mate will stitch him up, give him his walking papers."

Bannerman shook his head. "I want him kept there, under guard, until we're finished here and gone. If Billy sees him again, he'll probably have to kill him. And you, Mr. Grassi, will get the bill."

Grassi wiped his brow and nodded. "Speaking of which," he said, gesturing toward the hill. "When's show time?"

"Have a nice night, Mr. Grassi."

They had reached the path to their suite. It had taken a while. More handshakes, embraces, a few introductions, invitations to meet at breakfast. Once outside, Billy paused to spit into a running stream. "Did you pack any Feenamint?" he asked.

Bannerman rolled his eyes, mentally. Tucker's ear had not mixed well with the paella. "I have some Rolaids. And some toothpaste."

Billy spat again. "I'm getting too old for this. Tastes like calamari. I hate calamari."

"You did fine." They walked toward their suite. "You even scared me."

Billy shrugged indifferently. "You should have let me do Grassi. He plays too many games. You can't let people do that."

I know, thought Bannerman. Reputations. Use them or lose them. But Grassi was harmless enough. Not dangerous. Just likes to know dangerous people. "I think he'll behave now. You heard him. He wants to see the floor show."

"That's another thing. We go out on a job, when did we start selling tickets?"

"You threw a party for Palmer Reid," Bannerman reminded him.

"And that time you invited Lesko and Urs Brugg. Tomorrow, they're coming again. Is this going to be a regular thing with us?"

"It does wear thin," Bannerman agreed.

"So what now?"

"We'll get some sleep. First I'll call Anton. If he hustled Susan out of Westport, something must be happening."

"Then what?"

"Show time."

— 25 —

The same evening. A six-hour time difference earlier. Westport.

At the window table in Mario's, Anton Zivic lingered over a cognac as he browsed through the current issue of *Art & Antiques* magazine.

The restaurant was full. The bar two deep in commuters. Several parties stood, drinks in hand, waiting for tables.

Zivic knew many of the faces. But not all. Twice, in the past ten minutes, the front door had opened and the light over the bar had blinked. Both were men who had come in alone. Business suits. Carrying briefcases as if they'd just come from the train. One stood at the bar, his back against the partition. The other stayed close to the pay phone near the entrance. Both held beers and were nursing them. The man by the entrance seemed more interested in the street outside than the company within.

Zivic frowned within himself. He touched the cognac to his lips and returned to his magazine. He was reading, with no small amount of envy, an account of two Flemish paintings, Brueghels, that had been looted by a Nazi general, vanished, and had apparently spent the last forty-five years on the wall of a Cincinnati barbershop owned by a former American corporal who had accepted them, reluctantly, in lieu of a $10 poker debt. Sotheby's put their value at $6 million.

A shadow fell over the magazine. It stood still. He looked up.

"Ah, Roger." He brightened. "How delightful." He rose to shake hands, then gestured toward a vacant chair.

Clew hesitated. "Can we go someplace?"

Zivic brushed the suggestion aside. He signaled the waiter, indicating another cognac for his guest.

Clew took a breath. But he pulled the chair out and sat. Heavily. "Anton"—Clew leaned closer—"where is everybody?"

An innocent shrug. "Is something wrong, Roger?"

"I've got to see Paul. Where is he?"

"He is unavailable." The drink was brought. Zivic caught the waiter's eye. A message, unspoken, passed between them. The waiter left. "Perhaps I may be of some help."

Clew didn't like this at all. No Billy McHugh or Molly Farrell behind the bar. No Paul Bannerman anywhere. His house dark. No one answering the phone. Anton Zivic here as if he were waiting for him. Polite, friendly. Almost too friendly.

"Anton"—Clew spread his hands, intending a gesture of openness—"have any of you been to Washington lately? Molly Farrell, for instance?"

Zivic's eyes appeared to go blank.

"Okay." Clew's jaw tightened. "Are Paul and the rest of your crowd now in New York, by any chance?"

The eyes came alive again. He shrugged, waiting.

Clew pulled Hagler's newspaper from his briefcase and placed it in front of Zivic. He pointed to the article. "Five Die In Drug War." Zivic scanned it with no more than polite interest. He looked at Clew. "Your phone message to Paul"—Zivic dropped his voice—"mentioned a threat to our security. I take it that these people are somehow involved."

Clew returned to his briefcase and produced a manila envelope. From it, he withdrew two photographs. He set one of these before Zivic. A black man. Zivic recognized Hector Manley but his expression showed nothing.

"Do you know him?" Clew asked.

Zivic ignored the question. "Let me see the other."

Zivic took it from his fingers. He saw a young man, early thirties, dark complexion, semitic nose, a large mole high on one cheek. He was dressed in military fatigues. In the background was a lifeless rocky landscape that was either the moon or the Middle East. He was, he presumed, looking at the man known only as "the Arab."

He returned to Manley's photograph, tapped the table next to it. "This one. Who is he?"

Clew held his gaze. "You don't know?"

"Tell me, please."

Clew seemed relieved. He gestured toward a photo of the same man, poorer quality, which appeared in *The Times* story. "Hector Manley. A Jamaican. A drug dealer. Also an urban terrorist trained in Cuba. Now in New York."

"And this one?"

"His name is Aba Jibril. His uncle is Ahmed Jibril, head of the—"

Zivic waved his hand, a gesture of dismissal. He knew of Ahmed Jibril. A former captain in the Syrian army. Joined the PLO in the late sixties, found them insufficiently militant. Split with Arafat to form the Popular Front for the Liberation of Palestine. Invented skyjacking as a weapon of terror. But even they were too moderate. Split once more to create a new faction called the Popular Front for the Liberation of Palestine—General Command. Made names for themselves in 1974 by pitching the bodies of Israeli children from the roof of an apartment house during a siege. Also specialists in booby-trapped packages, letter bombs, and, eventually, bombs in the baggage holds of airplanes. The nephew, Aba, was the man who romanced a young Irish woman then, once she was carrying his child, placed her aboard an El-Al flight with a time bomb in her luggage. The bomb, fortunately, was discovered in time.

"These men," Zivic asked, "what have they to do with us?"

Clew reached into his pocket once more. He produced an audiocassette tape. He pushed it toward Zivic. "It's from a

DEA wiretap. This one"—he touched the younger Jibril's photograph—"is hiring *that* one"—he touched Manley's—"to blow this whole fucking town into splinters."

Zivic pretended to be stunned. He leaned closer, whispering an occasional question, as Roger Clew described a plot to visit forty car bombs on the town of Westport.

"Why?" Zivic asked. "Why Westport? Why us?"

"You tell me. Did you ever hurt Jibril?"

They had indeed. Once in Athens. They'd found one of his factories, took two of his men alive. Russo had questioned them. They'd begged to die. But they were released, barely able to walk, at the gates of the Iranian Embassy. They made it through. The Iranian who was their control rushed out to meet them as guards followed with weapons drawn. The two men, now safe, bawled curses, threats, made obscene gestures at the idling car outside. Then the two men exploded.

But Roger Clew knew of that episode. Zivic did not bother to answer. He reached for the tape, a duplicate, no doubt, of the one he'd heard two days earlier. He picked up the photographs.

"Not those." Clew held out his hand. "I'll need them."

"So will we," Zivic said.

Clew moved to argue but the waiter returned. He placed a paper bag, lined with foil, on the table at Zivic's elbow. It bore the restaurant's name and a cartoon drawing of a frisking dog. Zivic pushed it toward Clew. Clew looked at him, puzzled. He had no dog. Neither, as far as he knew, did Zivic.

"Have you told me the truth, Roger?" Zivic kept one hand on the bag.

Clew's forehead began to glow. "How can you even ask?"

Zivic smiled. "A simpler question. Have you come here alone?"

"As always. Yes."

"You came with no escort? No bodyguard?"

"Paul says come alone, I come alone. Why would I need a bodyguard in Westport?"

Zivic frowned. "Then this is most embarrassing." He rose to his feet, placing one hand on Roger's shoulder and touching the doggy bag with the other. "Take this with you when you leave," he said. "Do not come back unless invited."

"Wait a second." Clew flared. "Who the hell are you to—"

"Please," Zivic said gently. "Nothing foolish. Just go away while you can."

Zivic walked to the front door. He waved toward the bartender as he pushed through it. The bartender waved back.

Clew touched the bag. It seemed heavy. Carefully, he broke the tape that held it shut. He opened it, glanced inside, and covered it quickly.

Now he reached, feeling with his fingers past the muzzles of two service revolvers until he gripped one of the two wallets that were in the bag with them. He pulled one out. Opened it. It contained a photo ID. Treasury Department. He extracted the other. Same ID, different name. He turned in his chair. He saw them at once. Two men at the crowded bar. Their backs to him. Heads slightly bowed, their arms at their sides. Not moving. They seemed to be dozing.

They almost seemed to be dead.

"Mr. Manley?"

"Yes?"

"Cover your face, please. I will turn on the light."

Manley sat up on his bed. He looked away as Anton Zivic turned the switch. Zivic approached him. An orderly, armed with a stun gun, stayed two paces behind.

Zivic held a photograph in his hand until Manley nodded that his eyes had adjusted sufficiently. Manley glanced at it.

"The Arab?" the Jamaican asked.

"You tell me."

Manley stifled a yawn, nodding. The nod stopped abruptly. He blinked, then looked again, more closely this time.

"That is not the man," he said.

"You are certain?"

"They could be brothers. But no. The man I saw had no mole."

"It could have been removed. What then?"

Manley shook his head. "The hairline is different. The nose is wrong."

"These too are cosmetic. They might have been altered."

"No," Manley was firm. "That is not the man."

"Thank you." Zivic turned toward the door.

"Mr. Zivic," he called.

Anton stopped and waited.

"Will you be speaking to Mr. Bannerman?"

"In a few minutes. Yes."

"I told him I would try to think of a way to reach an accommodation with Mr. Covington. I believe that I have."

"I think, so has he," Zivic said. "But I will tell him."

"Mr. Zivic. Will he spare my life?"

"He will try, Mr. Manley."

Zivic stepped from the room.

—26—

Martin Selly was becoming restless. And terribly bored.

Here it was, a perfectly delightful Marbella morning and he might as well be behind bars. As indeed he was. Wrought-iron bars.

Before him, viewed from the terrace, all the rest of the world seemed free to come and go, seeking its pleasures. There were women everywhere. In passing convertibles, on pleasure boats, on the beach far below. He watched them through his binoculars. Many of them topless. Oiling their bodies. Their hands languidly, proudly, kneading their breasts. Exciting him.

It had been nearly a fortnight since he'd had a woman. A fresh one, he thought. A clean one. There was always Erna, of course, but that was like saying there was always a pig wallow. No amount of bathing would make her clean. Sperm, in her case, probably died on contact.

Worse, her capacity for conversation seemed to diminish by the day. Her drug-cooked brain had gone from slow simmer to deep-fry. Not that scintillating chats were ever her strong suit. And not that she needed much of a mind to hold up her end during periods of financial distress. In Marseilles she'd serviced the entire engine-room crew of a Nigerian freighter. He'd wanted to boil her afterward. Or chuck her out once and for all. But every time he'd been at the point of doing just that she would show up with some new pretty, sometimes two of them, waving packets of cocaine under their noses and all they'd have to do for it was to take a lovely hot bath and if they made an effort not to scream we wouldn't have to tie them up quite so tightly, now would we. Makes it all the harder to scrub the little nooks and crannies.

He turned his binoculars to the grounds of the Puente Romano. Quieter now. Not like last night. So many cars arriving at all hours. Unusual this time of year. He'd been on the point of driving down, Signore Grassi's instructions notwithstanding, to see who they all were and what was the attraction. But then Grassi's Rolls-Royce came into view. His man, Weiss, driving. Another bodyguard, huge creature, in front. Left the Rolls in front, naturally. No hotel or restaurant ever parks a Rolls. Too good an advertisement. Grassi climbing out, greeting other new arrivals, most of whom he seemed to know. Selly thought he'd recognized two or three himself.

A party of some sort? A convention? Perhaps a business meeting. And perhaps, thought Martin Selly, this gathering had something to do with the assignment that Grassi had in mind for them. Or rather assignments. In the plural. Grassi had been clear about that at least. Be patient, he said. Sit tight, he said. You'll have all you can handle. All three of you.

Behind him, through the screen door, he heard the Algerian. Or rather his automatic weapons. One seldom actually heard Amal. Just the click and slap of those guns he was forever cleaning. You'd think they were women. To Amal, perhaps they were. All those orifices. Hidden parts. Nooks and crannies.

A delivery van had turned off the coast road. He checked his watch. Late this morning. But welcome nonetheless. Fresh croissants, his copy of the *Tribune,* and a supply of groceries. A nice Dover sole for lunch. He would bake it himself. Erna, like all Germans, would fry it into shoe leather.

Martin Selly had begun to lower his glasses when another movement caught his eye. Just below him. The second house down. It was shut for the season, windows sealed with white boards, but someone was there. In the back. By the swimming pool, hidden behind the hedge. Selly slipped from his chair. He stayed low, edging backward toward the screen. He was about to call Amal. Stop playing with your bloody toys. Put them together. Quickly. But then, rising from the hedge, he saw the head and shoulders of a woman.

She was looking up, but not toward him. It was the delivery van that had caught her attention. Selly heard the splash of water. He saw her turn, fingers to her lips, toward someone still unseen. The splashing stopped. Selly scanned the pool area. Then he saw it. A hiker's backpack. No, two. Stashed in the shadows of the hedge. He relaxed. Now he understood. Trespassers. Sneaking a morning swim, a welcome freshwater bath, in the pool of a shuttered house. The sound of the van, stopping so near, had alarmed one of them. But now it was leaving. Erna had paid for the delivery. He could hear her on the stairs, bringing his newspaper. Quietly, soundlessly, Selly opened the screen and stepped inside. He stood there, watching. Soon he was rewarded.

A young girl, judging by her figure, was doing a lazy silent backstroke toward the far corner of the pool. The morning sun glistened off her flat stomach and the creamy mounds of her breasts. She reached the corner. She stopped there, arms draped along the tiled edges. Her legs and stomach sank from view but not the breasts. They floated, buoyed by the water. She was smiling now. Seductively. Her tongue working the edges of her lips. Enticing the other hiker to her.

Another splash. Barely heard. The sound of wading. Ripples spread from its source. More nakedness appeared. A back this time, and a tight little buttocks. She was quite slender. But for the tan lines of a swimsuit's halter she might have been a young boy. She was swimming, toward the other, in a slow, tantalizing breaststroke. The other was smiling. No. It was more than that. An invitation. A seduction. Her lips were parted. Her tongue worked their edges. Now her head fell back. It began a slow, rolling motion as the swimmer drew nearer.

"Erna," he whispered.

She came to his side. He pointed. They watched in silence.

The swimmer reached her waiting friend. Hands found her waist. Her face, her mouth, found the other's throat. The other gasped. The face, the mouth, the tongue, explored the shoulders of the other, and then the breasts. The other squealed. Now the head reared up. It took a great breath. It sank from sight. Now the other moaned. A deep, throaty sound. It became a scream.

"Get them," Martin Selly said hoarsely. "Bring them."

"Lesbians? For you?" The German pinched her face. But her own eyes were glistening.

"The water there is old and dirty. They will want a bath."

Erna frowned. The temptation was strong. She had gone longer than the blond Englishman without softness in her life. And the American, Grassi, had not forbidden this. No calls, he said. Stay home, he said, until I need you. But she too had needs. Still, she was doubtful.

"They will not come," the prostitute said. "Not now. Drugs will not bring them. They want only each other."

"They are trespassers," he reminded her. "Take Amal with you. Say that we own that house and that you have brought a policeman. Let them see a gun on his belt. Say we intend only to question them, search their belongings in case they have stolen from us, and then they will be free to leave Marbella."

"But you must let them leave," she warned. "This place is too small. They would be found, and Grassi would know."

"Get them," he said through his teeth.

By the time Ronny Grassi had settled his bar bill it was nearly three in the morning. He had not returned to his boat. Better, he'd decided, to stay at the Puente Romano. Less likely to miss anything. The decision had probably saved his life. For aboard *Temptress,* a sixty-foot trawler of teak and chrome, B. J. Tucker was waiting for him.

The first mate, who had stitched and cauterized his ear and splinted his thumb, lay unconscious on the deck of his cabin, slowly suffocating, his windpipe crushed by a forearm blow seconds after Tucker had risen to see the results in a mirror.

There were no other crew on board, save the ship's cook. They were on shore leave, prowling the brothels of Malaga. Only a single guard had been posted and he had stationed himself at the foot of the wharf. Grassi had underestimated him. He would pay for it.

Tucker tried the door to the crew's quarters. It was locked. But he could hear the cook snoring loudly. The cook would keep. Tucker found the gun locker. He pried it open and smiled. There were two assault rifles, M-16s, two TEC-9 machine pistols, an M-203 grenade launcher, and a drum-loaded automatic shotgun meant for sweeping the deck of an unfriendly vessel. He chose one of the machine pistols, studied its workings, then took two magazines, each containing thirty-six rounds. He inserted one of these and fed the chamber. He put the other in his belt. Moving quietly, he stepped from the storage cabin and climbed to the main salon where he found a bottle of vodka that would ease the throbbing where his ear had been and the pain of his ruined hand. With the vodka under his arm, he climbed on to the flying bridge. From it, twenty feet above the dock, he could see the entire waterfront of Puerto Banus. And the access road where Grassi's car must enter. He sat heavily into a swivel chair and turned it in that direction.

He had no plan worth the name. First Grassi, hear him beg, hurt him first, take his money, his rings, then find that crazy fuck who ate his ear. After that . . . he didn't know. Ireland, maybe. The IRA. Or South Africa. Fight the niggers. Maybe play some rugby.

He was aware, at some level, that shooting makes noise. That there were many more guns in Marbella than his. That he could not kill two men . . . make that three . . . don't forget that faggot Bannerman . . . thinks he's king shit . . . called him stupid . . . and then just hail a cab out of town. But when he tried to consider things, to think clearly, all he could hear was laughter. He brought the vodka to his lips. He drank deeply, choked, then drank again.

They'd laughed at him. And they threw him a rag. Told him to get lost. Like he was nothing. He'd show them who was nothing.

He waited.

Drinking from his bottle. Nodding. Fighting sleep. Around him, lights blinked off. Waves lapped at the boat. His chin fell to his chest. He slept.

It seemed only moments later, although hours had passed, that he felt the sun hot on his legs and a hand on his shoulder.

He fired without looking.

She had spotted her father at once. He stood waiting, one arm raised, just beyond the glass immigration booth at Zürich's airport. Beside him, dwarfed by him, was the small, elegant woman who had so captivated him, and who, not a month before, had helped to save her life.

Elena stood, erect, chin high, cloaked in fur, both arms in slings that crossed her breast, the fingers of one hand clutching the sleeve of her father's coat, her expression at once eager and anxious, her father touching those fingers as if to reassure her.

There was no need. Susan's grin, first of recognition and then of pleasure, washed away any apprehension that Elena might have felt even before Susan reached her. They stood together, saying little, touching cheeks.

At last her father took her aside. She, he told her, would be taken to Elena's house. He and Elena, and Elena's uncle, had to take a short trip. They would be back, perhaps that day. Certainly the next. She would stay in Zürich. The Bruggs would take care of her. Susan gripped his necktie, pretending to straighten it.

"In a pig's ass," she said sweetly.

Her father shot a helpless glance toward Elena, who, her expression smug, was examining the ceiling. Susan guessed that there had been a wager. Her father had lost.

Within twenty minutes she was being helped aboard a Gulfstream jet by two young men, both named Brugg, who stared first at her and then at her father, then met each other's eyes with expressions that seemed to remark on the perversity of genetics. Susan was used to it. She answered with a pleasant shrug.

Inside the aircraft, strapped into a leather seat, a robe covering legs too small for the rest of him, was an equally elegant and bearded older man whose expression, directed at her father, was equally smug. Her father could only grumble.

They would land in Malaga, Urs Brugg explained, within two hours. From there, a short ride by helicopter to Marbella. Yes, Paul Bannerman is there. Yes, he is well. No, most assuredly, he is in no danger. Yes, he is expecting them, although not Susan, but none of them, especially herself, should expect to be welcomed with great enthusiasm. Yes, his purpose there is as she thought. She must not interfere. She was silent for several minutes. In the end, she gave her word.

Two hours flight time. Enough to ask and answer many questions. Susan answered those she could, about Westport and the events that led to her departure. Then the conversations turned private. She sat first with Elena. They spoke in whispers that were punctuated by grins. A few times, they laughed aloud. Lesko's ears began to burn.

The copilot served a light breakfast. Susan took it with Urs Brugg, at his request. He gestured toward the rear of the plane where her father now sat with his niece. He asked Susan if she approved. She hardly knew how to answer. She had never before seen her father with a woman other than her mother. She had never seen any woman, including her mother but excepting herself, regard him with such obvious affection and respect. She certainly liked Elena, she said, and she was glad for her father, the difference in their backgrounds notwithstanding. It was no greater than that between herself and Paul. Time would tell.

She asked what they would do, whether Elena would return to New York with him. Urs Brugg seemed to avoid the subject. Perhaps, she supposed, he did not know. He asked that, on arriving in Marbella, she stay close to her father, keep him out of trouble. This trip, he said, was an indulgence. Nothing more. He began to say that there were more important things her father should be doing but he stopped himself. Abruptly, she thought, he began pointing out the sights below. The harbor of Marseilles. Ahead, the coast of Spain. But she had heard him.

At the airport outside Malaga, two Bell Jet Ranger helicopters awaited them. The younger Bruggs took one, the rest of the party took the second. It seemed no more than minutes before the first settled down on a concrete pad at a place where a white man-made breakwater said "Roman Bridge" in Spanish. Susan's aircraft hovered above the gentle surf as the younger Bruggs, their hands concealed within raincoats, stepped away from their helicopter and awaited the approach of two other men, one thickset, dressed in a blazer and white slacks, the other slight and balding, dressed in a floral-print shirt, shorts, and sandals.

"The bigger man is Ronny Grassi." Urs Brugg spoke above the noise of the rotors. "He is a friend. The man smoking a pipe is Colonel Leonid Belkin. He is KGB, stationed in Switzerland. Also a friend."

"KGB?" Susan's eyes widened. "As in Russian?"

Urs Brugg smiled. "As you see, he does not have horns."

"But why is he here? Does Paul know him?"

"He is strictly an observer. He knows of Paul but they have not met. He is an admirer. Do not be concerned."

Susan could see other men. And a few women. Perhaps twenty in all, spread out along the beach. They seemed, at first glance, to be strollers and sunbathers. But then she noticed. None were looking in their direction. They were looking away. Toward the east, the west, and the trees and buildings to the north. As if whatever might come from those directions was of considerably more interest than the arrival of two helicopters.

"Those people down there," she asked quietly, "are they friends as well?"

He smiled. "You have a good eye, Miss Lesko."

The helicopter banked. The other was lifting off. Urs Brugg leaned closer to her.

"You know, I take it, what Paul Bannerman does," he said. "May I ask how you feel about it?"

"I wish," she said slowly, "that he were just a travel agent. But of course he isn't. Is he?"

"No. He is much more."

"And I know, although I'm not sure I've really grasped it yet, that he's here to execute three people who murdered your nephew."

"But then so is your father. The only distinction being that your father will not be given the chance."

"I know that, too. I know that they're alike."

"Would you try to change them?" Urs Brugg asked.

"I would try . . . to protect them."

"Miss Lesko"—Urs Brugg turned in his seat—"before you return home, could we have a talk? Just you and me?"

"About Paul?"

"In large part. Yes."

"In this talk," she asked, "will you tell me what you want from him?"

"That and other subjects. I think so. Yes."

"What else will we talk about, Mr. Brugg?"

"About the world we live in, Miss Lesko."

Ronny Grassi had waved off all introductions until Urs Brugg could be carried across the sand in his wheelchair and the group had safely reached a restaurant table in the open courtyard of the Puente Romano.

Around them, Susan saw, were more men and women. Some at other tables, some strolling about. Nearly all with their backs to them. Her father had noticed as well. She'd seen his hand brush over the bulge at his hip as he seated Elena. He remained standing behind her. But neither Grassi nor the bookish little man who was a KGB colonel seemed concerned by their presence.

Grassi seemed more interested in her father. He kept looking at him, his brow knitted, as if he were trying to place him.

"We had a little trouble here," Grassi said. He shot a meaningful glance at the people nearby, acknowledging for the first time that they'd been posted there. "My fault, maybe. Guy on my boat went berserk, shot my cook and nearly killed my first mate and a guard. We have people out looking for him. Better we stay close to home until they find him."

"I'm Susan Lesko." She extended her hand. "Does this trouble involve Paul Bannerman?"

"Lesko." He repeated the name. He looked once more at the man who hovered close to Elena Brugg. "You're not . . . you from New York? From the cops?"

"Used to be," he answered. "Retired. This is my daughter. What about Bannerman?"

Grassi answered but he was looking at Urs Brugg. "So far," he said, "the only thing Bannerman's involved in is ruining the hotel's business. This morning he makes the rounds of the breakfast tables and next thing you know half his old friends are heading for the airport." He turned back to Lesko. "Detectives, right? Raymond the Terrible. I'm from New York myself."

The KGB man looked up, his expression showing new interest.

"Small world," Lesko said indifferently. But to show Elena that he had manners, he extended his hand.

"Ronny Grassi." The other man gripped it. "Used to live in Brooklyn. Ocean Parkway. We had a mutual friend. You know Irwin Kaplan?"

"DEA." Lesko nodded, one eyebrow rising. "How do you know Irwin?"

"He grew up down the street. We kept in touch. We've done each other a favor here and there. You talk to him, tell him Ronny Grassi says hello."

Lesko relaxed a notch. Grassi was telling him that he was okay. Probably set up a drug bust or two for Kaplan. You have any doubts, call him. Lesko just might do that, he thought.

"Where is Paul?" Susan interrupted. Reunions are nice, but . . . "Is he here now?"

"Last I saw, he was up on his deck." Grassi pointed, but then thought better of it. "You better stay here though. He'll be along."

"Excuse me," she said.

Grassi watched her go.

"Your daughter, huh?" he said, almost doubtfully.

"Life's full of surprises." Lesko scowled.

But he wished she hadn't gone. He wished that he had not chosen between Susan and Elena. But he knew that he had.

— 27 —

Martin Selly opened the second of the two backpacks. The contents of the first lay on a glass-topped table before him.

The second held more of the same. But no sleeping bag. Apparently they had only one between them. He found spare clothing, not clean, damp with mildew. American jeans and a beaded denim jacket. Shorts and T-shirts. One cold-weather jacket and a poncho. An unused bikini. A two-liter bottle of Evian water. Junk jewelry, some of it rather clever. Tampons. A *Fodor's Spain*. And in this one, unlike the other, a packet of condoms. A lesbian, to be sure, but perhaps not beyond redemption.

A zippered plastic bag contained her toiletries. Within it, her passport. Also American. Several hundred dollars in traveler's checks, a few thousand pesetas, a few British pounds. No alcohol. No drugs.

He opened the passport. Issued two years earlier. Home address, like the other, Carmel, California. The Fodor's guide had been borrowed from a Carmel library. It was months past due.

Standing near, Amal between them, were the two women. Eyes wide. Terrified. Hands bound in front of them with a twining of electrical tape. Both still naked but for the loose-fitting shirts they'd scurried into at Amal's approach. The shirts, men's shirts, clung to their wet bodies. Water dripped to the tile floor. Fear and the chill had hardened their nipples.

Erna Dietz stood at the terrace door, her attention struggling between their well-toned bodies and the two helicopters that had hovered so long before landing on the beach of the Puente Romano. The helicopters lost. Her eyes were caressing the younger one. The one who had swam to the other. She tried to keep her expression stern. But her breath was catching in her throat.

They were young enough, thought the Englishman. Although not so young as he'd thought at first. Still, their bodies were firm. Breasts high and proud. Only the first hint of lines at the edges of their eyes and mouths. Their bellies flat. He liked bellies. He liked to rub them.

California girls. He'd assumed they were all blond. Or at least all deeply tanned. More than these two. And that they all had money enough not to travel off-season. But these two were designers, they claimed. Of costume jewelry. Precious little money in that.

"And you designed these, you say." He chose a sample. A tiny silver skeleton fashioned into an earring. The sort of thing seen in a discotheque.

One of the women, the one who had condoms, nodded, then chewed her lip.

He frowned. "Or do you steal jewels?" he asked. "Is that what you were going to do? Look for jewels in that house?"

"No," the woman insisted, her voice quaking. "Really. We just wanted to—"

"Bathe." He answered for her.

He stepped nearer. The one who spoke tried to shrink from him but Amal placed a hand against her back. Selly reached to touch her hair. It was worn short. A butch cut. Not recently shampooed. Bits of algae from the untended pool still clung to it.

"I believe you," he said gently.

The women stared.

"And I'm going to let you go."

They wilted in relief. The one started to speak. He brought a finger to her lips.

"But first"—he grimaced, picking at the algae—"we're going to clean you up properly. We have our standards here, you know."

She tensed. "Oh—that's okay," she said. "We can shower down on—"

The finger came up sharply, this time in warning. But then the gentleness returned.

"And after you've had a good scrubbing," he continued, his voice purring, "perhaps you can think of some way to thank me."

Her mouth fell open. She shuddered.

Selly moved to the second woman. Even smaller than the first. Frizzy hair. All the dirtier for it. The one whose pack contained knitting needles and yarn and a pair of dildos but no birth control device.

"And you," he said, "will make amends to this nice lady" —he gestured toward Erna whose chest was rising— "for all the trouble you've caused. You'll know how to do that, won't you?"

She swallowed. Then she closed her eyes. And nodded.

Bannerman, on the deck of the suite he shared with Billy, raised his Nikon to his eye and, touching a button, brought the telephoto lens into focus.

He could see no movement at the house on the hill. But they were there. He'd seen them earlier. First the blond man and the woman on the terrace. Next, the delivery truck came and went. Then he'd watched as the woman and the Algerian stepped from the house and walked to the one below where Bannerman had, before breakfast, seen a sleeping bag draped over the hedge. Airing out in the sun. The Englishman, he felt certain, had not seen the bag. The house would have blocked his view of it. But he had surely seen its owner. And her friend. Bannerman had watched as four figures scurried back up the hill. Two women in front, legs and feet bare, frightened, dripping wet, prodded from behind by the two who had surprised them during their morning swim.

He could do, he thought, with a swim himself. Some of

last night's crowd might be down on the beach. Those he'd missed at breakfast. Especially the two Israeli women and the two SAS men who were bodyguards to Princess Anne. He would ask them the same favor he'd asked the others. The more the better.

But then, Leo Belkin had sent a note asking if they might have some time together. Perhaps lunch or dinner. Just the two of them. Or, if Bannerman preferred a third party present, Urs Brugg could join them.

Speaking of whom, he would have to go and greet the Brugg party before long. Impolite not to. He'd heard them arrive. Helicopters. He did not actually mind. A face-to-face meeting with Urs Brugg was well overdue. They'd spoken only by telephone. And he was pleased at the prospect of finally getting to know Elena, whom he'd seen only twice. Once while being pummeled by Lesko and again, shortly afterward, while trying to stop the flow of Gary Russo's blood.

Lesko was another matter. But—Bannerman checked his watch—perhaps he'd be in better humor with his daughter now safely in Zürich. Perhaps Elena had managed to mellow him a bit as well. He would have called Lesko in any case. Given him, as he'd promised, the option of flying down to see the damage for himself. But only after it was done.

"Um—hi there."

A woman's voice. Sounded almost like Susan. Billy heard it as well. He put down the pistols he'd been cleaning and stepped out onto the deck. Billy saw her first.

"Hi, Billy."

"Guess who," the bartender said through his teeth. He waved, his smile more or less genuine, at Susan Lesko who had parted the top of an hibiscus shrub for a clearer view of their deck.

B. J. Tucker was on foot. His head and heart were pounding. His first thought, on shooting the cook who had startled him—not his fault—and then the guard who'd come running down the dock, was of escape.

All along the wharf, hatches had slid open, heads had popped up at the sound of the gunfire. He ran, gun in hand, waving it. The heads ducked out of sight.

He reached the parking lot. He found two cars unlocked but both were BMWs. Hard to hot-wire, even with tools and with two good hands. He had neither. He searched for hidden keys. There were none. But there were maps. A road map of Spain and a tourist map of Marbella and Puerto Banus. He took them.

The main road was some distance away. Few cars on it at this hour. He thought of going there, flagging one down, taking it. But to do that he would have to stand in the open. And he was a mess. His collar caked in blood. No one would stop.

The map of Spain showed no other road. But on the tourist map there was a thin dotted line running through Puerto Banus to Marbella. It was the old Roman road, the map said. It led to the Roman bridge on the grounds of the Puente Romano, cutting through several other beach hotels along the way.

Tucker tried to think. A part of him wanted to go back there. To empty one full clip into one of those who had shamed him. Even if he died for it. But he knew that was crazy. If he followed that old road, however, there would be other parking lots. He might catch someone getting into a car. And, better still, no one would be looking for him to come that way. He began walking.

He waited in the shadows of one hotel and then another. No luck. At a third, a gardener stumbled on him as he hid in the shrubs bordering the lot. Tucker clubbed him with the machine pistol. But the man, falling, had somehow grabbed his splinted thumb. He broke it again. Tucker's hand and brain were screaming. He staggered on.

Before he realized it, he had reached the Roman bridge. He went under it. He hid there, soaking his hand in the cool running stream, washing his face, drinking deeply.

A fluttering sound. Distant. He recognized it. A helicopter. He climbed the bank and looked, his first thought that it was searching for him. But no. There were two. One landing, the other waiting its turn. In the distance he could see Ronny Grassi, on the beach, waiting for them. His grip tightened on the machine pistol, the knuckles of his good hand turning white.

Tucker watched.

A man, bearded, was helped out of the second helicopter. Now two women, one young, the other with both her arms in slings. A second man, very large, almost Tucker's size, was helping them. Tucker rubbed his eyes.

"McHugh?" he whispered.

He wasn't sure. Something different about him. He'd wait. Get a closer look. They were moving toward the courtyard now.

He watched as the party disappeared behind the beach house and then came into view again. Much nearer. He could hear their voices. They had reached a table. They were sitting. He still could not see the big man clearly. His eyes were blurring from the effort. And they hurt. He felt his brain pressing against them from the rear. He needed something. Calm him down. He patted his pockets, felt the outline of some pills. They were bennies, he remembered. Not what he needed now. He could have used some dust to clear his head. Or some dillies for the pain. But he swallowed them anyway. All three of them.

The choppers.

Why hadn't he thought of them? The speed helped after all.

Screw grabbing a car. All he had to do is get to that table. Grab Grassi by the throat. Tell the rest of them he'd kill them if they moved. Which he might do anyway. Especially McHugh, if that's him. Blow both his ears off. Then his nuts. Drag Grassi down to the beach to that chopper. Get it to take him someplace. Ireland, maybe. France.

He didn't know. Someplace.

Throw Grassi out on the way. Make him beg first. Then hear him scream until he bounced.

Shit.

Then what?

Where could he go that they wouldn't find him?

You know who'd know?

The Englishman. Up in that house. And the other two with him.

Pilot could set that chopper down right outside. Street's wide enough. And it levels off up there. Make Grassi tell him what was going to happen to them. How he set them up.

Stupid?

You call me stupid, you fucking wop?

I'll show you who's stupid.

"Of course I'm glad to see you," Bannerman insisted. It was not quite the truth. It was not quite a lie either. But he made no move to embrace her.

"You're sort of glad," she corrected him, accurately. "I understand. I don't blame you."

Billy had gone down with him, after handing him his pistol. At first, Bannerman had refused it. Susan was likely to hug him, at least touch him. She would feel it.

"She's got to get used to it," Billy told him firmly. "Now's as good a time as any."

Bannerman tucked the weapon into the small of his back. He slipped into a blazer. But she had not hugged him. She greeted Billy first, kissing his cheek. For Bannerman, she waited. He kissed her lips, lightly. She touched only his arms. Billy realized that she knew. He excused himself and walked up the path that led to the courtyard restaurant.

They stood in silence, watching him go. Bannerman took a deep breath, his expression stern, hands on his hips, one thumb pressing on the butt of his pistol to keep it from showing.

She poked at his arm. "Say you're glad to see me. This time, mean it."

"Who brought you here, Susan? Urs Brugg?"

"Yes, he did."

"And your father let him?"

"I didn't give them much choice. Come on, Bannerman. Say it."

"Susan, we need to talk."

She held up a hand. "Do I know why you're here? The answer is yes. Do I understand that you'd rather I stayed home, pretty in pink, keeping the home fires burning? Yes again."

"The fact is—"

"The fact is," she interrupted, "I'd probably be doing just that if Molly hadn't hustled me out of town. That doesn't mean I would have liked it. Say you're glad to see me anyway."

"Fact is, I guess I am."

"That's progress." She made a show of examining his waistline. "Now say, 'I know you grew up with men who carry guns, Susan, so I'm not going to stand here like a dummy trying to hide the one in my belt anymore.' "

He closed one eye. "Susan—"

"I think this is where I say, 'Paul—be careful. Come back to me.' "

He looked skyward.

"Or I say, 'Paul, why can't we let the police handle those three?' But I already know the answer. You're Mama's Boy. You don't do courts."

"Susan—" He stepped closer to her.

"I know what you're going to say. Don't."

He shook his head as if to clear it. "Are you sure we need two of us for this conversation? Why don't I go back upstairs and you can finish it by yourself."

"I'm not leaving you."

"Fine."

"I mean it, Bannerman. I know too much. The phone calls. The blinking lights. Fortress Westport. I'm even on the run now so your pals in Washington can't—What did you say?"

"I said fine. We'll work something out."

"No more secrets? All or nothing at all?"

"We'll see about *all*. But you're right. *Nothing* is no longer an option. Why don't we talk about it over brunch."

"Brunch?" She stared at him, blankly.

"I have to go up and say hello anyway. We'll get some-. thing from the buffet. After that, let's find you a swimsuit and go down to the beach."

"Brunch." She repeated the word, tasting it.

He's here to kill three people, but only after brunch. *That's right, isn't it, Paul? You're going to shoot them?*

Uh-huh. Try the Eggs Benedict.

And it's your basic execution, right? I mean, we're not talking gunfight at the OK Corral here.

You got it. Care for a sticky bun?

No thanks. Too heavy. We're going swimming, remember?

Oh, yeah. Then maybe while you're dressing for dinner I'll run out and blow those suckers away.

Oh. Okay. Good plan, Paul.
Thanks, partner. Glad you came.
Oh, well.
She took his hand.
In for a penny, in for a—
She heard the sound. Like a New Year's Eve noisemaker.
Brak-brak-brak. Not loud. Not at all like gunshots. But she
saw, in Paul's eyes, that they were. He mouthed an order—
Stay here—raising a fist as if to back it up.
He had barely turned away when she saw the pistol. It
seemed to leap into his hand, his thumb already working its
safety. He raced, in stocking feet, toward the courtyard
where she'd left her father. He made no sound at all. She
had not even seen him kick off his shoes.
She kicked off her own and followed.

—28—

The Algerian raised his binoculars. Something had happened at the Puente Romano.

He'd heard nothing. Too great a distance. Nor could he see much within the hotel's grounds. But on the beach, strollers had suddenly stopped. Sunbathers in folding chairs, spread out to the left and right in a pattern that seemed too precise to be random, were, as if on signal, springing to their feet and turning toward the hotel.

Now, on each side, a person waving. Gesturing. As if directing traffic. The rest hesitated. Now a few moved toward the hotel. Others toward the two helicopters, one on the landing pad, the second on the sand fifty yards distant, as if to guard them. About half stayed where they were. At their posts.

Yes. They were definitely not tourists. He could see no weapons but nearly all carried beach bags or had towels draped suspiciously over their hands.

The Englishman should know of this, he thought. Even if it came to nothing. A fight, perhaps, between rival gunmen. Grassi was known to cause such fights. It was good, for that reason, that they kept to this house. Too many of those others despised the Englishman. Some would have mocked him. One or more would surely have challenged him. And the Englishman, who was a coward, would refuse. He would walk away, back to his room, to his bath, where he would try to scrub the shame from his body. He would make threats, take an oath of vengeance, but it would come to nothing. All he would do, he would send Erna to find a young woman and he would scrub her until blood seeped through her skin. Her screams would make him feel like a man again. Today, perhaps twice a man. Today he had two. Soon the screams would start.

No, thought Amal Hamsho. He would not interrupt the Englishman. Not for this. He would keep silent. He would wait. He would take his share of Grassi's money and then, he had decided, he would take the Englishman's share as well. And Erna's, which the Englishman kept in any case. He would cut both their throats. He would buy drugs. In Barcelona. But this time he would sell them. He would—

The Algerian turned at the sound behind him, his hand on the Uzi slung under his arm.

One of the Americans, one of the lesbians, had entered the room. Her shirt was gone. She wore nothing at all. The tape on her wrists still in place. Mouth open. Eyes wide. Behind her, the door to Erna's room. The American, too frightened to speak, pointed to the table on which the contents of her knapsack had been strewn. Amal watched, saying nothing.

"She—she sent me," the woman stammered. "f—for these."

Hamsho saw where she pointed. Two plastic devices. Powered by batteries. One very thin, the other very fat. These things disgusted him. Erna disgusted him. As did this woman.

He crossed to the open door. He saw Erna there. On her bed, face down, also naked. Legs spread wide. The right one was quivering, as if in anticipation of the things the American would be made to do to her. Hamsho spat, although inwardly.

Strange about that leg, he thought. He had watched men die, and women, and their legs trembled in that way as the

life went out of them. Sex and death. The beginning of life
and the end of it. Are they so alike?

He sensed a presence at his shoulder. He glanced. The
American, her toys held against her breasts, stood close to
him, waiting for him to let her pass. He hesitated. Something about her. Her expression. There was a new light in
her eyes. The fear seemed gone. What had replaced it? Was
it lust? Why no more fear? Was it possible that she had come
to believe that she had found a friend in Erna Dietz? A
protector?

Foolish woman. She would soon learn how much—

Erna.

She was making sounds. Bubbling sounds. And the leg
now more than trembled. It was in spasm. This was not
passion. This was—

He felt a tickle at his ear. And the colors of the room
exploded. He heard a screech. High and shrill. It seemed to
come from within his brain and push out against his eyes.
The room tilted crazily. His arms, before him, flapped like
wings. He wanted to bring them to his head, to the pain, but
they would not obey. Now his whole body floated. The naked woman with him. Her breath on his face. He felt her
hand against his ear. There was something there. It was
hurting him. She pulled at it. Another screech. A popping
sound. Now she was showing it to him. Something long and
thin. He tried to focus. He could see only that she was moving it, down past his face, under his chin. He felt it there.
Hurting him again. Stinging his tongue. The roof of his
mouth. His nose. They all screamed. More lights, red lights,
as it pierced his brain. Then his eyes rolled back and there
was blackness.

In that first minute, before the shots were fired, Billy
thought he was dead.

He had rounded a curve in the path leading to the courtyard, his way hidden from view by the thick tropical gardens. And there was Tucker, crouched low behind a shrub,
holding a machine pistol aimed squarely at his heart.

Tucker, he realized, had heard his footsteps. Had been
waiting for him. And yet he seemed stunned. Billy saw the
tables up ahead. Lesko there, facing in their direction but

his attention on the woman seated to his left. Billy understood. From this distance Lesko could have been himself.

Billy watched his eyes, waiting for the confusion to pass and for a decision to be made. He braced himself. His one chance—leap sideways into the thickest foliage and roll. He would surely take a hit, maybe several. But if he could free his own weapon, get off one shot, just one, that was all he would ask.

Tucker's eyes were wild. He saw fear in them, then hatred, and then a glee that bordered on hysteria. They were moist, blinking rapidly, as if bothered by the light. Now they changed again. A certain drunken slyness appeared. Tucker was on something. Speed, thought Billy.

"Go on, shit face," Tucker rasped. "Make a move."

What's this? Billy wondered. *You go to shoot, you shoot.*

"Go on," Tucker snarled. "Go for it."

Billy understood. The voice was low. Close to a whisper. He did not want to be heard. Nor did he want to shoot. Not yet. Not now. He had something else in mind. Slowly, Billy raised his hands.

Tucker seized a branch for balance. The touch shocked his ruined thumb. He stood, nearly erect, holding it out for Billy to see. His mouth twisted into a terrible smile.

"Ohhhh—yeah," was all he said. He raised the thumb toward the stump of his ear, turning his head as if to remind Billy of what he had done. The smile remained. It was making a promise. But still, not quite yet.

He waved Billy forward, using the machine pistol. An amateur, thought Billy. You don't wave guns. Billy took a step. Tucker waved again, indicating a point just beyond him on the path.

Good.

Billy saw it now.

Tucker wanted him. But he wanted Grassi more. Tucker would use him to get close to the table. He would be Tucker's shield.

Billy offered a silent hope. Let Tucker be so dumb, or so wired, that he sticks that gun in his back. Billy would take it from him before Tucker could blink, breaking a few more of his fingers, then hammer his teeth out with the butt.

Tucker was that wired. He was not that dumb.

He reached with his left hand, letting Billy see it, holding his weapon well back with the other. He patted Billy's waist, under his shirt, front and back. He found Billy's automatic. He took it, jamming it into his belt.

"Now," he said, jabbing at the seat of Billy's pants, "stick your arms down there. Under your belt, all the way, palms against your ass."

Billy obeyed.

He sighed inwardly.

Tucker had about a minute to live. Two at most.

The problem was, so did he.

The woman sat, not moving, listening.

Her elbows rested on the Algerian's chest. Her hands, still bound, gripped the butt of his Uzi but she did not take it from its sling.

She heard no sounds of alarm. Only the bubbling of the Jacuzzi behind the door of the master bedroom suite. A man's voice, barely heard. A woman now, whimpering. Softly pleading. She wet her lips, satisfied.

She reached for a thin cotton cord that hung between her legs. She pulled at it, steadily. Something white and heavy fell into her hands. She stripped away a covering of cloth. A switchblade knife. She opened it and worked its edge under the tape at her wrists.

She rose slowly to her feet, first gathering the vibrators that had fallen to the floor. These in hand, she stepped through into the room where Erna Dietz lay still. One knee on the bed, she reached to feel the pulse at the German's throat. There was a beat. Very faint. She counted three full seconds before she felt another. She moved the tips of her fingers farther down. They found the place where the windpipe had been crushed. She felt the damage, assessing it. Again, she wet her lips. Soon the pulse would stop. She put the knife aside.

She turned the German's head, parted her teeth, and forced both vibrators between them. She stood again and stepped into Erna Dietz's bathroom where she found three large towels. These in hand, she left the room, stepping over the Algerian.

At the table, she picked clean undergarments from the

pile and put them on. Next came her jeans and her jewelry.
She had chosen a blouse but she found a stain on it. Her eye
fell on another in the pile belonging to her companion. She
hesitated, her eyes rising to the door of the master suite. She
shrugged. Her friend would not mind. She slipped it on,
then took a brush and began teasing her damp and curly
hair into a fullness that approached its normal state.

That done, she returned to the body of Amal Hamsho.
Bending over, she retrieved the thin metal rod that had
pierced his brain. His flesh cleaned it as it withdrew. This
she wiped against his shirt.

She returned to the table, found its mate plus a skein of
white yarn, gathered the three towels and stepped out onto
the terrace. She shook out two of the towels and hung them
over the railing. The third, for the time being, she left
folded.

She settled into a deck chair, wondering briefly whether
she should first put lotion on her arms and face. The sun
was high, strong for February. But no, she decided. She
would not be there long enough to burn.

Unless Carla took her time.

She glanced at the unused towel.

Then Janet Herzog began to knit.

"Lesko?"

He heard Katz's voice. In his head. He cursed, silently.
Katz was all he needed now.

He was having enough trouble trying to make conversation and listen at the same time.

Elena on his left, telling him about Spain, all the places
she wanted to show him. Urs Brugg on his right, huddled
with the little KGB guy. They kept saying his name, and
Bannerman's, connecting the two, asking Grassi a question
now and then but not including him otherwise. He could not
get the sense of what they were saying, although he was
damned well going to ask if Elena ever gave him the chance.
He was almost getting the feeling that she was deliberately
keeping him from hearing.

"Lesko!!"

Katz's voice. Lesko groaned. He shut him out.

And if Elena wasn't distraction enough, here comes Billy

McHugh, up from where Susan had gone. On top of Mc-Hugh, he did not need Katz.

"Lesko! Wake up, already."

"Hey. Do you mind?"

Lesko blinked him away. But now he felt a chill. It was climbing the back of his neck.

Something was wrong. He knew that. And it was not, goddamn it, from Katz. His instincts had picked up on something, was all. But what?

He picked up a napkin, touched it to his mouth. He looked around.

The guards, all of Grassi's shooters, Bannerman's pals, showed no sign of alarm. But they weren't looking toward McHugh. They were—

Wait.

One of them just whistled. Softly. Tilting his head toward Billy who was—walking—hands behind him—like he was cuffed—big guy, bald head, with him—big guy looks a little whacked.

Lesko's fingers moved to his belt. They closed over the butt of the German automatic he'd extorted from Urs Brugg. He released the safety.

"Lesko?"

Elena this time. In a whisper. The fingers of her crossed arm tugging at his sleeve. She had seen it too. Two men— she wouldn't have known Billy—walking stiffly—not naturally. Off to the left, two of the guards, folding their arms, their hands finding weapons as well.

"I know," he said softly. "Drop your napkin. Bend low to pick it up. Stay there.

"Uncle Urs," she said, into Lesko's ear.

"I got him. Just do it."

She did as he asked.

Carla Benedict was weeping softly. Twice she had squealed in pain. The squeals were genuine.

He had done her chest first. He had used a scrub brush and a scouring cleanser that smelled of ammonia. It would make her skin smoother, purer, he told her, than it had ever been. His breath was coming fast.

She had tried to squirm away, fend him off with her

bound hands, but he had slapped her face, and he had choked her, pushing her under the water and holding her there until the last of her air bubbled to the surface. She very nearly had to end it then.

Time.

Janet would need twenty minutes at least. For the German to become absorbed by her. To taste her. More time would be better. Carla would stand this as long as she could.

He was doing her back and shoulders now. He had draped her over one end of the jetted tub. He knelt behind her, fully nude. She could feel his penis nestled between her buttocks but he made no attempt to enter her. She was, she knew, not yet clean enough. She tried, through her pain, to listen for sounds from outside the room. She could hear nothing. The rush of the swirling water was too loud and too close.

But now, a sound. A clatter. Something, it sounded like plastic, had been dropped. Not much longer, she thought. She closed her eyes and wondered about her skin. It would be a while, she was afraid, before it could stand the sun again. She wondered what she could wear. Soft cottons. None of her winter things. No silks.

The scrubbing stopped.

She felt the Englishman's fingers in her hair. Picking at it. His tongue clucking in disgust. The fingers appeared before her face. Bits of pool algae on them. "How could you stand to touch each other?" he spat.

"Please—" she swallowed a sob.

"You should thank me for this," he said, still probing. "Your friend should as well."

"Are you—will you let us go?"

"We'll see." He found the stem of a leaf. He tore it loose. "We'll have to see how you clean up first, won't we." He seized the hair in his fist. "Come on, now. Up you get. On your knees, facing me."

She pivoted, slipping. He held her up, painfully, until she was kneeling erect, her face at the level of his groin, inches away from his hardness. "What are you going to—"

He released her, then reached for bottle of shampoo. "I'm going to wash your hair now," he said. "You'll like this much better."

She waited, her hands low in front of her. She kept them there.

"You'll like it so much," he said, his breath coming in gasps, "that while I'm doing this for you, you'll want to do something nice for me."

He saw her stiffen. She dropped her head, turned it from him. He slapped her sharply. "You do want to be nice to me," he hissed. "Don't you?" He slapped her again.

A choking squeal. A rapid nod. She kept her face averted but her shoulders sagged. She had surrendered to him. Head bowed. He could not see the tiny smile. Or that her eyes were shining.

Martin Selly poured the shampoo. Using both his hands, he worked it into a lather. He took his time. Now he raised her head, tilting it backward, his hands at her temples. He guided it closer. She resisted, not much.

"Have you done this before?" he asked. "For a man, that is."

She hesitated. Then shook her head.

"It is done very gently. Much as with a woman. Use the lips and the tongue. Drink deep. I must never feel your teeth."

Her lips quivered. But she parted them.

"Who knows?" he purred, taking himself in one hand, guiding it toward her lips. "We may open whole new vistas for you today. Gently now."

He saw her own hands rising up from the water, covered with suds, twisting at their wrists so that one of them could be used freely. The other stayed below. She was taking him. Willingly.

He frowned, more than annoyed. He had not asked for her participation. It trivialized the event. This was hardly a romantic encounter. It was an act of corrective therapy.

"What are you doing?" He rapped her skull sharply with his knuckles.

She looked up at him. This time he saw the smile.

"I'm about to cut your pee-pee off," she said.

And she did.

A high-pitched shriek startled Janet Herzog.

She heard the splash of water, waves of it, more screams,

and a series of dull thumps as if someone were bouncing off the walls and floors.

The screams, though shrill, were those of a man. But the person being bounced, might it be Carla?

Janet was afraid of this. So was Paul. That she would play with him first. Let him know why he was dying. But not before she crippled him. What if she hadn't? What if she played too long?

She eyed the third towel, wishing she could hang it. Better go check first. She set down her knitting, except for one needle, and stepped through the screen door of the terrace.

Tucker saw the guards.

They were pretending, some of them, not to see him. But he'd heard the low whistle. And he saw where their hands had gone.

"Uh-huh. Okay." He smiled. It was more of a twitch.

I'm stupid, right? I'm blind, too. You want to play? We'll play.

He raised the machine pistol. He waggled it, letting them see that it was now aimed at the back of Billy McHugh's head. His left hand, with the broken thumb, had made a fist over Billy's belt.

The guards froze.

Thirty yards to the table. This was beautiful, he thought. No one there had even looked up.

"You see that, shit face?" He leaned toward Billy's ear. The one he would soon blow off. And then the arm. Off at the shoulder. If he had time, he'd make him eat it. "They're not going to shoot. You know why? You're their fucking hero, aren't you. They don't want to hit their king shit hero."

Billy said nothing. Tucker shoved him forward.

He could not look at the table. Had to watch the guards. One was Kurt Weiss. Little prick. Last night he just stood there. Enjoying himself. And the one near him, the Jew girl who cleaned up the blood. Probably the one who threw the towel at him.

Twenty yards.

He'd get them too. But first Grassi and the chopper. Then

make a fast pass. They'd still be running around. Chinese
fire drill. Still afraid to shoot. He'd empty a clip into them.
Shit.

Weiss's gun was out. In both hands. The Jew girl too.

Tucker crouched and fired.

Janet stood, taking in the scene. She lowered the steel
needle to her side.

It was a large bathroom. In the center, a wooden platform
housed a raised Jacuzzi. Toilet and bidet at one end, twin
wash basins and a mirrored wall at the other. There was
blood everywhere.

The floor was awash. The water was pink, clotted here
and there with a deeper red. Random sprays of blood
dashed the walls and ceiling. Carla's face and arms were
smeared. The blond Englishman seemed painted with it.

He was on the floor, near the toilet, still alive. Naked. On
his knees and elbows. Mewing softly. Trying to raise himself. He could not. The tile was too slick. And he would not
part his thighs.

Carla sat, equally nude, on the Formica counter between
the basins. Her knees were drawn up, her arms folded across
them, her chin resting on one arm, her switchblade rolling
carelessly between her fingers. She was watching the Englishman, her expression oddly at peace.

Janet slipped out of her shoes, leaving them on the bedroom rug where they would not be stained. She stepped
closer to the Englishman, assessing the damage that had
been done. He was in shock, bleeding to death, but slowly.
Blood oozed between his thighs. It dripped from both
hands, each deeply slashed, now useless to him. As were his
legs. She saw deep cuts, low on each calf, just above the
ankle. The calves were flaccid, their musculature gone.
Carla had sliced through both Achilles tendons, taking care,
it seemed to Janet, to avoid the arteries nearby. Janet
chewed her lip. Carla had played with him, all right. She
certainly had.

The distribution of the blood told the story. Carla had
followed him around the room. Taking her time. He had
tried to fend her off with his hands. She'd ruined them.
Then, when he could no longer use them, not even to stop

the hemorrhaging between his thighs, and when he slipped and fell, she went to work on his legs.

Janet Herzog turned away from him. She approached Carla who squirmed to one side, leaving room for her to sit.

"I was afraid he had you," she said, hoisting herself, leaving her own legs dangling. She kept her eyes on the Englishman. He was retching now. A string of spittle hung from his lips.

"He tried," Carla said. She took Janet's hand and guided it to the skin of her chest and shoulders. "But feel."

Janet had already seen the slickness and the soreness. She looked as if she'd had a peel. Her skin was hot to the touch. It felt like an underdone fish. Try to grab her and she'd squirt away.

"It's not so bad." Carla wet a finger and wiped at a smear of blood on her arm. "Most of this is Martin's." What was not still seeped from her pores.

"It'll grow back," Janet offered, "probably smoother than before."

"Remind me to thank him."

Janet moistened a hand towel. She dabbed with it, gently. "Let me do you before we leave," she said. "I have some Oil of Olay outside."

"You've also got my blouse," Carla noticed.

Janet made a face. "You wanted me to come in and ask first? It seemed a bad time."

Martin Selly collapsed onto one side. Fetal position. His thighs tightly clamped. Although in deepening shock, he could hear all this. It drove him nearer the edge of madness. His mind now worked to deny what had happened to him. It could not have been done. Not by this tiny woman. And that thing she had held up, dripping, instantly deflating, could not have been . . .

No! he screamed in his mind. Would they be sitting there? So calmly? Talking of skin-care treatments? Borrowed clothing?

The other woman. How could she be here? Where was Amal? Where was Erna? He screamed their names, this time aloud.

Janet patted Carla's knee.

"Let's finish up," she said.

* * *

Lesko heaved to his feet as Tucker fired his burst. He slammed one hip into the side of Urs Brugg's wheelchair, knocking him to the flagstone surface. Leo Belkin, breaking his fall, went with him. Ronny Grassi covered his head, uselessly, and tried to flatten against the table surface.

Lesko's gun was in both hands, held high, not yet aimed. He jigged to his left and hooked a leg over the shoulder of the crouching Elena, sweeping her to the ground behind him. She gasped in pain. He blocked it out.

As Tucker fired, Billy had thrown himself backward, spoiling his aim. Off balance, the younger man fell, Billy with him. They sat, legs splayed, joined as if tethered. Tucker—Lesko heard someone shout his name—made no attempt to stand. He wrapped one arm, thickly muscled, under Billy's chin. Billy bit it, tore at it with his teeth. Tucker chopped the side of his weapon against Billy's ear, stunning him, then jammed the barrel against his neck.

To Lesko's left, behind a molded concrete planter, Kurt Weiss was down, writhing, hands covering one cheek. A woman, not hurt, dragged him from the line of fire. Other guns were drawn. No one could shoot. Lesko dropped his sights onto a point just left of Billy's ear, now smeared with blood. He could see half of Tucker's face, part of one shoulder. An impossible shot. No chance.

"SHOOT HIM," Billy rasped. He meant anyone. All of them. Tucker clubbed him again.

No one fired.

Bannerman. Coming up the path. Making no sound. Gun ready. Sweeping the courtyard with it, assessing what he saw.

"LESKO!" Billy again. Their eyes had met. "SHOOT HIM."

Grassi panicked. He stood up. Tried to run, find cover. But he stepped into the armrest of Urs Brugg's collapsed wheelchair. It snagged his foot. He stood there, upright, trying to pull free. Tucker saw him, swung the machine pistol. Urs Brugg shouted. His strong arms reached up, seizing Grassi, trying to drag him down, lifting himself in the process. Leo Belkin, in turn, shouting, clawed at Urs Brugg. Tucker snapped a burst. The barrel kicked upward, stitching from the flagstone behind Grassi to a low palm above him. A sharp cry. He pitched forward. The machine pistol returned to Billy's neck. Lesko still had no shot.

"LESKO? SHOOT THROUGH ME. NOW."

He held his aim. But he could not.

Bannerman now. Creeping up. Fifteen feet. Come on, move, shouted Lesko in his mind. A few more steps. Slap that gun away and kill the fucker.

Susan—

On the path behind Bannerman. Coming up. No. Stay away.

It's as if she hears. She's ducking a little, moving sideways toward the cover of a bush. Reaching for it. No, he wanted to shout. Don't touch it. Just get down.

But she touched it. Bannerman hears. He's whirling, crouching, swinging his gun around—

"NO!!" Lesko wheeled on Bannerman. He fired. Bannerman spins, staggers, crashes down on the flagstone. Susan screams his name.

Tucker jumped at the sound. A shot and a scream. He hesitated between them. Then he fired toward the shot. Bits of tree leaf rained on Lesko. He waited, held his aim, then squeezed the trigger. Twice.

Tucker's cheek exploded.

And a part of Billy's neck.

The woman, the one with Kurt Weiss, ran toward them. Not breaking stride, she kicked at Tucker's weapon, then wedged herself between the two. Two muffled shots. Tucker's leg bucked once, then it was still.

Carla Benedict unfolded her legs and, carefully, eased herself to the floor. The Englishman squealed. He tried to back away. There was no place to go. He could only scurry, crablike, into the space between the toilet and bidet, eyes wide with terror as she approached, the knife still rolling between thumb and forefinger.

She knelt close to him, elbows resting on the toilet seat. He had covered his face, more mewing sounds. She waited until one eye peeked between his fingers. She glanced over her shoulder, just once, in the direction of Janet Herzog. Then she leaned closer.

"For the record," she told him quietly, "we're not dikes."

"Oh, for Pete's sake." Janet threw up her hands.

"I'm just telling him." She tossed her head self-consciously.

"Carla." An admonishing tone. "Who cares?"

She didn't answer. But she cared. No one knows what's on the other side. Who knows who Martin might bump into after she sends him there.

"Hey, Martin." Janet waved a hand, craning her neck to see past Carla. "In case you're wondering, this is for Gary Russo."

Carla turned. An angry glance. "Do you mind?"

"Do you? Can we get this show on the road, please?"

Carla turned back to the Englishman. His hands had dropped a bit. His eyes, duller now, beginning to cloud, showed no recognition of the name. Good, she thought. No harm done.

She reached one hand to his arm and eased it away from his face. Helpless, he did not resist. He stiffened only when he saw the knife. It appeared where his arm had been. It moved toward him, but slowly, not threateningly. The blade came to rest at a place beneath his jawline. She held it there.

"Last January." She reminded him. "The Elena Brugg hit. The one you screwed up."

He blinked, still confused. These two, he now realized, were professionals. Specialists. Amal and Erna, surely dead. And what this one had done to him. So calmly. He'd known it then. But he'd thought, to the extent that he could think, that they must have been hired by a parent—a lover—of some other woman he had taken and bathed. That much he might have understood. But by the Brugg woman's family? It was only a job. Not personal. She's even still alive. Professionals simply do not do this. Work both sides of the street. They do not—*humiliate* each other. He heard himself saying that. Bawling it. Screaming it.

She cut him.

Her hand had barely moved. It was clean and quick, nearly painless. The Englishman winced, nothing more.

"Dr. Gary Russo." She repeated the name. "He was in that car. He was my friend. You killed him."

"No—I would never—the two outside, they—"

She touched a finger to his lips. He flinched, and he was silent.

"My name is Carla Benedict. Have you heard of me?"

His eyes showed recognition. But he shook his head, slowly, as if to deny her as he had denied what had been done to him.

She raised the knife to his eye. "Say my name." A mock pleading tone. "Say that you know me."

"C—Carla Benedict," he managed. "With—Mama's Boy."

A tiny smile. "That's good, Martin," she told him. "It's good that you know who killed you."

She gestured with her chin toward the cut she'd made. He could feel it now. It was throbbing. Pumping. He turned his head, in anguish, fearing what he knew he would see. Fresh blood, in rhythmic spurts, arcing onto his hip. Blood that would never reach his brain. He clamped a hand against its source. He made cat noises again.

"I'll go hang the towel," Janet Herzog said.

—29—

The first Bell Jet Ranger rose from its pad. It hovered 100 feet above the beach. Urs Brugg, the pain in his side easing, one of the Israeli woman, named Tovah, feeling his pulse, looked down on the activity below him.

He could see the whole of the courtyard. As he watched, one man hosed blood from the stone. Two others walked about, picking up spent cartridges. Tucker's body was gone. It had been wrapped in a plastic tarpaulin and carried to the trunk of Grassi's Rolls. It would be taken to his boat where it would be suitably weighted, then disposed of in international waters.

At the front entrance, Grassi himself. Being helped into his car. He, too, had been shot. Twice. Low on the hips. The wounds, although painful, were not dangerous. At his side was the other Israeli woman, also, like Tovah, trained as a combat medic. It was that one who had finished the man called Tucker. Grassi's Israeli had fitted him with a sort of diaper made of material cut from a beach umbrella and packed with towels. Humiliating, perhaps. And well deserved. But no good leaving blood in the Rolls. The Israeli had agreed to stay with him until discreet medical attention could be arranged.

Also at Grassi's side stood Kurt Weiss, his driver. His left cheek bandaged but the wound not serious. Caused not by a bullet but by chips from a concrete planter. Tucker had fired wildly and with one hand; Bannerman's man McHugh spoiled his aim. Had Tucker been more competent and had it not been for Lesko, more might have died. Himself among them.

Many other cars leaving. Or preparing to leave. His own nephews were there, having solicited rides as far as Malaga, having been denied the second helicopter. There was a greater need for it.

It was lifting off now. It rose, over a maelstrom of sand, and banked immediately to the northwest. Fuel permitting, thought Urs Brugg, it should reach Lisbon within ninety minutes.

The departing cars again caught his attention. A few had turned east. But most were crossing the Cádiz road and climbing a hill that, as far as he could tell, led nowhere. Now he saw where they were going. Several had already stopped at a house halfway to the base of the mountain. He could see two men standing on the terrace, gesticulating to new arrivals. Their body language seemed to convey great enthusiasm. Urs Brugg could not think what the cause might be. The house was unremarkable. Except, perhaps, that its occupants used their terrace railing as a laundry line. Unusual for Marbella. Probably Italians.

The pilot looked over his shoulder, questioningly, concern on his face. Urs Brugg managed a smile. He raised his thumb, then turned it, gesturing in the direction of Malaga where his Gulfstream jet was refueled and waiting. His wound could wait. The bullet, steel jacketed, meant for Grassi, had entered under his armpit and exited high on his chest. It passed through four inches of his flesh, no more, deflected by a rib. It would be treated in Zürich. Meanwhile, he had Tovah. Then, too, there was Lesko, seated behind him with Elena. There was every reason to get Lesko out of Spain quickly. The helicopter banked and climbed.

* * *

From his place behind Urs Brugg, Lesko watched the scene below, without interest, his expression sad and distant.

Elena sat with him. She tried to soothe him.

"You did well, Lesko," she told him. "Susan will understand."

Lesko did not answer. In his mind he heard his daughter's scream. And he saw the look in her eyes. Disbelief. Then fury. Perhaps even hatred. He could not blame her.

"David?"

Katz would know. He knew Susan. Practically her uncle. He almost wished that Katz could go with her. Talk to her. Maybe he had. There was no answer.

The way they had looked at him, the rest of them, Bannerman's friends, he was lucky to be alive. Several of them, maybe six or eight, ran over to Tucker, ready to pump insurance shots into him. But his head was already all over the courtyard. Then they swung their guns on him. Elena yelled at them, stepped in front of him, or tried to. He held her aside, his own gun lowered.

But they didn't shoot.

He almost wished they had.

In the second Bell Ranger, Billy McHugh's head snapped up.

The hot sun strobing across his face, the whine of the rotors, had revived him. He glanced around him. The Mediterranean, he saw, was on his left. This helicopter was heading west.

"Wha—where we going?" he gasped, trying to rise.

Leo Belkin reached to restrain him, ease him backward.

"To Lisbon," he told him. "To the Soviet Embassy. We have a surgeon there. A good one."

The KGB colonel reached to adjust the field dressing that packed Billy's neck and shoulder. Beneath it, the wound had been crudely stitched. The collarbone pressed into place. No anesthetic. But the Israeli had worked quickly. And this man had not complained.

"Where's Paul?" Billy asked, pressing forward against Belkin's touch.

"Behind you. Resting. You must both sit quietly."

"Paul?" Billy ignored him. He raised his good hand to the space between the headrests.

"Right here, Billy." Bannerman took the hand in his. His left. Bannerman's right hand and arm were also useless.

"How bad? You, I mean."

"Not bad at all," he lied. "Just a crease. You relax. We'll be there before you know it."

"At the Russian Embassy? What for?"

"No police, no questions, a good doctor. Besides, there's something Colonel Belkin wants to show me there."

Billy met the Russian's eyes. Trying, through his pain, to read them. He saw nothing that gave him alarm. Nor did the Russian look away. But he saw Billy's suspicion. He shook his head. "You are quite safe," he said. "It is not at all what you must be thinking." Belkin gestured toward the empty seat next to Billy. Billy's automatic was there. "You may keep it if you wish."

Billy wished. And he wondered. What could be better than delivering Mama's Boy and Billy McHugh, wounded, mostly helpless, inside the walls of a Russian Embassy compound? But Paul showed no concern. Billy's mind turned to the last thing he remembered. The shooting, the chaos, at the Puente Romano.

"Paul?" he asked over his shoulder. "We lose any?"

"No."

"You're sure? Any sign of—"

"Three towels," Bannerman answered tersely. "Stay quiet, Billy. Try to sleep."

"Carla and—"

"They're fine, Billy. Show's over."

Billy nodded, satisfied. "Grassi." He closed one eye, remembering, a smile tugging at his mouth. "He got shot in the ass, didn't he."

"He'll live."

"Too bad."

"Billy—not now."

"It's his fault. Him and his games. If that dumb shit football player didn't pop him first, I would've before we left."

"Billy—"

"Or you would've."

A sharp intake of breath. "Billy—Susan's back here with me."

"Lesko?"

He heard Katz's voice over the slap of the rotors. He was no longer in the mood.

"David—Leave me alone."

"Just listen for once, okay?"

"No. Go away."

"Lesko, I saw. You did good.

"Bullshit."

"Bannerman's still alive. So's his gorilla. Nobody got hurt that bad except the redneck who was dead one way or another anyway. You did good."

"You saw how Susan looked at me?"

"What about it?"

"What about it? She sees her father blow a man's face off and she sees me shoot her boyfriend. What do you think, she grew up seeing me do this around the house?"

"I would've done it. Shot Bannerman, I mean."

"You would have yelled first. I didn't. Maybe I—I don't know, maybe I wanted him dead. Out of Susan's life."

"Will you stop?"

"Stop what? Maybe it's true?"

"Lesko"—Katz shifted in the seat next to him—*"Anything involving your daughter, you wouldn't know the truth if it bit you on your pecker. I have to draw you a picture?"*

"Just leave me alone."

"You're at this hotel, right? No regular guests. Most of the staff sent home except the ones in Grassi's pocket. Otherwise, nothing but pros. Old pros. The kind who stayed alive because they don't wait to yell warnings."

Katz had a hand on his arm. Lesko tried to pull away.

"Listen to me." The hand gripped him. *"Bannerman knows this. He knows none of his friends—only his enemies— would run up behind him without letting him know they're coming. So he hears a noise, his instinct says turn and shoot. The guy's on autopilot. By the time he sees it's Susan, maybe it's too late."*

Lesko squeezed his eyes shut. It had been so close.

"You did good. You also impressed a lot of people. Two great shots."

"David," Lesko said patiently, *"I aimed at Bannerman's head. Any lower and I hit Susan myself. It was luck I got his arm."*

"So? One great, one lucky."

"I aimed for Tucker's head, too. I got his jaw. And a piece of Billy."

"You want some advice? Shut up about luck. Let people think what they want."

He did not answer.

"Lesko?"

He felt the hand on his arm. Squeezing it.

Wait a second.

Since when does Katz touch him?

"Lesko?"

He blinked. Elena's voice. Her hand.

"Yeah?" He straightened. "Sorry—what?"

"Do you understand what I've said?" she asked, gently.

"Ah—what part?"

"That Uncle Urs is right. You did well. You were very brave. And that, concerning Mr. Bannerman, you had no choice."

"That was you? Just now?" He waved a hand as if to erase the question. "Never mind," he said, embarrassed.

She eyed him curiously, but withheld comment. "What is important is that you believe it."

"I'm more interested in what Susan believes," he said, gathering himself. "Maybe you could call her. Talk to her."

"I think Mr. Bannerman will do that."

"Square me with Susan? Fat chance."

She squeezed his hand, reassuringly. "May I rest against your shoulder?" she asked.

"You want a pillow? I could get you a pillow."

A deep sigh. She lifted his arm and, to the extent she was able, raised it over her head. She nestled against him. "No, Lesko," she said. "I do not want a pillow."

He allowed his arm to embrace her, but he kept its weight from settling. He was barely touching her.

"Am I made of spun glass, Lesko?"

"Sorry." He eased it down, finding the warmth of her arm. She closed her eyes.

"David?"

No answer.

"Were you here?"

Still nothing. Just as well. All in his head. Has to stop anyway. While Elena still thinks he's sane.

"A pillow?"

Oh, Christ.

"Lady wants your body, so you'd give her a fucking pillow?"

"David—"

"You're hopeless, Lesko. You know that?"

"I know."

. . . *I know.*

Susan had barely spoken to him. Nor he to her.

She had asked about his arm, how badly it was hurting him. He made little of it, saying hardly at all, but she knew better.

The right arm was broken, although not shattered. The bullet had entered at a shallow angle, just below his elbow, and drilled, toward his wrist, through several inches of muscle.

Like Urs Brugg's, it had passed through. Like Billy's, it had been roughly stitched. She had watched as two men held him still and the Israeli straightened the bone. She flushed the wound with vodka, then sewed it shut using what looked like an upholstery needle and dental floss. Susan would not turn away. She refused to let him see her do that. Only when the arm was splinted and wrapped did she leave, to get ice from the bar in a plastic bag. She went with him to the helicopter, boarded with him. He did not resist. Nor did he welcome her. She sat with him, strapped him in, and carefully placed the ice on his arm.

Billy, when he realized she was there, greeted her and was kind to her. He did not blame her. *"Grassi's fault,"* he repeated. He did not explain what the man she'd seen shot had done, or why he, or Paul, might have popped him for it themselves. She tried to believe that *popped* meant the same as *punch.* But she knew that it probably did not.

Nor did he blame her father. Billy had asked—insisted—that he fire. Whatever the risk. *"Somebody had to,"* he said. *"No one else would. It was his own fault,"* he said, *"that he did not duck away from the point of your father's aim."* But a wounding shot from her father was better than a killing shot from the gun pressed against his neck.

Susan did not believe him. No one could calmly accept a bullet. He was being kind again. But it was not, she agreed, her father's fault. Nor was it Grassi's. It was her fault. All of it.

Paul had told her to stay. She couldn't. She didn't.

But she would not have interfered. Or cried out. And she'd kicked off her shoes, as Paul had, to move without sound. She saw Billy and the man who held him. She saw the man shoot. She saw Paul, moving silently, creeping toward him from the rear. She was about to watch him kill a man. It must have dizzied her. She grabbed for a branch. That damned branch.

He pivoted toward the noise. He would have seen it was her. He wouldn't have fired. But her father shot him. Her damned father.

And his damned daughter.

"Paul, I'm so sorry," she said.

"It's okay," he answered distantly. He did not look at her. She sat in silence.

"Susan?" Billy's voice. "Come here a minute. Sit with me."

She hesitated. But Leo Belkin was rising. She unfastened her belt. Bannerman said nothing. He seemed relieved.

"No. You rest," the woman named Tovah insisted.

Urs Brugg shook his head. "The wound is trivial," he said. "I wish to speak with Mr. Lesko."

Lesko had already risen and squeezed past Elena. He stood in the aisle, frowning. His expression said that he sided with the Israeli.

"Five minutes," Urs Brugg said. "Then I will rest."

"Two minutes," said the Israeli. "No more."

Lesko waited as the former medic gave up her seat. He eased himself down next to Elena's uncle.

"I have been eavesdropping," said the older man. "Elena is quite right. Kindly waste no more time in self-reproach."

"How're you feeling?" he asked.

"Of all concerned, including Elena, my wound is the least serious. We will say no more about that either."

"No chest wound is not serious."

Brugg glared at him through hooded eyes.

"Okay." Lesko surrendered. "I did great. What else can I do for you?"

"What we discussed in Zürich. You have not changed your mind?"

Lesko shrugged vaguely.

"If I am incapacitated, Mr. Lesko, I will need you more than ever. Elena needs you in any case."

"I'll have to go home," he said. "Take care of a few things. But I'll be back."

"And you'll stay?"

"I'll stay." For a while.

"In that case, your consultantcy began yesterday. Young Willem will open an account for you. Whatever you need, it is yours. Mr. Grassi will provide names and addresses, warehouses, laboratories"—Urs Brugg winced—"enough to make a beginning."

"Are you okay?"

"It's nothing. Yes."

"Two minutes is up. Get some rest."

Billy McHugh made a calming gesture with his good arm.

"You got nothing to be sorry about," he told Susan, softly. "The problem's with him, not you."

She shook her head. "If I hadn't—"

"What happened there"—he stopped her—"is that something went a little wrong. Something always goes wrong. Most times, we handle it. This went wrong three different ways before you ever came up that path." He held up three fingers. "Grassi played games, I didn't finish the guy last night, I didn't go for him this morning when I had the chance."

"I got Paul shot. You didn't. I probably got you shot as well."

Billy ignored the reference to himself. They'd covered

that. "He doesn't care about the arm. Three, four months, it's good as new."

"I really don't think he's enjoying it, Billy."

He made a gesture of dismissal. "All he cares about, he almost shot you. He would have. Your father saved your life."

She drew back from him, doubtfully.

"I would have shot you too, Susan. It's true. It happens that quick sometimes. Sometimes even on purpose."

She didn't understand.

"We go on a mission," he explained, "the idea is to do the job and not take any losses we can help. Those two things come first. We try to be neat, but people get hurt now and then. People in the wrong place, wrong time. Maybe all they're doing is walking their dog. Or they happen to be looking out a window. Sometimes it's us or them. We try not to hurt them but . . ." His voice trailed off.

She waited.

"Molly—she told me once you ought to know this. She wouldn't say it herself because—she likes you, you like her. She wouldn't want that to change."

"And Paul?"

"Same thing. Yeah."

"I understand. I guess." No witnesses. My God.

"It takes time," he told her. "Another thing, Molly's going to be real proud of you when she hears you held up this good. Most would've fell apart. You're your father's daughter, for sure."

She started to speak. He saw anger in her. He slapped her knee.

"Next thing," he said. "Don't get down on your father. Switch places, him and Paul, and Paul would've shot him just as fast. Except Paul wouldn't have hit no arm."

She dropped her eyes. "He claims he's a bad shot."

"At targets"—Billy waggled his hand—"so-so. At people with guns, he's better. Thing is, he's glad your father nailed him. For your sake and for his. We get to Lisbon, you call your father. Tell him that."

"Billy? Why are you doing this? Being so nice to me."

"What's not to be nice?"

"I would have thought—that you'd just want me to disappear. Get out of Paul's life."

"That what you want?"

"I'm not sure I'm going to have a choice. I think he'll send me away."

"He can't now. He's stuck with you."

"Because I know so much."

Billy shook his head. "Because other people think you do."

She understood. She supposed. Truth be told, she really didn't know all that much about Westport. Certainly less than her father. And probably the Bruggs. And probably the fifty or so men and women who'd showed up in Marbella just because Paul was in town. There was a lot more to learn. If she wanted to learn it.

"Will you teach me?" she asked.

"Teach you what?"

"How to be useful. How not to make mistakes."

"I'll talk to Paul. But I think we better, yeah."

—30—

The bone splinter, barely longer than a thumbnail, had been driven nearly through the muscles of Urs Brugg's chest. During the flight to Malaga, it caused him pain.

But on landing, when he raised himself into his wheelchair and the muscles of his powerful upper body flexed and then relaxed the pain went away. Tovah, the Israeli, said that he must not use his strength. Flexing opens wounds. It causes new bleeding. It causes fragments to move.

He paid no attention. The bullet had bounced off him. There were no fragments. And a bleeding wound, a draining wound, hurts less and is less likely to become infected than one that is closed. That aside, it felt good to test his arms and shoulders. To know, wounded or not, crippled or not, that he was still the man he had always been. That he could still manage his affairs, guide his family, help his friends, be a burden to no one.

Still, he humored the Israeli. He let his crewmen, with Lesko, lift him into the jet and settle him in his seat. He let Tovah pamper him, cover him, check his dressing, feel his pulse, until at last she had a need of her own and made her way, in the sky over France, to the aircraft's lavatory.

Left alone, he tested his strength against the arms of his seat. He lifted himself, once and again, muscles flexing, then relaxing.

The bone splinter moved. It reached the fibrous wall of his aorta. It might have slid past. But his heart had quickened. It sucked the splinter toward it.

One more time, he decided, then I will rest so that my pulse does not give me away. He raised himself once more.

Good. He felt good. A bit light-headed now, and a fullness in his chest, but these would pass. He settled back. He turned his head to watch the clouds, his eyes half-closed. The clouds moved toward him. They settled over his eyes, fogging them.

Tovah found him that way.

The Bell Ranger, diplomatic clearance confirmed by radio, had followed the broad, tree-lined avenue leading to Restauradores Square in the modern section of Lisbon. Leo Belkin guided the pilot to a squat three-story building with a curved facade and a large painted circle on its roof.

Not thirty minutes had passed before X rays and blood samples of both men had been taken and Billy was wheeled into surgery. The Russians were efficient, thorough. There was not the one promised doctor, but three, among them a Soviet bone specialist and a Portuguese neurosurgeon.

Bannerman, for his part, was satisfied that he'd suffered no nerve damage. His fingers worked stiffly but they worked. His injury could wait. Billy's couldn't. Still, he welcomed the injection that deadened his right arm from the elbow.

Susan had born up well. Even Belkin had remarked on it. She'd helped Billy onto the stretcher, helped remove his clothing, took possession of his personal effects and his pistol. An embassy guard held out his hand for it. She answered with a cool shake of her head.

He wasn't sure what he'd expected from her. Certainly a measure of apprehension considering her surroundings. At the mercy of the sinister Russians. She seemed guarded but not frightened. Nor was Bannerman at all concerned. Those who'd seen them leave knew where they were going. Carla and Janet. John Waldo, wherever he was, would soon find out. There would be no duplicity. The price would be too high.

Nor was she unduly solicitous concerning his injury. That pleased him. What's done is done. You go on from there.

The same applies, he reminded himself, to the vision that had tortured him throughout their flight to Lisbon. Susan's body. Slammed backward. Sprawling among the shrubs of the Puente Romano. Himself frozen in place, unable to move, his back to Tucker, waiting for him to shoot, or for Lesko to shoot. Hoping one of them would.

But the body was here. Alive and well. Confident. Strong. No more apologies. Let's go, Bannerman, she seemed to be saying. Quit your moping. You would have missed me anyway.

Leo Belkin reappeared. He stepped to the door of the operating room. He opened it, holding it ajar. He spoke to the surgeon in Russian. Paul knew a few words, enough to get the sense of them. The surgeon answered him sharply, then ordered him out. The colonel approached Bannerman, his expression a trifle sheepish, the look of a man who had just learned the limits of KGB authority.

"It is going well," he told Bannerman. "He estimates two hours of surgery. Three if I pester him again." He glanced at Susan, a slight bow, then back to Bannerman.

"How are you feeling?" he asked. "Is your head clear?"

"More than it was." His eyes were on Susan.

"This thing I wish to show you. It is in the communications office, top floor. If you are up to it."

Bannerman chewed his lip. "Might Miss Lesko join us?"

The question startled Belkin. He had a sense that it startled Bannerman as well.

"That would be—imprudent," he said.

"I trust her, Colonel Belkin."

The Russian stepped closer. He dropped his voice. "This gesture—I understand it, of course. However—"

"It's not a gesture. I want her to know it. I want you to know it too."

Susan found a chair. She sat in it.

"If it's all the same to you," she said to both of them, "I'll stay close to Billy."

Leo Belkin looked at her. He bowed again, more deeply this time. "Thank you," he said.

"Thank *you*," she said to Paul.

"What's so important?" Paul asked. The elevator door closed on the infirmary floor.

The question, asked distractedly, annoyed Leo Belkin. He might as well have brought the woman. She was very much with him in his mind.

"You have an expression," he said. "Benefit of the doubt. I will ask only that. I will not ask for trust."

"I will listen."

"You will refrain from judgment as to my motives?"

"Until you get to the point of this, yes."

"Have you any knowledge of computers?"

"I'm a travel agent."

The Russian grunted. "Of course you are." The door slid open.

The communications room, emptied of personnel, resembled nothing so much as a repair shop for electronic equipment. Television monitors, scanners, radio receivers, computers, crowded every surface. Shelves were crammed with boxes, many with their original labels, much of it surveillance equipment. Most of the labels were in English, some in Japanese. The computers were by IBM and Apple.

Leo Belkin dragged a second chair to an IBM workstation whose power was already on. This, Bannerman assumed, is where Belkin had been while he and Billy were in X ray. Belkin gestured toward the nearest chair. Bannerman sat. Belkin took the other. He touched a key.

Three words, in Cyrillic, appeared on the screen. Bannerman knew only the first and third.

Belkin touched another. The same words appeared in English.

"What am I looking at, Leo?" Bannerman asked, stifling a yawn. Blood loss was taking its toll.

"You do not know?"

"It sounds like a computer game."

"You might call it that. Yes."

"Colonel Belkin—" He rubbed his eyes.

"Forgive me. Press any key. The rest is interactive."

Bannerman touched the "space bar." The words
                    THE RIPPER EFFECT
blinked on the screen.

He sat for an hour. Now fully alert. Fascinated. He made people vanish. He watched the effect. Most often, he knew what it would be, even before the screen told him.

"This is American?" he asked finally.

"Yes."

"It is operational?"

"No. It is still—a game."

"It's more than that. How did you get it?"

The Russian shrugged. "By hook or crook."

Bannerman looked at him, wearily. He waited.

Belkin took a breath. "It was taken from a telephone line. A modem. The data you're looking at were transmitted from the residence of Mr. Roger Clew to the residence of Colonel Harold Hagler."

Bannerman was impressed. And surprised. Electronic eavesdropping was a fact of Washington life. Roger should have known better than to bring this sort of work home from the office, let alone transmit it from his home without benefit of a scrambler. He would have had his lines swept regularly but there was always a way, especially in a private residence. On the other hand, nearly all communications from the State Department are monitored internally. Roger must not have wanted this monitored. He must have seen that as the greater risk.

"This Hagler"—the name was vaguely familiar—"His field is counterterrorism?"

Belkin nodded.

"Who else knows about this? Americans, I mean."

Belkin reached for the keyboard. "In the beginning, frankly, we thought you did." He tapped several keys. A message appeared. A series of them. Between Clew and Hagler. There were references to himself. And to Lesko. And to one Irwin Kaplan.

"Who is Kaplan?" Bannerman asked.

"Drug Enforcement Administration. As you have seen, the program seeks the elimination of the narco-terrorist as well as the garden-variety terrorist."

Bannerman reached to advance the screen. There were more messages. Abruptly, Belkin reached over his hand. He hit the "escape" button. The screen went blank, except for a hard-disk prompt.

"If you were to read further"—Belkin chose his words—"you would see that Roger Clew and Hagler and, to some extent, Kaplan, hoped to recruit you and your people as a sort of research team for the purpose of field testing the Ripper Effect."

"I gathered as much." Bannerman remembered Clew's visit after he delivered Susan and her father to Westport. He said, then, that he was working on something. He would not say what. Only that he might soon call in a favor. "Why wouldn't they simply ask?"

"What would your answer have been?"

"No."

"They knew that as well." He gestured toward the screen. "Reading further, you would also see a discussion of various measures, to be taken by them, which might persuade you to say otherwise."

Bannerman was not surprised. That sounded like Roger. "Why don't you want me to see them?"

"They are—inflammatory."

"As in sending car bombs into Westport?"

Belkin, startled, raised an eyebrow. Then he nodded. "That and more. Yes. Eventually, the man funding that assault would have been identified as a Syrian named—"

"Jibril. I know."

Belkin blinked. "But you realize that he is innocent."

"Only of this." Bannerman gestured toward the machine. "Tell me about Urs Brugg. Where does he fit in?"

"He knows nothing of this."

"Then what does he want from me?"

"Your friendship. Your help if he needs it." Belkin explained Urs Brugg's concerns about the future of Europe, Zürich in particular. "He admires Mr. Lesko. He also has a great sense of family. His hope, in my opinion, is that you will one day be part of it through Mr. Lesko. And, in consequence, feel obligated to it."

"I see."

"He is an honorable man."

"I hope so."

"Never doubt that, Mr. Bannerman," the Russian said firmly. "He did lure you to Marbella, he did let it be known, by the right people, that you were coming. They were there to protect you, even from me, his friend. They were also there so that he could meet them, perhaps recruit them. Had you had a chance to talk, he would have told you all of this."

Bannerman believed him. "And you, Colonel? What do you want from me?"

In reply, Belkin removed the floppy disk from the machine and called up a document from the hard disk. It was all in Russian. Belkin began scanning it. There were charts, lists, blurred photographs. In terms of content, it seemed to resemble the other.

"Your government," he explained, "has compiled a data base containing files on all known terrorists and drug traffickers. So has mine, although our computers are somewhat less sophisticated. Your government has done little with this information. Nor have they shared it with mine. There has been talk, since Glasnost, of doing so. It will happen, but slowly. Cooperation will be limited, not because of mistrust but because your system of government, your checks and balances, obviate any possibility of decisive action, to say nothing of confidentiality. Your most effective weapon, assassination, is proscribed by your laws."

"There are other weapons, Colonel. Believe it or not, killing is not my first choice. Sometimes they kill you back."

Belkin raised a hand, keeping to his train of thought. "This 'Ripper Effect' is clearly extracurricular. Not sanctioned by your government. The work of a few men who have grown impatient."

Bannerman waited.

"It is an excellent tool. Superbly done."

Bannerman said nothing.

"And you know it, Mr. Bannerman. In fact, you use it. Intuitively. Random terror, confusion, indirect action"—Belkin stopped himself; he closed one eye—"Speaking of the latter—those three who shot Elena—that house on the hill. I assume they are dead?"

"They are."

Belkin shook his head in appreciation. "Mama's Boy comes to town, he is thwarted in his purpose by the unforeseen, he leaves with his work unfinished, and still his enemies are destroyed and the legend grows. I rest my case."

Bannerman shrugged off the compliment. He laid his hand across the keyboard. "You're saying you want me to use this thing. But you want me to work with you, not Roger."

"My government will act. Yours will not." He held up a hand. "Please do not say no. Hear me first."

"Why should I do this? For you, or anyone."

"Because you can. Because it ought to be done. And because I think that your peaceful years in Westport have come to an end."

"I'm going back there tomorrow."

"You will be arrested. Possibly shot on sight. Mr. Clew knows that you know. He is certain that you mean to kill him."

"For that car bomb nonsense?"

Belkin fidgeted. He lit his pipe. "Ah—there is more, I'm afraid. There is the matter of your attempt on the life of Colonel Hagler."

Lesko watched as Elena, head high, eyes clear, followed her Uncle's wheelchair across the tarmac of Zürich's airport to the waiting limousine.

His driver and bodyguard, both grim faced, lifted him inside. Willem and Tovah were already seated. Willem pretended to be in conversation with him, nodding his head, gesturing, as he covered his lap with a robe. To any observer, Lesko realized, Urs Brugg was still alive.

He would be taken to his home. The family would be gathered at once. A decision would be made as to the timing of the announcement, first of an illness, and then, eventually, unavoidably, the death of Urs Brugg.

It was Elena who had given those instructions. *"When the powerful die suddenly,"* she told Lesko, *"there is often chaos. There are always vultures."* The cause of death, as yet undecided, will be such that he would have been alert to the end, giving instructions, making appointments, all duly witnessed by his surviving family and by his lawyer.

Lesko held back. He felt useless. Worse, he blamed himself all the more. Urs Brugg had been right. There was never a need for him to go to Spain. It had been an indulgence. And, ultimately, it had cost this good man his life.

The limousine departed. Elena watched it go. He wished that she had gone with it, leaving him there. He had his bag. He could just walk to the terminal, book a flight, and leave quietly. All this let's-get-our-stories-straight business had begun to sicken him. That's what it was. All business. Even Bannerman wouldn't have been that cold-blooded. Bannerman liked the guy. So did he.

Yes. That's what Lesko would do. First he'd see Elena home safely. So she could get busy. Not much question who's in charge now. Willem damned near clicked his heels. But at least he cried. Not so much as a whimper out of her.

She was turning now. Walking back toward him. The Godmother. Maybe he should kiss her hand.

"Listen, um"—he looked away—"Suppose I get you into a cab. Get you home."

She blinked. Her lips parted.

"I mean, you've got things pretty much under control here. And it's not like I'm family. I'd better—" He cocked his head toward a row of parked Swissair 747s.

Her chin began to quiver. Her color rose. Tears—finally, he thought—rimmed her eyes.

"Um—you want a cup of coffee first or anything?"

"N—No." She choked.

It wasn't just the tears. It was disbelief. It was fear. It was as if he'd slapped her.

"Look—I didn't mean—"

He never finished. A stuttering sob rose from her chest and tried to escape through teeth that were clenched, through eyes now tightly shut. Sobs wracked her body. Her arms, still in their slings, quivered helplessly. He saw pain as he'd never seen in any human being. The collapse was sudden. And it was total.

"Look, I—" His own hands flapped uselessly. She'd been holding it in. Now the dam had broken. "I—um—I didn't mean today."

Her face was red, almost purple. The only breaths she took came in tiny gulps and she was choking on them. He reached for her, afraid that she might fall. She yielded, burying her face against his chest, almost vanishing within his arms. Her fingers found his belt. They gripped it, tightly. She said something, he thought. Maybe it was just a sob.

"What was that?" His lips brushed her hair. "Never mind." He patted her shoulder. "It's okay. Really. It's okay."

The sobbing slowed. "Do—do you swear?" she managed.

"I—ah, I didn't hear."

She did not look up. "I said n—n—never."

He could barely understand her. She was trembling so. "Yeah, well—sure. Until you get things straightened out."

"Lesko?" His name came as a scream. She pulled at his belt, twisting it.

"Okay," he purred. "Okay, Elena—sweetheart."

The endearment, his first, ever, brought a deep building wail that caused baggage handlers to turn and stare. He held her. He could not speak. At last he heard her voice. It almost seemed to come from within himself.

"S—swear it, Lesko," she gasped. "I cannot—if you go—"

He swallowed. "I won't leave you. Not ever."

He held her tightly. Ten minutes later, neither had moved. And tears ran down Lesko's cheeks as well.

—31—

Bannerman listened to Leo Belkin's account of the bomb that was harmlessly detonated under Hagler's dashboard.

He should have been angry, he supposed, but he appreciated the tactic. Confusion to thine enemies. More Ripper Effect in practice. It probably kept Clew out of mischief and kept him from realizing that he had left the country. And, it got Belkin what he wanted, which was Mama's Boy, sitting down in front of this computer and listening to the proposal of a new alliance.

The Russian, thought Bannerman, was certainly right about the U.S. government's incapacity to deal with these sorts of problems. But Bannerman was not sure he'd have it any other way. The price you pay for an open society. Checks and balances. Congressional scrutiny. Effective action must necessarily be secret. Conspiratorial. And therefore illegal. The trouble with that is there's no such thing as a secret in Washington. Not for very long. Witness Leo Belkin's possession of these disks.

Belkin was working the keys again. "Some of this may upset you," he said. He pressed the "scroll" button until he reached the place that he had kept Bannerman from seeing.

A message came up. Clew to Hagler.

MANLEY MISSING, PRESUMED DEAD—BANNER-MAN/ZIVIC ARE ON TO US—MUST MOVE BEFORE HE DOES.

"When he says 'move' "—Belkin pointed—"one would assume that he means against Westport."

Bannerman nodded. The message certainly smelled of panic. And it was justified, but only to a degree. Bannerman would hardly execute, although he would surely chastise, two top government officials for what was ultimately an elaborate ruse aimed at forcing him into their arms. But then, of course, Belkin's "distraction" wouldn't have done much for their peace of mind.

Belkin scrolled forward. He stopped at the first of several profile documents. Bannerman's own. Those of about half his people—the rest apparently unknown, even to Roger. One for Lesko. One for Susan. Bannerman read it.

It was dated the previous November. Updated several times after that. The sense of it was that Roger disapproved of his involvement with her. No surprise there. Almost no one approved.

Reading on, Roger had learned that they planned a ski trip to Switzerland. Probably tapped her phone. Clew wondered, in his notes, what Palmer Reid might make of that.

More notes. Evidently taken from a computer analysis. These seemed to list Reid's probable courses of action.

Belkin was right. This did upset him. Here, Roger had calculated what Reid was likely to do. He knew about the Elena–Lesko connection. He knew that Reid had been involved with Elena. And he said nothing, gave no warning. But, the big question, did he deliberately see to it that Reid knew? Or was it just carelessness that he made that call, on an unsecured line, at exactly the right time?

Not likely.

"Colonel Belkin." He sat back. "These notes seem personal. Not meant for transmission. Why would he send them to Hagler?"

"He did not. This part, the profiles and notes, were transmitted by modem to the machine of Irwin Kaplan. It was done on the day of Palmer Reid's burial. Roger Clew left for

Westport directly from the cemetery. We believe that Irwin
Kaplan gained access to Clew's apartment."

"Any idea why?"

"There appears to have been an estrangement between
Kaplan and the others."

One would say so, thought Bannerman. Breaking and entering, theft of data, would tend to suggest a breakdown of
goodwill.

"Colonel Belkin," he asked, "would you ask Susan to join
me here?"

"You would show this to her?"

"I'd like to know what she thinks."

Belkin hesitated.

"About this," Bannerman told him, "and about your
proposition as well."

"For heaven's sake, why?"

"I told you. Because I trust her."

Bannerman stared at the phone. There had been something in Lesko's voice. A hesitation. A thickness. But Urs
Brugg was fine, he said. Sleeping comfortably. Elena was
fine. Everyone arrived safely.

Bannerman shrugged it off. Probably still upset about the
shooting in Marbella. He dialed the number Lesko had
given him. A woman answered.

"Mrs. Kaplan? This is Paul Bannerman. May I speak to
your husband, please?"

"Does he know you, Mr. Bannerman?"

Her voice had an edge to it. Probably having dinner, he
thought.

"I think so. Yes. It's quite important."

"One moment, please."

A long pause. Too long. Bannerman could hear whispers.
The voice came on.

"This is Irwin Kaplan."

"Good evening, sir. This is—"

"I know who you are."

"Mr. Kaplan, I've just spoken with Raymond Lesko. He
says that you're an honest man."

"Is he there with you?"

"No, sir. But I'm about to give you his number. I'm going

to ask you to gather your family, leave your home immediately, take your disk file with you, destroy it or not as you choose."

"Wait a minute. Why would I—"

"Go to a safe place, no relatives or close friends. Call Lesko from there. He will explain and he'll tell you how to reach me. I must hear from you within the hour."

"And if you don't?"

"I'll assume that you've been harmed. Or that you are my enemy. But at this moment, Mr. Kaplan, you have nothing to fear from me."

Silence. It had the sound of doubt.

"Get out of there, Mr. Kaplan. Call Lesko."

Bannerman felt a touch at his shoulder. Susan reached for the phone, took it from his hand.

"Mr. Kaplan? It's Susan. Susan Lesko."

"—Susan?"

"We've met. You've been to our house."

"Of course—I—"

"Please trust him, Mr. Kaplan. Trust me. And call my father."

"Give me the number."

"Get some rest, Paul," she told him, frowning. "At least get off your feet."

He'd rocked backward, nearly toppling a lamp in the guest room to which he'd been assigned. He looked at his watch. Susan had moved it to his left wrist. He kept the right arm elevated. A full cast ran from the tips of his fingers, to keep them from flexing, almost to his shoulder.

Two in the morning. Six hours ahead of Washington time. Kaplan should be calling soon. He had Belkin's word that the phone would be clear. He had to keep his mind clear as well.

"I think I'll look in on Billy," he said.

"I just did. He's out cold. So should you be."

"Soon," he told her. "You go to bed. We have an early flight."

Which was dumb, she thought. But at least he was leaving Billy. The doctor said two weeks before he could travel.

Bannerman said he'd probably kick his way out in three days without us here to sit on him. Speaking of sitting . . .

"Sit, Bannerman." She dragged a chair to within reach of the bedside phone and eased him into it.

"Did your father," he asked, "have anything else to say?"

She had spoken to him before he did. Paul had told him about the Ripper Effect. The American version. Not in great detail. Just enough. And that it was Susan who had recognized the name of Irwin Kaplan when she saw it on the screen.

"Not much. But Elena came on. She was very grateful. That you were so nice about what happened, I mean. And so considerate of my father's feelings."

A dismissive shrug. He said nothing.

"You *are* nice, Bannerman. You're a nice man."

He cleared his throat.

"And Elena's nice. So's her uncle. And Billy. Even Colonel Leonid Belkin of the dreaded KGB is nice. I still can't get over it."

"As Billy would say, what's not to be nice? It's not a weakness."

"How tough is Elena? Tough as my father?"

"I only know her secondhand. But the word I'd use is *strong.*"

"How long does it take? To get that way."

"You're already there, Susan. You were born with it."

She smiled, but remained doubtful. "If that's true, it probably needs to cook for a while. I'm way behind the rest of you."

"Time will turn it into habit. And then instinct. But it won't change you any more than it's changed Elena. You won't become hard."

She fell silent. She looked for something to do. She stepped to his end table where a thermos of water had been left, intending to pour it for him. She saw two paper cups but they each held pills. American made. She recognized the sleeping pills: Seconal. And the two yellow ones were Demerol. For pain.

"You haven't taken these? You've had nothing since the anesthetic?"

"After I speak to Kaplan," he said. He gave her a look that asked her not to argue.

His cast was sliding over the arm of his chair. She took his bed pillow and gently placed it in between.

"Have you ever been shot before?" she asked.

"Nope. First time."

"I've seen scars on your body. What are they?"

"Appendix when I was thirteen. Otherwise, just your basic collection of cuts and bumps, mostly from general klutziness."

"Is that true?"

"Scout's honor."

"Then you've been lucky. What you do is so dangerous."

He shook his head. "Not really. It's a lot safer than being a New York street cop, for example. Has your father been shot?"

"Twice. And cut a few times."

"There you have it."

"Bannerman." She curled her lip. "I've traveled with you twice in the past four weeks. And both times one of us almost got killed."

"For reasons totally unrelated to our purpose in being here," he pointed out. "Someone miscalculated, or jumped to a conclusion, or was careless or stupid. A planned mission leaves as little as possible to chance."

"You can plan for no Tuckers?"

"No. But it's why I pick my friends very carefully. It's the Tuckers and the Palmer Reids that hurt you. They're more dangerous than the enemy."

"Am I your friend? You know what I mean."

"More than that. You're *our* friend."

She knew that. Although it was good to hear. And although there might be an exception or two.

"What about Carla? Do you think she'll ever get off my case?"

"Eventually. Don't worry about it."

Calamity Carla. "I could probably learn from her."

Bannerman shook his head. "Learn from Molly," he said, "or from Janet Herzog if you can get her to talk. Carla's good but she likes to walk too close to the edge."

"And from you?"

"I'll teach you nicer things. I'm a nice man, remember?"

There were more questions she wanted to ask. Like, *Those three you went to Marbella for—does this mean you have to go back? Try again? Or did I miss something.*

And why did you, while speaking of Carla, cock your head in the direction of Marbella, not Westport?

Probably just tired. Disoriented.

But she didn't think so.

And what about us? The old one-day-at-a-time seems to have gone by the boards. Do we give some thought to—you know—or do we keep it unofficial? Or am I supposed to make my bones first.

Whatever.

Or how about an easy one. Like, *My new Russian diplomatic passport, even now being forged, which I'll need to slip back into the country tomorrow. My new name. Katya Khakov. Which has to be Colonel Belkin's idea of a joke. And do I get to keep it for a souvenir.*

The phone rang.

"Good," she said. "Now take your pills."

— *32* —

The TWA flight from Lisbon touched down shortly after noon, waking Bannerman, jarring his arm. As it taxied toward the terminal he could see the black stretch limousine, windows smoked, waiting near the gate as Leo Belkin had promised. An immigrations officer stood near it, clipboard in hand, waiting to record and clear their diplomatic passports.

He and Susan stayed in their seats until the last passenger had cleared the aisle of the first-class section and a wheelchair could be brought aboard. The wheelchair, and a feigned sedation, made it all the more unlikely that he would be questioned.

The officer's face showed nothing. No sign of recognition or interest. Perhaps the Soviet credentials were unnecessary. But better safe than sorry. They were cleared in less than a minute. The limousine, its driver a burly young Russian, huge hands, followed the signs to the terminal exit. Once there, Bannerman asked that he return to the entry ramp for departing passengers. At the far end of the ramp, Bannerman directed him to the curb. They waited. Seconds later,

Anton Zivic approached the door and, waving the driver forward, quickly stepped inside.

"Can you take us to Westport in Connecticut?" he asked in Russian.

The driver nodded. "I am to give every assistance."

"Are we being recorded?"

"No," the driver answered. But he shrugged and lifted one hand, palm up. Who knows? "There is vodka," he said. "Also there is tea in a thermos."

Zivic thanked him, then found the switch that raised the glass partition between them. He snapped open a briefcase, taking a plastic device from it. He turned a dial. A pulsating light showed that it was working, flooding the limousine's interior with inaudible harmonics. "Speak freely," he said to Susan, "but softly."

He reached for her hand, kissed it, and held it for a moment looking into her eyes. Perhaps appraisingly, she thought. But apparently satisfied. His gaze shifted to the cast on Bannerman's arm. He frowned. Bannerman waved dismissively.

"Colonel Belkin sends his regards," he said.

Zivic nodded an acknowledgment. "How is Billy?"

"Not so bad. John Waldo showed up at the embassy this morning. He'll stay with him. I saw Carla on the street outside and Janet at the Lisbon airport. They'll stick around a while as insurance."

Susan raised an eyebrow. She'd seen no one.

"Roger is in Westport," Zivic told him, "with perhaps two dozen men. Most of them are positioned as surveillance teams. The rest, with Roger, have occupied the clinic. They have found none of our people but they have Hector Manley. They are holding him, possibly for use as a witness against you."

"A witness? To what?"

"Kidnapping. My information is that he carries federal warrants on that charge, another concerning the theft of government property, and a third concerning a conspiracy to commit murder."

"That's not a federal crime."

Zivic waggled a hand. "It is alleged that you deprived Palmer Reid of his civil rights. It is all the same."

Bannerman sighed audibly. "What would have been wrong with a simple phone call asking if we could talk this over?"

Zivic's eyes flicked toward Susan.

"It's okay," Bannerman said.

"He tried. But he is now certain that you suspect him of that car bomb business. When he saw that you were gone, that nearly all of us were gone, he concluded that we were about to move against him. In his place, would you sit and do nothing?"

"He might still be innocent," Bannerman told him. "It could have been done by an associate of his named Harry Hagler. I have some computer disks to show you when we get a minute. In any case, that wiretap of Manley and Buster Bang came to us through a third associate, a DEA official named Irwin Kaplan who also happens to be an old friend of Lesko's. He had no role in it but when he heard the tape he suspected his friends of working a sting. There was also the chance that the plot could be genuine. Third, because he'd had a falling out with Clew and Hagler, and since the recording was done by DEA agents, it crossed his mind that they might be setting him up as well. The course he chose was to leak the tape to a narcotics cop who he knew, via Roger, to have been in Westport and who was very likely to go to Lesko with it."

"Roger is not innocent," Zivic answered. "I saw his evidence. And I saw his eyes."

Bannerman looked away, his expression uncertain.

"You have doubts," Zivic said. "What are they?"

Bannerman reached into his carry on bag and found an antimagnetic film pouch that contained the computer disks. He handed them to Zivic. "Hold on to these, by the way," he said.

Zivic opened the pouch and saw what it contained.

"Leo Belkin got those," Bannerman said slowly, "by tapping Roger's line. He told me that and I believe him. But how is it possible?"

"Technically, you mean?"

Bannerman shrugged. "Whatever the technology," he asked, "how does a tap on the home telephone of a senior

State Department official go undetected for a period of weeks, even months?"

"Did you ask Belkin?"

"I thought about it later. He wouldn't have told me anyway."

"Would Molly know?" Susan asked.

"She might." Bannerman reached for the tea. Susan helped him with it.

"What are we going to do now?" she asked.

"There are a few places in Westport they won't know about. We'll drop you off at one of them. You'll be safe."

"No chance, Bannerman. Not this time."

"Susan—"

"With that arm, I assume you're not going to walk in shooting."

"No, I'm not. I'm going to try to defuse it. But Roger is a frightened man right now and he has a lot of guns with him. It's a dangerous situation."

"If they see me with you, would they be as quick to shoot?"

He hesitated. "It's not worth the—"

"I'm staying with you."

One hour later, the sun still high behind it, the limousine veered onto the exit ramp at Westport, pausing at a stoplight. Bannerman leaned forward in his seat.

"To your right," said the driver. "Two men."

"Thank you." Bannerman had seen them. They were in a car, illegally parked. One held a camera and was peering through the lens. He could see nothing of the occupants but the diplomatic plates, Bannerman assumed, had caught their attention. He was not alarmed. Many diplomats lived in Fairfield County. Such plates were a common sight.

Bannerman watched as the light turned green. Neither man raised a microphone to his lips.

On directions from Zivic, the driver made his next left turn and continued on until they reached Westport's Main Street. Another car, two more men, were stationed not far from Zivic's antique shop. They went on. In a residential area just north of town, Susan saw two more such cars. She knew this street. Mrs. DiBiasi's house. The gray colonial.

She'd once seen Billy McHugh raking her leaves. Billy rated two cars.

The limousine worked back to the south, coming out onto the busy Post Road. Turning right, it passed Compo Shopping Plaza. The parking lot, Susan noticed, was full. Several windows displayed banners announcing final winter clearance sales. Across Post Road, several dress shops, a resttaurant, and Hermann's Sporting Goods store. Lots of shoppers on that side, too. Hard to spot a surveillance team. She saw that Paul's office was closed, the blinds drawn. He noticed it as well.

"What happened to—"

"Your staff? I furloughed them," Zivic answered. "I thought it best."

"Did they ask why?"

"Two airline tickets to island of their choice were sufficient explanation. You are a generous employer."

Bannerman grumbled. "I notice you're still open for business."

"Um"—Susan clapped her hands—"Children—"

"Never mind."

The limousine turned onto South Compo Road. A mile or so down, on the right, Susan saw the small brownish Cape Cod belonging to Molly Farrell. An unremarkable house were it not for an adjoining tennis court twice its size and, on its roof, an unusually complex antenna. A bit farther, an unmarked van, no doubt equipped for electronic surveillance. She was sure of it when Zivic, catching her attention, brought a finger to his lips. No one spoke until the limousine turned onto Greens Farms Road.

"Have you seen enough?" Zivic asked.

"I guess."

"What now?" Susan asked.

"Let's go get a beer."

"At Mario's?"

"Mario's."

Railroad Avenue is a short, one-way street running no more than the length of the Westport commuter platform. The station is at it's center, Mario's directly across.

The limousine pulled up outside, passing yet another sur-

veillance car. Bannerman reached into his bag. He found the
Belgian automatic pistol; he slipped it into his sling, the
muzzle against his elbow. Susan showed no surprise. With
their diplomatic passports, they had bypassed metal detectors when boarding the plane in Lisbon.

"Five minutes. No more." He told the driver. "We'll let
ourselves out."

Inside, a light blinked. At the bar, he asked for two beers.
Zivic walked toward the kitchen. Two men at a table picked
up ski jackets and followed. Bannerman raised his beer,
sipped at it, then left it untouched.

"Why are we doing this?" Susan asked.

"To let people know we're in town."

"Won't they all come here? Block off that street?"

"Not in time, no." He gazed at the overhead clock.
"Drink your beer."

In a room at the New Englander Motor Inn, Roger Clew
snatched at the phone and said his name. He listened,
frowning.

"At Mario's? Drinking beer?"

He listened further, incredulous.

"We're on our way. Stay with them."

"Hi." The man in the ski jacket rapped on the driver's
side window of the surveillance car, parked near the news-
stand at the foot of Railroad Avenue.

Two men looked up, startled. Instantly, the glass on the
passenger side exploded inward, showering them with fragments. An Ingram machine pistol followed. The man holding it, another ski jacket, reached in and lifted the door lock.

"Either of you guys care for a drink?" he asked.

Bannerman, Susan with him, not Zivic, returned to the
limousine.

"Just pull around the corner," he told the driver.
"There's another car waiting. We'll take that one. Your next
left will take you back onto I-95."

"Is it permitted to stay?" the big Russian asked. "I would
like to watch."

Bannerman hesitated.

"I can draw them off. Give you more time."

"It's not necessary, but sure. Do you remember my office? The travel agency?"

"That Colonel Zivic has closed, yes."

"Drive around town for fifteen minutes. If you're not intercepted, go there. Park and watch. Don't leave your car."

He turned in his seat, extending his hand. "My name is Yuri Rykov."

"Are you KGB, Yuri?"

"Of course."

Bannerman took the hand with his left. "Nice to meet you, Yuri."

Susan drove. At Compo Shopping Plaza they waited, briefly, for a parking space. Susan, taking Bannerman's keys, worked the double locks of the doors. Bannerman flipped on the lights, turned up the heat, then adjusted a mechanism that left the front door fully ajar.

He walked to the rear, to his private office, glass enclosed, and left that door fully open as well. He picked up a chair and placed it behind the heavy, oversize desk, next to his own, facing the street. He asked Susan to sit.

"What now?" she asked.

"Just relax. It won't be long."

"This is it? We sit and wait?"

He nodded, then held out a hand. "Could I have Billy's gun, please? You're breaking the law."

She made a face. Damned blinking lights. But they'd entered both places together. They blinked for his own gun. "How did you know?"

"Lucky guess. Put it in the drawer."

She hesitated, but did as he asked.

He gestured toward the front door. "Anyone comes in, if you see a weapon in their hand, or even if one hand is hidden, you drop right to the floor behind this desk."

"What'll you be doing?"

"I'll be there with you."

—*33*—

Roger Clew, his radio in hand, stared at the shattered glass. Farther up the sidewalk, an agent called his name. Clew turned. Two men, his men, were stepping through the front door of Mario's, their hands raised to their shoulders. He cursed.

"Is he in there?" he called.

They shook their heads, gesturing toward the far corner.

Clew spoke into his Motorola. "Has anyone seen that limo? Report."

"Unit six. We have it," a voice crackled. "Wilton Road, Merritt Parkway entrance. It just climbed on, headed north."

North, Clew muttered in his head. *To where?*

"Can you see passengers?"

"Negative. Only the driver . . . wait. He's exiting again. Exit forty-two, southbound."

Clew felt a chill. He turned to the two men, now approaching, their expressions fearful, disgusted.

"Who's in Mario's?" he asked.

"A few people. Not the ones who took us. They disappeared out the back."

The chill turned to horror. "Out of here!" he shouted. "Everyone!"

Bannerman. He likes to let you commit, come in behind you. Clew could almost see it. Cars, Bannerman's cars, sealing both ends of this little street. Guns on the roof, more on the station platform. Nowhere to go.

"Out of here. Now."

"Unit two," the radio crackled. "We have Bannerman and the woman. He just entered his office."

"You're sure? Confirm."

"It's Bannerman. We still see him. Door's wide open. No Zivic."

"Door's open? What's he doing?"

"Nothing at all. Talking."

"Three minutes. We're coming."

"Mr. Clew? There's a lot of locals here. We can't just—"

"The hell we can't." Clew ran to his car.

The first thing she noticed that was at all odd was the turning of heads in the parking lot outside Paul's office. Shoppers walking to their cars, suddenly stopping, looking behind them, then ahead, then quickening their pace. Whatever had startled them, a few seemed to be backing away from it.

Some, now, behaved as if they were being tugged. An unseen string, on either side of the doorway, seemed to be pulling at them. The same few, and a few more, resisted. They appeared confused, even frightened.

"Something's happening outside," she said.

Her hand was on his desk, her fingers running along its edge. The hand paused over the drawer in which she had placed Billy's pistol.

"Don't you dare," Bannerman warned.

"Well? Tell me."

"It's Roger. Trying to clear a perimeter. He seems to be having trouble."

It struck her, fleetingly, that more than a few outside were black or Hispanic. Unusual for Westport. And they seemed even more disoriented than the whites. Yes. Three blacks, two men and a woman, had backed against the window, as if trapped there, and were nervously eyeing the open door as a possible place of safety.

Now men were shouting. "This way." "That way." "Freeze." "Move."

"Bannerman—"

"It's okay. Easy."

She saw them now. A few in uniform. Most in civilian clothing wearing blue vests with large letters on the back. Most had assault rifles, all wore flak jackets.

"That's a SWAT team," she whispered.

"Treasury Department, I think." He craned his neck. He glimpsed the letters. "Yeah. ATF agents. That's Alcohol, Tax, and—"

"I know what the hell it is. Bannerman, why are you fucking calm?"

He winced at the language but kept his eyes on the street. "It's okay," he repeated. "We're rolling."

The shoppers, converging on the open door, now numbered about ten. Suddenly, they broke. A woman first, then the man with her. They dashed for the door. The rest followed. They scrambled through, elbowing, shoving each other. One man tripped against a desk. A monitor pivoted on its base and crashed to the floor in a spray of green glass. Bannerman winced again. Some hid behind desks. Some lined the walls. Others backed away farther, toward Bannerman, obscuring his view.

He rose to his feet, peering over their heads. Outside, all had gone quiet. Across Post Road, a crowd had gathered. A lone agent tried to herd them away. They ignored him. Several heads peered back at him from behind a black stretch limousine.

"YOU PEOPLE INSIDE." A bullhorn. Bannerman did not know the voice. "COME OUT IMMEDIATELY."

No one moved.

"YOU ARE IN NO DANGER IF YOU COME OUT *NOW*."

The black woman screamed. She began sobbing.

"PAUL BANNERMAN?"

Roger's voice. He'd taken the bullhorn. Through the blinds, Bannerman could see shadows moving. Figures, crouched low, were tugging at another, trying to pull him down.

"BANNERMAN, THIS IS ROGER CLEW. SEND THOSE PEOPLE OUT. NO ONE NEEDS TO GET HURT."

Several, on hands and knees, crawled to the edges of the door. Outside, hushed voices urged them on. A black man was nearest. He stopped. "Man here," he called to those outside, "say he shoot us if we try to leave. He say you talk, he don't shoot."

Susan blinked. She glanced at Bannerman's hand. It had made no move toward a weapon. He'd said not a word.

"BANNERMAN. THIS IS A LEGAL ARREST. YOU HAVE NO PLACE TO GO."

Bannerman cleared his throat. "Come in, Roger. Just you. Bring the warrants."

Silence.

But Bannerman could almost hear the whispered conference. Urgent voices, arguing. "We can't go in. People in the way on either side. More near his desk, in the line of fire." "No, Mr. Clew. Not you either. We can't let you."

"Roger?" he called. "You won't be harmed. My word on it. Just talk."

A long pause.

Shadows moved. A brief struggle. Roger Clew shook off a restraining hand and appeared in the doorway. But at once, two men with rifles pressed in front of him, shielding him with their bodies. They were just inside the door. "Talk from here," one of them snapped.

Susan, as he'd asked, had slid to her knees. Bannerman, still standing, eased into his chair. "No," he said. "I don't think so."

Suddenly, the shoppers rose. Making, Susan thought, a dash for safety. But the two men with rifles stiffened. They parted. The black man, rising between them, blocked Roger Clew from her sight. Now he was backing up, into the office, bringing Clew with him. She saw Clew's face, head back, eyes wide. The other two—their hands were rising. Their rifles, snatched from them, sailed through the air, tossed by two of the shoppers into the waiting hands of others. Susan stared, openmouthed. They weren't shoppers any more.

None of them. More weapons appeared in their hands. They moved quickly, expertly, taking positions as if they'd been assigned. The door swung shut. The room was silent.

Clew, searched and released, approached Bannerman's desk. His right hand, knuckles white, still gripped his radio.

"Have a seat, Roger," Bannerman said quietly. "Use that thing. Tell your men to relax."

"Bannerman—"

"Do that now, Roger." He drew the pistol from his sling and held it across his chest.

"You gave your word."

"Yes, Roger, I did." He nodded. "But if I hear one shot outside, you won't hear the second."

"What good is this?" Clew asked. He'd been searching the faces of the men and women in his office. He recognized none of them. "You have nine people. I have thirty. All legal."

Bannerman ignored him. He was reading the warrants. The charge of kidnapping seemed to intrigue him the most.

"Where is Hector Manley?" he asked.

"In custody."

"Where, Roger?" He raised his eyes. "Is he outside?"

"Down the road."

"Make another call. Get him here. We'll settle that one first."

Clew hesitated, but he raised the radio to his lips and gave the order. Someone argued. Clew switched him off.

Bannerman rose to his feet. He stepped into the conference room, returning shortly with a Scotch bottle and a single glass with ice cubes in it. These he placed in front of Clew. Clew's fingers twitched but he left the bottle untouched.

"What's with the arm?" he asked.

Bannerman ignored the question. He continued reading.

"If that's a bullet," Clew said, "I had nothing to do with it."

Bannerman said nothing. He sat back, his eyes closed.

Five minutes passed. He heard sounds outside. Shadows moved. The black man at the window raised a slat of the blinds. He turned to Bannerman and nodded. Then he backed toward a rack of brochures and sat. Another man held the door open. Hector Manley stood there, a disembodied hand on his shoulder. The hand pushed him forward. The door closed behind him.

"This way, Mr. Manley." Bannerman rose to greet him. "Straight ahead, please."

The Jamaican showed no fear. His expression was one of fascination, even amusement. He was dressed as Bannerman had first seen him. Long leather coat, white turtleneck, sunglasses, gray snakeskin boots with two-inch heels.

"Unfinished business, Mr. Manley." Bannerman tossed the arrest warrant aside. "I offered you your life if you could give me certain assurances. I'm afraid it's now or never." His manner was pleasant enough. Unthreatening.

Manley shook his head as if to clear it. He had seen the guns outside. He knew of the warrants. He had even sworn the complaint. And yet, here was this Mama's Boy acting as if he still had him chained to a wall.

"Could I—ahh." He paused, searching for words that would seem neither impolite nor foolish. "Might I see a bit more of your hand, Mr. Bannerman?"

"I think I'll need an act of faith, Mr. Manley."

He eyed the pistol. Then the man from State. "Mr. Clew?"

"He's not going anywhere," Clew told him. "And he won't shoot you. Not here."

Bannerman looked at his watch. "There you have it, Mr. Manley. You have two ways to bet. Please make your choice."

"Is it true that you won't shoot me? Here?"

"Yes. It is."

"And that I can walk out? Leave you to those men outside?"

"Absolutely. Please decide."

"What if I were to stay here with you? At your side."

"You might get killed. Anyway, that's not an option, Mr. Manley. You and I are some distance from being friends."

"Sad to say." Manley took a breath. "In any case, Mr. Bannerman, I think I would prefer not to be your enemy. Or Mr. Covington's. If he will meet one requirement."

"Name it."

"He must call me his friend and ask for my protection. If he will do that, I will see that no harm comes to him and that no drugs are sold on the streets of his association. If he calls me his enemy, I must hurt him or I will not survive. It will not matter much who kills me."

"Sounds reasonable to me." He cocked his head. "Mr. Covington?"

The black man stepped from behind the rack of cruise brochures. He walked toward Manley who, in recent days, had lost his capacity for bewilderment.

"Is it possible," the Jamaican said to Bannerman, "that this man has come to live in Westport?"

Bannerman shook his head. "Just visiting for now. A friend in need." He looked at the man from 153rd Street. "Mr. Covington, you heard?"

"Could I ask—what you'd do in my place?"

Bannerman shrugged. "The devil you know. I'd take the deal."

"Then the bastard's my friend."

"Mr. Manley?"

"Done. With the same sentiment."

"You needn't shake hands. Mr. Manley? Give me an hour. I'll drop you at the station. Mr. Covington? See me before you leave. I have another gift for you."

Bannerman had closed the glass door to his inner office, first signaling those outside that the meeting would be brief. He did not ask Susan to leave.

Clew poured the Scotch. He turned the glass in his hand, thoughtfully, trying to understand that business with Hector Manley. Letting him walk. It was not like Bannerman to take an enemy's word that he would behave. Especially when it meant betting his new friend's life on it.

It has to be the girl, he thought. Susan. She's gotten to him. He wants her to see that everything isn't killing and dying with him. That sometimes there's negotiation, sometimes there's forgive and forget.

Okay, he thought. *Let's give that a shot.*

"I want you to know something," Clew said quietly, still looking at his glass. "Zivic told you about the two men in Mario's? And he figured they were there with me?"

"They weren't. He knows that now."

"They were Kaplan's people, right?"

Bannerman didn't answer.

"Just so you know. I never broke that rule."

"Until today."

Clew sipped from his glass to wet his lips. "You were going to kill me for all this, weren't you? Even for that."

Bannerman said nothing. But he felt Susan's eyes on him.

"All I was trying to do today," Clew told him, "what I'm still going to do—is lock you up until you listen to reason."

"I'm listening now."

Clew sipped again, more deeply this time. "That thing with the car bombs," he said. "I didn't set that up. It was Hagler's idea. When he told me, it had gone too far for me to stop it. I might not have anyway. It might have been worth a shot if it would get you back in the game."

"At the risk of destroying this town?"

Clew shook his head wearily. "Give me a break, Bannerman. You talked to Manley. It never would have happened."

Bannerman said nothing.

Clew shot a glance toward Susan. She was still watching Bannerman. Maybe, he thought, her being there was keeping Bannerman from saying things he didn't want to hear. But it wasn't moving things along any. He cocked his head in her direction. "Does she have to be here?"

"She has a name, Roger," Bannerman hissed. "And you didn't worry about her being here when you brought up your SWAT teams."

Clew squirmed.

There were things he could talk about in front of her and things he could not. Things that even Bannerman wasn't supposed to know about. Except he did. Bannerman had never asked who Hagler was. Who Kaplan was. He knew.

"How much, Paul. How much do you know?"

"The Ripper Effect," he said simply. "Does that answer your question?"

Clew seemed to wilt. "Kaplan told you. Right?"

"Wrong."

Clew drained his glass. "Will you tell me who did?"

"No."

"Will you at least tell me what you think of it?"

"It's a good tool. It should work."

"Would you use it?"

"Maybe. But not with you, Roger. Those days are over."

Clew poured his second Scotch. He slid the bottle across the desk toward Bannerman.

"No, thanks." Bannerman moved it aside. "I have to fight my way out of here, remember?"

A deep sigh. "It doesn't have to be like this. Unless you killed Kaplan. Did you?"

Bannerman shook his head. "He's not afraid of me, Roger. He's afraid of you. And Hagler."

"What about me? Would you have killed me?"

"Not for the car bombs. Not even for this." Bannerman gestured toward the street. "But tell me about Palmer Reid."

Clew sat back. He shook his head slowly. "See that?" he said. "That's why I'm here with a fucking army. That's why I'm risking everything just to calm you down long enough to convince you I had nothing to do with that. None of us did."

"You saw it coming. Or your computer did."

"That's not true. Maybe that Reid would wonder how you tied in with Elena. Maybe that he'd put a tail on you or something. But that he'd have Susan here killed just to confuse the issue? That probability didn't even make the charts."

"Because it was illogical?"

"Because it was nuts."

"So was Reid. And you knew that, Roger. Here's what we're going to do"—Bannerman rose from his chair—"We'll take a walk outside, you first. You'll tell your people that it's a false alarm. You will tell them to put down their guns, pack up, and get out of town at once. Next—"

"I can't do that."

Bannerman ignored the interruption. "Next, you'll come back in here and call the judge who issued these warrants. Get them quashed. Then, call your office. Have your staff get on the phone to the media and to the local police, and tell them I'm not your man, mistaken identity, whatever."

"Paul—it's gone too far." Clew gestured through the

glass toward the men who'd been disarmed. They'd seen and heard too much.

"Promote them, Roger. Then transfer them." He waved off further discussion. "Tell the media that you're terribly embarrassed about upsetting the good people of Westport, to say nothing of me. The man you were looking for, my height and build, arm in a cast, has just been arrested elsewhere. Make it good, cite national security if you like, ask them to say nothing of this episode. I don't want to see one word in tomorrow's paper."

Clew reddened. He turned toward the outer office and made a show of counting Bannerman's force on his fingers. "Am I missing something here?"

Bannerman pretended not to understand.

"What are you going to tell me? If I don't, I get killed?"

"Only if shots are fired. You have my word."

"Then what? With ten people, you take on thirty and turn this whole part of town into Beirut? You don't think that will upset the good people of Westport?"

Susan was smiling. She was staring toward the street. The smile had grown slowly.

"Did I say something funny?"

"Sorry. I just realized—"

Bannerman touched her arm as if to silence her. "Come on, Roger," he stepped toward the front door, "Let's look at your thirty men." He pulled the blinds.

They were still outside, Susan saw. Still armed. But their weapons were lowered. And they'd moved closer, gathering in the parking lot, out of the street. Behind them, traffic moved normally. Around them, among them, stood twice their number of men and women dressed in civilian clothing. The civilians were chatting with them, physically touching them.

The scene called up an image of a high-school band awaiting the start of a parade. In uniform, milling about, instruments held carelessly, friends and classmates among them.

She scanned the faces. The federal agents in their lettered vests seemed sullen, confused. But they did not seem fearful. It was as if a rumor, as yet unconfirmed, had spread among the band members that the parade would be canceled. Next, she scanned the townspeople, half-expecting to see her father among them. He was not there. Nor were they townspeople.

"See anyone you know, Roger?" asked Bannerman.

Susan did. Molly Farrell. She stood, facing a federal agent, her fingers against his chest, casually conversing. Another woman stood with her. Susan recognized her as one of the two Israelis who'd attended to Paul and Billy in Marbella two days before. There were others she'd seen there as well. Glenn Cook moved through the crowd, shaking hands, slapping backs, exchanging hugs. Several black men, arms folded, hands hidden, more wary than the rest, had formed an outer ring between visitors and onlookers. Beyond them, across Post Road, the Russian chauffeur, Yuri, stood in stocking feet on the fender of his limousine, taking photographs, his expression one of boyish delight. Next to him stood a smaller man, wiry, with a bandage on his cheek.

"Isn't that Kurt Weiss?" Clew asked. It was more of a groan.

Susan followed his eyes. She saw Paul nod. With an upraised finger he was now picking out other men, and several women, reciting their names. Most of the faces were familiar.

Clew turned from the doorway. He had seen enough. "How many?" he asked.

"About thirty. Some couldn't get flights. Then there's Mr. Covington's block association."

"Are they armed?"

"Of course."

"Would they have fired?"

"That's the idea, Roger."

"Why is the European crowd here? Why else, I mean?"

"To look the town over, I suppose. Check out housing costs, the crime rate. That sort of thing."

Clew rolled his eyes.

"Roger—make your calls."

"Then what?"

"Make one more. Get Barton Fuller on the phone for me."

Clew's color rose. "Anything else?"

"No." Bannerman shook his head. "But drive carefully, Roger."

"Question time," Susan said.

She had to wait until Yuri, behind the wheel of the limo, finished gleefully recounting all that he'd seen and heard. Colonel Belkin, he said, would scarely believe it. But he had pictures, which Mama's Boy said he could keep. And soon, after taking them home, he would go and have lunch at Mario's, which Molly Farrell said he could do. As her guest. Perhaps she, too, would permit a photograph, a souvenir, of the two of them together. Perhaps the others, even Colonel Zivic, would sign his menu.

Bannerman fingered the switch that raised the partition but he decided not to bother. There was no point. And it would have been a rudeness.

"You want to know"—he nodded—"whether they would really have fired on federal agents."

"That wasn't it. But would they have?"

"They wouldn't have had to," he answered. "Too many of them. Too unexpected. But don't count on that working a second time."

"What about Roger Clew? Would you have shot him if his men had opened fire?"

"They didn't."

"Did me being there make a difference in what you might have done?"

"As things turned out, no."

"But if—"

He took her hand. "We'll talk about this. But it needs to settle."

"Bannerman," she said slowly, "I don't want to see you hurt anybody. But I also don't want to see anybody hurt you. Any time those are my choices, I can handle it."

"I know you can."

"One more. The man with the Jamaican accent?"

"Hector Manley."

"And he's a drug dealer."

"Yes. What about him?"

"I think you sort of like him. How come?"

"Within limits, I suppose I might. We've had some interesting talks. And he seems to be a man who keeps his word."

"Will he? Where Mr. Covington is concerned?"

"Yes."

"How can you be sure?"

"Just a feeling."

There was that, Bannerman thought. His capacity to judge character. But there was also the transmitter that he'd given to Wesley Covington, courtesy of Molly Farrell. And there were also the gray snakeskin boots whose hollowed-out heels were packed with a microreceiver and just enough Semtex to blow off both his feet should he reconsider.

Bannerman's apartment complex was just ahead.

"Let's go up and make a fire," he said.

"Can we unplug the phone?"

He nodded. "And no Vivaldi this time."

"But no Bolero, either. I should have picked up a copy in Spain."

"I'll hum it," he said.

—34—

In Lesko's Queens apartment, Elena watched, sipping tea, as he filled the second of the two large suitcases he'd purchased.

His daughter stood at the suitcase, opened on his bed, removing certain of the items he had packed, stuffing them into a plastic trash bag, replacing them with others. Lesko had stopped arguing.

Bannerman was in the kitchen with Harry Greenwald. They were packing cardboard boxes, adding them to the those already stacked by Lesko's door. The detective had agreed to store some, dispose of others. No one spoke much. Not since Elena had sat Paul and Susan down in Lesko's living room and told them, as gently as possible, of the death of her uncle, Urs Brugg.

Lesko had argued against her making the trip with him. It could still be dangerous, he said. Unfinished business. But she'd insisted. Bad news, she said, should be given face-to-face, where people could touch and give comfort through more than words. And, too, she wished to know this Mama's Boy as her uncle had.

Not the least of her reasons, although she denied it when

Lesko asked, was to make certain that he, once home, did not change his mind. She went with him to Rockefeller Center where he obtained an emergency passport. A legitimate one. Bannerman had arranged it. Next, to the Beckwith Regency Hotel where he resigned the position he'd held. She returned with him to Queens where he saw his landlord, settled his lease, and arranged for his furnishings to be given to charity. He did all these things in her sight and in her hearing. It was a burning of bridges. An act of faith.

One bridge remained, still unburned. It involved the partner whose death she had ordered in a different time, a different life. The ghost of that man, Detective Katz, still remained. Susan had told her about him during their first long talk as they flew from Zürich to Malaga. Later, she spoke of it to Lesko.

"Susan's got a big mouth," he had growled.

But it was not the betrayal of a confidence. Merely an explanation of her father's occasional odd behavior, his protracted mutterings, interspersed with attentive silences. The partner, Susan told her, had remained his partner, like it or not. Until now, the ghost of this Detective Katz was nearly all he had. But perhaps, thought Elena, that need will soon fade. As had his memory of her past. As had that day in Brooklyn.

Perhaps.

But perhaps it should not.

One could argue, she thought, in favor of keeping all such ghosts alive. This Detective Katz had become a part of him. That was not a bad thing, necessarily. To have such a ghost, and to not deny him, was to have an extra brain, an extra pair of eyes and ears. Even Mama's Boy, she felt sure, might agree with that. If it keeps you alert, he might say, if it gives you an edge, it is a friend. If Lesko is to honor his covenant with Uncle Urs, which he will and must, he will need such an edge.

Nor, thought Elena, her eyes on Lesko, should the ghost of her past be allowed to recede entirely. She will cook for him, make him smile, give herself to him, love him. But she is still Elena. The family now looks to her. It must not surprise him if this woman who shares his life and his bed, who teases him, pampers him, needs him, and who even now, God willing, may be carrying his child in her belly, will be, when she must, no less ruthless than he. For she too has made a covenant. And it will be honored.

Bannerman entered the bedroom where she sat. The sounds from the kitchen continued. He spoke briefly to Susan, and then to her father. He crossed to Elena and knelt at her side.

"Will there be a service?" he asked.

"Soon. Yes. Within two weeks, I think."

"May I come? With Susan?"

"Uncle Urs would be pleased. And I will insist."

"Thank you."

"It is not yet finished here, is it, Mr. Bannerman?"

"Soon," he answered. "I will end this on Sunday. With your permission, I would like to borrow Lesko for the day."

She frowned. "Come to Zürich now, Mr. Bannerman. Make a new life there, as I have."

"This *is* my new life," he said gently. "And it's my home. But if we may come visit you—"

"I will insist on that as well."

"Thank you. When will you be leaving?"

"You say you will end this on Sunday?"

"I think so, yes."

"Then that is when we will leave."

—*35*—

Saturday afternoon. Georgetown.

Roger Clew, unshowered, unshaven, stared at the screen of his Toshiba. He'd been at it, unable to sleep, since before dawn that day and for all of Friday. Trying to salvage something.

Anything.

He had also, since Westport, gone through intelligence reports by the score, looking for some piece of information he could use. Some item for which Bannerman might thank him. There was one, the report of a rumor, that placed Bannerman in Spain. Obviously untrue. No help there. And there was another, from Lisbon, placing Billy McHugh in the Soviet Embassy there. Equally unlikely. On the other hand, Clew could not recall having seen him in Westport recently. Perhaps it was worth mentioning. But he needed more.

He went back to the Ripper program, not sure what it could tell him or even what to ask. He'd tried everything. Plotting out one scenario after another, punching in every relevant name he could think of, asking the computer for predictions, assessments, most of which were of no use at all.

It told him, for example, that Harry Hagler, missing for three days now, was dead. Or 80 percent dead. That was the probability. But Hagler, he knew, was holed up in Fort Meade, waiting for this to blow over. Waiting for him, Roger Clew, to mend fences. But Roger Clew, according to this machine, was 90 percent dead himself. On the other hand, so was goddamned Hector Manley. That piece of shit. Walks away from Westport, free and clear, practically with a pat on the back while he, Clew, watches fifteen years of work, fifteen years of friendship, go up in smoke.

He sat back, bringing with him the pad on which he'd scribbled his notes. He read through them one more time, marking them and numbering them in order of importance.

They weren't much. But they were at least an excuse to call. A way to start mending.

He reached for his phone and, with one deep breath, tapped out Bannerman's private number. He listened, then sagged. The damned machine was answering.

But the greeting, Bannerman's taped voice, was friendly. More so, he knew, than a live voice might have been. Still, irrationally, he found encouragement in it. He cleared his throat and spoke.

"Paul—look," he read from his notes, "I have a report here that Billy is being held in the Soviet Embassy in Lisbon, possibly injured. On the chance it's true and you need —you'd *like*—me to put some heat on, let me know."

Silence.

"A few more things." He read them off, the report from Spain among them.

More silence.

He was not going to mention Hagler. Or blame him again. He could not find a way to say it, especially into a machine, that did not sound puling. Nor was he going to mention the Jamaican whom Bannerman, God knows why, allowed to walk. Maybe Bannerman thinks he might be useful to him someday. Whose word Bannerman took. The word of a drug dealer.

Jesus Christ.

Clew changed his mind.

"Listen—about Manley." He swallowed. "I've asked the

computer about him. It says you can't trust him. If you like, I'll show you what else it says."

He hesitated. Even to himself, his words had the ring of sour grapes. He tried strengthening his voice.

"He's a lot like you, Bannerman. That's what you see in him. And like you, he can't be hit without hitting back. Like you, if he shows weakness, he loses credibility. He's not going to keep his word, Bannerman. The computer only gives that one chance in six, and only then if he has something more to gain by it. People like Manley—"

He stopped himself. Enough. Too much about too little.

"Look." He took a breath. "I guess you know why I'm really calling."

Silence.

"You're going to see Fuller. Well—you don't have to. I'm out, Paul. He has my resignation."

A sigh.

"So maybe you'll believe me when I say that all I want to do now is square this. Fifteen years, Paul. Maybe we can . . ." His voice trailed off.

He broke the connection.

—36—

Sunday morning. Arlington, Virginia.

Fuller watched from his study as the limousine cleared his main gate and followed the crushed stone of his driveway. He had dressed in his warm-up suit. Force of habit. There would be no platform tennis. No chance of a decent foursome in this group anyway.

Bannerman crippled. No one seems to know how. Kaplan's game flaccid at best. And as for Lesko, if he should take it into his head to try the game, there would probably be no platform left either.

Kaplan was below, greeting him. And his daughter. Now, rather less comfortably, shaking hands with Bannerman.

Fuller shook his head.

It was Bannerman's business, of course, whom he chose to trust. And Lesko, according to Irwin, was a man of fierce loyalties to those he trusted in turn. The girl, however, was something else entirely. Too young. Too little experience, her travels with Bannerman notwithstanding. Worst of all, her very relationship with Bannerman will put them both at risk. She, as his Achilles' heel, a way to hurt him. He, as a man distracted.

Too young.

Still, he found himself envying Bannerman. Not least, for having a woman who loved him. But also for the world he lived in. One that relies on no outside agency, governs itself, polices itself. Defends itself, with finality, when necessary. And most of all, one free of moral ambiguity, at least by Bannerman's lights.

Nor, it seems, is it only Westport that aspires to that happy state. Zürich as well, by all reports. And parts of New York City. There seems to be a ground swell afoot. Communities, or at least neighborhoods, are taking shape throughout the country: neighbors banding together, choosing their own leaders, setting up their own patrols, having despaired of the capacity of the law and of politicians to protect them. Bannerman's new friend, this Covington fellow, was among these new leaders. And, oddly enough, with the blessing of some of those same politicians.

New York City's mayor, himself an advocate of community action groups, has called a press conference this very morning at which Mr. Covington is to be held up as an example to all. And, afterward, a block party at which the Manhattan Borough president is to award a citation to Mr. Covington and his 153rd Street Association. Speeches, refreshments, rap bands, and dancing in the streets, that sort of thing. Not the best weather for it, but timely nonetheless. The ray of hope that rotting city needs will hardly be found in a summer sky.

Fuller returned to his kitchen, uncovered a tray of sweet rolls, and returned with them to his study. He stepped to the painting that he had bought because Cassie Bannerman liked it. He smiled, as if to Cassie herself. Then he opened it on its hinges. He checked the panel behind, watching the dials. And then, satisfied that the surveillance cameras were working properly, he walked to his front door where he waited to greet his guests.

"You have your mother's eyes," he said as Bannerman eased into a chair. "Are you aware that I knew her?"

"Yes, sir. I am."

"Now that we meet, I can see a great deal of her in you."

"Thank you." Bannerman passed the pastry tray to Susan. She declined.

Oddly enough, thought Fuller, he could see a trace of Cassie Bannerman in the Lesko girl as well. There was a certain . . . strength to her. Polite enough. Gracious. No hard edges yet. But not at all in awe of meeting the secretary of state. Perhaps Mama's Boy is a hard act to follow. To say nothing of the redoubtable Raymond Lesko.

"You will understand," he said, "if I am less than comfortable having this discussion as a group. Especially in front of two people whose interest is no more than—peripheral."

"Sir, I trust them both. We're here to find out whether we trust you."

Kaplan stiffened. Fuller did not.

"I'm not offended," he said. "You have concluded, I gather, that I had foreknowledge of Mr. Clew's—invasion. I had none. I was in Brussels at the time."

Bannerman had played Roger Clew's message. He had not returned the call.

"What will you do about Roger?"

"I have his resignation. After this discussion, I will decide whether to accept it."

"Why would you do that?"

Fuller spread his hands as if the answer were obvious.

"If you'll forgive me," Bannerman told him, "you should not accept it and I don't think you will. Not while he knows about the Ripper Effect. The same applies to Mr. Hagler."

Fuller raised his cup to his lips. He sipped slowly. He dared not look at Kaplan. "The Ripper Effect, you say."

"Mr. Fuller"—Bannerman let out a sigh—"if we're wasting each other's time, we can leave now."

He sipped again and swallowed. "Forgive me," he said. "Do I gather that both Mr. Lesko and this young lady are familiar with that—exercise?"

Bannerman looked at his watch.

Irwin Kaplan cleared his throat. "We're not trying to be coy," he said to Bannerman. "Clew told us you know. We just don't know how much and we didn't figure you'd tell—" He gestured vaguely in the direction of Lesko and his daughter.

"I'll say again"—Bannerman filled his cup—"I trust them. I trust you, Mr. Kaplan, because Lesko says I can and because you've been straight with me. But only within limits. I appreciate that your first loyalty is to Mr. Fuller."

"That's not true." Kaplan tapped his fingers against his chest. "My first loyalty is right here. They can have my job any time they want."

Bannerman studied him. "But you'd rather keep it?"

"I'd rather do it. That's not the same thing."

"How would you feel about working with me?"

"Can I ask you first how much Lesko knows about the Ripper Effect?"

"He's seen it. I've explained it to him."

"Lesko?" Kaplan asked. "Would you use it?"

"Yeah, Irwin. I'm going to."

"Then, no offense," he said to Bannerman, "I'd feel better about working with him."

"No offense taken, Mr. Kaplan." Again, Bannerman glanced at his watch. "Mr. Fuller? Could I ask where your loyalties are?"

"They have not often been questioned, Mr. Bannerman."

"They certainly don't extend to Roger Clew or Harry Hagler. Are you ready to tell me the truth about that?"

"Which truth would you like?"

"Did you set them up? To be killed by me?"

"No."

"What did you do, Mr. Fuller?"

"I tested them."

"They're both good men, you know," Fuller said. He was on his feet, pacing the room. He seemed drawn to the IBM workstation on the stand beside his desk. "And you are correct. I do not want their resignations. But if you tell them what is said here today, they will surely leave of their own accord."

Bannerman waited.

"That would be a waste. They are, in their positions, what Mr. Kaplan here is in his. Entirely dedicated. Unselfish. Like Mr. Kaplan, they are also frustrated. But *unlike* Mr. Kaplan, those men tend to be buccaneers. I had to know——" He stopped himself, pausing once more at the IBM machine.

"How much of the program have you seen, Mr. Bannerman?"

Bannerman hesitated. "Enough, I think."

"But you won't tell how you found access to it?"

"No. I won't." Nor would he mention that, in his pocket, was a silver lead-lined envelope containing another disk, handed to him that morning by Yuri Rykov. "Jibril," Rykov had said to him. "This is how it can be done." Bannerman had been tempted, more than once, to throw it away.

"You're aware, however," Fuller was saying, "that it has other applications beyond terrorism and drug trafficking."

Bannerman nodded. "It can work against any criminal organization, including corporations."

"Against corporations," Fuller corrected him, "whether they are criminal or not. That application begins to stretch the point, don't you think?"

"I would think. Yes."

"I had to know two things. First, given such a weapon, how far would Roger go? Would he step over the line? Where, indeed, *is* the line?"

"And the second?"

"How far Mama's Boy would go."

"So you had Roger watched."

"Every step of the way. I think you know that, Paul."

He did. The two in the bar. "And you wired his apartment."

"Only after Irwin came to me. He'd had a meeting with the others. He feared that they were about to cross that line."

"When was that?"

"Late January. A few days after we—um—lost Palmer Reid. When Irwin learned of a supposed DEA tape that no one in the DEA knew anything about, that business about the car bombs and Westport, he felt sure he saw their hand in it. On the chance that your Jamaican friend might have actually gone through with it, we decided that you should be alerted. We chose to do so indirectly through Mr. Lesko and his former colleagues."

"Why didn't you simply stop it?"

"The truth? To see how you'd respond."

"Another test."

"Yes."

"Was it the first, Mr. Fuller? Or did you test me as well when you learned that Susan and I were going to Switzerland?" Bannerman checked the time.

"I—don't get your meaning."

The telephone rang. Fuller's private line.

"It's for you," Bannerman said.

"Hold it." Lesko pushed to his feet. He looked into Bannerman's eyes, suspiciously. The phone kept ringing. "Suppose I get it," he said.

"It's for Secretary Fuller."

"Yeah—well." Lesko stepped to the desk. He picked up the handset. The earpiece was not the kind that twisted off. Probably no dart. Still, he held it gingerly, moving it closer to his ear but keeping it pointed toward the ceiling. He heard only static.

Fuller, frowning, glared at Bannerman. "Is he in danger?" he asked.

A small shrug. "If it were me, I'd drop that thing on the floor."

Lesko blinked. Then he felt it. The phone in his hand was becoming hot. He let it fall, then stepped away quickly. The earpiece spat flame. Only for an instant. Then it was out. Black smoke rose from the ruined carpet.

Fuller's color rose steadily. "You did that?" he said to Bannerman. "You've been in my home?"

"Someone has. Yes." Bannerman gestured toward the painting that was Fuller's favorite. "Your security system must not be working properly. Go look at it."

Fuller sighed. "And what will I find there, Mr. Bannerman?"

"I think it's been shorted out."

Fuller didn't bother. He walked instead to the partially melted telephone, prodding it with the toe of his tennis shoe.

"Would this have killed me?" he asked.

Bannerman shook his head. "It was a demonstration. And a warning."

"Against what, for God's sake."

"Games. Too many games." Bannerman rose to his feet. "Drive carefully, Mr. Secretary."

* * *

"Hey, Bannerman. Hold it."

Kaplan's voice. Angry.

Bannerman, one hand on the car door, turned. He waited as the DEA man approached, glaring at him, one hand balled into a fist.

"Tell me something," Kaplan said, fuming, stopping inches from his chest. "Just who in hell do you think you are?"

Susan blinked. Bannerman said nothing. He had half-expected this.

"How dare you," the smaller man sputtered, "how *dare* you talk that way to a man like Barton Fuller?"

"Um—Irwin—" Lesko stepped forward.

Kaplan waved him off, his eyes locked on Bannerman's. "Tell me what makes you so goddamned superior." He jerked a thumb toward the house. "No. I'll tell *you* something. Barton Fuller is an ass-breaking public servant who does his damnedest for this country and what you are is an arrogant, self-indulgent son of a bitch."

Lesko raised his hands. Kaplan ignored him.

"You want to be left alone?" he asked. "You got it. You want Westport? It's all yours. We don't need you. For my money, we never did."

A small nod toward Susan. Almost an apology. Kaplan turned his back and stamped toward the house.

Lesko went after him. Susan followed.

—37—

No one had spoken.

Lesko, at the wheel of their rented car, retraced the route to Washington's National Airport. On his right sat Bannerman, staring ahead. Susan sat behind, a pad on her lap. Occasionally she would jot another note. Mostly, she watched Bannerman's face in the rearview mirror.

He felt her eyes and met them. He softened his expression. "Go ahead, Susan," he said. "Ask."

"I'll flush this when I'm done." She held up the pad.

"Whatever."

Her eye followed her pen to the top of the page. What she wanted to say was not there.

"Those things Mr. Kaplan said"—she bit her lip—"you didn't deserve that."

Bannerman only shrugged, a bit sadly. He turned toward Lesko. "You were right about him. He's a decent man."

"Irwin? Yeah. He is." Lesko looked at his hands. "Um, about that, what he said—"

"It's okay. Forget it."

"Yeah, well—" Lesko grimaced. "Up to a point, he's right. You've had things pretty much your own way. He's got drug agents dying in the streets. And Fuller's got a whole world to worry about. All you got is Westport."

Bannerman chose not to argue.

"By the way—" Susan held up her pad, signaling a change to another subject. Any subject. "What's with all this 'Drive carefully' lately? You also said that to Roger Clew."

"Just a figure of speech." And a small game of his own. They still didn't know who'd placed that bomb in Hagler's car. Might as well make use of it.

Susan twisted her mouth doubtfully. The phrase sounded suspiciously like *Don't fuck with me*. It even rhymed. But Mama's Boy doesn't say bad words.

"Okay." Her eye returned to the top of the sheet. "What was that stunt with the phone?" Then, to her father, "And how did you know what would happen?"

Lesko didn't answer. He looked out the window. At the sky. Imagining himself aboard the next Swissair flight to Zürich.

"Just a bit of theater," Bannerman told her. "To let him know that he could be reached as easily as he could reach me."

"But why? What were the games?"

"Too much manipulation to suit me. And he lied about when he placed that wire on Roger's phone. Leo Belkin tapped it well before January. Molly says the only way the KGB device could have gone undetected is if the sweepers never thought to look for a tap on a tap."

She said nothing for a moment. "Just before it rang, you asked him a question about the vacation we took. He turned white."

Now Lesko was watching him.

"You think he set up Reid?" he asked. "To go after you, I mean?"

"I don't know."

"What was the point of asking if you weren't going to wait for an answer?"

"I'm not sure. I guess I really don't want to know."

Lesko blinked. *A human Bannerman,* he thought. *God save us.* On the other hand, he wasn't so sure he wanted to know either. Enough was enough. One more hour, a short hop up to JFK and Elena, and he was out of here.

He wasn't even sure why Bannerman wanted him to come. Except to put Kaplan at ease. For all the good it did. It sure as hell didn't put Fuller at ease. Still, it let him spend a little more time with Susan. Better than nothing.

Kaplan had kept on defending Fuller. Out in the driveway, before they left. He said Fuller would never have hurt Bannerman. Some weird thing going back to Bannerman's mother. Maybe that works both ways. Maybe it's why Bannerman pushed but didn't shove.

"For the record," Bannerman said quietly, "I think Barton Fuller is a decent man too. But so was Roger, once."

No one spoke. Susan was staring at him, thoughtfully.

"Paul?" She took his hand. "Who was your father?"

Bannerman understood. He had to smile. "No," he said. "Nothing like that. My father died when I was fourteen. Fuller never laid eyes on my mother until I was twenty-four or so."

"About the time she was killed?"

Bannerman nodded. "According to Billy, and I just found this out, he was infatuated with her. Not long after she was killed, someone passed Billy a list of those involved. Billy thinks it was Fuller who gave him the list. I just heard that for the first time as well."

"McHugh went after them?" Lesko asked.

"We both did. John Waldo and a few others pitched in."

"How did Clew figure?"

"Apparently"—Bannerman shrugged, as if this had been another recent revelation—"Fuller decided we'd done enough damage and offered to mediate a peace between us and the CIA. He sent Roger with a white flag. One thing led to another and Roger's been our case officer ever since. That's until he caught whatever bug infects people down here."

"But ever since, it's really been Fuller, hasn't it. Fuller's been your godfather."

"Fuller created me," Bannerman said wistfully. "It's a heck of a time to realize it, but he created Mama's Boy."

"So? He didn't create Paul Bannerman. What stops you from hanging 'em up?"

"You know better, Lesko. There isn't any more Paul Bannerman. Just like there isn't any Raymond Lesko who can stop being a cop."

They walked with Lesko to the gate of his connecting flight. Lesko stopped to use the washroom. Bannerman joined him. As Lesko prepared to leave, Bannerman offered his hand. "I'll leave you alone with Susan," he said, "until you have to board."

"I appreciate it."

"Do you think you'll stay? In Zürich, I mean?"

"Nothing is forever. But it looks that way, yeah."

"Good luck, Lesko. In everything."

Lesko nodded. "I might call you," he said. "Any suggestions you might have about Zürich, who I should hire, maybe something out of that computer, I wouldn't say no to some help."

"Kaplan will help you. But sure. I owe you one."

Lesko looked at the arm he'd broken. "You don't owe me shit, except you take care of Susan."

"Then I owe Urs Brugg. And one more to Leo Belkin. But as for Susan, I think I'm going to ask her what she wants me to do. Whatever that is, I'm going to try to do it."

"If she says quit? Become a hairdresser?"

"Within reason." Bannerman smiled.

Lesko relaxed his grip. Bannerman held on.

"What?" he asked.

"You won't get mad?"

"I was born mad. What?"

"What if we should think about—"

"Getting married? Forget it."

"Just thought I'd ask. Good-bye, Lesko."

Bannerman watched him go.

"A hairdresser?" Susan took his arm.

"Or a mud wrestler. I haven't decided."

She smiled. A long silence, alone with her thoughts. They followed the signs to the Trump Shuttle.

"Or anything else I want?" she asked, at last.

"Within reason. And after I clear up a few things."

"Would you quit if I asked? No more guns?"

"I'd try. Yes."

"You'd do that for me?"

"And for me. I think."

"What would happen to Billy? And the others."

"Anton is pretty much running things already."

"All those people from Europe. Molly says some of them want to stay."

"We'll have to deal with that. Get them settled in."

"Then there's giving my father a hand in Zürich? And your debt to Leo Belkin?"

"As I said, a few loose ends."

"You know what I think?"

"What's that?"

"You're never going to quit."

"Oh yes, I will. I'm—" He fell silent.

They continued on, Susan waiting for the rest of his rebuttal. He said nothing more.

They arrived at the shuttle gate. Donald Trump's name and picture all over the place. Even a couple of posters promoting his book and some dumb board game about making deals. But that's okay, she thought. He's what he is and he's good at what he does. And so is Bannerman.

The departures board showed the next flight at half past twelve. They had almost forty minutes. Bannerman nodded in the direction of the Admiral's Club lounge.

Loose ends, she thought. Where do they stop? And all those new people in Westport. What does he think they're going to do there? Take up golf and tennis? No way. They like their own game too much.

They reached the lounge. Bannerman signed in. There was a TV set, its volume low, tuned to CNN. She took a seat near it while Bannerman filled two coffee cups at the small buffet table, his black, hers with Sweet'n Low. She watched as he dropped the empty packet into a covered wastebasket. He seemed to be looking at it, the basket, thoughtfully. Now he reached into his pocket and withdrew something that was square and silver. For a long moment he held it in his hand, gripping it as if to crush it. But he didn't. He returned it to his pocket.

Another loose end, she thought.

But the biggest one was probably Barton Fuller. With Roger Clew, he'd ended it. Clearly. Unequivocally. It's over,

Roger. But not so with Fuller. What he'd done, although he might not admit it, was leave that door open. Just a crack. Maybe the memory of his mother had something to do with it. Maybe not. But all he'd really done was let Fuller know he was on to him and warn him to behave. He'd gone to Fuller's house with three other people, none of whom really needed to be there, to say "These people are my friends. Don't f . . . Don't mess with them either."

He returned with their cups, one at a time, and sat. She leaned toward him.

"You said that Mr. Fuller is a decent man. What if he—I don't know—tries to put this right?"

A shrug. Not a no.

See?

"You know what else I think?"

"Mmm?"

"I think you're—" She didn't finish. She heard a soft gasp coming from behind her. The Admiral's Club hostess had risen to her feet, peering over Bannerman's head, looking at the TV screen. Susan followed her gaze. She saw a street in what must have been Medellín or Beirut. Bodies everywhere. Wreckage. Ambulances. A car, barely recognizable, shattered and burning. Too awful. She began to look away. But it struck her, suddenly, that the people she saw were not Arabs or Latins. They were black. And the street—it seemed to be in Manhattan.

Bannerman, noticing her expression, had turned. She saw him stiffen. He leaned toward the television console and punched up the volume.

". . . at least two explosions . . . possibly three . . . tore through masses of local residents gathered for this . . ." The camera showed what had been a speakers' platform, made of plywood, flattened, its sections strewn like playing cards. On top of them, and beyond them, were more bodies. Several were nearly nude, their clothing torn away by the force of the blast. ". . . confirmed dead . . . Manhattan Borough President Alvin Hicks . . . Councilman Andrew Lehman . . . thirteen others . . . many more injured . . ."

The camera panned over the fronts of tenement buildings. It showed one, all its windows blown out, even some of the frames. Tattered remnants of curtains. Bannerman knew that building. A week before, he'd taken Wesley Covington home to it. The pan continued, down to the street in the other direction. A second car, blown to pieces, another burning. More police cars arriving, fire engines, having trouble getting through. More bodies, several of them moving, some as yet untended, some at least a block away.

The picture cut to a studio. A black man, a blond woman, their jaws tight. The man was speaking. ". . . at eleven-fifteen this morning, at what was to have been a salute to the efforts of one community action group in cleansing its streets of drug traffic, two powerful bombs, believed to have been detonated by narco-terrorists . . ."

Bannerman sat, frozen, barely hearing, barely seeing, except in his mind. He saw Wesley Covington, shaking his hand, thanking him, being thanked in return. He saw Covington's niece, Lucy, the brave one, who had wanted to stand up to Hector Manley on the night he came to the dry cleaning shop and who had pretended to be terrified by the SWAT teams surrounding his Westport office. They had both come to help him, to protect him. And now, almost certainly, they were dead.

". . . the death toll, now confirmed at seventeen, is expected to rise. The Columbia University Medical Center has issued an urgent call for blood donors . . . the New York City police department warns of the risk of secondary explosions and asks all . . ."

He felt Susan's body against his back, her hands on his shoulders, squeezing them. "Oh, Paul," she whispered.

She could not see his face. It was well that she could not. Bannerman's eyes had turned dead.

—38—

There was a small color TV in the limousine that met their flight. Bannerman turned it on, searching the network channels for a news program. There were none. Mostly movies. He selected a local station and sat back, waiting for bulletins.

Susan took his hand. "You couldn't have known," she said gently.

He nodded. He didn't speak.

But he should have known. He'd even been warned. But he'd dismissed Roger's call as an attempt to ingratiate himself, a grasping at straws.

Could he have anticipated that Manley might do something like this? Something, yes. That was the point of the Semtex in his boots. But this? A slaughter? Dead city officials, probably dead cops, dead reporters?

No.

Yes.

He remembered Hector's screams, strapped to that table, naked, terrorized, humiliated. He remembered him later, chained to the basement floor of the clinic, very calm now, resigned, docile, reasoning, showing no sign of the hatred he must have felt. Or which Bannerman had failed to see. No man ever forgives you for making him beg.

"We are not so different, you and me." Manley had said that. And he was right.

Both were outlaws, fine distinctions aside. Both would fight, kill if necessary, to protect what is theirs. When threatened, hit first. When attacked, hit back. Fast and hard. Massive retaliation.

They were not so different.

Manley's act—if it was indeed Manley—was not so unlike his own against Palmer Reid. Except for the numbers involved. And the innocents who were killed.

Manley—if he did it—would probably deny it. But his eyes would smile. And his enemies would know. The Dandy Man did this. And yet a part of Bannerman still could not believe it. An act so terrible, on such a scale, was not likely to go unpunished. The police, the FBI, would never rest. They were not like the Arab terrorists, whom Bannerman now despised all the more, who had all of Syria and Iran in which to hide, protected by governments.

Someone had to have bought the explosives, made the bombs, driven the cars. Materials would be traced. Someone would talk. Only a madman would think that he could—

A news bulletin: Videotape, now, of the actual blast. Cameras had been recording the ceremony. There was Covington on the platform, his family, his neighbors, up there with him. Politicians. A band. Then a thunderclap and they were gone. Camera tumbling. Buildings, smoke, sky. The cameraman among the dead.

The movie flicked back on. The limousine was approaching Westport.

"We'll stop at Mario's," he said to Susan. He had called from Washington. The others would be gathered there, watching this.

She said something, intended to comfort him. He barely heard. Instead he heard Irwin Kaplan. *What makes you so goddamned superior, Bannerman? You arrogant, self-indulgent son of a bitch.* Lesko, later, agreeing with him. Up to a point.

And they were right.

His arrogance had killed all those people. He had *tamed*

Hector Manley. They *understood* each other. Manley *liked* him. He would be no threat because Paul Bannerman, that superior judge of men, had said so.

If it *was* Hector Manley.

A part of him, a part that he did not much like, still tried to believe that it was not.

The sign said Mario's was closed. A private party.

Molly Farrell had seen the limo arrive. She opened the door for him. She held it open for John Waldo and Janet Herzog who entered seconds later. They had returned from Lisbon that morning and had waited at LaGuardia to cover his return to Westport. Paul, she realized, had not even noticed.

The stools at the bar and the tables to the right were full. The television, mounted above the far end, visible from either side of the partition, was on. A New York cable station was providing continuing coverage. The Police commissioner was addressing reporters: ". . . cooperating with the federal authorities. Whoever is responsible, wherever they are, in whatever hole in whatever country, we're going to find them . . ."

Or I will, Bannerman said in his mind.

Anton Zivic approached. He greeted Susan. "There is at least some good news," he said. "Billy is flying back today, although against the advice of his doctors. Colonel Belkin is escorting him. Kurt Weiss has taken Mrs. Dibiasi to meet his flight. We've told her, incidentally, that he had a tumor removed from his neck."

Bannerman grunted. It would be good to have Billy home. Leo might be useful as well should Manley decide to hide out in Cuba.

"Irwin Kaplan has been trying to reach you. I spoke to him. His message is, 'Forget what I said this morning. Anything you need, any time, it is yours. That goes for Bart Fuller as well.' "

Bannerman said nothing. But he was grateful.

"Also"—Zivic gestured toward the screen—"Mr. Covington's body, I'm afraid, has been positively identified. But several members of his family have survived."

"He had a niece," Bannerman said hopefully. "Her name is Lucy."

Zivic nodded. "Injured, but not so badly. She was standing directly behind him when the bombs exploded."

Bannerman closed his eyes. "Whatever they need, Anton. The family—"

"I will see to it."

"Money, a place to live—see if they'll come out here." He turned around, surveying the bar once more. "Where's Carla?"

Zivic frowned. He asked Susan if he might have a minute with Bannerman. She excused herself, moving to the middle of the bar where Molly stood watching the screen. It was showing older footage now. Something about the force of the blasts. ". . . casualties, severe damage, even two and three blocks away from the source of the . . ."

Zivic eased him toward the front window. "You are allowing this to consume you," he said quietly.

"No. I'm okay."

Zivic shook his head. "Whenever you ask for Carla Benedict, those in need of organ donors rejoice but the rest of us wince. Carla, in any case, is keeping an eye on Belkin. She is on the same flight."

"Anton." Bannerman stared out onto the street. "I want him."

"Have you considered that he might be innocent of this?"

"I have. He isn't."

"The man has competitors, enemies, perhaps even in his own organization. How very convenient for them that a drug dealer known to be Mr. Covington's enemy will soon be one of the world's most wanted men."

"Anton—he knows what I must be thinking. He would have called by now. He would have denied it."

"You say that"—Zivic tried to put it gently—"because you know the man?"

Bannerman understood. And the question stung him.

"But as it happens," Zivic added, "I tend to agree with you. If Manley did this, he is a psychopath who hates you far more than he hated Mr. Covington. What, therefore, might he do next?"

Bannerman chewed his lip. He might have said *hide*. But

Zivic, he knew, was driving at something else. "Wait for me?" he asked. "Knowing that we'll come?"

"*We,*" Zivic said firmly, "will *not* come. We will follow you in most things, Paul, but we will not indulge you."

Bannerman darkened. That word again.

"Nor, indeed, will Manley wait for you. There are now thousands of policemen combing all of Manhattan above Central Park, river to river. He would hardly sit waiting for them, to say nothing of you."

Bannerman's eyes had narrowed. But now they were blinking, growing wider. They fell on the row of cars parked outside at the curb. One of them, a red Honda just off to his right, had New York plates. A part of him wanted to back away from the glass.

"Precisely," Zivic said at his ear.

"Why now?" he asked slowly. "Why now and not before?"

"Before, it was foolish. Now it is vengeance. And now, only two or three cars would be required. Not forty."

Zivic was right. Bannerman realized that. Certainly about his lack of detachment. He glanced once more at the television screen ". . . adding to the horror . . . freakish effects of the blast . . ." and at the men and women crowding the bar. Some were looking at him. Waiting. He could not afford to have them wonder. Or to see in him what Zivic had seen.

"Okay." He took a breath. "Priorities." He squeezed Zivic's arm, thanking him with his eyes. "Let's get most of these people into cars patrolling the streets of Westport. I'll tell them what to look for. Send Molly to get whatever she needs in the way of detection equipment. I want Glenn Cook and two other marksmen covering the turnpike overpass on the chance that any bomb would be detonated, or at least witnessed, from there. Then get—"

"Paul?" Molly's voice.

Her head was turned toward the TV screen. One hand was raised, beckoning him. He tried to finish his thought.

"*Paul.*" Now Susan's voice, more urgently. "Look at this."

His eyes followed her pointing finger. On the television screen, a man, injured by the explosion, sat on the sidewalk, the camera some distance away. A uniformed policeman, hat missing, face blackened, was crouched in front of him, doing something with the man's legs. Other men stood watching, all wearing sunglasses, the wraparound kind. They watched helplessly, their expressions stunned, confused. Bannerman moved closer. Something about the one on the ground.

The man holding the video camera moved in as well. ". . . freakish—a full block away . . ." It focused now, not on the man but on a spot on the sidewalk. Two stains. Blood. Bits of bone and tissue. The stains were fan shaped, radiating outward. At the base of each the concrete was blackened, cracked. Now the camera moved to the man's legs. ". . . flying shards of steel and glass—one man— watching from a distance—had both feet . . ." The policeman had tied one leg off below the knee. He was looking at the men standing near. He seemed to be pleading. A black man, sunglasses, threw him a belt and backed away.

Bannerman reached Susan's side. "Wait," she said. "They'll show him again." But he knew.

The camera panned upward. It framed the victim's head. It was lolling, side to side, jaw slack. "Isn't that . . . ?" Susan whispered.

It was.

Hector Manley.

The head came up slowly. The eyes, glazed, in shock, seemed to notice the camera for the first time. They stared into it. They widened. A wildness appeared in them. Hector Manley, pushing with his hands, tried to back away. The policeman held him, urging him to be still. But Manley fought him, striking him, shoving him to one side, his eyes all this while locked on the camera lens. But in his mind, Bannerman knew, it was not the camera that he was seeing. He was seeing a man from who he could no longer run, no longer hide. He was shaking his head, perhaps in denial, certainly in fear. His lips parted, probably to moan or cry out. But it struck Bannerman that he was asking *how*. How was this done to him?

Bannerman caught Molly Farrell's glance, his own eyes asking her that question. In reply, she made a pressing motion with her thumb, then turned the thumb toward Manley. She shrugged.

Bannerman understood. She was not sure, exactly, how the Semtex in Manley's boots had been detonated. All that was clear was that Manley had gone there, to a vantage point he presumed to be safe, to watch Wesley Covington die. He had brought his friends, perhaps even his competitors, so that they could see and tell what the Dandy Man does to those who put hands on him. And they had seen it. But they had also, in that instant, seen Hector Manley lose eight inches of his height. Perhaps, for a moment, he had even remained upright, bone against concrete, before toppling backward.

It might have been, Bannerman realized, that the frequency Molly had chosen and the one used for the car bombs were the same. Or, possibly, that the sound waves from the explosion had set off the microreceivers in his heels. Or, as he preferred to hope, that Wesley Covington had seen him, and the thugs with him, and that Covington's thumb, as the bombs took his life, had been poised on the transmitter that Bannerman had given him.

—*39*—

He needed some air. Some time to think. Saying nothing, he slipped through the front door onto Railroad Avenue and crossed to the railroad station. A train was just leaving. He would have the platform to himself.

Susan found him there ten minutes later.

He stood leaning against the railing on the platform's north end, his cast and sling resting on it. She rested against it as well, folding her arms. She did not speak. Ahead of them, a block or so away, was the I-95 overpass. Traffic hummed in both directions. Off to her right there was a willow tree, its long pendent branches just on the edge of turning green. Life goes on, she thought.

"There was this kid," she said quietly, "in our building in Queens. Twenty years old. Rotten kid. A sneak-thief and a bully."

Bannerman waited.

"Once, while he was on probation, his mother caught him taking money from her purse. She tried to get it back. He punched her in the face. Kicked her. She told my father."

Bannerman sighed. He knew what was coming.

"My father wanted to put him away. But the mother was

too afraid of what he might do when he got out. So my father found him, dragged him up on the roof and—um— had a talk with him."

Bannerman nodded. "Until they reached an understanding."

"Yup."

"But this kid ended up killing his mother anyway."

She shook her head. "Some other old woman. Followed her home from the bank and cracked her skull with a Coke bottle. By that time, as it turned out, he had robbed and beaten at least five others. My father—"

"Blamed himself. I know."

Another shake. "I was afraid that he might. But he said he didn't. He said he knows he isn't God."

"He lied to you."

"I know." She reached a hand to his neck, rubbing where the sling cut into it. "But he still knows he isn't God."

An Amtrak express train roared by behind them.

She didn't know what more to say. She was reluctant to bring up that drug dealer's name. The one he'd said he liked, sort of. Or to ask if it was true that he, Paul Bannerman, had done that to him. She knew that it was true, somehow. Everyone in Mario's seemed to know it. She saw the awe, the appreciation, on their faces. The legend grows.

And she'd heard many of them talking, openly, satisfied, she assumed, that she was one of them. The way they spoke, this was only the beginning. The Jamaican's legs would not be enough. And they were glad. Excited.

She heard Irwin Kaplan's name in reference to his promise of anything Paul might need. Something about a hit list. Open season. No interference. Several references to the drugs and money that would be found. Torch the drugs, the laboratories, their homes. Split the money. She began to doubt that retirement was uppermost in their minds.

Someone mentioned Leo Belkin's name, wondering why he was coming. Another answered with a rumor that it meant more work but no one seemed to know the nature of it. She heard no hint that they'd been told about that computer. The Ripper Effect. Nor, she felt certain, would Paul or Colonel Belkin ever tell but a few. Molly, probably. Surely Anton.

It seemed to her that all this should have troubled her. One way or another, it would mean more killing. Much more. But the face of Wesley Covington, the touch of his hand, were still fresh in her mind.

"You know what I wish?" she asked.

He turned his head.

"Never mind," she said.

A sad smile. "So do I," he told her. "I really do."

She hesitated. "Down at Washington National, just before all this came on television, I was about to tell you something."

He waited.

"That I know you'll never quit. Maybe because you don't want to. Maybe because they won't let you. And maybe—"

He opened his mouth to argue. She shushed him.

"And maybe," she continued, "as long as there are people who do things like that—maybe you shouldn't."

He was silent for a moment. "You don't mean that," he said.

"I don't love it, but I think I mean it."

"What about tomorrow?"

"Ask me then."

He turned to face her. "It wouldn't be for long, Susan. Not much more. Just a few—"

"Loose ends. I know."

She took his arm.

"Let's go home, Bannerman."

ABOUT THE AUTHOR

JOHN R. MAXIM lives and writes in Westport. He is the author of five previous books including *The Bannerman Solution* and *Time Out of Mind*. He is currently working on a new novel about the Westport group.

READ AN EXCERPT FROM JOHN MAXIM'S NEW NOVEL:
BANNERMAN'S LAW
Coming in the fall of 1991.

The secrets housed in the mysterious mansion Sur La Mer were better left undisturbed. A rest home for elderly (and often deranged) movie stars from the golden age of silent moviemaking, Sur La Mer, however, proves irresistible to a beautiful college student who is doing her thesis research on film history. The knowledge she unearths is deadly, because those who protect the secrets of Sur La Mer cannot allow her to leave its grounds alive.

Made to look like one of a set of serial killings, Lisa's murder might have gone unavenged—but her murderers had failed to account for one small factor. Lisa's sister is Carla Benedict— Carla of a group of deadly assassins that the U.S. government has retired to Westport, Connecticut. And the head of that group is none other than Paul Bannerman.

The following is an excerpt from
Bannerman's Law:

Lisa could see sky now through the sugar pines. Quietly, but for her own labored breathing, she climbed forward. She saw the roofline of the château.

It occurred to her that the greased rocks and the trip wires she'd passed would be just as effective at keeping people in as at keeping people out. Not that any of the *members* could have managed that slope, trip wires or no. She thought of the two, the younger ones, with the bandaged faces who seemed to have been breaking a rule by merely sitting on the terrace steps. Could they have been prisoners here? Committed here? Lisa doubted it. They seemed too . . . confident for that. And that other man had seemed intimidated by them.

She stopped, still inside the trees.

The old actress was on her bench, waiting, as if she'd never moved. Same hooded coat, her back to Lisa, keeping an eye on any movement from the main house. Lisa looked over the grounds. No sign of Richard Bellarmine. No one else in sight either. Seemed strange. She was tempted to wait for another member or two to be wheeled out, some sign of business as usual, but Norma, suddenly, raised a gloved hand. Must have heard her. Or sensed her. She was motioning her forward, signaling her to stay low beneath the hedge. Lisa, crouching, stepped from the trees. Her own eyes on the château, she followed the beckoning hand. She saw it open, as if to take her own hand in welcome. Lisa reached for it.

The old woman's grip, the strength of it, surprised her. Norma's body half-turned. The other arm came up, reaching behind her neck as if to embrace her. No. Seizing her. The fingers were gripping the hood of her running suit, pulling it down over her eyes, jerking her forward. Now Norma was rising, wrestling with her, driving her sideways until her legs struck Garbo's bench and her body slammed against it. Lisa cried out, more startled than afraid, but a hand, a third hand, now reached in from the side and clamped firmly over her mouth. She saw a flash of red. A sweatshirt. Her eyes widened. It was that man. The jogger from Tower Road. And the woman. It wasn't Norma at all. The face was younger, darker, the skin deeply pitted.

Suddenly all fear was gone. She felt a warmth. A heaviness. The marble bench began to soften. Her body was sinking into it as if it were a bed. She saw, or thought she saw, a syringe being drawn from the flesh of her forearm, now bare. She wondered, vaguely, what it might be doing there. Then, in seconds, she no longer cared.

It seemed to her that she was dreaming. Home in bed. Dreams that annoyed more than they frightened. She tried to wake up, to shake them, but she could not. She was in a white room, like an operating room, strapped to a table, and she felt no clothing against her body. It seemed that it, her nakedness, should have bothered her more than it did.

There was a single bright light above the table. A doctor, an older one, was talking to her, asking her questions. Most were about school. The woman with the pitted face was there. And there were other people who came in, looked at her. The woman showed them her recorder and some things from her purse. That was funny. Lisa tried to think. It seemed to her that she'd locked the purse in her car.

The doctor asked if she had family in the area. Did she have a boyfriend? No? Then whose warm-up suit was that? She did not mind answering.

One of the men who came in held out his hand for her keys. She tried to see his face but she could not move her head. Then he stepped closer and she recognized him. It was the man in the red sweatshirt except that he had showered and changed into a sport jacket. It was also the man she'd seen the Sunday before, arguing with the bandaged man.

With his free hand he reached out to her and, his eyes becoming glazed, began exploring her body, feeling the slight mound of her breasts, the flatness of her stomach, touching his fingers to her lips. The woman spoke sharply to him. He stepped back, sighing. Such a waste, she heard him say, as if from a great distance.

Time passed. Minutes . . . hours, she wasn't sure. The lights came on again. The dream continued. The man who had touched her was back. Asking more questions. Who was her professor? Had he seen any of her work? Had she spoken to him, or anyone, about Sur La Mer? Did she have a locker at school and what was its combination? As he asked these things, he sorted through notebooks and papers that Lisa thought she recognized. Yes. They were hers. From her apartment. He was scanning them, discarding some, selecting others and making a pile of them on her bare stomach. Next came two yellow Fotomat envelopes. He went through the photographs that she had taken seven days earlier. He selected several, laying them out across her thighs.

Her mind was clearing, slowly. This wasn't her bed. And she was not dreaming. The doctor came forward. He held a syringe. But the man she'd seen jogging waved him back. No more, he said. Leave us alone now. The doctor seemed as if he might protest. But he didn't. He left the room.

"Go get Norma," she heard him say. "Bring her down here."

"What good will that do?" The woman's voice.

"I want to be sure. I want to see her face when she sees that we have this one."

"Mr. Dunville"—she hesitated—"in one week, Norma will remember nothing of this girl."

"She remembers more than you all think. Bring her."

A pause. "The Weinbergs are with her. They are watching films."

"So?"

"Mr. Weinberg has . . . *asked* us . . . not to bother her."

Henry Dunville bared his teeth. He snatched at one of the photographs, his fingernails gouging the inside of Lisa's thigh. She cried out. He ignored her. He thrust the photograph toward the woman.

"Show this to him," he hissed, "and then ask him if he would rather be bothered himself. Ask him, while you're at it, just who in hell he thinks he is."

More time passed. The waves washing over her brain were coming less frequently. She could feel her body. It ached in places and burned in others. Her thigh, she thought, was bleeding. The realization that she was naked—not just dream naked—became more focused. They could at least have given her a sheet. Not just those papers. She heard voices. Two men. One was much deeper than the other and slightly muffled. Something else about it. She tried to listen but the voices stopped.

A white mass floated above her. She squinted at it. She saw an eye. Oh, yes. The man with the bandaged head. Same white robe. He was looking, closely, at her face. Then her body. The head stopped above her thighs.

"She took these pictures?" she heard him ask. A trace of an accent. That was it. German, maybe.

"They were in her apartment," the jogger answered. "All this, too." He gestured toward the many papers. "Even a map of our security system."

A snort.

"It caught her, didn't it?" came an icy reply, petulant.

A wave of the hand. Dismissive. "Who is she?"

"A film student, or so it seems. Apparently doing some sort of thesis."

The larger man straightened. "A student? That's all she is?"

"If she's anything more, she'll tell me. I'll especially find out what she wanted with pictures of you and your wife."

The man known as Weinberg was silent for a long moment. When he spoke, it was very quietly. "Why," he asked, "did you not simply take her to a room and question her, threaten her with arrest, as you would any other intruder?"

"Because she spoke to Norma. More to the point, I think Norma spoke to her."

"That is not likely."

Dunville shifted some of the papers on Lisa's stomach, uncovering a pocket-size notepad, left open. He jabbed his finger, jarring her, at several lines written in her hand.

> *Victor D'Arconte?*
> *Victor Dunville?*
> *Daughter / b. 1931–2 / strawberry birthmark*
> *Who are "those people" in the house?*

"Where," asked Henry Dunville, "would she have gotten that information if not from the old woman?"

The man called Weinberg closed his one eye. The bandaged head shook slowly, wearily. His hands reached for the papers and photographs that covered Lisa's body. He gathered them all, then stepped to a cabinet where he found a supply of linens. He shook out a light cotton blanket and covered her with it.

Next, taking a full five minutes, he scanned the notes and photographs, including those that Dunville had discarded into a separate pile. This, Weinberg noticed, seemed to make Dunville ill at ease. He soon discovered why. There, before him, was a shot of Henry Dunville, mouth forming a silent curse, his middle finger extended at the backs of Weinberg and his wife. He smiled beneath his bandages. The photograph, he sensed, was taken to no purpose other than a conviction that cowardice should not go unrecorded. He was beginning, he decided, to like this girl.

"Has it occurred to you," he spoke at last, tapping a finger against the open notepad, "that this is not information at all? That these are simply questions based on rumors, legend, which she came here hoping to have answered?"

It was Dunville's turn to snort. "Why, then, would she have taken your picture?"

"Because she had a camera," he answered patiently, his voice pained. "And because I was there. She photographed everything she saw, Henry, from the main gate, to old Mr. Bellarmine's red seascape, to your rude little gesture."

Dunville's jaw tightened but the chin came up, defiantly. "Well," he sniffed, "we'll know soon enough."

"What have you given her?"

"Heroin. Scopolamine."

"How long until her head clears?"

"Two hours. Maybe less."

"I'll question her then." He raised a hand to stay any objection. "Why is she naked, by the way?"

The other man shrugged.

"Is it because you've been playing with her, Henry? Or does that come later?"

His tan deepened but he said nothing.

Weinberg reached an arm around the smaller man's shoulder. He stiffened but did not pull away. Weinberg guided him toward the door. "Henry," he said, shaking his head, "I'm going to try to explain what you've done here . . ."

Lisa listened to the fading voice. The man who had covered her. She did not want him to leave.

"By the way . . ." The man called Weinberg paused in the corridor outside the surgery, "when your little assistant asked me who I think I am, she wasn't speaking for you, was she?"

No answer.

"Because if she was, I'll tell you. Or would you rather I showed you?"

"What you are," he managed, the chin rising again, "is a guest in this house. Kindly keep that in mind."

"A paying guest," Weinberg corrected him. "And wouldn't you

say that all that money should entitle Mrs. Weinberg and myself to a little peace and quiet?"

"It does not entitle you to interfere—"

The bigger man squeezed his neck, silencing him. "A little college girl comes up here . . . making it past that wonderfully sophisticated security system of yours . . . because she's doing a term paper about old movie stars and, quite naturally, she thought she'd try to talk to one or two. She gets in here but she has only anecdotes to show for her trouble. She has spoken to a blind old man about marble benches and to a nice old lady who can't talk back and who, even if she could, is in another world. Are you with me so far, Henry? Just nod."

He nodded.

"Enter Henry Dunville. You learn that this little girl has been up here, having bested you, and you overreact. You make poor Norma stay inside and you get your little friend to sit out there every day for a week in case she comes back . . ."

"It wasn't that way."

"Correct me."

"We recorded her license plate when she first came to the gate. We had her checked out. When we learned that she was a film student, we knew that she must have been the one who spoke with Bellarmine. We kept her under surveillance. When she left her home this morning, heading this way, obviously outfitted for a return visit, we were alerted, we were ready for her.

"And you got her, didn't you, Henry?" Weinberg punched his arm, lightly. "You jumped her, drugged her, strapped her naked to a table and you burglarized her apartment. In the end, Henry, do you feel that this will make her less curious, or more curious, about Sur La Mer?"

"We can't let her go. Not now."

"Tell me why."

"Because she's seen you. And for all the reasons you just mentioned."

"What she's seen is gauze, Henry. And anything she's seen or heard since you drugged her will have been through a fog. She's not going to die for that."

"We can't take the chance. What if she . . ."

Weinberg squeezed him again, very hard, shutting off his air. "In a little while," he said, "Mrs. Weinberg will come down. She will rap that girl smartly across the back of the head and then she will put her clothes back on. Your surgeon will put a few stitches in her scalp. When she revives, you will tell her that she hit her head when you grabbed her, which you regret, and she's been in the infirmary ever since. Whatever she seems to remember, you and the doctor will assure her that no such thing happened. I will then come in and, standing behind a light, I will play bad cop. I will threaten her with arrest on a trespassing charge and with a lawsuit for the emotional damage she's inflicted on our patients. I will scare the shit out of her, Henry. In the end, she will probably not even report the burglary of her apartment."

"But if she does . . ."

"Let her. You know nothing about it."

"Sh . . . She's been injected," Dunville said, flustered. "What about the marks?"

"Give her a tetanus shot and a painkiller. Use the same holes."

Dunville appeared to consider it. Then his jaw tightened. He began to shake his head. The man called Weinberg reached for his right hand, forced it open, then wrapped his own fist around the offending middle finger. "Must I put it another way, Henry?" he asked, gently.

"N . . . no."

"My bandages come off in three days. One week after that, Bonnie and I . . ." He corrected himself. "Barbara and I . . . will be gone from here. Until then, promise me, Henry, that you will do nothing to compromise us."

"Let go of me. Please."

"Promise?"

"Yes."

Weinberg patted his cheek. "Thank you, Henry."

Lisa heard banging. First a door, slamming. Then muttered curses Then things being thrown.

A face came into view. Her eyes were slow to focus but she knew from the deep tan and the color of the shirt that it was the jogger.

"You little cunt," she heard him say. His fist was raised as if to strike her. But he did not. Instead, the hand lowered, slowly. She felt it on her hip. It moved to her stomach, her chest, feeling her through the cotton blanket. And the face was changing. The anger was gone. Something else in its place.

Henry Dunville had made a decision.

Now she felt him unstrapping her. First her ankles, then her wrists, then, last, her head. It had been held in place with a belt wrapped in thick terry cloth. More rolled up towels had been packed against her temples. She was free now. She raised one arm. It felt so heavy. She let it fall. The fingers seemed to work but not the arm.

She felt his hands reaching under her, lifting her. The blanket fell away. She was out of the light now. She could see better. The ceiling turned and she felt herself being lowered onto something cold. She felt its texture. A leather couch. He stood over her. He was only a shadow now against the light but she could see that he was undoing his clothing. His trousers fell. His belt buckle struck the floor. He stepped out of them. The shadow lowered itself on her. She screamed, cursing him.

A door opened. A woman's voice. The pockmarked one. *No*, she shouted. *Don't do that.* He turned his head. *Get out*, he said. *Right now. Out.* The door slammed. Angry words from outside it.

She felt him trying to enter her. Roughly. Clumsily. She made herself relax so that it would not hurt so much. Yes. That was better. She felt herself becoming moist. He felt it as well. He entered her.

She listened, her face turned away, as his breathing became rapid. She felt him raise himself on his elbows. His hands, which had gripped her shoulders, now moved to her throat. It frightened her. She looked into his face, saw his eyes searching her own, and she knew what he intended. She squeezed her own eyes shut.

Carla, she thought, desperately.

What would Carla do?

She would use her teeth. Tear at his face. Bite into his neck with a pit bull's death grip. Drive the heel of her hand against his nose. But she could do none of these. She still had no strength. Except . . . except in her fingers.

"Open your eyes," he gasped, softly. "Look at me."

She squeezed them harder. She felt one hand come free from her throat. It slapped her, viciously.

"Open them," he snarled. "Open them wide."

The eyes, she thought. Yes.

She obeyed. She let him peer into the light that he wanted to watch as it flickered and died. The hand that had slapped her returned to her throat, joining the other. His grip tightened. He quickened his thrust. He was coming.

She saw her own right hand. She willed it to stop floating, to make a fist, thumb extended, to strike at his eye.

He shrieked.

Drive deep, she said in her mind.

She watched, almost curiously, as her long thumbnail felt its way, sinking in to half its length. Blood spat from his eye. She felt it on her face.

More shrieking. His hand clawed at her arm. His other hand, now a fist, tried to hammer at her face but his body slipped on the wetness between them and the blow glanced off her forehead. He steadied himself. And he seized her. By the throat. She felt his thumbs pressing, digging, much deeper than before. Inside her, she heard something snap. And she heard another sound. The door again, slamming open.

She heard a woman's voice, from a distance this time, through a wall of pain and flashing lights. It was not the same voice. This new woman was shouting, kicking, trying to help her.

Carla?

No. Not Carla. Through a red veil she caught a glimpse of blond hair, bandages, white robe. And this woman was calling a name. It sounded like *Alan.*

She heard it again. Farther away. It faded into a distant echo. Everything was fading but for the bursts of light inside her brain. They were the last thing she saw.

Henry Dunville was on his feet. Backing away. Sniffling. Moaning.

He was bent over sideways, his left elbow pressed tightly against his ribs where Barbara Weinberg had kicked him. The ribs were broken. Blood dripped from his face.

The blond woman stood before him, moving with him as he tried to circle her, blocking his path to the door. His left hand held the waistband of his trousers. He tried to tug them up but he could not. They barely covered his thighs, hobbling him. His right hand held a small brass lamp by its neck. He gestured with it, threatened with it, but the woman, her expression cold, almost lifeless, did not retreat.

The man known as Weinberg knelt at the leather sofa, his face against Lisa's, his chest heaving as he tried to breathe life into her. He straightened, watching. She showed no response. Now he pumped at her chest although he knew it was useless. After a while, he stopped. He reached to close her eyes. Slowly, he pushed to his feet. He turned to face Henry Dunville. Dunville raised the lamp.

"See this?" Dunville cried. He turned the left side of his face to the larger man. The eye was like a red prune, oozing, clotted. More blood smeared his cheek and had soaked through the collar of his shirt. "Do you see what she did to me?"

Weinberg didn't answer. "Please wait outside. Watch the door," he said to his wife.

She shook her head. She gestured toward his own face under the bandages. "If he hits you," she said, "he'll ruin it."

"He's not going to hit me. I'm going to hit him."

"No," she said firmly. "You can't see to the side. You wouldn't see it coming."

He hesitated.

"Touch me," Dunville gasped, "and you're finished. Both of you."

"You wait outside," the blond woman said. "I'll finish this." She walked to a cabinet. She opened a drawer. He heard the metallic rattle of instruments.

"What do you have in mind?" Weinberg asked, turning to her.

"I'm going to take his other eye," she said.

The door to the surgery had muted the screams. A second door, leading upstairs, would block them entirely.

The man and woman named Weinberg waited there, not opening it, until Henry Dunville's screams became sobs and until the sounds of crashing furniture became less frequent.

That done, the man called Weinberg fully realized that he had a problem. Given their condition, his especially, there could be no question of running from it. And they had an investment to protect.

The surgery on their faces, the new documents, the weeks of coaching to prepare them for their new lives as Alan and Barbara Weinberg . . . had already cost them nearly $400,000. Add to that the cost of two new homes—the house in Santa Fe, the apartment in France—which were part of their new identity and, therefore, could hardly be used if they ran. It would be a million-dollar write-off at least. And even then, where could they go, how far would they get, looking like this?

By any standard he knew, the punishment of Henry Dunville had been just. The man had committed a useless, stupid murder. The girl had posed no real threat. She'd discovered nothing that could not have been explained, denied, or ignored. Worse, he'd had her followed to Sur La Mer by someone who would soon conclude that she must have died there. That person might now have to be silenced as well. All because Henry Dunville liked to play with helpless women.

He could only hope that the other Dunvilles would see the wisdom of cutting their losses. Keep Henry alive if they wished. As a new and permanent member. Let old Mr. Bellarmine teach him to paint. Or kill him and be done with it. He had nearly done that himself after Bonnie . . . Barbara . . . finished with him. But Barbara had said no. Let it sink in, she said, that he's done this to himself.

Weinberg doubted that allowing Henry time to reflect on his sins would lead to a spiritual awakening. Or to an insight for which he would thank her. It was really, truth be told, that Barbara tended to regard a quick death as a mercy rather than as retributive justice. And yet this is a woman, as he'd mused more than once, who will capture household moths and spiders alive and then release them out of doors. Then, too, she is a quasi-feminist at heart . . . who thinks women should smell good and be sent flowers and have doors opened for them but should not be raped unless the rape was their idea.

He had yielded to his wife, letting Henry live, because she asked him to and because it might not be a bad idea to let the other Dunville's learn of his stupidity from his own lips. But a bit of insurance wouldn't be a bad idea either.

That in mind, he and Barbara proceeded through the second door and up to the main entrance hall where they relieved two security guards of the pistols they wore under their blazers. They had the one who could still walk drag the other to a padded holding cell where they were invited to quietly pass the remainder of their shift. They returned to the administrative section and the office of Carleton Dunville, the younger. They knew that both Carletons were away, hence Henry's temporary stewardship. The father was in Mexico, probably fishing, and the son, the smart one, was in Palm Springs preparing a fund-raiser for the Motion Picture Relief Association. He had long served on its board and had rotated, this year, into the chairmanship.

Their purpose in going to the younger Dunville's office was to get at his safe, which Barbara felt sure she could open given thirty minutes or so, and to get at the cabinet in which the heavier weapons were kept. Weinberg had seen them when, on arrival at Sur La Mer, he was required to surrender his own. A third purpose was to use the telephone.

But after entering the richly paneled room, they found the phone in use. Henry's little friend—he'd only heard her called Ruiz—was standing at the desk, her back to them. Weinberg waited, listening. She was recounting certain of the day's events to, he assumed, the younger Dunville. Twice she used the word *idiot* in connection with Henry. She was clearly distressed. So, from her manner, was Carleton, although neither, as yet, knew the half of it.

Weinberg cleared his throat. She turned, startled. He made a time-out signal with his hands, using the guard's pistol to cross the *T*. The woman with the bad skin blinked. Weinberg asked for the phone, then, realizing that it would not fit around his bandages, handed it to his wife.

Barbara Weinberg identified herself. Then, making herself comfortable, she explained to Carleton Dunville, the younger, why his half-brother had no eyes.

* * *

It was a comfortable office. The desk faced a couch and two chairs set around a low table in a conversational grouping. The door seemed sturdy enough. Two large windows looked out on the front lawn and gave a clear view of the driveway. The office had its own washroom. While Carleton Dunville made up his mind, it would do nicely.

As his wife busied herself with the safe, he had the woman Ruiz order a plate of sandwiches and two pots of coffee from the kitchen. He told her exactly what to say. He listened on an extension, satisfying himself that no alarm had been given. Still, it was only a matter of time until Henry found his voice again, or managed to unlock the door and come groping his way up from the basement.

Weinberg opened a narrow coat closet that was built into the paneling. Inside, hidden, was the cabinet that contained the guns.

"Do you have a key, by chance?" he asked the woman named Ruiz.

She shook her head, her expression sullen.

Barbara Weinberg looked up from the safe. Rising, she stepped to the coat closet and glanced inside. "Just kick it in," she said.

Weinberg, under his bandages, made a face. He had expected a measure of artistry. He braced himself, raising one leg.

"Wait." Ruiz winced. She reached into her pocket, producing a ring of keys. "I'll open it," she said. "But you won't need guns."

"We share that hope," he said. "Open it all the same."

It was, he thought, a rather odd collection. A dozen or so pistols, including his own, all different models. One Heckler & Koch MP-5 submachine gun with a sound suppressor, two Ingrams, two Uzis. He took the MP-5 for himself and one of the Ingrams for his wife because these two had extra clips while the others had, in some cases, no ammunition at all. And they'd been dumped into the cabinet carelessly and at random. Ruiz appeared to read his mind.

"He doesn't like guns," she said.

Weinberg said nothing. He checked the action of his weapon.

"He doesn't like Henry, either. Vengeance will not interest him."

"What will?"

"Containing this."

"What will he do about Henry?"

"He will ask me to . . . give him something for the pain."

Weinberg looked at her. He believed her. Still . . . the matter of insurance. He asked Ruiz to take a seat on the sofa. He sat at the desk. There was a Canon fax machine behind it. He moved it onto the desk. He found a blank sheet of paper and began writing on it in large block letters.

"What's your first name?" he asked.

"Luisa. What are you doing?"

He fed the paper into the machine and punched a series of numbers. The machine hummed. He caught the sheet as it cleared the stylus and held it up for her to see. It read

BOX 617
IF NO MESSAGE, MY VOICE, AT WEEKLY
INTERVALS, PLEASE ASSUME WORST. ASSUME
C. DUNVILLE, JR.,
AND ASSOCIATE L. RUIZ, SUR LA MER, SANTA
BARBARA, RESPONSIBLE.
KILL THEM. PAYMENT GUARANTEED, CJP VIA THIS
NOTE.
REGARDS, STREICHER.

Westport, Connecticut. The next afternoon.

Paul Bannerman, one hand resting gently on the shoulder of Carla Benedict, walked with her, slowly, along the road that ran parallel to the town's public beach.

They had it largely to themselves. At the water's edge, a young woman dismantled a windsurfer, the late April breeze having faded to a whisper. One couple walked with a golden retriever. In a week, the beach would be closed to pets. Parks Department vehicles would begin combing the sand for their leavings and for the winter's flotsam.

The sun seemed to hover in the western sky. Carla, Bannerman saw, could not keep her eyes off it. He could only imagine what she must have been seeing there.

"Would you like me to go with you?" he asked, hugging her.

She shook her head.

She was a small woman, no larger than her sister, of whom he had only seen snapshots. Same color hair, almost a bronze, but worn in a pixie cut while Lisa wore her hair longer. Seen together, in flattering light, one would guess that Carla was no more than five or six years older. Carla looked thirty. But she had just turned forty.

She was crying softly. Bannerman had never seen Carla cry. Not once in more than fifteen years. Not even when she took the call that told her of her sister's death. But here, arriving at this beach, she had collapsed, utterly, in unimagined pain. He had held her, tightly, against his chest, enduring the fingernails that dug into his flesh, feeling the deep, wracking sobs that welled from so far within her that he thought her lungs must surely burst. But she was better now. Not yet in control. But better.

He glanced at his watch. Her flight would leave in less than three hours. Molly Farrell had the tickets. They would meet her at Mario's, perhaps get Carla to try to eat something, then leave from there.

"I want you to stick with Molly," he said, squeezing her shoulder. "Except for private times, like seeing your father, I've asked her not to leave you alone."

"Seeing my father is when I'll need her," she said, swallowing. She gestured toward the horizon with her chin. "He's sitting out there, right now, wondering why it couldn't have been me."

Bannerman chewed his lip. "Don't talk that way," he said. "I'm sure it's not true."

She didn't argue. But she knew better.

"Paul?"

He waited.

"Lisa liked me."

"I'm sure she did. And so do we."

"No," Carla Benedict said firmly. "You *accept* me. You *tolerate* me. Lisa *liked* me."

Bannerman stopped walking. He turned her so that she had to look at him. "At least four of us, me included," he reminded her, "would be long dead if not for you. We do love you, Carla, each in our own way. There's not a thing in the world we wouldn't do for you."

She leaned her face into his chest. A shudder rose from deep inside her. He felt new tears soaking through his shirt.

"Will you . . ." She swallowed. "Will you help me find the son of a bitch?"

She had asked him that before, within an hour of the phone call from a neighbor of her father. He answered only that he would do what he could. Make some phone calls. In the meantime, see to her needs.

He wanted to help her. They all did. They would have liked nothing better than to find and slowly dismember the animal who had done this to her sister. Raped her. Strangled her. Left her body, nude, spread-eagle near a Ventura Freeway off ramp in Los Angeles, a grotesque smile cut into her face, just as he'd done to six other young women, all college students, over the past two years.

But this was a police matter. The police had a task force, organized after the third of these murders. The FBI had one of its own. Between them they had all the experience and all the tools. They had the psychological profiles of past serial killers, their behavior patterns, they had all the accumulated physical evidence, forensic data, the killer's DNA fingerprint from his semen, all on a computer. Bannerman's people had nothing. They would get in the way.

"I'll see what I can learn," he told her. "If we can help, we will."

"You could call Lesko," she said into his chest. "He probably knows about things like this."

"We'll see. I'll ask him."

No harm in asking, though he did not think it would do much good. Lesko had been a good street cop, but he'd mostly worked narcotics. New York, as far as Bannerman could recall, had never had a serial killer. Not that one would necessarily be noticed there. They all seemed to come from the West Coast. And Lesko, in any case, was now living in Zürich.

Still, Lesko had made a national reputation for himself. Bannerman had never met a cop who hadn't heard a story or two about him. He might well, therefore, have a connection or two on the Los Angeles force. Someone, at the very least, who could help keep an eye on Carla. Anyway, he would probably want to know.

"Listen . . ." Carla fingered his lapels, "about Susan . . ."

Susan Lesko. Lesko's daughter.

"I'm sorry I gave you so much shit about her."

"Forget it." He shook his head. "That's in the past."

"She's been great about this. Everybody's been great."

It was Susan who'd made the flight reservations. And suggested that he send Molly with her. And had gone to Carla's house to help her pack the things she'd need. All this in spite of the fact that Carla made no secret of resenting her presence in Westport, telling him how foolish he'd been to take up with Susan, an outsider, unproven, untested, no skills. But Susan, over the past year, had more than proven herself. Everyone had acknowledged that but Carla. Until now.

"Maybe Susan's okay," she said.

"Thank you."

"Don't tell her I said so."

Bannerman made a face.

"I'll tell her myself. When I get back."

"That would be nice," he said. He steered her toward the parking lot where he'd left his car.

"Paul?"

"Umm?"

"Did you mean what you said?"

"About what?"

"That you love me. Except when I make you crazy, I mean."

"Even then." He leaned and kissed the top of her head.

"Don't take this wrong, but if Susan ever dumps you . . ."

"I'll come crawling," he said.

Look for *Bannerman's Law* in the fall of 1991, wherever Bantam books are sold.